BLOOD DRAGON

by

Amber Anthony

Print ISBN 978-0-578-51591-5
eBook ISBN 978-1-39398-113-8

Credits
Cover Artist: Kelly A. Martin, kam.design
Editor: Professional Editor Services
August 2020
Published by Amber Anthony
Printed in the United States of America

Praise for Blood Dragon

"This book has so much life. Amber Anthony knows how to bring characters' inner demons to the forefront and challenge their every move. That is what makes a good author. From Adam being the Master Dom of kink and Willow on her massive journey of self-discovery Blood Dragon is shifter crème de la crème…. Only Amber Anthony, I tell ya." – I.C.-NDP Book Review

"Fantastical world-building makes for the perfect backdrop in this thrilling adventure. Richly woven scenes provide a lovely tapestry for the drama to unfold. I could honestly hear the roar of dragon wings and witness the beauty of the rolling hills of Scotland. My head was spinning by the time it was all over. I would love to see Blood Dragon on the big screen. To sum it up simply: I love this book!" – AMD, USA

"Tall, blond and dangerous, he stole my heart with his reluctance and then his bull-headedness.

This story took me from Scotland to Ireland to Chile with some of the most colorful characters I've seen in a romance.

Yes, the romance sizzles right along with the snappy patter. I couldn't put it down, and I have gone back to it as my go-to BDSM read." -L.R. USA

Follow Amber Anthony on
All Author
BookBub
BookSprout
GoodReads
The Romance Reviews
https://AmberAnthonyWrites.com
Adagio Teas, Amber Anthony, Romance Writer, Special Blends

Dedication

To the animals we love,
magical and mortal.

1

Adam Lachlan was irritated. He got to the Dublin Airport on time, but the security line moved glacially, and even the number of travelers in the Pre-Cert line shuffled in place. When he handed his passport and new boarding pass to the security agent, he realized his seat assignment was altered. He went to considerable trouble and expense to be sure he had the bulkhead seat on every flight. His muscular six-foot-six frame didn't travel well even in first-class accommodations.

Placing him next to a woman from the age of twelve to death, inevitably found him prodded into a conversation on a wide variety of topics. He prided himself on not letting his good looks do the heavy lifting. He wanted to engage with people. He wanted to know their stories. He simply didn't want to do it while trapped in a metal tube thirty-three thousand feet in the air. In his work, he interacted with women all night long. He hoped today he'd sit next to an eighty-year-old foreign gentleman who did not speak English.

Adam found the mortal world fascinating and stimulating in a way his world could never match. He'd amassed a fortune, studied at the finest universities, become a shipping magnate. As the need arose, a lawyer affiliated with the Underground Railroad. Excitement called him to be a successful gold prospector in California. Introspection sent him to study and become an esteemed psychotherapist. Most recently, as Master Dominant for the Consort Group International, it was the role he liked best. But that was true for most of the occupations he'd held until he had to shed that identity and move on.

Once through security, he loped toward the gate agent. The middle-aged man was straight out of Irish central casting. His fiery red beard and mop of unruly hair topped a diminutive, stocky body.

Great. I have to deal with Darby O'Gill.

It was one more line to stand in before he could address the problem with his new boarding pass.

Adam pulled his original from his breast pocket. "You can see here." He pointed a long finger at the seat assignment. "I'm supposed to be One A. I paid for this assignment online. When I checked my bag, they gave me this new one."

Adam towered over the increasingly sour gate agent.

"I regret to inform you; seat One A was sold to an earlier purchaser."

"Very well, I'll take any seat in row One."

The agent sniffed and looked at Adam's name on the screen. "Dr. Lachlan, all of the bulkhead seats are sold."

Adam felt his ire building. He took a deep breath to calm himself. He knew, from years of training, conflicts were never resolved with anger. The gate agent predictably had something of a Napoleon complex. He wasn't going to bend without a very good reason, so Adam attempted logic. "Why would your website sell it, if it were not available?"

"Unfortunately, mistakes can be made. We could place you in an exit row in coach. They have a bit more leg room."

Adam blinked. He gestured at his height and stuck out a long leg. "Do I look like I'd fit in a coach sized…"

* * * *

One bushy red eyebrow rose as the gate agent's lips turned downward. At the adjoining gate desk, a strikingly tall woman halted her typing and craned her neck to look at Adam. Her tongue skimmed her bottom lip before she spoke.

"Angus, would you escort this guest to baggage?" The woman placed a hand on the gate agent's keyboard and insinuated herself into the helm. Angus reluctantly receded from his position of power and headed toward the guest in the wheelchair.

"Welcome to Ireland Air, sir. I'm Siobhan, the shift supervisor." She retucked her scarf further into the deep V-neck of her figure-hugging uniform, and her voice was breathy when she spoke. "How may I help you?" She visually ate him up.

His penetrating aqua eyes were framed by waves of golden hair falling just below his collar. A genuine megawatt smile enlivened handsome, symmetrical features. His bright white shirt collar encircled a long, strong neck. The muscles of his shoulders and arms were elegantly contained in a tailored tweed sports coat, and not an ounce of bulk showed at his trim waist.

He presented both boarding passes along with his quirky smile. His deep, rich baritone pled his case. "You see my problem. Can you help me out?"

Siobhan played with a loose curl from her updo and nodded. She tapped at the keyboard, while alternating sneak peeks at his broad chest. "Give me a moment, please, Dr. Lachlan." She picked up the microphone. "Paging passenger Willow Greer, to the gate desk. Willow Greer, please."

* * * *

The standing crowd split as the lithe, young woman approached the desk. She was gamine, with dark, playful eyes and long thick lashes. Her frame was athletic, but every curve was exactly where it should be. Willow's dress and manner sang with a delightfully coltish grace. She glanced at Adam, and he swore he felt the breeze from her eyelashes. He was enchanted.

I'd give up any seat to sit next to her.

"You paged Willow Greer? I'm Willow." Her doe-eyed gaze caught his and held just a moment too long.

Siobhan dove in. "Miss Greer, it seems your bulkhead seat was sold twice. As you can see, Dr. Lachlan would find most seats confining."

"I can understand that."

Adam expected a sweet-pitched gentle voice. He was excited to hear her words drawn out in deliberate, smoky tones. Willow looked him up and down.

"Could we entice you to exchange seats?" Siobhan continued. "You'll still be flying first class, just not in a bulkhead seat. Of course, we'll compensate you for your flexibility."

I'd like to test her flexibility, Adam mused. "I'd be happy to pay any difference in price..." He infused his resonate baritone with all the charm he could muster. Willow eyed him with a devilish smirk.

"That won't be necessary," Siobhan interjected.

"I wouldn't hear of it. I'm happy to exchange seats." Willow turned from him.

He drew her back. "I want to do something to thank you. At least let me pay for an onboard drink or two."

Willow smiled. "Thank you, but I don't drink."

Siobhan's smile was less bright, sensing competition. "Very well, it seems we've resolved this situation." Her smile vanished completely as she watched Adam admire Willow, and her face grew stony. "Please, let me issue your new boarding passes." She handed them the new cards. "Dr. Lachlan, do you have a contact number at your destination, in case there's a problem with your luggage?"

Adam withdrew a chromed steel card holder from his jacket pocket. He slid out two cards and passed one to each woman.

"I'm afraid my destination is remote, you may have to leave a message, but I'll return your call when I get within range."

"Very well." Siobhan slid the card into her pocket and glanced at the irritated travelers behind Adam. "Next, please."

"Thanks a lot." Adam flashed another smile. He turned to thank Willow, but she was already gone. Looking over the chairs at the gate he saw one open seat next to Miss Greer. He focused on the play of light dancing over her short, dark hair and set off with long strides in her direction.

"Danny, watch out for…" A woman warned her four-year-old as he threw his ball across Adam's path. The youngster barreled into Adam at his knees and the two twisted in midair with surprising grace. Adam scooped up the little shrieking child and handed him to the harried mother. "I believe I have something of yours." With a look over his shoulder, he watched the seat he coveted become occupied. *Rugrats!* He thought in frustration. *Did she sneak a smile at me? She's only pretending to read…what is it? Backpacker's Magazine? Would backpackers pack a magazine?* With that question looming in his head, he made for the open seat across from her. He strode carefully, wary of any other toddlers, and dropped into the seat.

"Hello, again." He nodded, and his golden blonde hair fell in front of his ears.

* * * *

Willow retrieved the card from her pocket. She scrutinized the kid finish engraved calling card. *Not a business card, a calling card.* One nimble finger ran over the engraving's relief. *Ivory, kid finish with black engraved letters?* She tapped the card on her knee. "Hello. It says here you're Adam C. Lachlan, Ph.D. What's your doctorate in?"

He smiled. "Psychology."

"Do you practice?"

Adam looked at the airfield and back at Willow. "How would I expect to improve if I didn't practice?"

Cute! Willow smothered a grin and turned the card around. "I didn't see humorist listed."

"That's my hobby. With a face like mine, I have to make a lot of jokes." Willow shook her head and slid the card into a safer place.

"Are you an avid camper?" He pointed to the magazine on her lap.

I would camp on the sun if I thought you would be at the same campground.

"It comes with the job." She smiled shyly as she slid the magazine into her carry-on and her laminated University of Florida luggage tag revealed her name, Willow Greer, Ph.D.

"Are you a happy camper?" He stretched his long legs toward her.

She leaned forward. "Depends on the weather."

"Well, this time of year in Scotland isn't great. You need to come back when the heather blooms in September, the days are still quite long. It's light till 7:30 or so."

"If only my subject would cooperate."

"And, what is your subject?"

"Zoology."

"That explains the camping…"

The gate agent's voice cut in over the loudspeaker. "Ireland Air regrets there will be a ninety-minute delay in boarding flight 201 to Inverness. Please, do not leave the terminal, announcements will be forthcoming."

Willow exhaled. "I've been sitting in this terminal all my life."

Adam stood. "Why don't you let me buy you dinner before there's a stampede at the restaurants?"

"Sure." Willow rose and caught up her carry-on.

"May I get that?" He reached for her bag and when they slipped away from the mass of complaining passengers, his hand gently guided her at the small of her back. "What do you like to eat?" His voice was whiskey deep.

"I'm mostly vegan, except for fish. Will that be a problem here?"

A guy his size no doubt eats steak and eggs every morning.

"I know just the right place. It's a bit of a walk, but worth it." He had a spring in his step as he kept to her shorter stride.

"I was dressed to dig right into work. I'm wearing my walking shoes."

I'm good. I'm stinking grand. *Is it my imagination, or is everyone watching us? The public looks at him as if he truly is that handsome.*

"I recommend the truffle and kale rice or the seafood crepes. But you have to leave room for the half-baked chocolate cake with vanilla ice cream." His aqua eyes danced at the mention of cake.

"What do you generally enjoy?"

Enjoy? He moves like he has about twelve percent body fat. Does he eat?

His reply was thoughtful. She could see him juggling a variety of favorites in his head. "We ate mutton constantly when I was young, so I judge a chef by his lamb. If it isn't offensive to you, I hope they have a slow roasted lamb shank saved for me."

"I'm not one of those rabid vegans. It was a choice I made in college; it was cheaper, and I fought off the freshman fifteen. I wish I could visualize chocolate as meat. I could fight the cravings easier."

No man wants to hear about a woman's battle with her weight. ARGHHHH.

Adam guided her around a corner, and there was a provincial façade in the modern airport. The stained-glass sign advertised The Rustic Chef.

"Mallory." He waved at the hostess as she returned from the kitchen hall.

Dear God, he knows hostesses in airport restaurants.

"Dr. Lachlan, good evening to you. Will you be joining us for dinner or are you just stopping to see what Kieran's cooked up?" She tilted her smiling eyes at him.

He has an effortless charm.

"Dr. Greer and I have about an hour and wanted a delicious dinner, she's never eaten here, and I thought we could turn a delay into something wonderful."

He already has.

* * * *

As she swept the last piece of the half-baked chocolate cake into her mouth, the burly chef approached their table, wiping his chunky fingers with a clean kitchen towel. His voice was good-humored. "Was it worth the walk, Cale?" His kitchen whites were exactly that and the name embroidered in black over his breast was Kieran Russell. Adam rose and bent to embrace the man who was a head shorter. Their dialogue sped up, and their accents became undecipherable until the two of them stopped to chuckle.

"I'm sorry, Dr. Greer, Kieran and I grew up together. While I was doing bad things with fermented fruit, he was butchering and cooking."

The dark-haired man turned to Willow. "It's my job to remind this oak tree of a man I knew him when he was a stripling. No wonder he ne'r uses his middle name, Cale, it was all we ever heard, he was such a prankster."

She winked at the chef.

Saints in Heaven, everyone loves this guy. I'm having too good a time.

She surreptitiously checked her watch; they had twenty-five minutes until their flight would board.

Adam caught her glance and reached into his trousers. "Kieran, we've got to make a flight, what do I owe you?"

Kieran put his chunky fists on his broad hips. "You and your friend aren't goin' anywhere tonight. The news just posted a walkout. Pilots union walked first, and then the flight attendants struck in solidarity."

* * * *

The walk to the baggage claim area was exceptionally long. Adam let Willow pass him to hold a place at the luggage carousel. It gave him the best view. Her hips swayed, and her head bobbed to some internal tune. The carousel groaned as it started, and bags belched out. He paused to watch her bend over and retrieve a coat from her carry-on bag.

Okay, Sparky, slow your roll.

A newspaper shielded his trouser front as he shook one leg. He yanked at the handle on his bag and nearly stepped back on Willow.

"We have the same bags." Willow pointed to the bag at her feet. "You see the Nature Conservancy tag? It's the sole difference." She pointed to a small luggage tag secreted under one of the handles. I appreciate the dinner, especially since it was made just for us by your friend. I hope this hotel," Willow waved the hotel voucher, "isn't horrible. I've got to do some finagling to get to Scotland for my sabbatical."

He smiled disarmingly and hoped his next suggestion would charm her. "This sounds like a come on, but honestly, it isn't. I know a resort, not far from here. I have some sway and could get you a deeply discounted rate while you make your plans."

Willow flushed and gave a self-conscious laugh. "Can I get a cab there?"

"There's a phone at the tourist desk, goes straight to the resort. They'll send out a car. If my presence is too intrusive, we can ride separately."

Her brow rose suspiciously. "What's the name of this resort?"

* * * *

Adam stood at the transportation desk and used his cell phone. His best friend picked up the call directly. "Rick, did you hear about the airline strike? I'm coming back until I can make other arrangements. I've got a favor to ask…"

* * * *

Standing at the passenger pickup area, waiting for the resort shuttle, Willow looked up to the man who was quickly becoming her infatuation. "It's absurd to take separate cars, Dr. Lachlan. I can see this is all on the up and up. The brochure is breathtaking. I've never stayed at a castle." Willow watched the shiny black SUV roll up to the sidewalk accented by a stylized coat of arms painted in gold on the hood. The chauffeur stepped quickly around the limo and checked his phone. "Picking up Dr. Greer and Dr. Lachlan? My name is Charles." They nodded, and he held the door open for them to step up. The smartly uniformed man closed the doors and got them rolling toward Erne Castle. "There's bottled water in the center console or a selection of whiskeys."

Willow laughingly passed on the whiskey. "I can't swallow another thing, thank-you."

Charles' pleasant and understandable accent complimented his well-rehearsed script. "Erne Castle is the original home of the Fitzjarrald Dukedom. It is one of the oldest castle hotels in Ireland, situated in the rolling Kildare countryside, an hours' drive from Dublin. The castle's history dates to 1180. Today, the castle is proud to be renovated into a luxury castle resort with a fully equipped leisure center. We can make clubs available if you wish to play our 18-hole golf course, we also have a limited equestrian center, a pool, and a gym. Each guest room is uniquely designed, with a selection of rooms in the castle itself and some within the specially designed courtyard buildings. Do either of you have any special requests or questions?"

"No, thank you, Charles," Willow demurred quietly, and from then on, Charles was silent.

* * * *

The water was so warm it felt like a lover's caress. His toes dug into the sugar-white sand as he ran the length of the beach toward Willow. Adam noticed the forty-two-foot sailboat as she dropped anchor and rode the raft to the shore. Her skin was kissed by the salt water and the warm island breezes. They collided sensually as island birds twittered a love song.

"You waited for me." Willow's lips whispered into his ear as he bent to kiss her.

Adam felt the gauzy fabric tied at her waist. She was topless, and her nipples grazed his six-pack abs. The vixen grabbed at the waist of his board shorts, running her gentle hand up and down his front to bring him to life.

"I could take you right here." Adam murmured as she untied his waistband.

"I could take *you* right here." Her voice was husky with desire as she dropped to her knees.

Adam caught her before she could remove his swimsuit. "I want you in the water. I want to take you as the waves beat around us."

She nodded and finished removing his trunks, and then dropped her gauzy wrap. Holding hands, they ran into the ocean. Waves invited them to wade up to their waists. She caught his ready erection in her hand as his fingers sought her waiting sex.

"I want to feel every inch of you…"

* * * *

Willow slid to the far side of the SUV, and even with its generous size, Adam appeared folded up while he dozed. It didn't bother her; he'd been more than gracious today. She sent out emails about her new plans and caught up on the latest news. Periodically, the sleeping man beside her snuffled or sighed pleasurably. When the artistically lit castle came into view Willow's heart fluttered. "Dr. Lachlan, we're here. It's…it's more than I expected."

* * * *

"Your room, Dr. Greer, is on the fourth floor, our bellman will take you up. Our dining room opens for breakfast at six, and there's a menu to hang on your door if you would prefer breakfast in your room." The welcoming desk clerk slid the key to the bellman and handed the folio to Willow. Clutching it to her chest, she sent Adam a parting smile and followed the bellman into the elevator, retrofitted to appear as if it was original to the twelfth-century castle.

Willow's spectacular brown eyes widened, and she gasped at the room. Shades of pale blue shone through the thick area rug over the wide planked floors. Her gaze traveled up the periwinkle walls where framed, inked scenes of Irish countrysides hung. The canopied bed invited peace and rest, swathed in ivory and a light water wash of cerulean satin. Once the bellman gave directions for the TV, clock radio and steam shower, he made a small bow.

Willow was mesmerized by the luxury accommodations and impeccable details at every turn. Slipping the bellman what she hoped was an adequate gratuity, she kicked off her shoes and ran from point to point. When she came down to earth, she unpacked. Even if she was only here for one night, she was going to live in every square inch of this room.

* * * *

There was a discrete knock on Adam's second-floor door. He expected a bellman with the beer he'd requested. He opened the door to see his friend, Rick Hiatt, head down, rocking on the balls of his posh loafers. Well-manicured hands held a six-pack of Guinness. "Delivery for Dr. Lachlan." He stuck his head into the room. "Is there a Dr. Lachlan staying here?" Adam stepped back and let his long-time best friend into the room. "What's with the title, Sparky?" Rick put the beer on the desk and made himself at home. After all, his international conglomerate owned the resort.

"Yeah, I have a title, I don't advertise it as a Dom, doesn't mean I never use it. I should get a little respect. After all, I *am* paying for this room." Adam defended.

Rick stroked his chin and arched a brow. "Why did you use your company credit card on your room?"

"To keep up the façade, I'm a guest. Hey, we get the points!" Adam poured a Guinness into a glass and sat across from his friend.

"I saw your traveling companion arrive. Dr. Greer. Are you suffering from some malady that you now travel with a physician?"

"Primarily, you know for a fact dragon shifters don't suffer from human maladies. She's a zoologist."

Rick pondered the ceiling for a second. "Funny, she doesn't look a bit like Jane Goodall. Does she study dragon shifters in their natural habitat?"

"You better hope she doesn't study vampires, especially vampires who own BDSM clubs across the world."

"Is that even a thing? Seriously, she is heaven on two feet. When did you plan on getting those feet of hers in the air? Am I intruding now?"

"That is not appropriate, Mr. Married Vampire. You can't live vicariously off me."

"Oh, bugger off, Sparky. Just because you've got us all on the down low, don't play Dr. Manners with me."

"Look, I only wanted to strike up a friendship with her. She's smart; she's a good conversationalist and…"

"She's built like a brick house."

"Doesn't mean I'm going in her direction." Adam played with the wedding ring he wore.

"Dear boy, you need to park the ring."

"I can't do it again, Rick. I've watched too many of the women I love die in front of me. Shifter longevity has a downside."

"We could turn you." Rick's hands flourished. "Imagine a fire-breathing dragon with fangs."

"Thanks, buddy. I've already got fangs." Adam paused between sips to consider the possibilities. "You could turn *her*, I mean, with her approval. But then this fire and ice thing is going on. Nah…I like my women alive."

"Fielder's choice." Rick shrugged. "So, what exactly are we hiding from her?"

Adam paced as he drank. "Oh, everything…"

Rick affected a German accent. "I vould loff to psychoanalyze you…" He dropped the accent. "But I'd rather ride the hell out of this. You've just met the doctor? No psychosis, no hostilities, no guilt complexes yet…"

"Who's the psychotherapist here?"

"I've been out in the world a good deal longer than you, dear boy. You weren't at the Gaoler when Dr. Bonner studied Dom/sub interactions for use in game theory."

Adam grinned. "You know everybody, why haven't you found me a shifter woman?"

"I like you more when you're lean and hungry, but back to the woman on the fourth floor. What's up?"

"There's a pilot strike going on. After we have a couple of good days together…" He gave Rick a stern look, "just as friends—could Matt fly us over to Inverness?"

Rick's lips curled into a devilish smile. "Ah, it's good to have friends with resorts and helicopters, isn't it?"

Adam popped off his shoes. "Yeah. I know *you* thought it was good when your dragon shifter friend flew over the Irish Sea to rescue your wife. I'm glad my vampire friends can keep their fangs and whips in the closet for a couple of days."

Rick rose and straightened his tie in the mirror over the desk. "Anna said the other day—" The room phone trilled. The men looked at each other. "My room, my phone." He caught it up and smiled. "This is Adam." Rick's vampire hearing didn't require him to hover.

"Oh, Adam, I feel like I've died and gone to heaven!" Willow sighed. Rick dropped his fangs and chomped his teeth together twice. Adam frowned and motioned him away.

"You like the room?" Adam's face flushed.

"Have you been in the bathroom? I just took a steam bath in my bathroom! Then I took a cold shower, you know, like they do in Sweden?"

Adam's voice dropped to sultry. "I'm imagining you there…"

Willow was silent. Rick threw up his hands.

Willow cleared her throat. "Well, before we go to bed…" Adam's eyes closed as his cock saluted. Rick's smirk told Adam he'd never live this down. "Dr. Lachlan, I want to thank you for bringing me here. I would never have found this place on my own."

"Please, call me Adam—we're sleeping under the same roof tonight. I'm glad you find it satisfying."

"Please, call me Willow."

Adam closed his eyes and turned away from Rick. "I'd be happy to. Will you join me for breakfast, Willow?" Rick circled Adam and grinned at him, he made a heart shape with his two hands and pumped it in front of his chest. Adam spun away, tangled in the phone cord.

"Do they eat as late as 9:30? I'm a little lagged."

"We can get breakfast at 9:30 at night if you want it. See you then?"

Willow yawned. "Sure. I want to hit the sheets. G'night."

Rick leaned into Adam and elbowed him. "I know what you want to hit."

"Stop it! Give Anna my best, and then you can give her some of you, too."

"Alright. I can rattle some chains, make Dr. Greer think her room is haunted. She might need your comfort…"

"Go, now, Rick. From here on out, you are Mr. Hiatt." He pushed Rick toward the door.

Rick held his place in the door frame. "But I'm Mr. Hawt in everyone's heart. I hope you don't sleep too hard."

Adam gave him a push. "Out. Now. Before I call the manager." Adam got the leverage to close his door.

2

When Rick bought Erne Castle and brought it into Consort Group International, he was buying the home he was born in, the year of our Lord 1513. Rick and his business partner Matt Brenner, both vampires, began in 1922, Los Angeles, with a speakeasy where mortal donors traded their blood for the sexual rush of the vampire's bite. By 1934, when prohibition was a thing of the past, the speakeasy developed into many BDSM clubs and resorts all over the world, becoming C.G.I.

The back-service elevator doors opened, and Rick proceeded to the security area of the undead sector of the club. If one L.A. vampire required several donors, the world vampire population required legions. Rick and Matt's clubs, resorts, and more, now served the needs of vampires and mortals alike, netting them billions in the process. Rick, Matt, and their wives were about to take advantage of the perk of feeding fresh whenever they desired. There was a time; he remembered uncomfortably when vampires killed their victims to eat. Now, they thrilled their victims to eat, and everyone was satisfied.

Rick accessed the palm print panel at the door and entered the informal feeding room. Everything in this room was designed for comfort, both mortal donor and vampire. Sensual, soft fabrics adorned yards and yards of horizontal lounging space. Muted lighting, restful colors and conscientious attendants made the experience enjoyable in every way, not to mention the unparalleled orgasmic thrill of a well-delivered bite. The vampires had their choice of donors, famous for blood pure with balanced diets and clean living. It was a win-win for everyone.

Rick smiled and nodded at his new bride and fledgling, Anna, and headed over to the area in which she, Matt, and his mate Cat, waited. "Good evening, everyone! I hope you aren't fainting from hunger." He bent to kiss Anna's forehead. "You, Cupcake, are one radiant fledgling. No one would believe six hours ago you were mortal."

"You fed me quite a bit upstairs; I'm not truly hungry." Anna sat prettily, her luxurious titian hair flowing over her ivory shoulders.

Matt held his own fledgling mate in his arms. "Your initial fresh feeding should be just a snack."

Cat nodded in agreement. "You're fortunate you have an intellectual understanding of all this." She gestured around the room.

"This time, we want you to learn the sensation of the bite and how your donor reacts." Rick touched the mark of her turning feed on his wrist. "If your bite is anything like the one made on me, they'll be in heaven! I'll treasure your mark forever." He kissed her cheek.

Matt shrugged. "You're killing my appetite. Where is my friend, the big bad vamp?"

Cat elbowed him. "Stop it! Be nice. This is a celebration." Matt laughed and nuzzled her neck.

Rick's gaze was direct and sincere. "As a sire, I'm kinda choked up to see how our family has grown."

"Yeah, yeah, old man. Let's get this dinner started. I'm hungry."

At Matt's nod, the attendants led their donors into the room. Anna smiled at her male donor and sat beside him on the chaise. "So, Fitz, what kept you?" She picked up her donor's arm and scented it, as Rick had taught her.

"I was doing something for Adam." Rick sat with his giggly, slightly inebriated donor and couldn't help but smile at her antics. He looked at his wife.

"Adam? What's he doing back? We just dropped him off at the airport." Anna studied the road map of veins in the donor's muscular forearm.

Cat licked her well-tanned donor's wrist, "Where did you acquire such a fine tan this time of year in Ireland?" She looked back at Rick without waiting for a reply. "Oh, I did catch the news just as I was getting up. There's a pilot strike. I'll bet that's why he's back."

Matt winked at his donor who blushed profusely. He stared at her neck for perhaps a second too long, but licked her palm instead, making her gasp.

"I can always take him over in the chopper."

Rick lowered his donor's arm, which caused a disappointed sigh, and announced, "Actually, he brought a stray home with him, Dr. Willow Greer, and asked if he could keep her for a couple of days." All the others stared at him in shock. "I think the young man may be in love!"

Fangs, that a moment ago had been ready to sink into flesh, instantly retracted, leaving their donors bewildered. "What?" Anna asked incredulously.

"Yep. Adam wants a couple of days with this woman. You know, just a little vaca…"

The impatient murmurs of their donors drew the distracted vampires back to their dinner. "In twenty-five years, I've never known him to spend even a night with a woman for romance," Matt observed.

Rick sank fang into flesh, and his donor gasped. He paused. The donor's eyes flew open. "Oh, there are two floors between them. He claims it's all platonic."

Matt's donor squealed in pleasure when he bit and drew steadily.

"What did he smell like?" Cat asked keenly. "Did he smell like sex?" Her donor groaned with need and absentmindedly, she bit, eliciting an immediate high. "Umm, this is damn good A Positive." She glanced at the donor who was already approaching ecstasy. "Did you have a Guinness tonight? You taste like chocolate." The donor lay back, replete.

Rick paused again to answer, teasing his donor, delaying her orgasm. "Nope. No sex, but plenty of pheromones. Matt, you look like a hungry boy tonight," Rick surmised watching him take his limit from one donor and call for another.

Matt moved to another seat. "I irrefutably believe in love at first sight." He winked at Cat.

Anna looked suddenly appalled. "Oh, I spilled some of my dinner." She waved at the attendant. "Anton, may I get a clean-up over here, please?" She looked at her donor. "I hope I didn't get any blood on your clothes." The man leaned into the corner of the conversation chair with a satisfied smile.

"I think he's okay, Cupcake," Rick observed wryly.

The quartet rose to have their after-dinner drinks up on the patio. Rick considered the unusual turn of events that led Adam back to them. Adam served as the Master Dominant in their flagship Los Angeles club, the Gaoler. Rick and Matt tried to draw him out at various times to discuss his business-only policy regarding sex. The most they could get from him was his long life, possibly spanning thousands of years, made emotional attachments with mortals too painful. When they'd suggested vampire women as an alternative, all they got was "not my kink."

"Did you scent anything different about her?" Cat pursued.

Rick shook his head. "I only saw her from afar."

Anna whirled around. "What if that's it? What if she's a shifter?

Rick rolled a fine cigar between his thumb and forefinger and then cut the end of a Cuban for Matt and himself. "Even in my five hundred years, I've heard of shifters, just like I've heard about elephants at the zoo, but seeing one…"

Rick lit his cigar, and Matt took up the discourse. "Right, you don't just run into one every day. We don't know their secret handshake."

Rick spoke as Matt accepted the lighter. "Intellectually, Adam shared with me that he was a shifter, but until the massacre at Barranquilla, I'd sure as hell not seen a dragon shift. Adam said he hadn't shifted in two hundred years."

Anna shook her head. "It's impossible to imagine what powerful and majestic creatures dragons are until you see one. I'm gonna ask again. Do you think it's possible she's a shifter?"

The group stared at each other in thought.

* * * *

The day had certainly not gone as he'd expected, yet Adam wasn't entirely disappointed with the outcome. These last few months felt like a trial by fire in many ways, with unexpected happenings and strange turns of events. Meeting Dr. Willow Greer was perhaps just another one of those. Still, he hadn't found himself enticed by a woman in over half a century. What was it about this doe-eyed sprite? He sighed with exhaustion. Perhaps tomorrow would tell.

* * * *

Barranquilla, Colombia
Ten Months Ago

The Lust for Life resort. Vampires out of control, engaging in the most horrific acts. Humans were torn apart, their tortured eyes pleading for help. Adam was unable to answer their pleas. The mob would have torn him apart as well if he had not shifted. He could not save the mortals, but he could save himself and his best friend, Rick Hiatt. Adam's flesh warmed to ombre shades of carmine and gold. His spine undulated and lengthened. Each leg turned outward as it muscled and formed claws. Clenched hands rested at his hips as wings extended from his back. Muscular arms lengthened into front legs, brawny and long, each ending in three vicious claws. Great curved horns grew from his skull, and his neck lengthened. Adam's gaze swept the ballroom as his mace-like tail unfurled. Mighty leathery wings, tested their flexibility and completed his transformation into a Blood Dragon.

With a definitive stomp of one great foot, he arched his dragon neck, crouched low, and with his snout, rolled Rick onto his broad, armored back. Massive feet plodded over the dead toward the balcony. Fierce claws balanced on the precipice. Then, with a bunching of his powerful haunches, he leapt into the sky. His wings caught the air, beat against the downdraft, and soared above the treetops. His shifting had been blessed deliverance.

* * * *

Damn fool! Adam thought. *The next time I check into a hotel, I'll remember to close the blackout drapes!* Adam rolled over and squinted at the clock—07:49 A.M. He clutched the pillow over his head and rolled away from the offending sunlight. He wanted to roll away from the dream. It replayed in a loop until about five minutes ago, it seemed, turning over and over. Even this comfortable bed did not put him back to sleep. He was awake.

Stretching and scratching and looking at his naked body in the mirror, he grinned.

What a waste of morning wood! I could be upstairs ravishing every square inch of that goddess!

He dug for his jammer swimsuit and prepared to do laps in the twenty-five-meter pool. He slid into his resort robe and grabbed his locker key.

How much sexual tension will I have to work off this morning? About seventy laps worth. Enh!

He found the pool pleasantly deserted at eight in the morning. Adam took a racer's stance and dove crisply into the pool. Around the fortieth lap, he reflected, *my pace isn't too bad for being almost a thousand mortal years.*

There are perks to being a shifter. He burst out of the water and caught his reflection in the mirrored wall. It was good to be a shifter in his prime.

Even with his exertion, Adam noted the water was a little too cool. He'd have to speak to the maintenance staff. He grabbed up his towel and began to dry off, noticing his ring became loose in the cool water. He worried it with his thumb. After five love matches, all of which ended in mortal death, he resolved to wear his last wedding ring as a deterrent to the bolder lasses who pursued him. In his mind and heart, he determined never to fall in love with a mortal again. His current incarnation as a Dom fit him perfectly; it allowed a certain intimacy and often sexual release, without requiring emotional commitment.

Willow probably saw my ring. No wonder I'm getting mixed signals. It's better for her if I keep my resolution, but how can I say I'll never fall in love with another mortal when there are challenges like Willow Greer?

Adam groaned with frustration when he realized he had a breakfast date in less than an hour and no suitable clothes in his locker. He might as well wear his robe back up to the room and get ready there. As long as he was the first one up, he'd take a manager's walk through the lobby to make sure everything was ready for the new day. He was, after all, an officer of the corporation and Rick and Matt couldn't have their eyes on everything twenty-four/seven. He saw the day shift as his time. He envied his vampire friends. Within the last year, he'd watched them court, marry, and turn mortal women into vampire immortal mates.

Unfortunately, this would not work for Adam, you were either born a shifter, or you weren't. There was no 'turning' involved. Could he entice one of his own dragon women to join him in this wide, wide world? Maybe, but probably not. Dragon folk were extremely reticent about coming into the mortal world.

* * * *

She hadn't had this dream in a long time, Willow thought, as she let the warm rainwater shower soothe her. It was simply a reliving of a series of high school and college encounters that left her insecure about a string of bad romances. Her latest wounds from a crush-gone-bad propelled her into choosing her solitary sabbatical in Scotland.

She liked Adam. It would be effortless to fall into those amazing aqua eyes and those strong arms. He was insightful, charming, funny, and even-tempered. Great qualities in a man, but she would walk away, she thought sadly. The fantasy could not outweigh the risk. Besides, he was wearing a wedding ring, and what was that story? No, far better to enjoy a platonic day while she arranged new transportation to Scotland, and then say goodbye forever.

Never the less, she, who rarely wore cosmetics, dragged out the smoky pencil liner. There was peach blush, and she slathered on a heavenly layer of coriander body lotion she found in the bathroom. Lastly, she dug out a slightly uncomfortable pair of jeans she would never wear in the field. She'd bought them because they made her ass look great. She pulled on her favorite cashmere sweater in deep cranberry. *Yeah.* She examined her reflection in the mirror.

I look good. Why am I doing this?

Playing with fire, her conscience taunted.

* * * *

Adam watched the elevator door open from across the room.

Oh, man, Rick was right. Heaven on two feet.

The space between them went silent; he listened to his own heart beat faster the closer she came. Suddenly, he was tongue-tied.

"I almost missed you! Are you hiding in the corner over here? Ducking the house detective?"

"I wanted to have a long look at you as you got off the elevator and walked toward the dining room."

Willow blushed and glanced down, her long lashes fanning her cheeks. "Oh, you silver-tongued devil, I think you've been kissing the blarney stone!"

"Ah, ah, ah! You earned the compliment; take it."

Willow paused; her face went neutral with shock. "So, what's for breakfast?" She asked, flustered.

"Well, since you're vegan, let me tell you about their fabulous scones with wild strawberry jam…"

"Emm. Sounds delicious! I'd kill for some coffee!"

"Comin' right up."

The coffee arrived, and Willow's eyes got round when she heard him order steak, three eggs and a side of bacon. She followed his recommendation for scones, yogurt, and wild strawberries, but looked at him seriously after the waitress left. "You keep eating like that; you'll have a heart attack before you're forty."

Adam waved away her concerns. "I come from a long line of carnivores with high metabolisms. Don't worry about me."

"I've been enjoying the room so much; I haven't turned on the news. Has the strike ended? If not, I need to book a ferry ride."

"Speaking of transportation, I have a line on a helicopter tomorrow. It'll take us right to Inverness, no charge. Of course, we do have to wait."

"Free of charge? How can that be?"

"Oh, it has something to do with their Grand Opening week. It's part of the Resort's services."

"My, they certainly are comprehensive…"

"You have no idea." Adam drained the last of his coffee. "The concierge would be happy to get you a cramped ferry seat next to a crying baby. You'll only have to stand in line with everyone else who can't fly out…" He watched her reaction from over the coffee mug.

"The crying baby was the over-sell."

"Too much?"

"Yeah, kinda."

"Okay. Your choice. Which one do you want?"

Willow gave him a sly smile through her lashes. "I do hate sitting next to crying babies…I choose the helicopter for five hundred, Alex."

"Your Jeopardy question is, what is more convenient than airline strikes? You wanna get out of here? I'll show you around the resort."

* * * *

Willow stared out at the placid blue sky with nary a wind. She turned as he exited the restaurant. "Wow! What great weather for February!"

Adam looked out the picture window. "You know, you're right. Do you feel like a walk? We may spend all the rest of our time inside if the weather report is accurate. You have a warm coat?"

She gave him an incredulous look. "Adam, I'm going backpacking in Scotland in February. Of course, I have a warm coat."

"Just asking." He led the way to the elevator. "Why don't you go up and get your gear and I'll meet you back here in five?"

* * * *

As warm as the day looked from the inside, despite the sunshine, there was still a damp chill permeating her bones. Willow pulled on her gloves, and her hands were comfortably warm, but she kept them inside her pockets as they walked along. The temptation was too great; they might end up holding hands as they strolled.

"There's the pond," Adam pointed. "It used to be part of the moat, which they got rid of centuries ago." A huge black and tan behemoth of a dog sprinted past them on his way to heckle the geese on the banks.

"That's a brave dog. Most of them are afraid of geese. They can be mean."

"Oh, Player's pretty brave. He loves to chase, but I've never seen him catch anything."

Willow gave him a suspicious look. "You know an awful lot about this place. Why do I feel these are not details you picked up in the brochure?"

"I spend a lot of time in Dublin, and I enjoy places off the beaten path."

"Didn't you say this was their grand opening?"

Adam rubbed his thumb between his brows. "Did I say that?"

"Yes."

"Um…I might have something to do with the restoration of the resort."

Willow gave him a skeptical glance. "As a psychologist?"

"No. More as an amateur historian."

Her skeptical look continued. "What don't I know?"

"I imagine we could write books on the things you don't know."

Willow shrugged and turned away. "Okay, keep your secrets. None of my business."

He capped her shoulders with his hands and turned her back toward him. "Oh, don't be like that. The owners are friends of mine, okay? It's been a fun project. Everyone should do something a little out of their comfort zone now and then, don't you think?"

His aqua eyes were mesmerizing, and all Willow could do was stare. *He's going to kiss me,* flashed into her mind. *I really want him to…I really* don't *want him to…* She watched his perfect lips come closer, and then his gaze searched hers, he hesitated and then withdrew.

Gesturing over to the pro shop he asked, "Do you like golf?"

"No!" Willow's answer was a little too quick, and she wasn't sure which question she was answering, so she clarified. "No, I've never been interested in chasing a little white ball. I like golf courses though; I always imagine myself galloping over those luscious hills." She bit her lip at his odd look. "But…but…that would be wrong, of course. The golfers wouldn't appreciate that…"

It was Adam's turn to be skeptical. "Right. Okay, if you like to gallop, do you like horses? Would you like to go for a ride?"

"Yes, I do like horses. The brochure said the stable was not finished yet."

Adam gestured in a different direction. "It's not, but we a have a few horses. Enough for you and me to go for a ride. If we can find a horse big enough for me…"

* * * *

The stable was warm, obviously heated for the horses, well-lit and well ventilated. Everything was spotlessly clean, but the two horses the large stable currently housed were stamping in their stalls. Willow could tell they longed to be out in the sunshine today. She caught the look of surprise on Adam's face when she marched directly up to a huge Clydesdale gelding and breathed gently into his nostrils.

"What…"

She held her palm out. "This is how horses greet each other."

"And you know this because you're a zoologist?"

"I know this because I'm an equestrian."

"Oh. A woman of many talents. I haven't ridden in ages."

She turned to him. "And you want to go riding with me in February?"

He shrugged. "Well…"

"Why don't you see if you can find the groom?" She suggested over-brightly, and Adam took off to hunt him down.

Willow took the time to introduce herself to the mare in the next stall. She opened her mind and heart to the communication she learned before she could walk. She'd been talking with horses since puberty.

She turned to the Clydesdale, who could easily carry Adam, looked at his nameplate, and telepathically asked, "Mephisto, do you ever carry people on your back?"

The gelding tossed his head and sent questioning pictures. "Saddle? Bridle? Man?"

"Yes, like that. You saw the man with me. Would you and…" She looked at the small mare's nameplate. "Princess, like to go for a nice walk in the sunshine with us? No running, unless you want to, just a nice walk?"

Princess head-butted her gently. "Yes, I think it would be fun, too. But Mephisto seems a little grumpy. What's that about, buddy?" Pictures flashed to her from Princess. "Oh, I see, they weren't gentle with you, were they? I promise those things won't happen with us. In fact, I doubt they have a saddle that would fit you. What if we ride bareback and amble along and enjoy the day? No whips, no spurs, I promise."

Adam returned with the alarmed groom who spoke up instantly. "You can't ride that brute! That animal's a menace even in his stall."

The tension between the animal and the man was palpable. Willow ducked into the stall. "What are you talking about?" She demanded, as hostile as the horse supposedly was. Both men reared back at her reaction. "This horse is as gentle as a lamb." Mephisto nudged her amiably and nickered softly. "Get me his bridle. We'll have a nice mellow stroll in the sunshine."

"He's got no saddle." The groom protested.

"We won't need one."

Adam swallowed. "We won't?"

Willow laughed. "No. If you can ride a bicycle, you can ride this horse with no problem."

"What about you? Who are you gonna ride? Or are you going to gallop alongside me?"

She narrowed her eyes at him. "No galloping. A nice walk. And, Princess deserves a little time out in the fresh air too."

Willow did an easy vault from the groom's hands onto Princess's back, but mounting Mephisto was a little more laughable for Adam. There was no mounting the Clydesdale from the ground, but a mounting block got Adam up and over. Adam didn't look too sure about all this, especially with the groom muttering about the horse being a killer, but Willow swore to him, "all will be well." And she was right. The worst was when the horse stretched down low for a tempting bit of grass, and Adam nearly tumbled forward.

Willow laughed and admonished Mephisto. "Oh, Mephisto, be careful, remember, the man is a beginner."

"You tell him."

"Well, he hasn't been out in a while because they're scared of him. He wants some green grass, but he'll plant himself and give you a warning before he reaches again."

"Unh huh. And you know this because…"

"I told you, I'm an equestrian. I have a way with horses."

"Really? Why don't you show me? Do something an equestrian would do."

Willow looked at him in shock and realized she'd gone too far. She needed to rein it in considerably, or the jig would be up. "Something an equestrian would do? Okay." She turned Princess, rode into the field, and did a series of dressage moves followed by jumping a small stone wall with perfect form.

* * * *

Mephisto let out a long, horsey groan and shifted his weight to balance on three legs. Just that small movement convinced Adam he was not an equestrian.

Willow trotted back to them. "Anything else you'd like me to do? Maybe trick riding?"

"Remind me never to challenge your claims." He nodded at Mephisto who was pulling at the reins to get to the grass. "He seems hungry. I don't know how he can eat with a chunk of metal in his mouth."

Smiling at the horse fondly, Willow loosened her reins to let the little mare graze and gestured toward Adam. "You can hold your reins loosely, like this, and let him walk along and eat if you want. It's not good equestrian form, but I don't think he's been treated kindly. Just because he's big, they think he's mean. He's not at all mean, as you can see. If you know the owners here, you should talk with them about their stablemen."

"Again, you know this. How?"

Willow shrugged. "I know it, okay?"

"Sure." Adam decided to change the subject. "So, what are you researching in Scotland? Blackface mountain sheep?"

"No. Plenty of research has been done on them, and frankly, they're a little boring. They're sheep." She looked away from him when she disclosed, "I'm studying wildlife in the lochs."

"In the lochs? You're not one of those Nessie searchers, are you?"

"Well, as a matter of fact, yes. I'm working to show Nessie and the other creatures supposedly seen in the Highland Lochs are either a hoax or simply large fish."

"I thought scientists were supposed to withhold judgment until they have facts." Adam raised a golden brow at her.

"You're not happy if I'm a Nessie searcher or a Nessie debunker. Which is it? Who are you rooting for?"

Adam shrugged. "Really none of my business, but I can tell you right now, you'll need warmer gear than you're wearing. It's freezing in the Highlands this time of year."

Willow looked him up and down with a challenging smirk. "Variations in temperature don't bother me." She glanced across the field. "And I'll be living in a motorhome most of the time. Thanks for the warning, but this isn't my first rodeo."

"Oh, I see." He stabilized his seat as Mephisto moved along, following the mare. "You're an experienced outdoors-woman."

"Since childhood. It was part of our family." The conversation lagged. "What was your family like?"

Adam frowned, searching for a way to describe his upbringing. "My mother was from the old country, and she held onto formality. Lots of protocol." Adam was astonished at his revelation. For two hundred years, and through dozens of encounters where he'd made up a Norman Rockwell style family life, whose members were all tragically dead, he'd never come this close to revealing what his family was like. *Why now,* he wondered in self-analysis. *Why with her?*

She bubbled up with ironic laughter. "Why, was she royalty or something?"

"You'd think!"

"Where was the old country?"

Why did I open my mouth? "Scotland. You know those commercials for researching your genealogy?" She nodded. "Don't do it."

"But I'm sure it must be interesting."

"Not really."

"She must have been some kind of gentry or royalty or something, even to know the protocol?"

"No, I think she's probably just neurotic."

"Ewe. Is that a professional opinion?"

Adam was uncomfortable. "I probably shouldn't say. Are these horses through eating yet?"

She flashed him a sideways glance from those fabulous eyes. "You getting cold?"

He faked a shiver. "Kind of."

"Well then, let's go back to the barn." She looked at Mephisto who suddenly lifted his head, alert, nostrils flaring. "A nice, sedate walk back to the barn," she warned. Miraculously, the horse dropped his head and plodded pleasantly along.

When they delivered the horses into their stalls, Willow had a stern warning for the groom -- treat Mephisto with respect. Behind her back, Adam supported her by giving the groom a firm nod. He guided her out toward the courtyard buildings.

* * * *

"Is it time for lunch?" Adam asked enthusiastically.

"We just finished breakfast!"

He glanced at his watch. "Two and a half hours ago. I can't help it if you wanted to stay in bed all day…"

She punched him playfully. "Do you always think of food?"

"No. I don't think of it at all when I'm eating. I think of it in between."

"There's something neurotic about that."

Adam shrugged. "Maybe I'm orally fixated." He winked, and his voice dropped an octave. "Or, maybe I'm a sensual guy who enjoys flavors and textures." Willow combed her fingers through her hair and thought, *could his voice get any deeper*? She smiled but looked away. "Oh, you must have some other things that make you happy. You said you enjoy chocolate. Isn't part of loving it enjoying that velvety sensation when you just let it melt on your tongue?"

He closed his eyes, tilted his head back and thought about the melting sweetness. "I'll admit, I like to keep one M&M in my mouth until the shell melts and I can feel the chocolate between my tongue and the roof of my mouth."

That is so hot! She gave an involuntary shudder and pulled herself together, but her voice was still slow and husky. "You can eat one M&M at a time?" He drew his tongue slowly over his bottom lip.

Omg! I know he wants to kiss me!

She hastily unwrapped a peppermint she always kept in her coat pocket and popped it in his mouth. "That should hold off your hunger pangs a little while longer."

His aqua blue eyes penetrated hers. "You would think that," his voice was a gruff murmur. "But it's not an M&M."

"Sorry." She looked away, stepped back, and pointed. "What's over there? Is that the conservatory?"

* * * *

Adam mentally clenched his jaw in frustration. *Damn! I'm pulling out some of my best moves, and she's not even meeting me half-way. What's the deal?*

He walked in the direction she pointed. "Yeah, there are some great exotic flowers in there. I know. I planted them."

"Is there anything you can't do?"

I can't get to first base with you!

"I'm not great at horseback riding. Let's go into the conservatory. You can enjoy the butterflies in there, and I'll get us some lunch. We can lounge under the blue sky in the tropical warmth."

"I guess I won't need my coat."

At least I can get something off you…

* * * *

The colors of the butterflies were startlingly blue and vivid orange and yellow. Willow was caught up in watching their graceful flight and wished she could talk with them. She found herself unable to talk with fish or insects. She mentally shrugged. Probably just as well. She didn't know if she would enjoy talking with a scorpion, though butterflies would be interesting.

Adam came in through the chain curtain carrying a blanket, and a small basket. Inside the basket were two rather large wine glasses, some cut fruit, a bottle of club soda, and a small bottle of wine. He spread the blanket on the floor and motioned her down. Willow pulled off her coat and joined him.

"This is lunch? No wonder you think about food all the time." She gestured toward the basket.

"Oh, no. They're bringing lunch. This is just something to wet your whistle." He poured half a glass of chilled sparkling water, carefully squeezed in a little lime, a cherry, and then added a conservative amount of white wine. He handed the glass to her and began making his own.

"No, thank you. I don't drink—alcohol."

"This is kinda like soda pop."

"Really?" She reached for the bottle of club soda and took a swig. "Why don't you enjoy mine for me?"

"Well actually, I enjoy mine straight up." He poured himself a generous glass of wine and lifted the glass in a toast. "To new friends." She clinked glasses. "Why don't you drink? Not that I'm pushing it. I don't want you to drink if you don't want it. Just curious. Is it for religious reasons? Are you in a program?"

Willow laughed. "For someone who doesn't want me to drink if I don't want to, you have lots of questions. But no, I'm not in a program, though I think the programs are great. It's not for religious reasons. Those were my parent's reasons, but not mine. I don't enjoy the taste of alcohol, and I don't enjoy the feeling of being out of control."

Adam studied her lowered eyes and serious face. "What happens when you're out of control?"

Willow's gaze flashed up to his in surprise. "What do you mean?"

"There must be a reason you always want to be in control. What are you afraid will happen if you're not in control?"

Anxiety palpably mounted in her. "It's just that I've watched people when they drink, and I think alcohol makes them stupid."

"Everybody?"

"I don't know about everybody. The people I've seen."

Adam stretched his long legs out, drew one up letting him rest the hand holding the wine glass atop his knee. "I'm guessing the people you're speaking of were in college. Right?"

"Most of them. Some were at the department Christmas party."

His laugh was a hearty bass. "The two worst examples of alcohol consumption from which to conclude."

"Why are we having this debate? I don't like to drink alcohol. I don't insist that you not drink it."

Adam shrugged, the epitome of interested innocence. "Just interested."

"I'm interested in something."

His turquoise gaze met hers. "What's that?"

"You wear a wedding ring on your left hand. What's that about?"

He looked down at the ring. "Yeah, there's kind of a story about that."

"I'm listening."

"I'm a widower."

Willow wasn't sure exactly what she'd expected him to say. She was stunned; there was a pause. "Oh my God! I'm sorry! That was so thoughtless of me."

He shrugged. "It was a long time ago."

"It can't have been that long ago, you're not that old."

He shrugged again. "Twelve years ago. We were high school sweethearts." He smiled sadly. "I suppose I should take this thing off now. I feel—naked without it, in a way."

"I'm so embarrassed, and I didn't mean to bring up painful memories…"

* * * *

Adam was disgusted with himself. There was a reason he wore the ring, and a reason he kept mortal women at arm's length. He was getting way too emotionally intimate with Willow Greer. He stood. "I'd better go check on lunch." He saw the devastation in her eyes as he left the room. He spun around from her to hide his hard-on, it would be difficult to explain. *What in blazes am I thinking, anyway?*

He peeked through the window to be sure she was all right. She added some lime to the bottle of sparkling water and sipped. *It's none of my business why she's afraid of losing control, and I need to shut up about it.*

3

The jacket of bronze, muted gold, and black was a St. John knit. She'd never owned a garment this expensive. There was a hook provided beside the closet door for whatever a guest needed to hang, Willow, supposed it was intended for robes. She placed the hanger holding her new jacket there, to see the dazzling effect from the front. She cringed when she looked at the price tag. The original price was twelve hundred dollars, and the castle boutique discounted it to seven hundred and then to five hundred. She couldn't believe she intended to spend big money on an item she would rarely wear. *Well, I suppose I'll be wearing this to every Christmas party, Department reception, luncheon, and college reunion for the rest of my life.*

She nearly dropped her wallet when the sales clerk ran her room number and gaily announced there was another discount, making her entire purchase with tax, one hundred and seventy-eight dollars. She couldn't believe it!

How is that even possible? The boutique has to be losing money on this! She admired the cut and the way the light caught the metallic thread. Her little black non-wrinkle dress from the travel catalog was unnoticeable under this gorgeous garment. *And, I won't embarrass Adam in front of everyone*

She wished she'd been able to purchase the pair of strappy Jimmy Choo's that looked suicidal for actually walking. Still, she'd blown her disposal income on the jacket, so she'd make do with her little black roll-up flats. Luckily, she was tall.

She decided to take a bath and rewash her hair since it was wind-blown and gently slobbered on by her horse. She ran the bath water and while the tub filled, reached for the toiletries basket. She noticed the one from this morning was replaced by a much more elaborate selection this afternoon.

Humm…I think warm vanilla would be lovely. And, I guess I'll add a little hair gel for definition.

It was something she barely used, as a rule, she didn't like the feel of gel, but why not? This was special. She even decided on dramatic makeup for the night. She rarely wore it. With her black eyes, heavy lashes, and naturally pink cheeks, she usually didn't need it, but it was fun. She was in the mood for some fun.

Walking out of her bedroom door, Willow felt gorgeous! There were undoubtedly a bunch of chichi people here tonight, and she knew her appearance could rival any of them. Plus, she smelled positively edible.

When the elevator doors opened in the lobby, she followed the musical sound of clinking glasses, subtle laughter, and live piano music. She paused at the doorway, wondering what the seating situation was and glanced around a truly spectacular room. She hadn't given Adam the opportunity to escort her around all the castle's points of interest. She'd love to know the history of this 'library' as they called it. The most compelling feature was the thirty-foot mirrored, vaulted-fan ceiling. The intense colors of the Fitzjarrald family crest, in the center, were vivid even thirty feet below. The hanging brass chandeliers bounced light off the glowing woodwork. The room buzzed with laughter and conversation. A tall staircase across the room led to the second level of ancient books in ten-foot bookcases, accessed by sliding ladders. Waiters, in tartan waistcoats, weaved in and out among the revelers, balancing trays of champagne. Waitresses, in peasant blouses with tartan sashes, circulated with scrumptious-looking trays of canapés.

Willow glanced around for any friendly face, but Adam wasn't there, and neither was anyone she recognized. "Champagne, Madame?" the waiter asked.

"Do you have anything without alcohol?"

A deep voice from behind, his breath sending a chill up her spine, answered. "Especially for you, we have sparkling cider." Adam glanced at the waiter. "Travis, would you please bring a glass for the lady? I'll take your tray." The waiter bowed graciously, and Adam sat the tray on a vacant standing table and picked up the two remaining glasses of champagne."

Willow gave him a teasing smile. "You think you're going to need double-fisted champagne?"

Adam inclined his head. "Really, I thought our host might enjoy a glass." He extended it to someone just behind her.

Willow jumped and clutched her heart. "Oh my God, I didn't know you where there."

Rick smiled the smile that got him his way with women since he was in the cradle. He took the champagne from Adam. "It's the rugs; they completely dampen the noise. Aren't they divine?"

Adam grinned. "Not everyone shares your love affair with floor coverings." He gestured between the tall, elegant man and Willow. "Willow Greer, meet Rick Hiatt, our host."

Willow extended her hand in greeting and Rick kissed the back of it, and lingered, holding on, while the gaze from his whiskey-colored eyes met her ebony. She sucked in a breath. "Hello. Nice to meet you. Your resort is…" she searched for a superlative, "is…supernatural!"

Rick assessed the room's atmosphere as if for the first time. "That was our goal, Dr. Greer. We aim to amaze."

"Please, call me Willow. This place is spectacular."

Rick bowed and released her hand. "We're delighted you could join us this weekend."

"Where's your beautiful bride?" Adam asked impatiently. "We can't have you flirting all night with the guests."

Rick grinned, ignoring the amicable abuse, and said mildly, "She's doing the final fussy touches, I think. She'll be along." The waiter reappeared with the sparkling cider for Willow, and Rick swooped it off the tray and handed it to her with a flourish. "We've contracted with farmers in Kilkenny, and this is traditionally made with their finest apples. I do hope you enjoy it." He pressed Willow's hand into his elbow and led her away from a gaping Adam. "Have you seen some of the historical features of the castle?"

"I've been to the conservatory. Your butterflies are beautiful! It was thoughtful of you to let us ride when your stables aren't officially open."

"I hear you have quite a way with horses. Even old Mephisto. I believe you're a zoologist?"

"Yes, that is my area of study. You must be a history buff?" She looked around at the crowd, many of whom were almost in costumes. "Was this supposed to be a costume party? Adam didn't say…"

Rick negated the thought with a jerk of his head. "Oh, no. Some of our guests have a flair for the dramatic."

Willow looked at the women wearing gold mesh choker necklaces with delicate locks and low-cut clingy sheaths with slits up to their thighs. Several of the men wore beautifully tailored leather trousers, Edwardian shirts of fine linen, and some wore waistcoats with pocket watches bordering on steampunk. On the other hand, Rick was almost austerely dressed in elegant wool trews and a deep wine velvet jacket. Adam looked delicious as usual in a modified tux, trousers, pleated shirt, jacket, but no tie or cummerbund. A light dusting of dark blonde hair snuck out of his open shirt.

Does he honestly not button the top three buttons of his shirts? As tailored as it is, I can see the definition of his pecs. If we were dancing, what would stop me from slipping my hand into his shirt? If I didn't know better, I'd think some of these people were Doms and subs .She dismissed the thought. That's impossible.

Within seconds, a spectacular redhead in a clinging emerald sheath and sky-high black patent leather heels appeared at Rick's side. "Please excuse my interruption. Fitz, we've received a call from the monitor below. There's a problem with the Baron. I think his companion feels unsafe, and he's refusing to acknowledge it."

Rick swore under his breath. "I'd rather not have to ban someone on our grand opening weekend, but God's nightgown, one more incident with this problem child, and he'll be on his way for eternity." He turned to Willow and nodded respectfully. "Please, excuse us, Willow. I'm afraid I have to take your date as well; Adam and I are needed below."

Willow turned a suspicious glance at Anna. "What kind of trouble can people cause in the basement?"

"Oh, sometimes they get carried away in the work-out room." She deliberately and on the dot changed the subject and Willow hid a grin. "You must be Willow. I'm Rick's mate, Anna. I'm pleased you came with Adam this weekend."

"Nice to meet you. I'm not actually with Adam; he recommended the resort; it's been a memorable visit."

"That's nice to hear. We love this place. A grand opening is a whirlwind." She gave Willow a sly glance. "You're sure you're not with Adam? You should be. The two of you look like you're made for each other, and he's a prince of a guy."

"I don't think he's looking for a relationship. And I know I'm not."

Anna smiled serenely. "Circumstances change." She waved at someone in the doorway. "Look! Here comes Cat!" She nodded toward a spectacular silver blonde in a riot of lace and chiffon, her peasant shirt slid off one shoulder, and her layered skirt was gathered outrageously high on her shapely thigh. Anna gestured her over and made the introductions. "Did Matt get called into the Baron situation, too?" She turned to Willow. "Matt is Cat's…er…husband, and Matt is Rick's partner."

"I see." Willow smiled, but it was impossible to ignore the mounting evidence that screamed BDSM to someone experienced in the lifestyle. Before she drew another breath to broach a question about it somehow, all three men appeared in the doorway, a little breathless and straightening slightly disheveled clothes.

"Here you are!" Rick accused brightly as if they'd been the ones to leave the party.

"Everything okay?" Anna asked.

"The Baron is leaving; peace is on the horizon. His companion will be enjoying a complimentary spa experience for the rest of the weekend."

"Is she okay?" Cat blurted out. "We don't need to be sued on our opening weekend."

Matt shrugged. "Apparently she didn't fully grasp how irritated the Baron can get when you try topping from the bottom."

Oh, good God! Willow whirled around to stare at the man she assumed must be Matt. *Dear Lord, each one is more handsome than the last!*

* * * *

Adam watched Willow's eyes dilate and saw her lick her lips at the mere mention of 'topping from the bottom'.

Son of a bitch, my little teetotaler, may not be as pure as she seems.

Though in fairness, she never claimed to be pure. He caught Willow's hand and drew her to his side. Leaning down, he whispered in her ear. "You look beautiful tonight. Sorry about that call to the playroom." His use of words was deliberate. He watched for her reaction, but Anna's swift intervention blunted it.

"Adam, you mean the work-out room."

Adam smiled lazily into Willow's eyes. "Do I?"

The four vampires stared at him. Decisively, Rick cleared his throat. "Anyone care to dance?" He and Matt led their ladies away to the dance floor.

Adam bent to Willow again, admiring her high flush. "How about you, Dr. Greer? Would you care to dance?"

"Sure," she replied weakly.

Adam held her securely in a dancer's embrace as they began a slow foxtrot. He could feel her heart beating wildly against him, hell, he could almost hear it.

Oh, she knows what's going on now, and her physical reactions indicate she likes it. What's her conscious reaction?

"We're protective of all our guests. Sometimes, people get a little rough during playtime. Some guests like that and others don't, but we never allow anyone to take advantage of another person. You understand that, don't you, Dr. Greer?"

Willow stared at him in astonishment, jaw momentarily slack. She lost the beat of the music entirely, and tread heavily on his foot. "Oh, I apologize." She gasped.

"You must be getting weak with hunger. Why don't we go into dinner?"

Willow swallowed hard. "Sure," she said weakly, again.

Adam grinned. "See there; you've even lost your flair for conversation. We have to feed you!"

They walked to the lobby, and Willow stopped dead, rubbing her temple. "I'm sorry, Adam, I need to go upstairs and lie down. I've developed a crushing headache."

"Maybe some food…"

"Yes, I'm sure you're right. I'll order some room service. I hate these migraine headaches. They never fail to come at the most inconvenient times, but I do need to take some medication and go to bed."

What can I say, if you're gonna run, you're gonna run.

"You know our helicopter flight tomorrow is at 7 A.M. Will you meet me here in the lobby at 06:30?"

Willow stepped into the open elevator. "Six thirty. Yes, I'll be here without fail, and then you won't need to worry about shepherding me around any longer."

Adam gave a small bow of departure. His aqua gaze held hers all the way down and back up again. "Shepherding you was a pleasure." The elevator door closed, and Adam returned to the library.

Rick turned when he reappeared. "Well, that was interesting."

Adam gave a wry smile. "She all but ran into the elevator to get away from me."

Matt let out an exasperated sigh. "I'm sorry, man, I forgot…"

Adam clapped him on the shoulder with one great paw of a hand. "Don't worry. Her reaction tells me, she knows about submission, she likes it, and she wants it." He chuckled. "She wants it from me."

Rick gave a skeptical smirk. "That much is obvious by her departure."

This has been one calamity after another. Maybe Willow is right. Maybe we need to stay the hell away from each other.

* * * *

As he repacked for Inverness, Adam reflected on the last time he'd made the trip from Scotland. It was the early 1800s, the docks were more treacherous than any airport, and he was expelled from home in semi-disgrace. He distilled strawberries in crockery and used the wine to seduce the fair Belinda, who was betrothed to the prince of the Fisherfield clan. The dragon-shifter clans held temperance and chastity in the highest esteem. When the dashing Prince Adam entertained and deflowered their would-be princess, the Fisherfield's demanded Adam's head. In a valiant effort to save her son, his mother, Queen Petra, sent him off to live in the mortal world until the hoopla died down.

That was two hundred years ago, and last week she sent for him. She was his mother, and the Queen, and of course Adam obeyed, but he'd already decided he had no intention of leaving the mortal world to live primitively with dragonfolk. It was enough of a shock to his senses when, in the treacherous situation in Barranquilla, his inner dragon took over and shifted. His initial attempt to head for home was interrupted by the pilot's strike, but nothing would interrupt him tomorrow. He was bound for Flight's End and whatever crisis awaited him there.

* * * *

Dominants haunted Willow's tumultuous dreams. She dreamt of Rick and Matt exercising their will over her in sultry Dungeon scenes. Her sweet release, under Adam's control, shook her awake. She stumbled to the bathroom for a cool cloth and stared into the mirror. She could almost see the shackle marks left on her by the spanking bench. She sniffed at her wrist, and it was there, the scent of lavender body wash.

Oh, what delightful spankings they were! Oh, good God, what other sensations had they awoken?

Matt and Rick's attention began with bathing her. She knelt in the steamy, lavender-scented bath water, facing Matt as he smoothed creamy lavender soap over her body, into every hollow and over every curve. His relaxing, strong hands made her skin glow. "Lie back." Matt coated her sex with bubbles and ran his fingers between her legs. The Doms' gazes met over her, and she heard their silent conversation.

"Let us begin with…"

"Orgasm deprivation." Their words were in perfect unison, two Doms with one mission. In an instant, her hungry flesh waited for them in an enormous four-poster bed.

Like bookends, their bodies sandwiched her, both athletic bodies, hard and cool. "Do we get to train *his* sub?" Matt murmured over her shoulder to his friend. Rick was ready, his flat hand poised over her flushed flesh, feeling the energy she radiated.

"You're going to question the opportunity to have her submit to you?" Rick scoffed as he rose to his knees and took Willow's waiting body in full view. "I agree …orgasm deprivation it will be." When Matt's body rolled away from her, she felt the mournful loss of the play of his chest hair on her back.

"Then, if she's not a brat, we can work those exquisite nipples until she pops." Rick's words were warm honey.

He pulled her to a standing position. The four-poster bed was gone, and they stood on a plush and ornate oriental carpet. They began to dress her in the clothes Adam chose. First, a sheer black open-nipple bra, one that almost completely exposed her breasts, pushing them upward and forcing her nipples to protrude brazenly.

Matt leaned down and alternately drew already-erect nipples into his mouth and gently bit and sucked them until they were incredibly engorged and distended.

Then, Rick gently attached a tiny gold tweezer clamp to each nipple, and she gasped with pleasure. "You like that? You know, this …" Rick flicked at her nipples extruding from the clamps, "…delicate gold chain connects the two clamps." He playfully pulled the chain stretching between her breasts, setting off a reaction in her core. It didn't hurt, it stirred her craving, for Rick, for Matt and yes, Adam somewhere in the background. Instinctively she arched her back.

From somewhere else, she heard Adam's voice. "Those breasts should feel beautiful, desired, like precious jewels."

Next, Rick's index finger held out a butterfly thong. Matt's cool breath assaulted her ear. "You're already so wet that before he pulls these gorgeous black panties up to your ass, he's going to have to lick you clean."

Rick stopped to blot her anxious flesh with a black silk scarf. He slowly dragged it between her legs and up to her rich, plump lips. "You smell hot, sugar sweet." His voice was a husky whisper as he brushed the cool, damp silk across her flushed cheek. "Lick it. Taste your cream." Rick wound the scarf around her neck, and then pulled the panties up over her fine ass and hips.

Matt took a long time to position the straps perfectly, the horizontal one across the small of her back, the vertical one straight and tight and deep in the crack of her ass. He gently parted the split crotch of the panties to expose the rose-pink of her lips.

She heard Adam's voice in her head. "Your flesh is like the petals of a rain-glazed rose." The skirt Adam chose was also black. A straight skirt, made of a pliable, figure-hugging fabric, so short it barely covered the apex of her thighs. Now, ebony fabric gripped her tightly over her rounded ass, and the straps of the thong were visible.

Rick stood, balancing two sky high-heeled shoes in the palms of his hands. "These high black heels will make those legs of yours feel longer, sexier and stronger if that's even possible." Matt held her hands as Rick knelt and bid her to step into them. Once she wore them, she arched her back, pushing that ass outward to mirror and balance her prominent breasts.

Rick unwound the silk scarf from her neck and used it, still rich with the scent of her searing, wet pussy, to blindfold her. "We're going somewhere that you've never been. You trust us, don't you, Willow?" And although she heard his voice within her mind, not with her ears, she nodded and felt each of their lips on her forehead.

She felt the bench at her hips, heard the sounds of the plush manacles closed around her wrists. The sound of a zipper, the noise leather makes when slipped down naked, hard hips and then the pleasure of Rick's sweet breath at her ear. "I can smell your arousal, your hunger. I know how far you've slid into euphoria and I'm going to have you trembling…" She heard the sound of lube on hard flesh. "…on the verge of that climax." His cock's thick head nudged at her wet lips; she felt the straps of her split-crotch panties spread as his length pleasingly filled her. The satisfying arch of his flesh stroked at her g-spot, and she shivered. "Oh, no, no, no, my sweet. I'm going to pull out if you try and sneak even a hint of an orgasm. So… Do you want me deep inside you?"

"Yes, Master, I want you deep inside me!"

Blindfolded, Willow's senses whirled. As unaccustomed as she was to high heels, she felt powerfully female, even at the hands of these mesmerizing Doms. Now, bent over the spanking bench, Matt's voice chilled her ear. "Those breasts of yours, they look…lonely. Perhaps, I can test your resolve. Would you like my hands on your breasts as Master Rick fucks you?"

"Yes, Sir. I would like your hands on my breasts." She heard his footfalls before her, then the sound of rustling denim and the lavender-mint scent of his shampoo as he drew closer. He was so close his wavy coffee hair grazed her face. She bucked at the feel of his masterful fingertips dancing over the tops of her breasts. Creamy flesh nearly fell out of the lace cups, the nipple clamps holding them rigidly in place.

Rick's thick cock withdrew abruptly, and his palm slapped her right buttock. Willow gasped at the twin sensations, the loss of his cock and the pleasure of his slap. She felt the heat of his phallus sheltered between her thighs and cried for his thrusts.

Matt chuckled. "Master Rick must have felt unwanted. Don't you want my hands and his cock?"

"Yes, Masters. I want your cock, Master, and your hands, Sir."

And the dream was unrelenting. They commandingly worked every sensual nerve in her body within a centimeter of orgasm, only to pull back to stark and abrupt sexual abandonment, her body limp and lonely in the shackles of the spanking bench.

When Willow's feet fought to balance, she ground out a long-expelled breath. Matt stood, and she expected to hear him unzip his trousers. She felt his hands slide the silk scarf off and there were casual steps outside the corona of light around them.

Adam strode into the light's circle. He was gloriously naked. Every aspect of his body was an example of perfection, from his muscular arms to his powerful thighs and carved calves. There, from a thatch of deep blonde hair, his erection curved tantalizingly up to his flat, muscled stomach. "Lolo, do you want to feel the blessed relief of your tits and your pussy exploding in orgasm?"

Now, she didn't cry at the loss of Rick's insistent cock, or the butterfly touch of Matt's fingers and lips. Looking up at the god-like body of the man who hijacked her heart, she swelled a deep inhalation and groaned back out. "Yes, Master Adam. I want to feel everything you want me to feel."

* * * *

The elevator doors opened on a virtually empty lobby. Willow's cheeks still burned from the memory of the overwhelming dream. After all, she barely knew these men. Rick and Matt were married, for God's sake! Even though she realized she couldn't control her subconscious, she wore her shame like a skin. Dragging her luggage, head down, she aimed for the front desk. Distracted, she nearly walked into the counter when she heard a too familiar voice.

"It's impossible for anyone to look this radiant early in the morning."

Her chin raised, and she gaped at Rick.

Why, God?

"I regret we've met under these unusual circumstances…"

"What?" she asked, bewildered.

Don't say, Master, don't say, Master…

"The pilot strike of course. If you were arriving as most of our guests do, we would have the pleasure of your company for a minimum of seven nights."

I would never survive.

Willow pulled out her credit card. "That would be lovely, but on a professor's salary it would also be impossible." Rick slid the printed invoice for her two nights and her purchases and meals toward her. She picked up the pen on the counter, preparing to sign, and saw the invoice marked zero. She slid her card toward Rick. "I don't see where you've charged my card."

Rick raised a halting hand and shook his head. "We couldn't possibly charge you—we've had so much pleasure in your company."

You, too? I'm a homewrecker! A complete slut! I'm going to Hell, and their wives will send me there.

"That's generous, but this is hundreds of dollars," Willow mumbled.

Rick's lips curled upward delightfully. "It's our pleasure. Your participation is payment enough."

"My participation?" She asked weakly.

Rick gave her a perplexed look. "Yes, your participation in our grand opening celebration. We have a highly selective clientele. We appreciate your mentioning us to your friends."

"Can't I get you to change your mind?"

Rick placed his cool hand over hers. "No, Willow. This adventure was on us. A satisfied guest is our highest compliment."

Willow swallowed hard. "I can certainly say I was satisfied." She swallowed again. "This resort is transcendent, Mas…Mr. Hiatt."

Rick crooked his head. "Why so formal? Please, call me Rick."

Willow looked at her feet. "Okay, thank you…" She slowly stowed her credit card and wallet.

Adam burst through the main doors. "Good-morning, Willow." He waved as he approached, grinning broadly. Willow glanced at his mountain-man attire.

He's so damn hot, why are all these men lethally attractive?

His face flushed, his golden hair windblown and that damn smile of his forced her to hold on to the counter.

Rick smirked at his energetic friend. "Ready to get on with it, Sparky?"

Adam shook a long finger at him. "Have you ever known me not to be ready, old man? Don't I always finish what you start?"

They glared at each other. "Who's calling who old?"

"Well, I'm ready…" Willow groaned inwardly. The men stared at her. "… to go…" She finished awkwardly.

Adam reached for her luggage, while Rick held her gaze with curious interest. "I'll get your bags.

Rick preceded them to the door. "I'll see you out."

* * * *

"Whattaya want, I'm doing my preflight," Matt answered Rick's call.

"There's a heat-seeking missile heading your way."

Matt stopped in mid-step and frowned. "What?"

"I'm not sure what spirit visited her last night, but when the elevator door opened, the scent smacked me in my junk."

Matt shook his head dismissively. "It was probably Adam."

"That wasn't what I scented. I mean he's part of it. She spiked when he arrived. But on approach to the counter, she radiated submissive satisfaction, oozing with shame once she saw me."

"Really? You think she's trained?" Matt moved through his other duties as he spoke.

"I'd bet the Dungeon on it."

"Well, this is getting interesting."

Rick's voice turned ironic. "You have a safe flight. The atmosphere could be highly charged."

Matt paused to consider. "You think Adam knows?"

"He's a trained Dom, it would surprise me if he didn't, but he doesn't have our heightened perceptions. He can't scent the pheromones, or the past as we can."

"I thought he was calling it quits with her once they landed?" Matt watched Adam and Willow approach on the resort golf cart.

"You've always had a detective's nose. Read her and see what I'm missing."

Matt grabbed the clipboard to resume his official work. "Oh, yeah. Because I work for you, right?"

"You know you want to. Later." Rick closed the call, leaving Matt hungry for more. He looked up as the golf cart glided to a halt.

"Good morning, passengers! Thanks for flying CGI Air. Are you ready for about an hour's flight?" He held out headsets to each of them. "It's noisy up there. This is the way we communicate."

Willow stepped into his space, and his casual posture stiffened.

Good old Rick. He can read a sub like I read weather reports. She's a sub, and she's sated, and now, in front of me, she's embarrassed.

She declined the headset. "I have a book on tape I want to finish, thanks anyway."

Matt shook his head and firmly contradicted her. "It's a safety requirement. You can keep one ear open if you want, but you're wearing it."

She grabbed it from him. "Yes, Sir."

There it is.

He and Adam exchanged looks over her head. When Matt lent a steadying hand to help her into the cockpit, he felt a jolt of energy rush between them. Her neck and chest reddened. Adam took the two seats in the back. Matt scented three things from him. Frustration, desire, and resignation. Adam was not a sexually satisfied man.

If you have one sexually stymied Dom, and one sexually satisfied sub, colored with shame and embarrassment, you have… Matt considered. A fantasy? No, a dream. His tongue swept his bottom lip, and his thumb wiped away his smirk as he powered his headset. He chuckled heartily. "Everyone ready for lift off?"

* * * *

After the way the flight to Inverness began, a quiet flight was almost a disappointment. Adam and Willow thanked Matt and wished him a pleasant flight home and then turned to resume their separate lives. Adam looked down at his cowed, erstwhile girlfriend. "You said you have a rental car waiting?" They headed toward the rental counters. He and Willow booked from different providers. He looked up from the papers he was signing when he overheard…

"I apologize, I'm from the United States, and sometimes I have a hard time understanding your accent. Did I understand you to say you're out of vehicles?"

Adam knew the voice. He didn't even need to turn around to know it was Willow, and he could imagine her dismay at deciphering the thick Highland accent. He walked back to the desk. "May I be of help?"

"Is that right? They're out of vehicles?"

Adam held, what must sound to her, an incomprehensible discussion with the rental agent. He turned back to her. "Yeah, there's a sheep herder's convention in town. It looks like I got the last car."

"But that's not possible! I updated my reservation. Look." She handed him the reservation email. Adam showed it to the clerk, who earnestly tried for pronunciation. Adam watched Willow's incredulous expression out of the corner of his eye. She turned her shining eyes on him.

"Alright, thank you." He turned from the clerk. "This is a motorhome reservation." She nodded. "Apparently they aren't kept here at the airport. He can arrange for the service to take you to it, but it will be about an hour's wait. I have a car. If you'd like to ride with me, the drop off is on my way."

Eros is with me! I owe you one, buddy!

Willow balked. "I think I'd better wait."

His expression was captivating, his tone engagingly soft. "I hope you don't have to wait too long." He glanced out at the sky. "Looks like a downpour is coming."

Willow followed his gaze to the angry-looking clouds barreling down on them from the west. "Oh, dear. If I hit mud on those dirt roads, it won't be pleasant." She gave him a sheepish glance. "If the offer's still good, I would appreciate a lift."

Just then, a car pulled up at the curb, and the attendant brought keys to Adam. He picked up her heavy bag. "I'll take this. Climb in."

Adam checked his mirrors and headed into traffic. "Have you ever driven in Scottish terrain before?"

Those fabulous ebony eyes flashed at him. "Hills are hills. I'm frequently in the wilderness. Motorhomes are a luxury. Most of the time I hike into my sites."

Adam quickly glanced at her and his gaze arrested on her enchanting face. "You know, you're far too pretty to be hiking the Scottish Highlands alone." A car horn blasted at him, and he corrected his steering.

"Do they let you drive where you're from?" But there was a telltale blush on her lightly tanned cheeks, and the saddle of freckles over her pert nose seemed to deepen.

"I have the license to prove it. Where are you going that you might be mired in mud?"

"You surely have a lot of questions."

"Just making conversation."

"I'll start in Loch Lomond, from there, certainly Loch Ness, and maybe Loch Morar if there's time."

"That's ambitious. What are you hoping to find?"

Her eyes were mesmerizing. "Dinner."

"There are most likely a lot of big ugly sturgeon. Do you fish?"

She nodded. "I often catch my dinner."

He pointed to a gas station, flanked by an adjoining lot of motorhomes with Rental Company decals emblazoned on their sides. 'Here's your home away from home'. He pulled into the main parking lot and ran around the car to assist her with the bag. "I'll say happy fishing and hope you stay dry and find something interesting."

She looked at him curiously. "Where did you say you were going?"

He leaned in closer to her. "I didn't say." She took a step back. "It's isolated; you wouldn't have heard of it."

Is she blushing?

"Oh. Well, thank you very much for the ride… and everything" She waved and turned to walk into the office.

He gave her his best parting smile.

Well, God dammit. Are you just going to walk away from me?

"Wait a minute, Willow." It was time for his Dom voice.

She stopped and turned. Said nothing but waited.

"Do you let people just walk out of your life?"

She looked at him in confusion. "I'm sorry; I've been preoccupied all morning."

He moved in on her. "I think you're exceptional, Willow. I want to say we'll meet again, but I think that's unlikely."

She said nothing, just watched him with sad, moist eyes. He hadn't expected to kiss her, and she wasn't expecting it either. He lowered his head; she drew back. He manacled her wrists with his large hands, and she stopped abruptly, allowing him to lower his lips to hers and then go further. He drew her hard and fully against him, not caring that his erection throbbed between them. His tongue caressed hers, tasting, tangling, playing, saying goodbye. Then he released her.

"Have a good life, Adam. I think you're exceptional too." She turned and walked into the rental office.

4

Adam accepted the inevitable since there was nothing he could do to change it. He was on a mission after all, and it was time to get on with his life. He remembered he had phone messages he hadn't checked. His phone had reasonable reception, and he doubted he would find better service anywhere else. The first message was from Helen, the gatekeeper at the Gaoler, in Los Angeles.

It was prime Helen, irritable. "Adam, you have a woman who says she's your sister. Here's her info. She was steamed. I wouldn't give her your cell number. Do me a solid and call her before she calls me again."

Adam saw the number was a UK country code, and he dialed it.

"Do you know how hard you are to locate?" Isadora's voice was light and young.

His heart lifted. "Is this Izzie? My baby sister? Where are you? Don't tell me they have cell phone coverage in the crater."

"Dumdum, I'm in London! I'm on reflection, and I've…reflected…I don't intend to go back. Could you be a big brother and take that message to Mum?

"Hold on there. I just got a Royal summons, and I'm right outside Inverness. I'm not going in unless you're by my side."

"Then, you're going to have a long wait."

"No, Izzie, I'm not leaving until the two of us have a face to face. Take the train to Edinburgh, and I'll pick you up."

"I have plans this evening."

"Break them. You don't want your brother to fly in breathing fire do you?"

"Well, all right, but I don't know what good this is going to do. I'm still not going back to that hole in the ground."

"We'll talk terms when you get here. I'll count on seeing you on the 5:30 evening train. Don't make me come and get you." He used his Dom voice.

Izzie snorted most disrespectfully. "Oh, my, where did that tone come from?"

"You're not too old to take over my knee."

"You would have to catch me first, Dumdum. But I'll come, for all the good it will do."

* * * *

It was raining in Edinburgh, of course. The wind blew in twenty mile per hour gusts, making Adam long for the beaches of California as he pulled his coat closer. He'd forgotten how miserable Scotland was in February. He could even forgive Izzie's reluctance to come home.

Parking in the hotel carpark, he walked across the street to greet her train from London. It was two hundred years since he'd seen her, and she'd been an awkward seven hundred, still in braids. She'd probably changed a great deal since then, at least he hoped she had. Possibly, she could recognize him.

The train arrived and released twenty plus tired travelers who dragged toward the taxi stand. Finally, he recognized Izzie's posture, though not her appearance, dressed in layers of finely woven wool, covered by a colorful angora poncho. Above her black leather knee boots, she sported beautifully crocheted knee warmers. Her hair was a pixie on acid; vivid rubine red spikes flew from every direction on her perfectly shaped head. Her lipstick matched her hair. She saw him first and let out a war cry of a greeting.

"Dumdum!" Her long stride threw her in front of him.

"Izzie?"

"Who else calls you Dumdum, or has the rest of the world figured that out too?"

He scooped her into a bear hug. "The rest of the world calls me Master Adam."

"Ooh, la la! Don't expect that from me. I'm hungry, and I'm not diving for eels at this time of day. You are going to feed me, since I've come this far, right?"

Adam caught her bag and hugged her again. "I've got a suite at the hotel across from here, and a room service order that should be delivered in about fifteen minutes."

"A suite! Haven't you moved up in the world?" She poked his chest.

"I've had two hundred years to work on it, and it was a lot of work, but I do okay for myself. What about you? You've been on reflection for a year. How can you afford to live in London?"

* * * *

Izzie removed layers of wool outerwear in the warmth of the suite. She gazed out the window as rain assaulted the glass. "I hate this time of year. Too dark and too wet. Must be a hard adjustment for you after Los Angeles."

Adam rolled the room service cart to the small table by the window. "Gads, yes. But, how do you know about Los Angeles and me?"

"I have clients on Rodeo Drive. I don't know how they wear it, but they snap my stuff up. Who wears wool in Los Angeles?"

Vampires, like Rick Hiatt, he thought. "Those skinny actresses who shiver like Chihuahuas from the smallest draft."

"Now that you mention it, I think you're right."

"Little sister, tell me more about this business of yours. You're obviously prospering." Adam pulled the cover off a plate of salmon and spring vegetables and slid it toward his sister.

She plowed into it, making short work of a soft roll and butter. Adam took his place and waited for her story.

"When I left Flight's End on reflection, I decided I wanted the excitement of London. My only real skill was weaving, and I found a loom literally in the alley. It was trash, and I dragged it back to my room and rebuilt it over the weekend. I was spinning and weaving within that month. First, I sold lengths to a tailor shop, and then he got greedy and wanted me to weave faster with cheaper wool. I dropped him like a rock." Izzie stopped to eat.

Adam chewed and nodded along. "What was your next step?"

Izzie drew a long drink of wine and patted the napkin to her bright pink lips. "I started weaving for an art gallery, and it was better money than the tailor. Then, as it caught on, women wanted wearable art. If I disappear off the face of the garment district, I'll have a few pissed clients."

Adam nodded. "Rodeo Drive? Really?"

"I was surprised myself. So, what are you doing in La La Land?" Izzie asked slyly and buttered another roll as she waited for her brother's answer.

"I manage a private club. Rather like a nightclub."

"Interesting name, The Gaoler." She swept the roll through the sauce on her plate and rested her chin on her palm. "If it's like The Gaoler in London that should be entertaining."

Adam put down his fork. "How did you get into The Gaoler?"

She paused and looked up at him through her eyelashes. "Is that why they call you *Master* Adam?"

His voice dropped into the Dom register. "Answer me, how did you get into the Gaoler?"

"It's not hard. I've made friends in London."

Adam sat back and touched his napkin to his lips. "Do your friends drink blood?"

"Not from me. That's not what I'm there for." She gave him a level look over her wine.

"Do not play games with me, little girl." His voice was totally commanding.

Izzie didn't blink. "Do not take that tone with me, Adam." It was an unmistakable Domme voice.

Adam guffawed and lifted his wine in a toast. "This will be interesting. We're going to see who out-doms the other. Of course, I have a few decades on you. Is that how you found me?"

"Well, your picture in the London office is quite flattering." She attacked her dessert.

"Do they know we're related?"

"Not unless you told them. Being a Domme did provide a good subsistence income while I was getting my business up and running. Now, I do it for fun. I'm surprised we haven't run into each other."

"Have you been to the Gaoler in L.A.?"

Sweet Jesus, say no!

"No, there wasn't time. But, you can see why I say, I'm never going back to rule over an archaic and repressed society. In fact, no one I know, except

Nessa Clark, Princess of Fisherfield Forest, has gone on reflection and returned home again. Geezers populate Flight's End."

"Why do you think Mother called me home?" Adam worried the stem of his wine glass.

"Time for me to return, and my messages haven't been affirmative. I suppose, 'I'm never coming back,' made her think—ya, know, I'm never coming back."

"And, that's why she wants to change the line of ascension? Well, I have news, I'll visit, but not to stay, and certainly not to reign. You say Nessa went on reflection and returned, of her own free will?"

"Nessa has always been a healer and a nurturer. If anyone should reign, and frankly, I think it's time for democracy, it should be Nessa."

"I met her recently. I hadn't seen her since she was a fledgling. Her dragon is stunning in flight." Izzie cocked her head trying to imagine what incident would throw them together. "There were women in trouble, and we couldn't have saved them without her help."

Izzie nodded. "If there's rescuing required, Nessa will do it. She's also wise and compassionate. The perfect candidate, really. It would be nice if she could choose a consort from Flight's End and unite the clans."

"Don't look at me."

"No, Fisherfields have long memories. You are still very out of favor there. Seducing their poor Princess. She did have a hefty clutch—three queens among them."

Adam winced. "I didn't know I left her in a family way. I didn't have a choice at the time; they were after my head. It was exile forthwith."

"Communications weren't like today. You were gone, and she was mated to Prince Alexi of Mount Denali. I hear they're quite happy." She tsked at Adam. "No thanks to you."

"Hey! I was bored, and she was appealing. It turns out strawberry wine is rather potent." They finished up their food and poured the rest of the wine. Once the cart was rolled out of the room, Adam got down to business. "If our kind are to continue, we have to bring the clans into the 21st century."

"I'm not the one to push that agenda. I'm definitely not their escort into the big wide world."

"I'm thinking we need to convince Mother that Nessa should succeed her."

Izzie took the pin out of her shawl and slid out of her boots.

She looks less formidable now.

"Well, good luck with that. Her Majesty has not gotten more tractable over the years. Her word is law, and that's that."

* * * *

The next morning as they drove to their ancestral home, their moods were as dark as the weather. Adam's early years began in the dragon's homeland, hidden within an extinct volcano, in the middle of Scotland's Cairngorm National Park. Flight's End was the name of the village which served as a gateway to their hidden crater home. The village was punctuated by the largest of the stone buildings, which housed the petrol station, post, and grocer.

A one-room schoolhouse stood outlined by neatly whitewashed stones, surrounded by one lane of cottages. A select few dragon shifters made a home there, the majority of residents were fey humans who shared the desire to be helpful but discreet. The human's psychic abilities allowed them to interact with fairies, nature spirits, and of course, shifters.

The little village hadn't changed much in the two hundred years Adam was away. The petrol station was new, it was a livery stable in his day, and the grocer stocked salted meat and fish rather than frozen foods. Essentially time bypassed the sleepy burgh. He pulled into one of the three parking spaces.

Adam and Izzie approached the round, pleasant clerk at the cash register. She watched them with bright blue eyes. She curtsied. "Good day, Your Royal Highness."

"Hello, Rachel, you look well."

"Yes, ma'am, I am."

Adam cleared his throat. "Yes, I've been gone for a spell, too."

Izzie gave him an amused glance. "Rachel, this is my brother, Prince Adam."

Rachel did a sharp intake of breath.

I see my reputation precedes me.

She dropped a cautious curtsy. "Good day, Prince Adam."

Well, that was nice and stiff.

He gave her his panty-dropping smile. "Good day, Rachel. We'll need two hut keys and a place to park my rental car."

Rachel held onto the counter's edge and looked up through her lashes. "Aye, Sir, there's a parking lot close to the huts. Here are your keys, Sir."

Adam held up a five-pound note. "Does this cover it?"

"For how long?" Rachel asked meekly.

"I can't imagine it will be longer than two nights."

"Oh, yes, Sir." Her small hand reached tentatively for the bill.

* * * *

Adam stood on the precipice of the land he left over two hundred years ago. His penetrating aqua eyes scanned the craggy mountainscape. The hallow holding the watch-dragon was still in use. The breeze blew back the waves of his golden hair. He stood naked in the noon sun as he summoned his dragon. Adam's cool Nordic looks warmed to ombre shades of carmine and gold. His transformation took place, and with a bunching of his powerful haunches, the blood dragon leapt to the sky.

Adam felt invigorated by the rush of wind, the crisp Highlands air, and the joy of buoyant flight. He circled the extinct volcano crater a few times, sweeping and swirling to enjoy the fact that he could. Izzie was a great deal less joyous. He could tell the impending meeting with their mother was weighing on her, and for a good reason. He'd been out from under the royal thumb for two hundred years. Although Izzie ruled as a Domme in the real world, she was still a daughter to be ruled at Flight's End. In the distance, he saw fledglings with their flight instructor learning to dive and rise. He offered them a telepathic challenge. "Catch me if you can!"

The irritated flight instructor recognized him in nothing flat. "Prince Adam, do not think you'll teach my fledglings your bad behavior!" she scolded and turned to Izzie with a much more welcoming tone. "It's good to see you, Princess Isadora."

He watched Izzie land and shift while he continued to taunt the fledglings, totally disrupting their class, as was his nature. Adam chuckled all the way to the settlement commons. He landed and shifted back into human form. Things were unchanged in two hundred years, except a freshly made woolen robe was hung on a peg under his name. Adam slipped into the robe and tightened the belt.

I'm home for now.

"Adam, you scoundrel! You've returned to the scene of the crime!" Magnus vigorously shook Adam's hand, until they patted each other in a bear hug.

"Magnus! You old berry picker! Are you still brewing contraband?"

Magnus put a finger to his lips. "It's still contraband, but I have about twenty-five regular customers." Adam tilted his head in question. "Adam, old man, we number about one hundred and twenty, now."

The prodigal son looked back at the class in flight. "With or without fledglings?"

"Without, but the striplings are every bit as rambunctious as we were. I guess our elders were right..."

Adam nodded. "Payback is a bitch!"

Magnus nodded toward the Queen's chamber. "I suppose you have things to settle with your mother, but when you're free, come around for a taste of my latest. It's been a good year. You know where to find me."

Adam waved as he walked in step with Izzie to see their mother. "I'll catch up to you."

* * * *

The lanterns lighting his way to the Queen's chamber were a new addition to this primitive world.

I wonder who convinced them to use these?

In his youth, the way was lit by torches. Wouldn't battery-operated LED lights amaze his mother?

His mother's Prime Counselor bowed to them. "Princess Isadora, Prince Adam." She intoned gravely. "Her Majesty has been awaiting your arrival."

Adam and Izzie bowed in return. "Mistress Carmichael. It's good to see you." He turned. "Mother!" He walked ahead; arms open. "You look wonderful, as ever." He embraced her and noted with a shock she was lighter and frailer, her hair now streaked with white. Her face was a map of a lifetime of responsibility.

"The human world has induced you to employ flattery." She patted his back and ignored Izzie. "Have you eaten? Let's sit before the fire and dine."

I know better than to decline a meal.

Izzie's lips were a thin line. "No word of welcome for me, Mother?"

Petra ignored her daughter entirely and turned to Adam. "Bridget has made her mutton stew. I know it's your favorite." Adam hid his grimace.

"Mother, I could have come here alone, but Izzie agreed to come with me. You need to respect her as your daughter and my sister." His voice was unassailable.

Petra stared into Adam's eyes and was implacable. "She has broken my heart, and I am done with her."

"Oddly enough, I think you have a stronger heart than that, but if we three can't converse and resolve this situation, I'll leave now and take Izzie with me. It's up to you." Adam held the chair out for his mother, awaiting her answer.

Petra's gaze swept her children imperiously. "You have learned disrespect for the Crown in your travels."

Izzie stepped forward. "It's not disrespect for the Crown. We are a family first, and royalty second. We must solve our issues together, as a family.

Adam recognized with amusement Izzie's authoritative voice. *She's more like our mother than she admits.*

Petra stepped close to Adam. "Please tell her…"

"No, mother. You will speak with us directly or not at all." He turned to Izzie and took her elbow. "Let's go."

Petra waited until they were nearly out the chamber door. "Wait." She sat elegantly at the table. "I will speak to her." Adam and Izzie expelled held breaths. She directed her speech to Adam. "A parent wishes their children would find happiness within their clan. Sadly, my heir," Petra gestured to Izzie, "will soon complete her period of reflection in the human world, and she has already refused to rise to the throne."

"Mother, I'm doing swimmingly as an artist and designer. I enjoy the world above."

Adam looked at his mother with compassion. "I'm sure we've both been a disappointment to you."

"I'm not going to live forever, children. I need one of you to come home and assume your responsibilities." The servers brought their food.

"And what do you consider our responsibilities to be?" Adam spoke, as a bowl was set before him.

"There are crops to be planted, herds to manage, fledglings taught, disputes settled. Someone must learn to rule."

Adam broke the large crusty loaf of bread and passed it to Izzie. "I'm sorry to tell you, Mother, if I were to rule, our homestead would be brought up to today's standards. Primarily, we would have communication with the outside world. There's no reason our fledglings should remain uneducated. Why should we live primitively without modern conveniences?"

"You disappoint me, son. If we were to modernize, it would be only a few years before we'd be discovered."

Izzie spoke up. "The settlement probably has been discovered, already."

Petra gave her a look of alarm.

Adam picked up her train of thought. "In fact, with satellite photography, our settlement is visible to anyone who wants to view this area. That doesn't mean we have to be revealed as shifters. Many other shifter species have survived for thousands of years within the human world."

Petra sniffed. "They live remotely."

"No, not all of them. They take advantage of the modern world. If you want to keep your people primitive, you'd best be Queen forever," Izzie declared.

Adam was curious. "How many other young dragonfolk have gone into the world for their period of reflection and chosen to stay among the humans? How many?"

Petra's face was a stony mask. "What are you suggesting?"

Izzie spoke softly but firmly. "This is an antiquated system, and unless we modernize, our species will eventually die from attrition. At least agree to some modern conveniences."

Petra pushed the meal away from her. "The matriarchal system has always worked well for our kind."

Izzie gestured with her spoon. "That's not what I'm challenging. You need a queen, a young queen, who can lead the clan into the 21st century."

* * * *

Anna and Cat twittered in Anna's spacious walk-in closet, picking out their best garden party dresses. "I've never met a real Duke, before." Anna giggled. "I don't know how to act."

"I know. Neither have I. Are we supposed to curtsey?"

"Excuse me?" Rick demanded, incredulously. In the sixteenth century, he'd been the Duke of Erne, Earl of Mayo, and the women had known that fact for months. Rick looked so adorably indignant; Anna had to laugh. He filled the doorway with his hands on the frame. His athletic physique complimented by the fawn riding breeches and tall leather dress boots accentuating his long legs. The warm, burnt sienna and gold in his tweed jacket and vest gave life to his pale vampire complexion. Anna was sure to supply him with a russet shirt to further heighten the effect. Standing imposingly, he was the epitome of handsome Irish aristocracy, with his caramel-colored hair and whiskey-brown eyes.

"Oh, I know, Fitz." Anna gave him a perfunctory kiss on the cheek. "And I suppose from your point of view, Ian Fitzjarrald is the interloper and you're still the real Duke. Unless we explain vampires, though…" Anna dropped her cute fangs at her mate. "…I don't believe he'll concede the point."

It was a year of enormous change for all of them. Anna, a girl from the heart of Ohio farmland, could never have imagined her life with a sophisticated and cultured vampire of five hundred years. She was sure Cat also never envisioned her love-match with an unconventional and spontaneous vampire like Matt. Even at one hundred and twenty years, with his matinee idol good looks, he was the free spirit of their circle. He fit Cat perfectly; they would have made the covers as America's sweethearts if they'd been in the entertainment business. As word of the renovations at the castle spread, British photographers were hungry to snapshots of the beautiful people bringing the estate into the 21st century.

The pre-opening meeting with the current Duke and Duchess of Erne would lend legitimacy to the re-purposing of the castle. In this day and age, Irish royalty couldn't afford to maintain their traditional estates but welcomed their transformation into resorts everyone could enjoy. All the media were eager to document the grand opening.

Matt ambled into the master bedroom. "Where is everybody?"

Rick was still up in arms. "Can you believe these two wondered how to treat a Duke when they've been living with one for at least six months?"

Matt bowed to him solemnly. "It's a travesty, your Grace." Cat ducked under Rick's arm and hugged her husband. They were the perfect opposites of dark and light. She looked up and down his tall, strapping frame.

"Going casual today?" She teased, checking out his denim jodhpurs, flannel shirt, and fleece gilet.

Matt shrugged. "If we were home, I'd be wearing a cowboy hat and chaps."

Cat got a wicked grin. "And you could bring those chaps back to the bedroom."

Matt nudged her with a hip. "You got it, baby." He looked over to Rick. "I don't have to put on airs for this guy, do I?"

Rick smirked at him. "Certainly not, I'll just tell him you're the stable hand."

Anna shook her head. "Don't listen to him, Matt, he's just cranky because he doesn't get to be the Duke."

Rick dropped his head and danced his tongue along Anna's ear. His voice was dark honey. "Don't you want to be my duchess?"

"Oh, Fitz, you're always the Duke in my book."

"He's welcome to the title. Just a lot of folderol and government red tape, if you ask me." Rick checked his tie in the mirror. "I feel sorry for the poor guy. He's got the title and some property with no money to maintain it. I hope he's got a good job."

"I read he's an excellent polo player." Cat popped Matt's flannel collar over his gilet.

"Maybe you two can bond over horses, after all, you are cousins." Anna chimed in.

Rick arched a brow. "Very distant cousins."

Anna dismissed his objections with a wave of her hand. "Well, they'll be here soon, and we ladies need to get dressed."

Cat consulted her calendar on the phone. "I have the photographer scheduled for eleven this morning."

Anna checked her watch. "Mornings are a bitch for newly-turned vampires."

Rick turned to leave the walk-in closet. "You ladies have been real sports about being up all hours during this renovation. Especially newly turned, we should be letting you rest. Your hours simply don't mesh with the mortal world, unfortunately."

Anna winked at him. "But after the grand opening, the staff will take over, and we'll get to relax, right?"

Rick winked back. "I have a few moves that will relax you."

* * * *

Willow parked the motor coach and saw the line of changing huts. These were the same huts she'd seen on the webpage, although the photo was from the previous season. The shape of the ridge was the same, but in the winter, the colored huts stood out prominently. Now they looked just like the huts on the beach back home, but there was no water in sight. She ran to the beginning of an incline and was gratified. It was the mouth of the extinct volcano she saw in the photos. She decided to take a break for lunch before she started up the hill.

Yesterday's internet-breaking news piqued her interest. She was aware the article could have been fake, but it was interesting it showed photos from Google earth of 'large flying lizards'. If this was not an out and out hoax, it was certainly an unusual species for Northern Scotland, where the weather was cold, and the lone existing lizards were six inches long at most. Nor did they fly. What interested Willow was the possibility, if they did exist, they might account for the "monsters" in the lochs. She was determined to follow up the source to its conclusion. After she ate, she grabbed her walking staff and headed up the roughly two-mile climb.

She'd gone less than halfway to the summit, surprisingly winded by the steep incline. In early February, the sun would be setting soon.

What good will it do to get to the top, if it's too dark to see anything? And, I'll probably break my damn neck descending this path in the twilight.

Willow retreated to the warm comfort of her compact motorhome. There was something about the wet chill of the Scottish landscape even hot tea and a goose-down comforter could not combat.

* * * *

A much more relaxed Adam and Izzie sat with their stiff-necked mother, who continued to resist their arguments. "Nessa would make an excellent Queen." Adam pressed.

Petra looked pained. "I agree she'd be excellent, which is why her mother, Queen Zora, has been grooming her to take over Fisherfield these past few years. Unlike my ungrateful children, Nessa has not shirked her responsibility."

Izzie sighed. "Flight's End and Fisherfield are a stone's throw from each other. Would it not benefit both clans if they were combined, modernized, and ruled as one?"

"My subjects would not hear of it!" Petra declared.

Adam shook his head. "Have you asked them? Let's put it to a vote."

Petra drew herself up regally. "This is a Monarchy."

Adam was undeterred. "It's a dying Monarchy. It could be a thriving

Republic of two clans." His gaze searched Petra's. "Mother, are you so power-hungry that you're afraid to let your people think for themselves?"

Petra turned a stony face his way. "It's not about power. This is the tradition."

Adam shook his head. "In the name of tradition, you'll leave your people leaderless?"

Petra thought for a moment. "The most expedient way to join the clans would be for Nessa as Queen, to marry Flight's End royalty." She cast a meaningful look at Adam.

"I'm not the one-woman man you need."

Adam thought for a beat. "What about Jude? Did he come home from reflection?"

Izzie rolled her eyes at the suggestion. "What? Jude was always the voice of reason, and he comes from solid lineage. When I last saw him, he was working wonders with crop rotation. He understands the Earth and our connection to it. Up top, in the human world, he was a voracious reader. He would understand the balance of two clans coming together."

Petra shook her head at Adam. "And you'd saddle another man with your responsibilities, again?"

"If he wanted it, I'd give another man the opportunity to mate with a beautiful and noble Princess and help both their peoples survive and thrive. I would never ask him to do it without his full enthusiasm."

"Humph." Petra glanced at him sideways. "If you have it all worked out, why don't you ask the people?"

"Let's call a clan meeting tonight." Adam agreed.

"Let's go put the word out." Izzie set off to start the ball rolling.

* * * *

Petra was shocked at the enthusiasm of her subjects for the proposed marriage, bonding the two clans. Nessa and Jude welcomed a marriage and were thrilled at the suggestion. The current queens saw the future, and it became clear, the future would be crafted by the young, who were keen to modernize.

Petra made the announcement. "By mutual consent, the bride and groom will divide their time between Flight's End and Fisherfield Forest. The ceremony will take place on the Vernal Equinox." The communities cheered in agreement.

Adam stepped forth. "I wish to honor the happy couple with a honeymoon at Serenity Retreat." The crowd murmured at his generosity.

Jude nudged Nessa. "Where is that?" Nessa shrugged.

Adam gave them a wry smile. "It's in the Peruvian Andes, a magical place for all supernatural beings, and I have it on the best authority from personal friends, a spectacular honeymoon spot."

* * * *

The sun struggled to show itself through the clouds and fog of the early February morning. Willow opened the door of the motorhome just in time to see an unbelievable spectacle.

What am I seeing? Massive wings carrying a…dragon? Is that a dragon? Wow!

Willow pinched her forearm and looked around.

Am I where I parked last night? Have I been transported through some vortex?

She walked boldly, if uncertainly, out to the end of the treeline.

I hope he isn't the fire-breathing type…

To her surprise, the creature seemed headed for a changing hut. The dragon made an elegant landing, and in front of her astonished eyes, the air around the creature shimmered as his human shape emerged. It was a form she'd fantasized about since their fortuitous meeting at the Dublin Airport. Willow held her breath as she spied on Adam from behind a tree.

He stood in the meager sunlight and rolled his shoulders, shook out his arms and crooked his neck from side to side. He looked over one shoulder, and then the other as if searching for something. Finally, he paused, and bellowed "Who's there?" He turned and looked directly at the tree hiding her. "I know you're there. Show yourself."

Willow sheepishly stepped from behind the tree's shelter. "Good morning." She crossed her arms in the morning chill and stood there in her pajamas.

"Are you following me?" Adam stood, hands on his slim hips. The pose accentuated his eight-pack abs, flat belly, and highly toned obliques.

Willow caught her bottom lip between her teeth.

Leapin' lizards, you are perfection!

Of course, it didn't hurt the rays of the sun seemed to radiate from him. She was momentarily speechless.

His voice was low, deep, and commanding. "I asked you a question, and I expect an answer."

"I think we have something in common." Her thumbs slid her pajama bottoms down her thighs, and as she stepped toward him, she wiggled her sweatshirt over her head. She could feel his eyes all over her, and she grinned behind the sweatshirt.

He huffed out a breath and shifted from one foot to the other. "Are you a dragon?"

Her impish smile emerged as she tossed the sweatshirt aside. "Not exactly."

* * * *

Adam watched her extend her arms forward, the air became highly charged, and her flesh began to mutate. Long, coltish arms and legs ended with horse's hooves, her pixie face elongated, and a brilliant black mane spread down her elegantly arched neck. With a flip of her black and white tail, Adam saw a dainty black and white paint Arabian mare where a woman once stood. At least he thought she was a horse until she lowered her head and whinnied as a pair of luminous, feathery, snowy wings with black tips extended from her withers. She trotted up to him and bumped him in the chest with her muzzle.

He put out an incredulous hand to touch her forelock. "Pegasus?" Her flashing black eyes, so like her human self, challenged him. "Okay."

5

The air tingled around him as he shifted and in two steps they were off, soaring above Flight's End. Willow followed him as he glided over the Crater Lake, he made room for her to fly wing tip to wing tip with him, careful not to interfere with her flight. *Welcome to my home.* Adam inclined his head toward the settlement below and spoke telepathically.

So, you are real. It's not a hoax. Willow arched her neck and flipped her tail, and he could not help admiring her graceful flight. He watched the human forms below them point up to her excitedly, the children, especially, jumped up and down as they pointed.

Adam projected. *I think you're a hit.*

They've never seen a Pegasus. Willow shook her shimmering mane. *Let's give them a show!* Her speed accelerated as she launched herself into a half roll. *If you can't keep up, I'll understand.* Her black and white markings tumbled like a dancing harlequin as she slipped into a split-S maneuver. She watched over her shoulder as Adam followed, pulling sharply up before his tail slapped the water. With a whip of one wing, he splashed the water at her and laughed delightedly at her indignant snort

I may not be as quick as you, Lolo, but can you do this? Adam swept in a circle over the lake and projected a stream of fire, blood red as his deepest coloring

Willow snorted again. *That's hardly a test of agility, but I will give you points for originality.*

She was off again, Adam hovered in place as Willow beat her wings to fly a lazy figure eight above him. *If she's this limber in the air, I can only imagine how we'd tear up the sheets.*

Willow's flight abruptly halted, and she hovered muzzle to muzzle. In the air over the crater, the mighty size of his dragon contrasted by her petite Pegasus, yet she was undaunted by his commanding wing spread. *You know, I can hear your thoughts. And yes, I can be more flexible than you'd ever imagine.*

Damn! C'mon! Adam led her back over the crater's edge and low over the rooftops of the waking village, where school children waved to them as they headed into class. They rose over the treetops of the forest that retained their pine scent even during the winter. Adam loved their crispness. They dipped low over a sparkling, rushing river, and saw eagles grabbing their breakfast from frigid waters. Then soared up again, over a snow-dusted mountaintop and buzzed the remnants of an ancient castle sitting at the mouth of the loch. Elk looked up at them as they flew back toward home.

Our flight is exhilarating. What a beautiful place this is! Why would you ever leave? Willow exclaimed, touching her dainty hooves in a perfect landing.

Adam landed and shifted straight away. "It is beautiful when I can share it with you!"

Willow shifted and grabbed her clothes up before her, while Adam dug in his duffle for jeans. "All this flying has made me hungry! Have you eaten breakfast? Would you like to join me in my motorhome?"

I'd be a fool to admit I ate my weight in breakfast before I left.

"I'd love to share some breakfast with you."

Adam stared at her intently as she dressed, and finally stepped into his clothes. She was shivering.

Are these shivers from cold or anticipation?

He instinctively wrapped an arm around her but noticed she was barefoot. "Where are your shoes?" He slung one muscular arm under her knees and proceeded to carry the laughing woman to her motorhome.

When they got to the steps, she demanded. "Put me down. I promise you'll bang your head on the door if you don't."

Adam let her feet hit the dewy grass. "It wouldn't be the first time."

She pulled open the door and looked over her shoulder. "I'll say mind your head, anyway, this might be a tight fit for you."

Adam stood on the bottom step and poked his head into the motorhome. Looking both ways and up, he leered. "I like tight fits. It's cozy, but it has every modern convenience."

"With the equipment I saw, I'll bet everything's a tight fit."

Adam crooked a devilish grin and stepped into the cramped interior. "I'd be happy to evaluate your equipment." He immediately bent his knees to avoid hitting the ceiling.

"We'll see." She shrugged.

Adam plopped into the first seat he saw. "This is comfortable."

Willow opened the narrow storage door. "Granola with almonds or granola with raisins?"

"No granola with bacon for me?" Adam made a face.

"You were the one who said we'd never see each other again. Do I look like I carry bacon to catch men? Coffee?"

"Coffee's good."

Willow retrieved the four-cup coffee maker from the cabinet and set about brewing it. Adam watched her graceful movements in such a small area. He rose silently to stand behind her and scent her after-flight musk. He noticed her short chocolate hair dewy and curled at her neck. He was gratified when she bent over to grab the soy milk from the tiny refrigerator. Her round and firm buttocks nailed him in the groin.

She squealed. "Adam!" She grabbed for the counter, off balance. He steadied her by catching her hips. She taunted him, "I've got it now, you can let go, thank you."

"No, I'm fine here."

"Well, I'm not. Let go." Willow shrugged out of his hands.

She pointed to the passenger's seat. "Why don't you just sit down by the table where you're safe?"

Adam slumped close to her, his right hand on the counter. "I'm completely comfortable right here, in case you need something from the top shelf."

"You're *so* helpful."

"That's my game plan; I'll be so helpful you can't live without me."

"What does a girl have to worry about with you?" Willow leaned her hip against the opposite counter, arms folded over her sweatshirt. "Are you—too hot to handle?"

"I've been told I have smoldering bedroom eyes, but not that way." Adam leaned against the cabinet wall. "For days I tried to send you signals, I kept getting the brush-off. So, I'm not sure if it's me or if you're otherwise involved."

Willow's gaze homed in on his left hand. "Your ring is gone." Those big brown eyes narrowed at him.

Startled, he looked at his left hand. "Yeah, but the mark will take a while to fade."

She handed him his coffee and sat in the opposite chair with her cup. "So, where do we go from here, Adam?"

"We're both shifters. You must know we outlive mortals by hundreds of years. I wore the ring to discourage messy emotional entanglements."

Willow nodded appraisingly. "What makes you think I wouldn't be a messy entanglement?"

"We have more in common. You're not going to age and die in fifty years." Adam watched her reaction to his words. Willow frowned and worried her bottom lip, and then took a large gulp of coffee. She was quiet for longer than he expected.

"I have no idea how long I'll live. Do you? Have you ever met a Pegasus shifter?"

"No. Mostly I've been with dragons, recently with eagles or orcas." He watched her expression change from guarded to curious. "I've spent the last two hundred years in the company of mortals and vampires."

* * * *

"Vampires? Who live in castles?" Awareness dawned with her words. "Like those four friends of yours?"

Adams brows rose, and he smirked. "Ya caught me! Guilty as charged." He waited for a beat. "Any questions about that?"

"Not right now." She returned to drinking her coffee. After a few moments of silence, she raised a finger. "Are orcas the basis for mermaids?" she asked brightly.

"No, mermaids are their own species." He looked at her closely. "This is all pretty much standard shifter stuff. Why all the questions?" Adam sipped his coffee.

"I was born to shifters, of course, but they died before I was two years old. Mortals raised me. I've never known another shifter. I didn't know anyone else existed."

"How old are you?"

"I'll be thirty-two my next birthday." She looked him up and down. "How about you?"

"You've never met any other shifter?"

Willow shook her head. "God's truth. I thought I was a freak. I guess that's why I study zoology. I thought maybe I'd find out what was wrong with me."

"From where I'm sitting there isn't a damn thing wrong with you!" He turned serious. "Have you aged from say, age twenty-five?"

"Not that I can tell."

Adam nodded. "Most dragons don't age after thirty. Not until we're two or three thousand years."

Her enormous eyes grew even wider. "Holy crap! Then, how old are you?"

Adam shrugged. "Uh…nine hundred and ninety-five on my next birthday. Listen, about that moment we had…" She blushed. *He's a shifter.* All those forbidden longings were now real possibilities. "I'm sorry if that touch was inappropriate. In my line of work, I'm direct about what I want." Adam swallowed the last drop of coffee.

"What line of work would that be? Psychologist? Historian? Gardener?"

Adam shrugged. "You really were listening when I gave you the tour. My true role is as the Master Dominant at our Los Angeles club."

Willow put her cup down and leaned forward, filled with interest. "The Los Angeles club? There's one in the basement at the resort, right?"

Did my dream unconsciously pick up on the vibe?

"Yeah, but I'm not Dungeon master there."

Willow grinned knowingly. "Who is? Rick? Matt?"

"They're that and much more. They originated the BDSM model as Consort Group and then went international. Erne Castle is just their most recent addition. Of course, Rick and Matt keep their hands in play. You realize, exchanging donor blood for BDSM sex is one of the ways vampires eat?"

Willow gaped at him and smiled slowly. "Wow! That's genius!"

"I thought so, too." He extended a long arm and caught her hand. He raised it to his lips, holding eye contact with her. "What does this mean to us?" He paused, and when she was silent, he continued, "Have you been looking for a Dominant shifter?"

"I never thought I'd meet one. It would be nice to be in the hands of a man who knows what he's doing."

Especially one who looks like a Norse god!

Adam's grin spread across his face, and her grin answered. "Am I that man?"

"How's your Shibari?"

"Ah, a devotee?" he asked, intrigued.

"We all have our little kinks. What's yours?"

Adam's blonde brow arched as he assessed her reactions. "I'm a Dungeon master, I can do anything, but if you're asking about my personal preferences, I know more knots than a boy scout, and I am a Dominant."

"So, you've never been tied up?"

"I wouldn't say that. There are more ways than one to fly."

Willowed gasped. "You know about flying?" Her voice was eager, her eyes wide.

"Did I pluck a nerve? Is that your ultimate kink, Lolo?"

She shivered. "Maybe someday you'll find out."

He laughed haughtily. "I'll find out today."

With those words, she overfilled her cup and jumped at the mess she made. With a calm sigh, Adam grabbed the dish towel and began mopping up.

Willow sat at the table, agog. "You must have a lot of sex."

"Generally, no. Not more than once or twice a day." Adam dropped the dish towel in the sink.

"You must know all kinds of things…" Willow watched his graceful movements in such a cramped space.

If he can move like that bent over, dear God, what other moves has he got? "On vacation do you avoid sex?"

Adam chortled. His blonde head threw back, and it grew to a guffaw.

"I mean you don't want to take your work home?"

Bring it on, bring it all on!

"Love your work, and you never work a day in your life." Adam's aqua eyes twinkled.

I don't dare do this, do I?

"Oh, yes, you can." Adam laughed.

"Are you reading my mind?"

"Lolo, I don't have to be a telepath to read your mind, right now." He took her hand and led her to the unmade bed. "Strip." He reached out to the band of her sweatshirt.

"Do I have to call you Master?"

"I don't remember permitting you to speak at all. But, since we're getting to know each other, let's say what comes naturally."

As her arms rose to release the shirt, she shivered. His head dropped down to her cheek, and he trailed soft, warm, kisses to her mouth, and pulled her tightly against him. "Let's get rid of those too." His thumbs invaded her pajama bottoms and dropped them to the floor. He helped her balance as she stepped out of them.

Willow couldn't wait to get another glimpse of his phenomenal body. She visually ate up the soft blonde hair covering his pecs, and her gaze followed the inviting line of hair disappearing behind his belt buckle. The sight of his perfect torso intoxicated her. He took her hand and placed it on his belt. "I like it when a woman takes the initiative…"

Willow rubbed the front of his jeans. "I wanna feel every inch of you!"

She released his belt buckle and jeans, eager for another look at his package. The glimpse she saw before he dressed was impressive, hugely impressive. Even better than her dream. Her hand abandoned his jeans to stroke his proud, thick, cock. He pulled away to step out of his pants, and then, with a cheeky wink, replaced her hand on his imposing sex.

"I want to feel this inside me," she whispered.

"It will be there soon enough."

Willowed gasped. "Did I say that out loud?"

"You sure did, and I like that. Don't hold back your thoughts and feelings from me." His voice was deep and resonating.

"'Kay…"

"I hope you have food here, 'cuz I'm gonna make you come all day long."

"I've never been with an expert before." Willow giggled.

"Does that excite you?"

"You excite me! Look at you! The fact that you're an expert at what you're doing is icing on the cake!" Willow trailed a fingernail down the center of his chest to the root of his hefty erection, "So, yeah, I'm excited."

"What a nice thing to say." He rumbled. "I've wanted this from the moment I saw you." He kissed her deliberately, his tongue carving through her soft lips. She answered with her own playful tongue. He drew her down to the bed.

"You have any long socks?"

Her eyes sparkled. "What did you have in mind?"

"You leave that to me, Lolo. This isn't exactly the Dungeon, but I aim to please."

She left the bed and returned with a pair of utility knee highs.

"Do you trust me?"

"Until you give me a reason not to."

Adam leaned in for a quick kiss. "I'll never give you a reason not to. Left ankle, please." She allowed him to bend her leg back behind her. "Right wrist." He secured her arm to her leg, which was not painful, but was quite restrictive, and allowed him to do whatever he wished with her."

"What's your safe word?"

She gave him a sly smile. "Zeus."

Adam smiled back. "Okay. Lie back, Lolo. I'm taking you for a ride."

In the excited haze of their intoxicating new intimacy, his hands explored. His fingers upon her body, his lips following closely. The silence was broken by the beating of hearts, excitement's heavy breathing. He felt the warmth of her body next to his, his head on her shoulder, their legs intertwined. His lips were strong yet gentle in their explorations.

"Your body is soft where a woman should be soft, and round where a woman should be round." His hands glanced admiringly over the hill and slope of her hips. His commanding grasp held her firm cheek.

She caressed the length and breadth of his aroused shaft with her left hand. "Your body is hard where a man's body should be."

He laughed. "I sure hope so. If it weren't, I'd turn in my man card." He slipped the knot on her hand.

Feeling her pressing into him as their lips met, kissing deeply, his hands ran down her arms to let their fingers mesh. Her body submitted to his body's commands. Adam's breath imparted a primal heat on her skin. His chest received her soft kisses, as their intensity, passion and desire fueled their primitive electricity.

Willow put a silencing finger on Adam's lips. "Before you drive me wild, I want to get a good close up." She crawled down to the end of the double bed and came back up between his legs. She licked him from balls to tip, lingering to swirl her tongue several times around his head.

"Oh, fuck!"

She flicked her tongue at him. "Yes, I believe so." She caressed each ball and sucked them into her warm mouth.

Willow heard his fist pound the mattress. "Is everything okay? I didn't hurt you, did I?" she joked.

Adam's head thrashed on the pillow. "I hope you take as good as you give!"

"Oh? I'm just admiring an outstanding example of a man's body." Her lips covered his erect flesh as she took him deep in her throat.

"Alright! C'mere!" He pulled her up to him. She did relinquish his pulse-pounding flesh to climb and straddle him, catching his hard cock under her wet flesh. She playfully shifted from side to side as he let out a surrendering roar. "You're going to make me come before I even get into you."

"I thought you said you were gonna do this all day. We can't do that unless we get started early."

"I had no idea you'd take me literally." Adam's fingers playfully circled her nipples.

"Don't think you're getting out of this bed. You promised me all day."

"Yes, ma'am, a promise is a promise." He flipped her over on her back as he knelt on the bed. He looked around. "I hope we have enough space. We might need to drive this cracker box to a proper hotel."

"Before we go to the trouble of putting on clothes to drive somewhere, why don't you just wow me with a preview of larger coming attractions?"

With a wicked grin, he thrust her legs apart, invoking her gasp. He shuddered as he tasted her nectar for the first time, the warm, salty tang of her innermost fluid contrasting strangely with the cooler flesh of her lips. She caught her breath, hips rolling, yearning towards him as his tongue dove down into her depths. He licked up wickedly, sweeping the full length of her slit in one long stroke. Her petals opened under his questing mouth, greedily unfurling, and his tongue aimed itself unerringly at her bud.

His tongue circled it hesitantly, teasing her, until her hips thrust into his face and she voiced hoarse commands, demanding he pleasure her. Smiling devilishly, his tongue danced upon her sensitive clit, lips pulling and suckling at her button until her hands were locked in his long hair, her heels beating a frantic tattoo on his back.

Suddenly, she arched upward; her panting voice lost in a keening wail as she thrashed beneath him, trembling with the force of her release.

Quick as a flash, he turned her onto her chest. His hands slid under her belly, reaching up to cup her breasts, fondling her as he split her sheath with one sure plunge.

If she thought she knew pleasure before, it was nothing compared to this. He spread her thighs wide, the hard muscles of his belly slapping into the firm flesh of her ass as he thrust into her. Still trembling with the aftermath of her first orgasm, she was stunned to find herself approaching a second within moments.

She moaned. "What are you doing to me?"

"Exactly what you want," he said, hands busy on her magnificent breasts, fingers pulling her nipples until they were rigid.

Dipping his head, he plunged into her, hips bucking as his restraint gave way at last, and he drove toward his climax. His lips, gentler than the rest of him, caressed her shoulders and neck, and then her cheek and lips as she turned her head to meet his. Overcome by passion and desire, he lost control and thrust mindlessly, the thick length of his cock plunging into her.

Willow gasped, her muscles aching, spasming, gripping his sex as her release bore down upon her. At the same time, Adam felt his cock stiffen and grow, rigid with lust.

With a shuddering moan, their orgasms hit them at once, a thundering crescendo of pleasure, and Adam shouted hoarsely as he felt his passion's rush leave him. At the same time, she writhed in his grasp, shaking as the force of her climax swept over her, leaving her limp with joy.

She collapsed on the bed and rolled to the outside to grab a water bottle, while Adam stretched out diagonally, watching her. He lay against the headboard; one arm crooked behind his head, his hair a golden halo silhouetting his flushed face, smiling triumphantly, unabashedly exposed. In this pose, Adam personified a stalwart explorer captured on a tintype photo from a naughty photographer, casually masculine and tender of heart. Their completion came as easily as the right key turns the lock tumblers. This was where their purest love started…

Willow climbed back into the bed. "Does 'master' mean expert?" She raised a challenging brow at him.

"I think I did pretty well if I do say so myself. You seemed to enjoy it."

"For our first time out, I'd have to say; you took me by surprise. I'd have to experience the whole thing a few more times to rank your consistency."

"Is that a challenge? Because, you need to know, I'm *very* competitive."

"We'll see…"

"Oh, the game is on, Lolo!"

* * * *

As the dawn's light warmed the motor coach, Willow stretched carefully and wobbled toward the refrigerator. She was sure she'd used some dormant muscles in the past twenty-four hours. She needed a shower, badly. She looked at the sleeping Adonis in her bed, yes, it was definitely worth a few overworked muscles to run a sexual marathon with him. Even now, flaccid, and asleep, his magnificent cock issued a wanton invitation to rise and shine. As she stood before the bare cupboard, her stomach growled. She was famished. She regarded empty plates where they'd grazed on cheese, crackers, and fruit. An empty wine bottle, bought in memory of him only yesterday, was next to the bed. *Maybe a little wine, alone, now, and then, would be medicinal.* They took turns, drinking directly from it. She was enveloped in his tantalizing spell. Being with another shapeshifter, her need for control evaporated. *Bring on every intoxication!*

Adam silently stepped behind her and wrapped his long, strong arms under her breasts. "I need food. If you expect me to keep up this pace, I have to eat." Willow settled back into his embrace and sighed. "I've never been with a woman who can meet my challenge."

"It would be worth it to dress and go into town where I'll undress you again and start all over. Plus, the cupboard is bare."

"I hate to leave our love nest." His fingers stroked her sides unconsciously.

Willow turned within his touch, alive with a memory. "I need to show you something important, and I'll need the internet to do it."

Adam nodded as he began picking up his clothing. He sat on the bed to re-dress. "I need to leave my rental for my sister. Give me ten minutes, and we'll ride into Newtonmore. There's a nice little hotel. We can enjoy a hot shower, and a hearty meal—with meat," Willow made a face, Adam gestured at his physique. "I need fuel to keep this body working." She playfully slapped at him as she found clothes.

* * * *

The room was available directly, and as Adam opened the luggage, Willow booted up her laptop. "Check this out."

Adam watched as she opened her Google page. Under news, this was the third story. "Breaking News! Do Dragons Live Among Us?" She clicked the teaser, and a web news site appeared. Under the headline was a large, grainy picture of a dragon flying toward one of the lochs. The caption read, "Is this the Loch Ness Monster?"

"By Odin's missing eye! It was just a matter of time." Adam looked at Willow. "What is this site?"

"As far as I can tell, it's one of those conspiracy sites. You know, Loch Ness Monster, Big Foot, Aliens. Whatever's hot."

"Maybe nobody will notice?"

"I noticed. It brought me right to you. Now, granted, there aren't a lot of people who are going to head to upper Scotland in the middle of winter, to chase Nessie, but by summertime, adventurers will start to appear."

Adam nodded grimly. "Even if this gets discredited, we'll have the lunatic fringe circling—no offense to you."

"Yeah, right. You should see the discussion boards. He's fostering a number of his fans, and he even has a fundraising page to get a few together for an expedition this summer."

"We've got to put the kibosh on that."

"The way I see it, you have about two months to discredit this account enough to discourage expeditions. You'll have to warn your people because as you said, there will probably still be some who will try to catch dragons. They'll certainly find the settlement in the Cairngorms."

Adam sat heavily. "You're right. Our people have always been careful to fly at night or at least pre-dawn, but we're going to have to be even more cautious now. We need to develop a plausible reason for our settlement in the crater. This changes everything."

"Well, go shower, and then we'll have some breakfast. You'll think better on a full stomach."

* * * *

Darla, the receptionist, craned her neck into the open door. "Oh, Boss?"

"Yeah, come on in, Darla. What have you got?"

"I just signed for twelve boxes, here's the one with the packing slip." Darla placed the three-foot-long box on the desk. Rick read the label and a leering smile curved his lips.

"Darla, have the other boxes delivered to the Dungeon Master's office." She nodded and left the room.

Matt cocked his head at Rick's curious expression. "What'd you get?"

Rick used the letter opener to cut the packing tape. Once the flaps were up, he reveled in the scent of the dozen lambskin floggers. "Ahh, the virgin scent of untried lambskin!" His eyes closed in delight. Matt came beside him to view the delivery. He slanted Rick a dubious look. "I've never seen you wax poetic over leather before."

"Then you weren't paying attention, dear boy." Rick extracted the crimson and ebony flogger from its packaging. "There's nothing I like better than an untried flogger." Rick reverently placed one in Matt's hand and then chose another for himself. "Feel the tail edges, so soft." Rick closed his eyes and flicked the flogger over the back of his hand. "That kiss comes from the way it's tanned."

"It could be tanned on the beaches in Miami, and I still couldn't convince Cat to let me use this on her. I doubt you'll convince your fair Anna." Matt moved the flogger around in the air like he was playing badminton, then he proceeded to flog the furniture, walking from piece to piece.

"Have some respect, dear boy." Rick savored the sensation the flogger administered. "Listen to the plush, loud thump when you strike something."

Matt playfully aimed a blow at Rick's backside. "Yeah, a good thump."

"If you think you're good enough with this little toy, I'll wager a bet." Rick ran the thongs through his fingers as he leaned against his desk.

Matt dropped the flogger back in the box. "A bet? What kind?" His hand flew protectively into his pants pocket for his money clip.

Rick's devilish smile reappeared. "Loser submits to Mistress Payne at the next demonstration."

Matt folded his arms over his chest. "You're a whip man, not a flogger. I bow to your skills with a bullwhip, but I've got you hands down with these babies." Matt gestured to the box of floggers.

Rick arched a brow at him. "Technique has nothing to do with it. The winner is whoever gets to administer the flogger on their partner…"

Matt pumped his fist in the air. "Then I won, I just nailed your ass."

Rick dropped his chin and looked up at Matt. "Dear boy, I'm not that kind of partner. For clarification, you must flog your lovely Cat before I flog Cupcake. The demonstration is a week from tonight. The clock is ticking, dear boy."

* * * *

Fed, showered and refreshed, Willow and Adam drove back to Flight's End. She parked the motorhome next to Adam's rental car. "My sister, Izzy is still here. You'll get to meet the fair Princess Isadora."

Willow waited for him to alight from the passenger side and locked the doors. "I was unaware I was dealing with royalty."

"It's not Buckingham Palace down there. In fact, it's more like the Flintstones."

"You know what? If we could hack into a university research program, you could disguise your settlement as an ongoing research project into primitive lifestyles."

Adam's eyes lit up. "I think I love this idea. The University of the Highlands would be perfect. They're new and not going to turn down a large financial gift. We'll take care of this mostly with a website. That and dropping the grant and research criteria into their catalog ought to do it.

"Yeah, that gives that settlement a legit reason to be there. What about the second settlement?"

Adam nodded. "We can call Fisherfield a control site."

Willow's doe eyes studied him seriously. "You know, this is a temporary fix. They won't be able to shift, at least not frequently. Scotland is way too populated to maintain your presence here."

Adam sighed. "I know if they want to continue to live as shifters the colonies will have to move to a much more remote site. A long way from Europe."

"It's hard for me to believe that in this day and age, any group could remain secluded from the global network."

Adam shrugged, "Look at the Amish; they choose it."

Willow shook her head and grinned. "The Amish live without modern conveniences; they don't shift and fly from one community to another."

Adam nodded somberly. "I'd be afraid what governments would do with a few of us on their side. We do need to get my people connected online and with cell phones as an early warning measure... No, they need a crash course in the twenty-first century."

* * * *

Anna caught Cat's attention while she settled into a Victorian Tête-à-Tête chair. The face to face seating made it comfortable for the vampress to face her male donor and catch a snack from the wrist.

Todd and Emery, a newly married couple celebrating their honeymoon, won the feeding lottery tonight. "Oh, Todd, you smell enticing." Anna scented gently along his bared forearm. She winked at Emery. "No wonder you snatched him up."

Cat laughed as she caught up Emery's arm. "Don't worry; he gives as good as he gets." She licked along a vein. "Humm, delicious."

Emery settled comfortably into the chair and smiled with satisfaction. "Nobody in New York is going to believe this."

Cat teased him. "That's because there's no such thing as vampires, right?"

He laughed. "Right."

Anna did her due diligence. "Okay, guys, now to be clear, we're just going to take a little snack to see how you like it. This is your honeymoon; we don't want to make you weak. That's what you're looking for, right?"

"I can't wait. After this experience, what's the big deal with kissing the Blarney Stone?"

Anna's fingers reached out and caught Todd's jaw. "Just relax and think of Emery." When Todd's eyes closed, and his posture relaxed into the overstuffed upholstery, Anna's fangs dropped, and she confidently bit his wrist. Her snack lasted as long as a song's chorus played in her head. The sensation for the donor wasn't the orgasm a full feeding would give, but it was enough to arouse Todd and kick-start his foreplay with Emery.

Emery, who was more nervous than his spouse, watched Cat carefully when her fangs dropped. "It won't hurt, Emery." Cat soothed. "Try to relax." Emery let out a sigh and closed his eyes. They flashed open again for the bite, and a wide grin spread across his face.

"Oh, my God," he murmured.

"I know," Todd agreed.

Cat and Anna sealed the shallow punctures with a sweep of their tongues and laid their satisfied donor's arms down on the armrests. They left the happy couple for a few moments to get them juice and fruit from the bar. When they returned, the men were alert and talkative.

Todd's bright eyes flashed from under sinfully long eyelashes. "This is quite a head start on what will be our most memorable night."

Emery chuckled in agreement. "We have an entire night booked in the Duke's Dungeon."

Anna smirked at the name of the Dungeon and turned to Cat. "Did you know there was a Duke's Dungeon?"

Cat shook her head. "I didn't write any of the copy on the dungeons."

Anna giggled "Aren't you curious about what they have down there?"

Todd's mouth fell open. "You live here, and you haven't been down in the Dungeon yet? It's the first place I would have checked out."

"Now, honey, maybe that's not their kink. Have you seen their mates?"

Cat blushed at the comment. "Anna and I did all the decorating, but the dungeons were done to Rick, Matt and Adam's specs. We weren't involved."

Anna whispered conspiratorially "They got another delivery today; I didn't see what it was."

Todd arched his eyebrow, "Well, you two should just amble down there and check it out. The Dungeon is soundproofed; you won't disturb us."

The ladies nodded in anticipation.

* * * *

Willow left the motorhome and walked into the sunshine to wait for Adam, who stayed inside on a phone call. Twenty-four hours with the shifter showed her "different" was good! Her face flushed at the thought of exposing herself to him, otherworldly as well as physically. She covered her face with her hands, amazed at being a shifter, and a woman who fell into a rapturous bed with a… stranger.

Adam plucked more than a few nerves with his plundering kisses and on-point sexuality. His confession that he was a professional Dom was initially daunting. Then as he played her body like a master with a Stradivarius, she responded to the best of her abilities, leaving him spent. Still, her hesitation to admit her peccadillos took a while to thaw. When she orgasmed for the umpteenth time, her fetish skittered into a dark corner like a bothersome bug.

Standing in the crisp air after a day and night of phenomenal sex, Willow conjured the one feeling Adam did not administer. As the breeze picked up, she could swear she felt the silk rope defining her breasts, separating, and lifting the flesh Adam adored with his lips and hands.

She missed the aesthetics of feeling the rope when she was bound. The position was important. Her previous Master, Jordan, was schooled in specific katas and aesthetic rules. He was a fan of graceful and symmetric positions. In those days, her long chocolate tresses were integrated into the pattern. Willow was acutely aware of heightened sensuality and amplified attention to her body, to each lick of rope, each tightened boundary. The journey of his hands was as satisfying as their destination, when he would orally pleasure her while she swayed, suspended over his bed. Her previous Master let his ropes become a loving extension of his hands. But, that "Master" was gone, and she ceremoniously cut her hair, if she no longer had Master Jordan, there was no need for the hair.

"Just got a few details nailed down. Are you ready to meet my people?" Adam began disrobing for his shift.

Willow turned and enjoyed the view; indeed he was spectacular and perhaps, just perhaps, he might be a reason to grow her hair again.

6

Jude, assuming more responsibility within the clan, took copious notes on the new additions to the crater settlement. "Your idea to label this a living history research site is phenomenal."

Petra sat, still unnerved by the idea she might be forbidden to shift and fly again in her lifetime. Adam comforted his mother with a sincere hug. "Don't give up hope, Mother. We're going to do what we can to discredit these reports. We'll be searching for a new home for the Scottish clans. It's clear; we can no longer stay here. Your support is crucial in helping your people adjust."

Petra bristled her face a stony mask of condemnation, and said, "I'm giving you conditional agreement. For now. Until my Counselor gathers more information…"

Willow stepped into what was about to become an ugly scene. "Your Majesty, I assure you, Adam has your clan's best interest at heart, and he's doing all he can to keep you safe in a world where all secrets are revealed."

"And you've known him, how long?" Petra tapped her foot.

Izzy stepped into the fray. "You sent him out two hundred years ago in disgrace, penniless. In the human world, you cannot imagine the desperate situation you put him in. He owes you nothing. I wouldn't blame him if he completely ignored your summons. But instead, he came, and he's spending the bulk of his worth, money it took centuries to accumulate, to save our people."

Jude walked to Petra and wrapped a brotherly arm around her stiff shoulders. "It would be far easier for Queen Petra to accept Adam's indifference to our plight. It's much harder to save face when you accept help from a prodigal son." Jude took Petra's hand. "Queen Nessa and I will ensure the clans survive, and it's because of Adam's generosity."

Petra gazed at Jude respectfully. "I accede to your judgment, my son."

Adam bristled, his spine growing stiff, his jaw resolute. He felt Willow slip her hand in his, offering support. Izzy stepped up with a warm hug and kiss.

"I'll be waiting to hear from you, Master Adam." Izzy winked. Petra turned and walked away in frosty silence.

Jude stepped up, "I don't know what to say about her attitude. It's simply unimaginable to her that people on the other side of the world would poke their noses into our business because of what we are."

Adam stood stoically. "You have your work cut out for you. At least you've been paired with a true helpmate in Nessa. Tomorrow, the helicopter will deliver a generator, the computers, and cell phones. We hope you don't need help before then. Within a week motorhomes will be delivered to the village for dragonfolk who want to live outside the crater."

Jude shaded his eyes from the setting sun. "I think it's exciting Izzy will be giving jobs to a few of our spinners and weavers. It will help keep their minds off our problems."

"Leave it to Izzy to turn a crisis into a cottage industry." Adam chuckled.

"Hey, life gives us lemons—we're just weaving the bags to carry them!" Izzy retorted.

Adam circled the crater lake in the golden twilight. He watched Willow shift into her Pegasus self. What a comely creature she was, in all forms. She rose gracefully to circle in tandem with him, and Adam wondered if this shift would be their last for an extended period. He would miss flying with her, and though they certainly found delight in each other's human bodies, there was something to be said for the arousal of flight followed by a romp in the sheets.

* * * *

Anna activated the hand-print identification on the Dungeon security door. She turned to Cat. "I was afraid we wouldn't have universal access."

Cat looked right into the pinhole camera. "What's good for the goose is good for the gander." They slipped into the anteroom noticing the stacked boxes behind the reception desk. Cat read the label. "Oh, these are eleven of twelve boxes of assorted floggers." Anna's green eyes went round.

Cat sliced into the box with her thumbnail. "Have you ever seen a flogger?"

Anna shook her head. "Only on the internet, never in real life."

Cat sifted through the box's packing. "Has Rick ever used a whip on you?" Cat's tone was secretively probing. Anna shook her head. Cat cast a glance at the empty demonstration stage. Only the downlight glowed on the empty whipping post. "Before I was turned, Matt and I fought, it was a knockdown drag-out argument, and Rick sent us into Matt's playroom to settle it." Cat paced back and forth before the long picture window. "When we came out, I was ready to call the cops on Rick." Anna's face grew serious. "But Matt demanded I watch." Cat's eyes cast up, recalling the memory. "I couldn't believe how incredibly hot Rick was when he dropped his shirt and delivered those licks with the bullwhip." Cat's focus went to the empty whipping post.

Anna was dumbstruck. "Go on..."

Cat picked up a lambskin flogger. "That sub wanted it. He escalated the whipping until he drew blood." Anna winced, as Cat continued. "Of course, the sub didn't see how hot Rick looked with that whip in his hand," Cat let out a long exhalation. "Once Matt calmed me down, Rick's total control spellbound me."

Anna's voice was thin and high. "Yeah, ...he has a lot of control."

Cat handed Anna a flogger to feel the supple lambskin. She drew the twenty-inch tails curiously through her fingers as she spoke. "Rick's aftercare was as erotic as his whip technique." Her voice evoked his sexual allure. "His tongue healed her welts, and then Matt thought we better give them privacy." She sighed, lost in the memory. Then shook herself out of it, to a pert finish. "So, I just wondered, has he done that to you?"

Anna's voice was dry. "No...He's never done that...to me. In fact, I was only in his Dungeon once, and that didn't involve sex. It's hard for me to imagine Rick whipping anyone."

Cat raised a brow at her. "Imagine it."

* * * *

Matt leaned over the billiard table. "I call solids."

Rick pulled the phone out of his back pocket—the alert stated: "ACH accessed Dungeon anteroom." He turned to Matt. "Are the ladies together this evening?"

Matt straightened up after breaking the billiard balls. "Yeah, they were snacking the last time I saw them. Why?"

Rick balanced on the balls of his feet with a widening grin. "Cupcake just accessed the Dungeon anteroom. Look." He switched to the closed-circuit feed.

"I see they got into the floggers; did you happen to put any aside for us?" Matt hovered and listened. "What's with them exploring? They've never shown any interest…"

Another alert read: ACH accessed Dungeon 1. Rick shook his head, "Children will play."

The two hung over the video and audio feed with bated breath.

* * * *

Anna giggled at the apparatus in the room, she and Cat flogged everything that stood still. "Anna, don't you wonder what it feels like?" Cat slid out of her jacket to expose her bare shoulders. She waved on Anna.

Anna dove into the box for the instruction pamphlet which she read aloud. "Lambskin…soft…perfect for titties and cocks…sensitive places…no directions, Cat, it looks as though it's a 'gentle and pleasurable turn-on'."

"Give it a try. I'll scream if it hurts."

"Okay, I've never done this…" Anna stepped back the length of the flogger plus an inch. "Okay, here goes…" Anna winced and turned her head away as she flung the flogger gently. Cat sighed. "That's it? A sigh? I was expecting more."

Cat laughed at their situation. "I think you have to hit me more, and harder."

Anna collapsed with laughter. "If you told me six months ago that I'd be a vampire, flogging my mate's friend's wife with a lambskin flogger, in an Irish Dungeon, I would have called the lunatic asylum."

"Don't you sort of wonder why people do this? I mean, mortals do it, too!" Cat and Anna wiped silly tears of laughter away, and the door flew open.

"Hello, ladies…" Rick and Matt stood in the doorway. "Did I hear someone has Dungeon questions?" Rick turned to Matt. "I know what you do in your playroom, but you've omitted quite a bit of fun…"

Matt would not be played. "Old man, I've got my own whip right here." He grabbed his crotch and grinned. "I don't need a Dungeon."

Cat asked. "Why do people do this? What's the sensation they're looking for?"

Rick took the flogger from Anna and handed it to Matt. "Okay, kid; show her."

Rick positioned Cat facing front in the hanging shackles. "If we were serious, you'd be nude. We'll forgo that…for now." He drew Anna back behind Matt. Cat and Anna watched with fascination as Matt assumed his Dom persona. He rolled back the sleeves of his shirt and further unbuttoned his shirt's front. Matt warmed up his arm with a swoosh or two. "You need a safe word; what is it?" His voice was firm, not quite threatening, but not the usual, jovial Matt.

"Demerits."

Matt shook his head at the word. "Let's hope you don't regret that."

"Well, why would I…"

"Silence," Matt commanded. "Unless you need your safe word, no talking."

Rick winked at Anna. "He's so strict." Matt squelched a laugh. *Whoosh, whoosh, whoosh.* Cat felt the thuds land on her thighs and hips and waist.

"What does it feel like?" Anna asked.

Matt frowned at her. "Silence."

Anna grimaced. "Oops."

Matt directed. "Cat, you have my permission to answer me. Are you ready for more?"

"Ummm, I guess…"

Matt hung his head, and shook it, sliding a look to Rick who was also desperately trying not to laugh. "We need Dungeon etiquette lessons." *Thwack, thwack, thwack.* His aim unerringly hit the mark on her arms and breasts, wrapping around her body with a sensuous embrace.

Cat crooned. "Ooh, that felt good."

"Sub, I have told you to remain silent. Believe me; I can use deferred gratification. I used it once before, remember? I can do it again. I can do it all night. This is your last warning. Nod if you understand."

Cat nodded emphatically.

"Good. I don't have control of any other subs in this room…" His gaze shifted to Anna. "But, I will suggest to the other Dom here that he keep his sub in check."

Anna glanced at Rick. "You hear that; be quiet."

Matt shook his head. "This is never going to work. You want the sensation, here it is. Chat amongst yourselves. I'm just here, being the Dom, entirely ineffectively."

Cat put on a stoic face. "I'm into it now, come on, go ahead… But, can I tell her what it feels like?"

Matt capitulated, "Whatever."

Rick's pocket buzzed. "Hiatt. Okay, okay, we'll be right up." Rick closed the call and waved at Cat. "The magazine is here for the shoot, and they need you and me topside."

Anna looked disappointed while Matt unshackled Cat. "Well, can Matt flog me while you're gone?"

Rick and Matt looked at each other in amazement as they answered in unison. "No."

Rick checked his collar and cuffs. "When you want flogging, I will do the honors. If Matt wants to get you acquainted with the lay of the land down here, fine. Understand?" He kissed her on the nose and waited for Cat to slide back into her jacket.

* * * *

Anna found herself following Matt through the largest Dungeon as he pointed out the variety of toys and equipment. She found herself uncomfortable with him for the first time. Cat saw a side of Rick she didn't know; this news was unsettling and brought up all those turbulent feelings she buried about Matt.

Matt looked down at her. "Is this equipment upsetting you, Anna?"

"No, why?"

"Because you're awfully quiet, you seem upset. What's wrong?"

"Do you realize this is the first time we've been alone, together, since that night?"

Matt stopped and hooked his thumbs into his belt. He nodded thoughtfully. "Is there something you want to say?"

Anna made a couple of faces displaying the weight of her questions. Matt waited.

"Cat said you met on January tenth." Matt nodded in agreement. "You know that's the same night you banned me from the Gaoler."

Matt replied slowly. "I never thought of it that way, but yes, I guess you're right."

"You hurt me." Matt blinked. "I crushed so damn hard on you, and you broke my heart. I don't feel that way now," she hurried to explain. "But jeesh, it was terrible at the time, and I guess my question is, why did you think I was worthless?"

"What?" Matt asked flabbergasted. "That's the last thing I thought. I was worried you were getting in too deep. I knew you didn't understand our feeder and donor relationship. I knew you had some fantasy…"

Anna nodded. "You're right. Knowing what I know now, as a vampire myself, I understand I had a fantasy about us."

"Right." Matt picked up her line of thought. "I'm sorry I hurt you. I didn't know how to make you understand we were never going to be a couple. I felt I needed to get you away from the vampire family before you got your heart broken. I guess I broke it anyway. I'm sorry." Matt bit his bottom lip. "Do you forgive me?"

"Yes, Matt, I forgive you." Anna drew in an unnecessary breath. "I have one other teeny question."

Matt braced himself.

"I know Cat had an accident, and you and Rick turned her to save her life. But…just how close were the three of you?

Matt weighed her question. "Could you be more specific?"

"Cat mentioned something about Rick that made me uncomfortable." They stared at each other for a beat. "About the night she watched him use the whip. He kinda turned her on."

Matt raised an eyebrow. "Did he, now?" He leaned toward Anna as a big brother would. "Let me tell you a secret about Doms. Doms are like actors; spectators project all kinds of feelings onto them. Those feelings have nothing to do with the Doms themselves. Being a Dom is playing a role. It's not real. So, even someone like Cat can fantasize about submitting to a Dom, but that Dom isn't necessarily Rick. It's her fantasy of a Dom. It might be a fantasy I can provide, whenever she wants to role play." Matt crossed his arms over his chest.

"And she knows that? Tell me, how close were the three of you?"

Matt's chuckle started low in his belly and came out in a guffaw. He held up his right hand. "I swear, there was never any sort of 'thing', ya know? But that night, Cat and I came out of my playroom sexually charged and seeing Rick with that whip was a turn on for me, too. I've never been drawn to Rick that way." Matt stepped back from Anna. "I'd like to think I jump-started Cat's attraction to Rick's domination."

Anna nodded slowly. "Then, when you were a Dom today, that wasn't honestly you?"

Matt roared. "Oh, honey, I could never truly be a Dom to Cat. She'd see right through me. Like she did today."

"I have to get over the fact that everyone wants to be with Fitz."

"It's not about Rick at all. He's that good at being a Master Dom. He's the screen they project their feelings on."

"I do get your point." Anna mused. "I saw enough women swoon for vampire role players to make me understand the principle. I mean, no woman in her right mind would fall for one of those cheesy guys."

Matt nodded. "Yeah, I met 'em. I would hope not."

Anna's eyes grew moist. "I love Fitz so much; I want to be the kind of mate he needs."

Matt smiled. "I've known him for a hundred years, and I've never seen Rick in love, it's a beautiful thing. We both found incredible women. There has to be some security in knowing you're the one he lays with at dawn. You're going to have a wonderful eternity together."

* * * *

Willow settled back in Adam's arms in the shuttle limo. It was a long day, and she was tired. It would have been less tiring to fly to Ireland under their own wings, rather than a commercial airline, but it would not have been safe. Adam ruffled his fingers through her short, coffee-colored hair. "You have such beautiful hair, and your website has pictures of it long. Why did you cut it off?"

"Don't you like it? I find it easier in the field." She ran her fingers through Adam's luxurious golden locks, past his collar. "All that long hair takes a lot to wash and dry in a cold shower and freezing weather."

"Granted. When we're in civilization, I'd love to see it long."

"I guess I can shift, and you can play with my mane."

"I wonder what it would be like to ride you in your Pegasus state." He quirked a smile.

Her look was impish. "What kind of ride do you have in mind?"

"Get your mind out of the Dungeon, I'm kinky, but not like that."

"Okay, I'll take you for a spin sometime if you want, but you're not a very good rider…"

Adam caught her hand and softly kissed the back of it. "I know you're going to enjoy getting to know my friends better. We're just about there."

* * * *

Adam left their bags with the bell staff and Willow followed him to the reception desk.

"Hello, Bridget. Will you get us checked into my suite? Where is everyone?"

The clerk looked up from her computer. "Good evening, Master Adam. I believe Mr. Hiatt and Mrs. Brenner just finished a magazine shoot. I'm not sure where they went."

"Okay, please have our bags sent up. I'm headed for the office."

Adam knocked respectfully and getting no answer, swiped his key card. He guided Willow to the desk and gestured at the security monitor panels. "Unless it's an early night we'll find them on the closed circuit." He started with the monitors in the lounges and gyms, finding plenty of guests, but no signs of the four. He paused. "I'm half afraid to look for them in the Dungeon."

Willow ran to join him. "Oh, let's look!"

"Don't get excited. I've never seen the girls there." He hit the Dungeon monitors.

"Well, I'll be damned. Come on!" He grabbed her hand and hurried to an elevator. Adam accessed the handprint reader at the Dungeon entrance and winked at Willow. "Let's see what they're up to…" They walked into the vampires gathered around a St. Andrew's cross. Rick pointed to the mechanisms as Matt demonstrated the placement.

"You can shackle the sub facing front or back; you can make the spread wider or narrower, you can make it a straight-out whipping post, too!"

Adam swaggered into view, and using his compelling Dom voice, said, "But first, you need to greet your visitors." The men exchanged surprised bro hugs, each of them eyeing Willow.

Matt extended his hand to her. "Welcome back…you remember my mate, Cat."

"I didn't expect to see you again this soon, but I'm delighted to be here!" Willow beamed.

Rick tapped his nose and winked at Adam. "It's a dream to have us all together again. I told you, Willow, this is a resort best enjoyed over a week."

Adam's gaze took in the newly organized Dungeon. It featured multiple apparatus for larger demonstrations. Adam nodded at Willow and assumed command. "You need a demonstration to explore this equipment adequately." Cat and Anna turned to Adam for his guidance. "Gentlemen, disrobe and assume the position," he commanded, a twinkle in his eyes. Rick and Matt glanced at each other, shrugged, and stepped out of their clothes.

Oh, dear, God. Willow fought to appear nonchalant, but there, in the flesh, were the two Doms from her dream, butt naked. She looked for the small heart-shaped birthmark she'd dreamed right above Rick's thatch of copper hair.

Adam looked at Rick, facing the cross. "Step up." Rick stepped onto the platform facing the padded cross.

Damn, he turned too fast!

Adam looked at Anna who watched in fascination. "Well, don't just stand there, buckle him in."

Anna looked at Adam through her eyelashes. "Me?"

"You can do this, Anna. Remember what I told you." Matt encouraged.

Rick's head turned toward Matt. "What did you tell…"

Adam clapped twice. "Silence, subs."

Anna returned with the flogger. "Sub, what is your safe word?"

Rick hesitated. "Monsoon, Mistress."

Anna looked perplexed. "Monsoon?"

Adam waved her on. The rest of them waited expectantly. Adam turned to Cat. "I don't know what you're waiting for; attend your sub."

Cat stepped meekly up to Matt, gloriously naked and waiting for her commands. Matt smirked as Cat approached to lock him in. "Step up, sub?" She said with a minimum of confidence. Willow squinted to examine Matt's forearms.

Oh, dear God, his hair is swirled exactly as I dreamed it! I should pluck out my eyes!

Adam instructed. "Say it like you mean it, Cat. Be the Domme." Cat looked sideways at Adam, and then her posture changed. She nodded and then approached Matt assertively.

It was a different tone of voice. "Step up, sub." Matt nodded and did.

"Don't just stand there, ladies. Get them buckled in. Then choose your instrument."

Rick looked over to Matt. "This could be a mistake."

Anna made a whistling figure eight with the flogger. "Silence, subs!"

Willow whispered into Adam's ear and then shrank back into the dark end of the Dungeon and stifled a giggle.

Adam stood between the two crosses and faced the Dommes. "There's a proposal on the floor." He grinned wickedly. "You're the Dommes, it's up to you, of course, but our new friend, who as it turns out is quite knowledgeable, has a suggestion for you. "You could do a simple scene of flogging and leave." His grin widened. "Or, you could tease your sub. You know them best. You could employ *orgasm deprivation…*"

Matt rattled his shackles. "Seriously? You're just blaming this on Willow!"

Rick's stare bore through the darkness, into Willow. "Oh, no, I think our Dr. Greer knows all about orgasm deprivation. Don't you, dear?"

Willow's voice was taunting. "I don't believe you have permission to speak."

This galvanized Anna into action. "That's right! Silence, sub!" She turned to Adam, and her lips moved silently. "What's orgasm deprivation?"

Willow waved to the women, and they left the Dungeon for a few moments. "Orgasm deprivation is just that. You rev 'em up again and again, and just when they get to the point of blowing, you dial it back."

Cat gasped. "Matt does that all the time! That bastard!"

Willow looked back through the window. "Nipple play?"

Cat nodded her head and shook her fist at her mate. "Yeah! All the time. And that's not all. He has this vibrating cock ring…" Anna gaped at them. Cat turned. "You're awfully quiet over there, girlfriend."

"I'm right there, and he just pulls out. Just like that." Anna smacked her hand on the glass and dragged her long nails down it. "I see handcuffs and ankle cuffs in Fitz's future."

Willow laughed. "Remember ladies, that door swings both ways. It's all in the way we use our talents and toys."

Both women turned to her, eyes wide. "Oh? You have some suggestions about toys?"

Willow shrugged. "If it were me, I'd go in there and let them sweat a little first."

The women smiled at each other. Willow loved enlightening them. Cat threw open the door and marched up to Matt. Anna copied her, her stance assertive. Cat nodded and asked. "Sub, what is your safe word?"

Matt held his head high and worked to squelch a smile. "Demerits."

Cat warmed up her arm. Adam stepped behind the two women, every bit of him in Dungeon Master mode, hands on hips, with a wide stance. Willow approached him and gently placed her finger on his lips, taking over as the instructor. "Ladies, the full range of impact play is from a feather's kiss all the way to whips and bloodletting. You can use those delicate floggers as gently as you would drag your hair over your lover. Get them used to the delicate end of the spectrum and then surprise them with an alternative sensation."

Anna walked up to Rick's back and dusted his shoulders with the soft, loose ends. Rick relaxed into the teasing, easy tickles. Just as his head dropped, Anna took a half step back and let him have a figure eight of full strikes. His body startled at the change of pace. His erection quickened. Anna followed with glancing strokes up each of Rick's thighs. His erection swelled as she escalated. Satisfied their play was well on its way, Willow turned to Cat.

"Hum, what's going on over here?" She asked as Cat circled Matt on the apparatus. Her long fingernails traveled in trails marking his flesh. She glanced off his back, across his buttocks into his hair and finally back around to the front. Using just one fingernail slipping from the cleft of his chin, between his pecs, along his six pack, and below his navel, she turned to Adam with a wicked smile.

"Hey, Adam, do we have nipple clamps?" Matt groaned. Cat spun. "Silence, sub."

"I'm sure we do, anything else while I've got the drawer open?"

Cat scurried to follow him. "What else is in there?"

Willow joined them. Adam slanted her a wry grin. She pointed to a drawer of cock rings. Adam laughed wickedly.

Matt yelled. "What are you getting me into, Sparky?"

Adam and Cat shared a look and answered in unison. "Silence!"

"Eyes down, sub." She directed, and then turned back to the drawer. "Oh, these are perfect." She held up nipple clamps with dainty hearts dangling from them.

Willow snickered. Cat leaned into Adam. "I think he used one of these on me." She pointed to a vibrating cock ring. Willow got a big smile, snatched the ring from the drawer and motioned Cat to her. "You can use this as directed or …" The rest of her thought demonstrated with Cat and Anna's backs to Adam and Matt.

Adam glanced over to Matt and saw his friend test the strength of the restraints. Adam shook his head sadly as if to say. "You're in for it, now."

Cat and Willow turned back around with a plan. Cat looked at Adam with surprise. "Where did Rick and Anna go?" Adam pointed to a private Dungeon off the main room "I think she got the best of him, or she's getting it now." He glanced at Cat. "You two need some privacy?" Cat looked up. "How would I restrain him?"

Adam laughed. "Each private Dungeon is kitted with equipment." Cat made up her mind and released the restraints.

"Then follow me, sub. I have plans for you." They disappeared.

Willow began opening and closing each of the cabinets. Adam's curiosity emerged. "What are you looking for?"

Willow opened a tall, closet door. "Found it." She brought out a large coil of thick silk rope.

"Tie me up, Master Dom."

Adam accepted the coil and pulled her close, he whispered in her ear. "I'll take you right now and explode in three strokes. We'll do a rain check on the rope."

Willow caught the front of Adam's khaki trousers. His erection was thick and pulsing. "Aw, let's not use orgasm deprivation on you." Without a word she dropped to her knees and had his pants around his ankles.

"This is a public Dungeon; anyone could walk in…"

Willow's gentle fingertips caressed his sac. "Then they'll see why they call you the Dungeon *Master*." Her lips scalded his flesh, and she swallowed his length. Adam steadied himself as her throat accepted him. His moans filled the room while her tongue and lips worked their magic. Adam lost himself in the feel of her hot mouth and the hypnotic appeal of her huge eyes. He caught his breath and moaned. "Oh, that's it…"

Willow giggled at his strangled words. The vibration of her laughter rippled through his rigid cock.

"Oh, God, don't laugh like that…"

Willow disobeyed with a wicked gleam in her eyes. Adam drove his splayed fingers into her short hair and held her right there. Her throat tightened as her tongue swept his root. She could feel his legs shake with the coming orgasm. She caught both of his balls in her hand and slowly stroked them as he began to bellow. She felt his orgasm down to her toes. The sound was music to her heart. His hands caught her shoulders as his scorching cum filled her mouth. He stood spent, and she had him in her hands and mouth. Gently, she caught his cock and danced the wet head over the tops of her breasts.

"You are a demon."

Willow bit her bottom lip. "I love the velvet touch of your cock."

Adam wavered in his stance. "I don't have the strength to tie my shoes…"

She made a pouting face as his cock trailed the last of his emission over her flesh. "I'll understand, as long as you let me have my way with you."

"Good God, woman, I can barely stand, now."

"Come on over here," Willow enticed. She caught his hand and led him to what she hoped was a private Dungeon and bedroom. "Let me rock you to sleep tonight." They stepped inside the private room and to the left of the St. Andrew's cross stood an imposing four-poster bed, which dominated one end of the room. She pulled back the silky duvet and guided Adam down to the bed.

* * * *

He shook, suspended in the heaven of one hell of a blow job. He listened as Willow moved around, heard her clothes hit the floor, and she was on him, bathing away her earlier work. She straddled his thighs and began working the loose ends of the lambskin flogger over his chest and neck. "Until I get my hair grown out, this will have to do." His face took on a sleepy smile of contentment. Then his hands caught her wrists.

"I think you better bring that rope in here because when I wake up, I'll be in the driver's seat."

Willow smiled at him. "Promise?"

* * * *

Rick paced the conference room. As Matt entered, he caught his shoulder and wheeled him around the corner, their heads close together.

"Hey, buddy, why so secretive?" Matt looked around like a detective.

"Did you catch the pheromone spike when Dr. Greer mentioned orgasm deprivation?" Rick arched a brow and whispered in subtones.

"I was preoccupied, you were closer."

"Don't cop out on this. I scented the same aroma when she stepped out of the elevator two days ago. Same damn, pungent hormones. Only, when she saw me, I caught a double shot of embarrassment." Rick punched Matt's shoulder with his index finger. "You never told me what you read from her."

"Yeah," Matt scrubbed at the back of his neck like a guilty schoolboy. "The second we touched, and she answered me 'yes, sir,' I thought something was up. Then I pieced it together. She's no innocent, but when I read the past, it looked more like a recent fantasy or dream she felt oddly guilty about."

"She called you Sir? Were you her Dominant in the dream?" Rick brushed his hair off his forehead.

"Maybe. But then, why was she embarrassed around you?" The light bulb flashed on. "Ooh. A little three-way action." He shrugged. "It was just a dream, but points for imagination."

Rick nodded with feigned confidence. "Nothing that will ever be acted out. Right?"

Nodding emphatically, Matt held up his left hand, thumbing his wide gold band. "Somebody doesn't like to share."

Anna swung behind the door and put both hands on her hips. "I may be a new vampire, but I can hear you two whispering over at the table."

"Just explaining away a little mystery." Rick drew her close.

She gave him a skeptical look. "So, at the reception, Willow sees a room full of Doms and subs. She has a headache; she goes back to her suite. I can't see a better way to get rid of a headache than a hot fantasy. Who could blame her? Except…" Anna narrowed her eyes at her mate. She smirked. "You two are over here surmising she fantasized about *you*? Charming. Well, Fitz, you are the star of every show and the groom at every wedding. You might as well be the star of her fantasy." Matt watched them, hands in pockets, jiggling his change and clearly enjoying their show. "And don't you stand there looking all cherubic. I know you two are lapping up every bit of the attention." Anna turned to Matt, who stifled a grin.

"A little harmless fantasy of our own… Let's agree to say, Adam's a lucky guy."

She narrowed her eyes. "Adam better be the only lucky guy."

Rick swept her into a deep dip and dropped his fangs. "Matt and I are incredibly lucky husbands."

"Nice save, Romeo." But her heart did flutter at the sight of her vampire lover.

"Thanks, I thought so." He kissed her nose.

"You guys about ready?" Cat swept around the corner. "What's going on?"

Matt drew her into a tight embrace. "I was just telling them what a fantastic wife you are. And a wonderful fledgling coach for Anna." His glance dared them to contradict him.

"That he was, yes he was." Anna nodded enthusiastically.

Rick broke the discussion up and headed for his seat at the conference table. "I bet Adam and Willow will be famished." Even with soundproofed dungeons, the keening wails of an orgasmic Willow reduced Rick and Anna to giggling vampires. The chef rolled in refreshments for the two A.M. meeting. Rick slid a tablet over to Matt and Cat. "Have you two recovered from your walk on the wild side?" Matt brushed at the front of his polo shirt and Rick piped up. "A little tender there, Sport? Did she make you leave on the nipple clamps? On second thought, where did she place them?"

"Old man, you know I don't kiss and tell," Matt smirked as he ran his hand up Cat's thigh under the table.

"Yeah, but one of these days I was hoping you would."

"Anna, what about you and that flogger?" Matt smirked.

Anna hid her face behind the tablet. "I've got nothin' for ya'."

Matt took a finger and pushed the tablet away from her face. "Nothing? Really? I thought I gave you sound advice in the Dungeon."

"I do appreciate your tutelage, but…" Anna broke out in giggles. "I don't flog and tell."

Rick leaned his chin on his hand. "Now that we've established our sexual boundaries let's get some work done."

Adam and Willow's footsteps came closer, the door opened, and two brightly flushed lovers entered the room.

Rick stood, and Matt belatedly got to his feet. Rick gestured to the sideboard and the food. "You two should probably hydrate after all your…

exertion." Rick handed Willow a large bottle of water. "I wasn't sure what you might be hungry for at this hour, help yourselves."

Willow wandered to the sideboard with interest. "Thanks, I'm starving."

Rick's brows rose, and Anna put her finger to her lips.

Adam looked at the offerings of cold cuts, cheeses, and fruit. "This is great." Willow plated cheese and fruit, and her fork headed toward the vampire's side of the buffet with blood aspic and other blood-based hors-d'oeuvres. She reached out for one.

Cat rose suddenly. "No, no, no! You don't want those!" Willow blinked her fabulous eyes at Cat.

"Oh, they aren't vegan?"

Cat held up her plate and pointed. "That's the vampire side of the buffet."

Willow made a comic face and nodded. "Just give me a loud shout out if I wander into vampire territory."

Adam sat down with his plate and accepted a tablet from Rick. "Don't mind me; I'm going to stuff my face."

Rick dropped his head and bit his lip. "I don't know what I'm going to do with you people. It's all sex, all the time."

"Don't give me that," Adam mumbled around cheeks full of food. He chewed rapidly and swallowed. "I don't even have vampire hearing, and I heard your howling at the moon, all the way down in our Dungeon." Adam mimicked Rick. "Cupcake, please, Cupcake, Oh my God…. Shall I go on?"

Rick gave him a sour look. "Exactly why are you back here? I think I liked it better when you were celibate."

The agenda was on the table, and Adam flipped through it. "Yes, we have to be prepared for the European Association of Hematologists. They begin to arrive tomorrow for their golf outing. Their conference starts the following day. It appears extra spa employees are on call for the mates who will not be attending the seminars." Adam flipped to the next page and winced. "We have a request for Rick's attention. His absence in L.A. has been noted, and a female sub has chartered a jet for a week's worth of discipline here."

* * * *

Rick reared back in the conference chair; his ankle crossed over his knee. He sipped intermittently on a travel mug. "A week's worth of discipline? Who would want that?" He winked at Anna.

"Says she's a Platinum Member." Adam drummed his fingers on the tabletop.

Rick's head dropped back as he contemplated Platinum Member Subs. He pushed back from the table and leaned over it on his palms. "Nope, never gonna happen. That's under your job description now, Master Adam."

"But she's a senior member of the high council. Her term began last December." Adam cocked his head.

Matt tucked his chin and ran his thumb over his bottom lip. "That's a bad one to refuse…"

Rick shook his head emphatically. "How did she get elected in December?"

Willow watched Adam seek support from Matt. Matt shook his head. "There was a runoff while you were at the beach house… It probably just slipped your mind."

Rick bellowed. "Don't tell me she won by one vote."

Matt arched a brow. "Look, bro, Adam and I aren't voting members. I begged you to run. It's out of our hands, and now she's going to be in your hands."

They're tossing billionaires and politicians and royalty around like monopoly money. What social circle have I entered? Willow thought.

"Oh, Fitz, I'm going on a junket to meet some breeders, we've got to have the stables stocked with well-trained hunters. You go ahead; business is business." Anna got a naughty sparkle in her eye. "Just be extra strict for me."

Rick carried his mug over to the bar and plunked it down. He spun around and waved a cocktail spoon at the men. "I've eluded Veda Bouvier Pierce for seven months. It's not just a discipline session; she does not detach."

"That's part of the discipline; you know that." Adam taunted.

"What's the big deal?" Cat asked innocently.

Rick's color rose, a mighty feat for the undead. "She's looking for her annual fuck-fest."

Cat pushed on. "When one contracts for a fuck-fest…" Cat flipped through the pages of the brochure for the item. "I don't see that on the menu."

Rick bent over the bar mixing blood types for the Everclear. His voice was sotto voce. "It's not a thing…"

Cat cupped her hand around her ear. Even with vampire hearing, Rick mumbled his words.

Willow watched with interest as Anna bit her top lip and shared a glance with Matt. His brow rose, and there was an almost imperceptible nod. Anna joined her mate at the bar. Her arm encircled his shoulder, and she gave him a little hip bump. "Oh, Fitz, everybody wants some of you."

He looked at her underneath his eyelashes. "Well, I'm off the menu. It makes me feel so cheap."

Anna turned to Adam. "Don't we employ skilled sexual surrogates? I mean, I can understand why she comes back year after year for a piece of this." She tugged at his belt loop and then went to sit down.

Matt made eye contact with Willow. "You picked a good time to get to know us."

"I've watched Dom/sub relationships before, but, you folks are truly progressive." Willow's wonderful brown eyes widened.

"Well, it's a role he played and lived for centuries. In fact, it is just a role." Anna winked at Rick.

He leaned his fine ass up against the bar and folded his arms over his chest. "I'd gladly whip her, but I'm not bumping uglies with her." He shook his finger at Matt. "Decades ago it was just a few heavily scented parchment envelopes, now, she thinks a cell phone is all she needs to be joined at the hip."

Matt shrugged. "Our clients won't be denied their release." He smirked. "I'll take the responsibility to tell her we are off the menu. We're mated."

"To women, not each other. Fine, Mr. Voice of Reason. She's like a bloodhound; I hope she doesn't find her way to our quarters."

****

Adam stepped in. "I'm going to hijack the rest of the meeting, Rick."

"But, of course." Rick gestured grandly.

"You'll find a PowerPoint presentation next." He directed the rest of the table. "I'm going to let Willow begin. She brought this information to my attention."

"If you'll look at the first page, you'll see a picture of Flynn Rail. He is a sleazeball 'journalist'," Willow used air quotes. "...who specializes in conspiracy theories. This guy investigates all kinds of conspiracies. Who killed JFK, Area 51, Bigfoot and most recently the Loch Ness Monster."

Matt interrupted. "What does that have to do with us?"

"There's a lot more to this, bear with us." Adam stood and took over the meeting. "I'll tell you more about how Rail bilks money from the unsuspecting public, but first, he got lucky and homed in on shifters."

Suddenly, the entire group was with him. "Flip to the next page. He's got pictures of one of The Flight's End dragons diving into Loch Ness."

Willow took the floor. "This is a poor time of year for fair weather explorers. I'm on sabbatical and was in the area doing other studies when I made a series of deductions that took me to Flight's End. Once the weather improves, and amateur explorers organize to travel in these remote areas, Scotland could be crawling with theorists."

Rick nodded seriously. "That's why you wanted the expedited equipment."

The table was silent, and Adam nodded. "But, I think we can do better. Hear me out before you laugh."

Rick's demeanor darkened. "Does this include moving the clans?"

"Eventually, but in the short term, it's extremely important to discredit this guy. Not only because of dragonfolk but because he's bilking millions of dollars through his podcasts. He's got a channel on MyTube that refers people to his GiveABuck page. His followers are being fleeced."

The cop in Matt woke up. "Is this guy being investigated by the police?"

"They say there's no basis in law against what he's done. We want to discredit him, so it goes no further."

Rick folded his hands in front of him. "I told you a few weeks ago we'd always have your back. What can we do?"

Adam grinned broadly. "He wants a conspiracy; we're going to give him a conspiracy he'll never forget. Everybody got their passports?" The group nodded. "We're headed to Chile."

Matt closed his eyes and threw his head back. "Don't send me back to Khuno!" Cat stifled a laugh. Rick and Anna exchanged glances and Adam and Willow were mystified.

7

Adam went down the timeline. "Rick, while you are fending off the lovely Veda, I'll be flying to Scotland with computers and generators and setting up trailers. Anna, about that junket to the breeders—you mentioned you weren't looking forward to going alone. Willow has some special gifts she could share with you." Adam raised a brow, seeking permission from Willow and she nodded and smiled. "Willow is a Pegasus shifter."

The room sat in stunned silence. Anna shook her head. Adam's grin spread across his handsome face. "What are you thinking, Anna?"

"Pegasus is mythology. There's no such thing…"

Cat chimed in. "… as Vampires? Dragons?"

Anna smacked the tabletop. "If I weren't a vampire, I would *so* want to be a flying horse."

Adam shouldered a nudge to Willow as she replied to Anna. "I'm not sure there are any other of my kind. Until I met Adam, I thought I was a freak."

Rick shook his head at his mate. "You don't want to be a Pegasus; you want to *ride* a Pegasus."

"Oh, I do, I really do. Can I do that?" She looked at Willow. "Is that possible?"

Rick patted Anna on the shoulder. "Willow, whatever you do, don't let her brush you when she's mad."

Willow looked from Adam to Rick to Anna. "I'm sure there's a story in there somewhere…"

Adam nonverbally prodded Willow to speak up. "I can speak telepathically with the horses; it would give you the edge on knowing their temperament and who would be happiest in a setting like this. I could make it a more equitable interview with your future equine staff."

Cat threw up her hands. "No way, you can talk to animals? I've gotta see this. PLAYER!" The sounds of the mighty beast's toenails approached at high speed. The partially closed door thudded open and bounced back. A massive black and tan Rottie barreled into Anna's lap.

"Who's my baby?" Anna scratched him under both ears and his chest. The dog's front paws embraced her on the chair, trying to crawl into her lap.

Willow laughed. "Oh, he adores you. He respects Rick, and he knows Rick is his master." Willow stopped for a drink of water and thought. The images kept projecting into her mind. "Rick, are you ready for what I'm about to say?"

"Please, do not tell me Veda's immortal soul has entered that sweet dog's body."

Willow shook her head. "He loves Anna. But, there's a little rivalry with you over her affections. He has deep gratitude for you getting him out of a cage…he loves you for that. And…he enjoyed some time in the snow? But the orange cat terrified him. Does that make sense?"

Anna's attention calmed Player. "Did Bonkers make you crazy?"

Willow nodded to Matt. "He sees you as another dog. He likes to play with you, especially at dusk."

Cat pointed from Willow to Matt to Player. "Excuse me, Player…" She addressed the dog with narrowed eyes. "You play with Matt like he's a dog?"

Matt hung his head to hide his grin. "We wrestle. When you take those long bubble baths, we take off and run…"

Cat narrowed her eyes at Matt, then flashed a smile at Willow. "I thought animals were afraid of vampires, and we couldn't have a dog."

Matt snapped his fingers under the table for Player, who ran to him. "…Depends on the animal…"

Cat tapped her finger for a minute. "Willow, what would Player think of a little Sheltie friend?"

Once Willow communicated it to Player, he halted and spun toward Cat. Player posed on guard.

Cat concentrated on the dog. "What's he saying to me? Yes, no, maybe…?"

Willow smiled at the news she delivered. "Player would like many friends; he'd like the first one to be a female."

Cat laughed in Matt's face and crossed her arms decisively over her chest. "Hah! We are *so* getting a dog!"

Player stepped over to Adam. The large dog's mouth hung open; a string of drool perilously close to Adam's pristine Gucci loafers. In his lighter Dom voice, he asked. "What do you want, Boy?"

Willow slid her chair back to make room for the dog. "Player sees you taking care of Rick. He thinks you're huge, but you're not huge fun. He wants you to be less serious."

Player sprung toward Willow and crawled over her lap. His vocalizing was definitely flattering and affectionate.

Anna made some notes. "I am canceling the junket, why listen to an 'expert' when I can listen to my future employee?"

"I am a veritable Dr. Doolittle who usually can't admit half of what I know. It will be a pleasure to be able to share."

Cat stacked the tablets and notes from the meeting. "I'm going too, there should be some dogs out there looking for a good home."

Matt folded his arms on the table and hid his head. "I can see it now; they'll return with an entire zoo."

Rick tossed a wadded napkin at Matt's head. "They took us in. If they want animals, I say we've got room for them."

* * * *

Willow made certain the mood was set. She had just enough time to light the candles and unwrap the scented soaps and lotions before Adam came back from checking the malfunctioning sprinkler system.

Matt cast shade her way when she asked about Adam's favorite scents. "That's not a guy thing."

She wished she could read people as easily as animals. Well, she'd heard men liked vanilla, so…

Adam's face wore a frown as he entered the suite, but not for long when he saw Willow standing in front of him, wearing nothing but his shirt and a smile. Candles were lit, painting her with the most delicious flickering shadows, and everything smelled like a cookie.

"Oh, look at that unhappy face. Let me turn that frown upside down."

He sighed happily. "You're the one who can do it! Come here, Lolo." He nuzzled her back against the wall.

Her hands glanced over his shoulders and chest. "You're all hot and sweaty. Come into the shower and let me scrub your back."

His lips descended sweetly on hers. "Mmm. That's not all you'll scrub…"

"This is business. Not monkey business…"

He pouted. "No monkey business?"

"Well, maybe later. I haven't been alone with you all day. I'm thinking a nice relaxing shower, and some wine and conversation, and then…"

"You told me on the airplane you didn't drink."

"That's funny coming from you. You're the one who drives me to drink."

"Right. Let's get to the 'and then' part!"

Willow cuddled into him and kissed his neck. "First talk, then 'and then'."

Adam sighed. "Okay. What's on your mind, Lolo?"

"You're leaving for Scotland tomorrow?"

"Yeah." He sighed gustily. "Ten A.M. flight. Just enough for a couple of hours of shut-eye—or 'something'."

"Umm." She rubbed against him. "Something." Taking his hand, she led him to an equally fragrant, candlelit bathroom, and started the shower.

"Dr. Greer suggests that Dr. Lachlan enjoy a stimulating shower."

Adam pulled his shirt from over her head. "I like the view."

"Well, then, let's get you out of these sweaty clothes, and into the steamy heat of…the shower."

"Umm. Steam heat."

"Yes. May I assist you?" Her busy fingers removed each piece as the cloud of her hot breath, and the casual glancing of her body stimulated every erotic area of his. Tired as he was, he sprang to life under her palm.

"I'm beat…will you bathe me?" Adam's smile was huge as he shuffled into the shower.

Willow set the shower stall to soft rain. She let it cascade over his smooth muscled flesh and could not resist a gentle bite at his pec.

Adam chuckled low, "You're not going to get me clean that way."

"I could give you a tongue bath." But instead, she grabbed the shower gel and poured it into her hands. She started at his neck, her fingers weaving through his thick golden hair. She worked the sweet-smelling soap into thick bubbles and massaged his neck and head as she went. "Aw, your muscles are tense." She worked soothing strokes into her massage, working down his shoulder to his right arm. "Doesn't this feel good?"

Adam groaned contentment as her thumbs pressed masterfully into his tight palm, she circled and tugged on each one of his strong fingers. He leaned back against the shower wall and closed his eyes. "Uh…feels good…"

"You're too stressed. Everything's gonna be okay."

One eye winked open. "You've met my mother, right?"

"I have. And she is formidable, but I know you can handle her. You can do this." She set to work on the left arm and hand. "I believe in you."

* * * *

Adam slid under her spell.

How does she know I can get everything done, but sometimes, I need someone here for me?

He sighed. "That feels great."

"Good. That's what I was aiming for. To do this properly, I need you lying down on a massage table. But for now, …have a seat…"

He lounged on the shower seat, his head lolled back and to one side, a relaxed smile on his face. His long-legged manspread sprawled before her. He could just about predict what was coming next…until she surprised him by sitting cross-legged on the shower floor. *This is a new approach—maybe she's going to use telepathy?* Willow caught up his right foot and propped it on her knee. Her thumbs began a ruthless assault on his tension. She began at the ball of his foot and swept strong strokes.

"What devil magic are you employing?"

"It's an ancient art, but effective, don't you think?" She stimulated the bottom of his heel and Adam felt a definite response.

"What are you doing to me?"

"Well, there are points on your feet that correlate to parts of the body. I touch you here, and…" Adam shuddered "You see? I locate areas that need relief and others that need…arousal."

"Well, it's damn effective," he said wryly, watching his cock stir to life.

"Yes, it is. We'll get back to the relaxation now. You're too big to do a full body massage in the shower, but I can handle a foot massage…Your feet are huge."

Adam grinned wickedly. "You know what that means…"

She gently squeezed the top and bottom of his foot, and then cupped his heel in the palm of one of her hands and tugged his foot toward her.

"I'm going to be in your lap if you tug much harder."

"Oh, I'm gonna tug hard, very soon."

She pressed her hands together around his foot and grasped it tightly three times. He groaned in ecstasy. She wrung the tension out of him. She started at the toes and used a slapping motion to tap all the way down his foot.

"That feels great!"

"I know. It's supposed to." Now, her hands were back to his body, massaging the back of his calves down to his ankles, and playfully hitting his bottom heel, making him crazy. His emotional tension dwindled as a tension of another kind took its place. She moved to the other leg and foot, repeating all her previous actions, incorporating those same marvelous sensations of relaxation combined with sexual tension.

Adam reached for the shower gel and smoothed it over his torso and legs. "I'm never gonna get clean your way!" He rubbed under his arms. "This is the rough stuff, anyway. You don't want to be there now."

"I wanna be all over you."

"Oh, yeah, how about you? You got any rough stuff?"

Willow stood and let the water run over her. She poured the cucumber scented gel into her hand and attacked first her chocolate curls, lathering, and rinsing. And then, in an unconsciously erotic dance, she swept her soapy fingers over both breasts, lifting them with her hands, her fingers making more bubbles underneath them. Adam's hands froze where they were on his lower abdomen, as he watched her show. Her fingers skimmed her aroused nipples, pulling firmly on their tips. Adam's eyes grew bright. He smoothed the bubbles from his abs to his thatch of pubic hair, his fingers scrubbed unconsciously, mimicking her actions. Willow extended one long leg onto the shower seat next to him.

"It's important to be clean inside and out," she said.

Adam's tongue licked compulsively at his lower lip. "Yeah. Do you want help with that?"

Willow leaned against the wall and made repeated circular strokes between her legs. "You look like you have your hands full."

"It's okay. I have big hands."

Her laugh was sultry, and the circles grew tighter, her breath huffed faster and faster as she laid her head back against the shower wall, giving in to the sensations.

Adam was riveted. His cock stood at full attention, his massive hand stroking the long, thick length of his shaft.

Willow's eyes slatted open as she watched him. "You have to pick up your pace if we're gonna finish together." Her gaze consumed him hungrily as her hips kept time with her intimate fondling.

His bright eyes watched those busy fingers, now sliding in and out of her hot sex. "Why rush a good thing?"

He slid into the corner and raised his foot onto the bench in silent invitation. He cupped his sack and grinned at her, catching his cock in a taunting embrace. Her responses were guttural as she worked her fevered flesh to the brink. "I wish those were my fingers. I would make you come *hard*," he teased. She grinned and giggled devilishly.

"You can't even speak right now, you're so close! I can see your pussy getting redder. Your lips are swollen, your nipples are hard little buds. I love the way you come. Show me!"

Willow slid into the opposing corner. Her fingers flew savagely as the other hand worked her nipple. She choked out, "Come with me!"

The Dom ceded to his sub's request. His strokes grew long and rapid as he cupped his sack. He recalled how her sex fisted the head of his dick and milked him. His fingers slipped slickly over his glans and frenulum, and Adam began to pant. The tingling started at the base of his spine.

"Yes, yes, yes!" She moaned, watching him. "Do that! Oh my God! You're so huge!"

His breathing hitched; his thighs shook. His foot on the bench moved to the wall as he stretched out his other long leg. "This is what you do to me." His essence erupted with brutal force. Watching him, Willow cried out and sank against him in the midst of her release. The shower beat on their exhausted bodies. "This was a lot more work than when we do it together…" His fingers cupped her satisfied sex.

"Maybe but look how clean you are."

He turned her in his arms and kissed her slowly. He took his time, he kissed her like she was the sweetest fruit on the tree. He kissed her as if only her lips sustained him. They sagged together under the simulated rain.

* * * *

Seven A.M. came too soon. Willow slept cradled in his arms, delighting in the feel of his sheltering body wrapped around hers. She never in her life felt dainty and delicate until she met Adam Lachlan. She scowled at the alarm clock.

"Catch a later flight."

"I can't, Lolo. I'll never get to Flight's End today if I do. Besides, you're going horse hunting, remember?"

She snuggled against his morning wood. "Oh…just one little…"

"Ut…ut…ut…I'm getting up now. I have to pack. Why don't you make me some coffee?"

Willow pouted, her lush pink lower lip covering the upper. Adam stopped in the act of pulling out his suitcase. "Now, that look will get you fucked!"

"Really?"

"Oh, yeah."

"I'll have to remember that unless you want me to ride in the limo to the airport?"

Adam groaned. "I'm afraid the limo will be filled with other guests…which now that I think about it, might be kinda fun for you to sit on my lap…"

"Adam Lachlan! I am not looking for an audience!"

Adam's eyes twinkled. "How do you know if you've never tried?"

"That sounds like your work to me."

"Love your work…"

"Yeah, yeah, I've got it. C'mon, Master Adam, I'll make the coffee."

"No limo?"

"Not this trip. We'll see, maybe later."

She brought his coffee the way he liked it. Adam stroked her forearm as she handed him the mug, and said, "I just have to get serious for a minute."

She frowned and stepped back. "No, it's good. I was touched by what you did with Player last night. It was genuinely kind and giving. They're vampires, you know, and vampires don't usually keep animals. It meant a lot to them to know that Player's happy and that they can make other animals happy. What a gift you share!"

"They're people, I don't see them as vampires. They're your friends."

"Oh, well, they were mortals first, but trust me, they are the top of the food chain."

"They were human first, and they still are."

He shook his head as he dressed. "You are a marvelous optimist."

"I can see the good in other people easier than I can see it in myself."

He drew her into an embrace and looked down into her eyes. "Lolo, then you need to see yourself the way others see you, the way I see you."

"What a gift that would be."

"We'll work on that."

* * * *

Willow propped her chin on her hand. She hadn't shifted this often in months. Her muscles complained over the demands she made of her body. Her past few days melted into hours of extended sexual pleasure, Adam's family drama, and adjusting to vampire hours. Her eyelids fluttered. Anna opened the car door and gave her a travel mug of coffee. "Here, you might need this. I know exactly what you're going through right now, converting your days to nights."

Willow accepted the cup and nodded. "Any Adderall in that? That's what I really need! I generally don't drink coffee in the afternoon."

"I'm afraid not." Anna climbed into the back seat. "You probably had only a couple of hours sleep today, right? Is this the first time you've kept the company of vampires?"

Willow's eyes widened. "Yeah, color me fascinated."

Anna nodded. "If there's anything you're curious about, just ask. Cat and I are fairly new at this. Until a month ago we didn't realize there was such a thing as Shifters. Let alone dragonfolk or Pegasus."

Willow nodded.

And trust me, I will.

"I didn't know there were other shifters either. I thought I was a freak. Then, I was in Flight's End. I woke up and peeked outside to check the weather when I see this dragon flying right toward me. I did not expect to see that at daybreak, let alone a dragon that shifted into a naked man."

Anna giggled. *Yes, he is a beautiful man, all six foot six inches of his muscled body.* Anna blinked. "When Rick showed his vampire to me, we were both fully clothed. I was scared shitless, but at least I knew where to look at him."

Willow shared her laugh, her hand shook, and she put down the cup. "Yeah, it was an eye-opener."

The subject attracted Cat to the conversation as she drove. "Are you and Adam dating? Because the men sort of put us in charge of finding him a woman. He's such a good guy and earnest in everything he does. It would be thrilling to know he found a soulmate."

Soulmate? Am I too jaded to believe in soulmates?

Willow's huge eyes sparkled at the idea of discovering more about the man who intrigued her. "Have either of you known him very long?"

Cat shook her head. "Last October, I was really distressed, and I passed out. The next thing I knew this giant of a man was standing over me in those tight tuxedo pants and a formal shirt that looked like it was painted on him. But, five minutes into our conversation, all I could feel was his kindness. He has a heart of gold."

Willow ran her fingers through her short hair. "Well, you know… I like him a lot. We'll see what happens. How long have you been with your men?" Looking at the two preternatural ingénues, she felt like a spinster.

As she drove, Cat played with the ring on her left hand. "Oh, Matt and I have known each other a little over a year." She made it sound like a long time. "We were mated, or you would say married last October."

How could you take a step like that when half the world's marriages end in divorce?

"Wow, that's sudden," Willow observed. *Do I sound judgmental?*

"Not really, we'd been through a lot by then," Cat countered gaily.

"I wasn't raised with shifters." Willow changed the subject, not wanting a debate.

Anna nodded sympathetically. "How old were you when it first happened?"

"My adopted family sent me to camp when I was eleven. I always loved horses, and I begged to go to a dude ranch in Montana."

"Well, of course, you would have loved horses. It was in your blood."

Willow continued. "Before daybreak, I woke up and felt weird, I wanted to be alone. I snuck out to find my horse broke his tether and took off. I went looking for Romeo."

The women were entranced.

"I've never told this story to anyone. I headed where I thought Romeo would go, and it wasn't too long before I saw his hoof prints. I found him by a stream, drinking. I knelt to get a drink myself, and the reflection I saw was this beautiful black and white paint, standing where I was." Willow shook her head as if reliving the event. "My clothes felt tight, and I felt like a swim, so I got out of my boots and jeans, and before I could get out of my underwear, the shift began. I felt my muscles and bones release; I felt a heat and a new energy. Before I knew it, I was in the water looking at a horse that was sprouting wings!"

Anna shook her head. "No way!"

"Romeo was beside me, his hoof pawed the ground, and he shook his head at me. Then, when I thought it couldn't get any weirder, Romeo spoke to me telepathically."

Cat drove and chewed her artificial nail. "What'd he say?"

"Romeo looked at me, and he said, 'What took you this long? I've seen this coming since you first got on my back. Didn't we share equine energy?"

"I told Romeo; I didn't know I could do this. And he said he knew it; the other horses knew it. Even the trail dogs knew it. They were waiting for it to happen. He asked me if my wings were strong enough to fly, and I had no idea. I certainly didn't know how to take off or land. Romeo took off running, and I chased him, and he ran to a cliff and skidded to a stop. I was so busy watching him, that, suddenly, the ground beneath my hooves was gone and the only thing left for me to do, was flap my wings." Anna and Cat gasped. "And I was flying. It was the ultimate freedom. Romeo just looked at me as I flew circles over him and then I realized I was exhausted. I wasn't sure how to land, I stopped flapping my wings and sank like a stone, it was an ugly landing. I was ass over elbows, and my coat was full of dirt and bugs. In fact, Romeo suggested I shift back, and he carried me to the stream where I could get a bath and get my clothes back on. He was such a sweetie, he suggested I talk to the hawks for landing advice. It took a lot of work, but they were great teachers."

"You can talk to Adam when you're flying?" Anna's mind was off proposing the possibilities of being a shifter.

"He is a prankster when he flies. It's a good thing he lives in the world, he'd be in trouble all the time."

Cat shook her head. "He seems like such a 'by the book' guy."

Willow drained her cup. "Oh, why don't you ask him why he's been in the mortal world the past two hundred years?"

Anna was fascinated. "He's two hundred years old?"

Willow bit her bottom lip. "Well, he told me his next birthday he'd be nine hundred and ninety-five years old."

Anna giggled. "I did some digging, and Rick finally admitted to me that he's over five hundred years old. He's just a youngster."

Cat's eyebrows rose. "Matt's not too far off from me, he's just a hundred years older. But, sometimes, his nineteenth-century mindset rears its opinionated head."

Willow smiled sadly. "I wish I knew where there might be other Pegasus shifters. Being like this alone is such a burden to carry…"

The ladies all spoke in unison. "…because who do you have to talk with about it?" Willow extended her hands to Cat and Anna. "And now we have each other."

"The vamp Family has vamp.net, perhaps we can do some research to see if shifters have an online community?"

"Well, zoology has shown me nothing, Adam is the first shifter I've met. I'm open to any ideas."

8

The four-lane road turned into two lanes, then to a wide swath of packed earth. The sign spanning the entry gate said Randolph Equestrian Center. A larger, garish sign stated *FOR SALE; Everything must go. All animals, tack, feed, and some fencing will be sold by February 28th. Auction March 1st.*

Anna read the classified advertisement. "They're school horses…mostly Irish Hunters and Connemara Ponies…they have some Cheviot sheep as well as the ram… They mention a sheepdog also available... It looks like the owner of this school died, and basically, everything that isn't nailed down is for sale."

The women alighted the car and went hunting down the heirs. They viewed two barns sharing a large round exercise paddock between them. Off to the side, was a jumping ring littered with knocked down rails. Sheep roamed a field surrounding their barn. A large sheepdog lumbered out of the barn to greet them. She huffed a breath and moved to Willow who knelt to rub her neck and ears.

Willow looked up at the women. "This is Bridget, she's lived here a long time. She's frightened because her home is being sold, and she doesn't know what they'll do with her. She doesn't like the adult children." Willow bent her head to Bridget's wet nose and carried on a telepathic conversation. "The other animals have elected Bridget to be their eyes and ears about their future."

Anna's eyes shone with sympathetic tears. "I could never imagine parting with our animals this way. It must be terrifying for them." Anna walked confidently to the first barn with the others following.

Willow was immediately struck with emotion and communication as soon as she stepped inside. She turned with wide-eyed excitement to the other women. "You know, we could stock the entire stable with this school alone. There may even be stable hands looking for work with housing. We'd be lucky to have hands that already know the horses."

Anna reached for her phone. "Let me call Rick."

Willow held up a hand. "Before we scare Rick with the wealth of this find, let's chat with the family." She looked at Bridget and learned the family spent all their time in the cottage, which was their next stop.

The Sheepdog stood stalwartly beside Willow as she rang the bell. A tweed-wearing gentleman of forty years plus, sniffed as he opened the door on the trio of women in wool and denim and muck boots.

"We're not hiring, didn't you see the for-sale sign?" He was about to turn and close the door when Bridget shuffled to block him. "Bothersome old bitch, head for the barn."

Anna's back stiffened at his words, and she stepped between Cat and Willow. "I am here to discuss the terms of your sale." He cast a look behind her at the shiny black Range Rover.

"Out with your Daddy's checkbook, dearie?" He folded his arms over his narrow chest.

"I have my own checkbook, thank you, as well as twenty plus years in farming."

He sniffed.

"Your sign says all must go by the end of the month. Are you in contract yet?" She patted her leather, saddle-bag-style purse.

He stepped out and closed the door behind him. "Who is your solicitor?"

Anna raised her chin at him. "My husband will handle that."

"So young, and with a checkbook and a husband?" The man flinched and held out his hand. "I'm David Randolph, and my siblings have charged me with getting the most out of this bucolic obstruction to progress."

Willow waved a hand. "I'm Dr. Willow Greer, and this is Mrs. Brenner." Cat stepped up with an outstretched hand to the Ichabod Crane of a man.

Willow dug back into negotiations. "I want to bring a Vet out here. Also, a mechanic to review the equipment and we…" She pointed to Anna, "Want to inspect the tack and your stock."

"Show me your earnest money, and you can spend a day here doing exactly that."

Anna stepped closer to him. "I want to see an inventory, and I want to meet your head groom."

"You do seem focused, Miss."

"It's Mrs. Hiatt."

"Hiatt?" His grey brow rose. "I had no idea the man had a child bride." His congested laugh trailed off to a loose cough.

"You know my husband?"

The man's lips pursed and released. "Of him, didn't the Duke visit and ride with him recently?"

Willow tapped her foot, and Bridget nuzzled her knee.

Well, didn't that double the price?

Bridget groaned and bit the air.

"Don't mind the dog, she's headed for the pound. The other animals are rather docile. Except that one fractious gelding that threw me the last time I hacked him."

Willow waved into the conversation. "What's your price for everything? We'll take everything but the buildings."

David Randolph's bloodshot eyes brightened.

"If we can get our people out here tomorrow, and our terms are met, you'll have a cash sale within forty-eight hours."

He rubbed at his thin goatee. "You Yanks come in and double-team us, don't you?"

Cat, who was roaming the general area, used her excellent vampire hearing and stepped silently up behind Randolph. "There's three of us here, we use a broad approach to negotiations. Let's get on with this, how much earnest money?" Randolph startled and jumped. Cat's hand nervously skimmed the side of her purse.

Randolph shook his head. "Young Hiatt seems trustworthy, how about ninety thousand pounds?"

Anna's fingers flew over her phone. In a short time, it rang. "Mr. Randolph, would you speak with my husband?"

He accepted the phone and for the first time exhibited any speed in movement. He clipped away from the women and headed to the far paddock. Willow grinned at her vampire friends.

Anna's brows rose. "Oh, I love the way my husband just sweeps in with diplomatic deconstruction."

Willow ruffled Bridget's thick coat. She divided her attention between the concerns of the dog and Anna's blow by blow account of the phone call.

Anna whispered. "Rick is telling him the market is flat, and the auction houses have been inundated with animal rights groups who decry sales of school animals to overseas meat packing companies. He says Randolph's stock is tailor-made for school, but not for shows or hunts, and he's asking show prices." Willow and Cat exchanged optimistic looks.

Anna dropped her head to smirk. "Oh, Rick is going for the throat now." Anna turned toward Randolph who covered his face with his hand. "He's going to cave, in one, two, three seconds. Rick has ended the call, and Randolph is showboating."

The man stomped back toward the women. "Young man, you cannot invade a country and inflict your west coast style of business. I insist." His words stopped as if he were listening to Rick. "I will accept a check from your wife. I will deposit it tomorrow at bank opening. Pleasure doing business with you, sir."

The women tittered at his posturing. Anna hugged herself. "One more actual minute on the phone with Rick and he'd be cryin' like a three-year-old."

Willow approached Randolph. "And, your decision?"

"We're still in negotiations. However, Mrs. Hiatt is to draft a check for thirty-five thousand pounds today. And you may see the stock, Dr. Greer."

He led the women to the stable, walked ahead of them, and engaged a hushed conversation with a burly bald man. The man nodded and walked toward the ladies.

"I'm Liam, the owner said I'm to take you to see the stock, glad you have your muck boots on, ladies. Follow me."

Anna took in the old barn and weathered equipment. She nodded to Willow who understood the stables' cleanliness was attributed to the conscientious stable hands. Willow stood in the center aisle of the barn, five stalls on each side. Then Liam touched his cap and went about his business, as well as the business of gossip.

Willow translated her observations to the women. "They tell me, they eat well…but since old man Randolph died, the portions are smaller… They pine for 'the Missus" she went first…and the 'Mister' was gone within weeks…"

Willow spoke to the horses. "It's no wonder it seems sad out here. I'm with the good women back there, and I've promised them I would do my best to share your feelings with them. They would like to take all of you to live with them in a castle…"

A pie-eyed paint stuck his nose out of a stall. If a horse could laugh, he was doing it. "They want us to live in the castle or the barn?" he asked amused.

Three more horses stuck their heads out of their stalls to join in the conversation. Bridget barked softly, and Willow chuckled. "In the stable behind the castle. You'd be ridden by the resort guests."

The redheaded vampire stepped closer and turned in a circle as she spoke. "The stables are beautifully done. Wouldn't you love to have a friendly home?"

After a short silence, Willow translated. "Will there be whips?"

Anna and Cat drew in shocked breaths. "No!"

"There will be treats!" Cat assured, and then turned to Anna. "What are horse treats?" Anna waved her off.

Willow smiled. "Well, that was a big hit!" Willow looked around at the horses in their stalls. "You all need to understand that your lives will be different, though in many ways better. But something you need to decide is if you're agreeable to working with vampires."

There was a general snorting and stomping on both sides of the barn. Bridget looked up at her. *What are vampires?*

Willow motioned at Cat and Anna, who crouched near the old girl. "These two ladies are undead."

Bridget crooked her head. *Undead?*

"Notice they smell different?" Willow gestured, and all three placed their closed hands to Bridget's nose.

Bridget drew her head back and stepped away.

They smell dead!

She stepped forward hesitantly.

It's true, they smell different, but I don't sense they're a threat.

She approached Cat to get some loving.

"No, no threat." Willow agreed. "Some animals are afraid of them."

Cat stroked the dog's thick coat. "Some of us—who are ancient—have a stronger scent. But, we mean you no harm."

Bridget climbed into Cat's crouch and licked her face.

Cat smiled. "We'd be thrilled to take all the animals to live with us."

Bridget's stubby tail shook her entire body. She turned to Willow. *"You know, my adopted son lives here, too."*

"Where is he?"

Bridget barked, and a scruffy Dandy Dinmont terrier tore around the corner and collided with Cat's legs.

"Who's this?" She picked up the young dog, who affectionately squirmed in her arms and licked her entire face. She looked at Anna. "I guess he's not afraid of vampires. Wait till Matt gets a load of this…"

Willow weighed in. "I think, as long as we explain to all the animals vampires simply have a different scent, they'll be fine. It's the scent that scares them. Obviously, no one here is afraid of you two."

Anna softly clapped her hands together. "Let's call Rick! We're taking everyone!" She began snapping photographs.

Liam approached, wiping his hands on his britches. "You know, we have a whole herd of sheep and one very randy ram."

Willow's fingers flew over her phone, to send a message. *Adam, what type of wool does your sister like? We're looking at a herd of sheep.*

She got no answer but slid the phone back into her purse.

Cat turned in circles, taking in all the countryside and livestock. "It's going to be like Rebecca of Sunnybrook Farm!"

Anna laughed as she wrote the check and clapped a hand on Cat's shoulder. "You like physical work that much, huh?" She headed toward the cottage.

* * * *

The ladies held what amounted to a doggie slumber party. The hotel clerk looked over his shoulder as Willow slipped a large stack of pound notes to the front desk for allowing the dogs. "I'm glad I asked for extra towels."

There was a shopping trip for dog wash, conditioner, new collars and leashes, brushes, and clippers. Anna pulled a set of clip-on bows from the shopping bag. "You're going to be so beautiful!" Bridget wagged her tail, and General groaned and laid down.

Anna took Bridget into the bathroom. "Okay, I'm going into the shower with her. Don't open the door, no matter what you hear."

For the larger part of an hour, Cat leaned her ear against the door, listening to every noise. Bridget emerged clean and dry. "Okay, Cat, you get to brush her, while I wash the General."

Cat looked bewildered. "I was raised in a convent. I have no experience with animals."

Willow winked at Bridget. "You'll be a good girl, and let Cat brush you out, won't you? We used plenty of conditioner, there shouldn't be too many tangles." Bridget sighed and laid down.

This is new to me, too. I've never been groomed before. I've been a working dog.

"You look beautiful! Prepare to be adored." Willow encouraged, handing Cat a brush, and picking up one herself.

Cat giggled. "Player will love having you and General for company." She glanced at Willow. "There was a time when Matt and I were first together when we would walk on the beach and play with a little Sheltie who lived by us." Willow raised a questioning brow. Cat sighed. "It's complicated. But at the time, Matt was on a drug that masked vampirism. And it was a real heartache when he said animals didn't do well with vampires, because, I knew we wouldn't be able to have kids, but I thought we'd be able to have a dog."

Willow smiled. "No wonder you were amazed when Player said he liked to wrestle with Matt."

"Right. And now we'll have a multitude of beautiful animals around us! Men are a mystery sometimes!"

"You're telling me! I haven't exactly had a great history with dating."

Cat shrugged. "I hardly dated at all before college, and not that much then. Matt and I met because a guy I'd just started dating became really inappropriate with me one night, and Matt intervened."

Willowed sighed. "It must be nice to have a guy come to your rescue. I never felt that."

"I think if the circumstance presented itself, Adam would be that guy. You two certainly had an unconventional meeting."

"Can't argue that. I like Adam a lot. Being what I am, it's been impossible for me to put myself out there. It started in high school, my boyfriend and I were making out, and he started to pressure me, and I kept refusing, and finally, he grabbed at my pants, and it became a wrestling match. I came this close to shifting because of the stress."

"Did he try to rape you?"

Willow frowned. "Rape is a strong word. Let's just say, I wasn't ready for it, and I didn't allow it."

"Good for you. But, almost shifting must have scared you. The fear of shifting in the middle of a sexual experience must be awful."

Willow nodded. "I stayed a virgin to a ripe age. In fact, it wasn't until I did some research and discovered bondage, that I risked it. I figured the bondage would keep me from shifting, and it did."

"Was your first sexual experience with a Dom?" Cat frowned. "That doesn't sound very romantic…"

"I couldn't afford the romance, but I wanted the experience…"

"By and large, the Doms I've met aren't interested in relationships. They have their subs, but almost always their emotional relationships are with their buddies—in a straight way."

Willow thought for a moment. "I never realized until you said that, you're right. Doms usually don't have emotional relationships with their subs, which is not to say they don't care about the sub, but there's always a wall, isn't there?"

"Yeah, as far as I can tell, a lot of these guys are just there for the kink. That's not where you're gonna find a lasting relationship."

Willow arched a brow. "What does that say for Adam?"

Cat was silent a long time. "I don't know."

"Yeah, I don't know either."

* * * *

Anna emerged from the bathroom looking wetter than the dog. "Willow?" She asked through gritted teeth. "Would you please have a chat with General about proper grooming etiquette?"

Willow laughed. "Of course." She took the soppy dog from Anna's hands and wrapped him in a towel. "Now, General, what's the fuss? Look how happy Bridget is to be brushed."

I am perfect the way I am. Submerging in water is not healthy!

Bridget looked over at him. *Stop your whining, boy! You might actually look like best of show once they're done.*

General grumbled. *I don't like clean, I like dirty.*

Willow roared with laughter. "Do you like sleeping in a soft, warm bed?" General's ears pricked up. *A real bed? Not a bed on the floor?*

"A real bed. But, you have to be clean."

Alright then.

* * * *

After the dogs were dry, brushed, fed, watered, and walked, they snuggled on the bed as if they were in the lap of luxury. Soon, Bridget was snoring softly, and General lay with his head in Cat's lap. Things became quiet, but it was just the beginning of the evening for Anna and Cat. Cat looked down at the dog whose legs were galloping in his dreams. "Awe, I hope he's chasing rabbits. His little body is warm and toasty next to mine."

Willow looked at her sympathetically. "I never really thought about it, but, it must be tough to live without the comfort of a warm man's body next to yours."

Cat winked. "Hard and cold is good, too!"

"Right, I learned a long time ago I'd better trust myself to meet my own needs, doubtful any man is going to do that for me," Willow observed cynically.

Anna brushed her hair as she walked around the suite. "Have you ever been in love, Willow? You know, head over heels?"

Willow searched the ceiling for the answer and shook her head.

Anna stopped short. "Really? Not even a crush?" She knelt on the ottoman in front of Willow. "Okay, have you ever just crushed really hard? Hoped he'd notice you?"

Willow shrugged. "Maybe."

"It's like being pregnant, you crush, or you don't. You can't crush a little." Anna waved a dismissive hand.

"You know, as a young woman, sure, I crushed. But it never worked out, and after a while, it became easier not to try."

Cat was astounded. "A beautiful, educated, kind woman like you? Who the hell were you meeting?"

"College professors, students, Doms… Never met someone I trusted enough."

Anna looked at Cat who closed her eyes and put her hand over her face. "That must be a lonely feeling. Do you like sex?"

"I like sex just fine, notwithstanding most of the men I've met, don't know how to do it right," Willow smirked.

"What about Adam?" Cat looked sly.

Willow chuckled. "Oh, yeah, he knows how to do it right."

Anna sighed. "Finally, some good news." She resumed brushing her hair. "So…how do you feel about Adam?"

"I've found that no matter what I feel in the beginning, it takes a while for men to show their true colors."

Cat nodded sadly. "Yeah, my college boyfriend, Brad took about three months to show his ass. Everyone's on their best behavior at first."

Willow shrugged. "I like Adam a lot, but, we'll see."

"It sounds to me as if you don't trust men." Anna gave her a searching look.

Willow nodded. "That might be true."

"I'm not sure you can find what you don't believe exists." Anna declared.

Cat considered it. "Well, actually, there were periods when I thought Matt and I would never work out. I loved him, but I was mortal, he was a vampire. It's true that sometimes you need more than love."

Anna crooked her neck at Cat. "But it did work out. Still, I know what you mean. I detested Rick at first. He scared the Hell out of me. In fact, the night we formally met, I straight out told him, 'I don't like you'. I still remember the look he shot me."

Cat lowered her head as if Rick was in the room. "You told him that?"

"He didn't take it well, scared me to death!" Anna grimaced. "You have no idea when love really begins. When I saw Rick with Player, I knew there was a side of him I missed."

Cat nodded. "I think with Matt it was love at first sight, although he did rescue me from a Dom wannabe, and that probably contributed to it. My hero."

Willow stared at them. "That would be really nice. We'll see how things work out."

* * * *

"Kill me now." Cat sighed dryly as she reached into the car for the cooler.

Anna shook her head. "We're both already dead. Do you mean, stake me now?"

Cat slung the cooler over her shoulder. "I don't know who to feel sorrier for, Willow or Adam." She passed a travel mug to Anna.

"They are both old enough to know what they want. Could it really be that it's all just sex for them?" Anna's brow rose. Together, they slowly proceeded along the garden path as the moon brightened the white stones of the walk. "I don't even know what to say to Rick."

Cat stopped in her tracks. "What has he asked?"

"Rick has been prodding me about them. He was silly as a teenager when he saw Willow wasn't sleeping in her room. But he says he's thrown all sorts of suggestions about romantic things to do at the castle, and Adam isn't catching one hint."

Cat pulled Anna along the path. "Maybe, Willow is right to be cautious. You know, Adam has worn that wedding ring for decades without being married…"

Anna waved her finger. "The ring is in Rick's safe." Both women raised their brows. "Adam left it there the day they flew out together."

* * * *

The horses, sheep and even the barn cats were relocated to Erne Castle by the end of the week. The grooms moved into bunkhouses, and shortly, the stable was running as smoothly as the Duke remembered it.

Player was in ecstasy with a puppy to romp with, and an old girl to fuss over him by the hearth. He loved chasing the horses, who, if they were not as enthusiastic over him, at least got some good exercise.

* * * *

Three Days Later

The group assembled around the conference table. "Hey, Rick, I heard you handled the Veda situation really well…" Matt couldn't help ribbing him.

Rick groaned and dropped his head into his hands. "She's still here, isn't she?"

Adam joined in. "Yeeesssss. But she's found a new boy toy, seems like Master Caleb has been making all her dreams come true."

"Yeah, he's about an inch shorter than me, but could pass for my brother."

Matt buried a laugh. "You jealous?"

Rick glowered at him over his paperwork. "I'm just stating she has a type…"

Matt tapped a pen on the table. "Yeah." He turned to Adam. "Sparky, what's happening with the grifter? Is he back in town after his expedition to find Bigfoot?"

Adam spun update sheets to each of them. "Yup, he's back in Vegas looking for a new scam. So I say, let's give the man what he wants. All of you ready to head to Chile?"

Rick clapped his hands together. "Seems like a good time for a vacation in the Andes."

Adam stood. "I'll schedule the jet; we'd better get packed.

* * * *

Adam brought some printed emails to Rick in his spacious walk-in closet. "I have confirmation on the chopper and the room reservations."

Rick assembled his wardrobe for the trip. As fast as he coordinated stylish outfits, Adam rehung them and found the most basic black suits, white shirts, and ties.

"You are cramping my style, Sparky." Rick shook his head as he blocked Adam's steps.

"Your role is to fly under the radar in your generic black and white uniform, not strut the international runways in your bespoke fashions. This is all you'll need for your part in the con. Remember, it's the mountains, you'll need jeans and flannel, too."

Rick's face dropped until Anna entered the closet. "C'mon, Fitz, jeans were originally sewn for gold miners. Just think of it as Halloween, and you're a gold miner."

Their trip to the Dublin Airport was jovial. Cat rode herd over Matt carrying all her camera equipment. "Did you remember the international power plugs?"

"Do you think I'm going to Serenity unprepared? This is a sting, and I'm thinking up things we won't even need. I feel like I've got my detective shield back."

The Consort Group International, as a mega-conglomerate, maintained company jets. Today, they used the Boeing 737-700 set conference-style, with sleeping accommodations in the rear. The fifteen-hour flight would be interrupted for fueling in Miami.

Once they were seated for departure, the jet was uncommonly silent.

9

Seated at the conference table, Adam directed their attention to the monitor. Photos of Nessa and Jude appeared. "Their marriage ceremony was three days ago."

Cat smiled at their images. "She was the dragon who helped rescue us. I wondered what she'd look like."

"I wish I could remember that part." Anna grimaced.

Adam passed out the con bios. "I gave the newlyweds a honeymoon at Serenity. I'm sure they won't mind helping us with a little photography. Our first priority will be to get to Mount Viejo, it's the most remote dormant volcano in Chile. We'll begin by taking pictures of flying dragons around the volcano crater." Adam nodded to Rick and Matt. "I've arranged an Agusta six-seater for transporting us in and out tomorrow." Matt pumped his fist at the chance to use his pilot's license.

"You each have your roles and your tentative scripts. Why don't we relax for a while and knuckle down after refueling in Miami?"

* * * *

Adam looked across the jet at Willow. She was in a particularly odd situation. In his two hundred years in the mortal world, he hadn't met a woman he could stand toe to toe with on so many points. He'd removed his wedding ring and put it away in Rick's safe. Her hand was drawn to his whenever they were together. Right now, as the jet refueled, he wanted to stow away in the back. *I long to caress her and breathe in her lovely scent.* Without really asking her, he'd included her in this unconventional exercise to discredit Rail. They'd been in step with each other since she warned of dragonfolk being discovered.

"Did they mean it when they said there were sleeping accommodations back there? I can't keep up with your friends." Willow sleepily smiled when Adam bent his knees to stand up in the jet.

"Sure, they don't expect you to. They'll be hitting the slab shortly, themselves. Follow me." The jet's sleeping quarters were simple. "The lavatory and shower are further back, but the hot water is iffy. Vamps avoid heat when they can." The door slid open to reveal a bed barely wider than a double, however it was longer for Adam's comfort. "I'm usually here alone, so we'll be sleeping fairly close, okay?" His arm encircled her waist and drew her closer.

Her eyes speak volumes, and her body language is a gift in itself.

Although he'd made private accommodations available for her at the castle, she hadn't spent a night in her own room. Her empty duffle bag had stayed in the center of the bed since the night they arrived.

She winked. "I'll be back in a few." She grabbed her toiletry kit and gracefully vanished. Slipping out of his chinos and polo shirt, he slid between the sheets and rolled on his side, his back to the wall.

If we get this job done, I can find out if she's here for the espionage or me.

He set the alarm on his phone and dimmed the light when she returned. She absconded with one of Adam's dress shirts at the castle, and it was her favorite nightshirt. He happened to like it too, their scents mingled provocatively.

"Nice, I never remember liking that shirt the way I do tonight." Adam held up the sheet for her to join him.

"You need to keep me warm." Her voice was a husky whisper as her lips danced over his ear.

I can do that.

She kissed him, it was a sincere kiss, not the inflammatory kisses she'd used in the last week to initiate Dungeon sessions that left his toes curled for hours. Once she settled back into his arms, it was all he could do to turn off his mind and actually sleep.

* * * *

Flynn Rail was a con artist. He exhibited the solid package of a great muscular build, smooth charm, a perfect set of teeth and a marvelously resonant voice. His piercing blue eyes gave his victims the idea they were the most important people in the room. With his six-foot-four-inch stature, he towered over his army of boiler room thieves. "This week's winner of a weekend at Buffalo Bob's resort is…" Flynn checked his clipboard, "Andy Dowd. Seems like Andy scored forty-nine thousand dollars in the Big Foot Caravan Drive." The chubby, hairless man lumbered from the rolling chair in his cubicle and accepted the envelope. Flynn held the edge of the envelope firmly and hesitated to release it. "Mighty fine work, there, dowdy-man. Why don't you clue some of our slow starters in on your technique?"

"Well, Mr. Rail, if I do that, I'll have to spend my weekends with my mother…"

Flynn slapped him on the back. "Way to go Dowdy! That's the Newsbuster's spirit—never give a sucker an even break!" Flynn's face clouded over. "Okay, enough celebrating Big Foot! Onward to Scotland and the Loch Ness Monster. This week we're twenty thou short of our hundred-thousand-dollar goal. Who's going to step up and bring us home?"

A timid hand raised. "I'm having a problem," the mousy girl whined. Flynn nodded. "People want to know if airfare is included."

"How could we score a great package like we're offering if we have to include airfare from the continental United States? I'd target your east coast leads because they don't mind flying one of those cheap flights from New York. Assess your mark. If you sell the luxury of this caravan, they won't scoff at buying their own ticket."

"Some of them want to know who the guide is. They're wondering if it's someone famous like that guy on Reptile Nation?"

"Hell no, we can't afford that—even if he'd agree. No, you tell 'em it's a genuine Scottish native. I'm sure, if the women think the guy wears a kilt, they'll be more invested. Remember, the Scottish caravan leaves in three weeks—who's gonna win the next weekend package to Buffalo Bob's? Ya know, The Busted Headlights are headlining there next week!"

* * * *

The travelers climbed aboard the Agusta helicopter headed for Mount Viejo. Introductions for Nessa and Jude were fondly made over dinner the night before, and they were firmly on board with the photo shoot. Matt hovered the chopper over the crater. "I see a few good spots to land. What's your preference, Nessa?"

Nessa pointed to the wide swath of flat earth within the crater. "If you shoot from this angle, we can fly over you." Within the extinct volcano, a series of concentric plateaus rose within. From the air, it looked like a giant's staircase. Matt landed the chopper, and their work began.

* * * *

Willow, Anna, and Cat sat with their laptops open. Anna chewed the straw on her travel mug. "I'll search his name if you take the corporation."

Cat nodded and began. "Well, it's a Nevada registered corporation based in Las Vegas." She looked up at Anna.

"The house always wins." Willow nodded.

"There's no property under his name. He's got a few lawsuits out there. No current wives or children." Anna frowned at his trail on the web.

Cat shook her head. "Any ex's we can pump?"

"His ex's all took back their maiden names and disappeared, except for Nadine Rail in Colorado." Anna snickered.

Willow arched a brow. "Must be love."

"I think it's more about settling her lawsuit." Anna shook her head. "She might be a willing participant."

"That's good news."

Anna thought for a moment. "You know, before we waste our time looking up all kinds of stuff, I'll bet we can get lots from the ex…"

"Do go on."

Anna confidently dialed the number, and within two rings, a woman picked up. "Good day, may I speak with Flynn Rail?" The phone was on speaker. Cat crossed her fingers.

"That bastard? Are you kidding me?"

"I'm sorry to intrude on your day. I really need to speak with him."

Nadine snorted. "You and everybody else, sweetie."

"You understand, I'm not at liberty to divulge the purpose of my call."

Nadine chuckled. "Honey, he owes everybody money, but you've been the first nice voice on the phone. I just settled my suit with him. You can have his address. I don't have a phone number; you'll have to catch him."

"Do you have the corporation name? And perhaps his home address?"

Nadine rattled it off like it was second nature. "Sky Hi Hopes, LLC, and he's living above his racket, 3316 Frontal Street, Las Vegas, Nevada. I had him served there last week, so I beat you to his money. Unless he's folded his tent again, he's still there."

"Thank you, Mrs. Rail. Have a good day." Anna turned, pumped her fist, and the ladies squealed.

Cat was in her element. "Now that we have the corporation name, which he probably has every utility under, we can hack into them, and get his phone number and private email address. That's what we really need…"

"How are you doing, Willow? Building that web page?"

She raised her thumb. "Now, you're certain this will come down shortly after he reads it, right? Cuz, I wouldn't want actual colleagues to see this."

Anna waved her hand dismissively. "Adam is a wiz with computers. I don't understand how, but he said something about he would hook your site as a Ph.D. in zoology to Cat's site, as a nature journalist, and then send it on to Rail's site. So, it looks like Matt sent you photos and a story, you verified and sent on to Cat, and Cat's sending it to Rail. And there's something about Adam being able to hide all that from the public."

"Well, God bless him, cuz I have no idea…" Willow shook her head. "Just as long as it doesn't get me in trouble with the University, I'm good."

* * * *

Matt pulled filters out of the camera bag. "If we shoot with distortion, we won't have to worry about them pinpointing the location. Once I get the camera set up, Rick, all you have to do is point and fire."

Rick nodded at Matt in his get-up. Both were dressed in resale hunter's gear. Rick tapped the trapper hat. "Are you going furry side up?"

Matt pulled the hat flat up, letting Rick shoot his incredulous expressions at seeing dragons. "Sort of flatters my pale complexion, doesn't it? Just be ready, Rick, Adam is going to pluck you up and rattle your spine. Be sure that coat is buttoned, you don't want to fall out. It's not going to be the gentle ride you had from Lust for Life."

The gang spent the remainder of daylight shooting the dragons circling and landing in the crater. They made the film of Rick, disguised as a guide, being abducted by Adam, and carried away. They would add screaming sound effects and strategic shots of Matt cowering from an approaching dragon when they got back to the main computer.

Matt guided the helicopter smoothly out of the crater. The flushed dragons laughed in high spirits. "If this doesn't rock his world, nothing will." Adam chortled. "Ladies and gentlemen, dragons live among us!"

* * * *

The room service cart was rolled out to the conservatory-style lanai, where the table was set for the four shifters. The glass enclosure provided a warm place for meeting and conversation with the chiminea burning brightly.

"A toast!" Adam stood and lifted his glass. "I'm sorry we weren't able to attend the wedding and toast you appropriately at the time, but, in true wedding tradition: May the best of your yesterdays be the worst of your tomorrows!"

"Here, here!" Willow echoed.

"Thank you, without you and Izzie there would have been no wedding, so we owe you!" Jude accepted for the newlyweds.

Adam rubbed his hands together and sat. "I'm starving. It's a relief to eat with others. When we're at the castle, I always imagine they're listening to us chew."

Nessa dabbed at her lips with her napkin, laughing although her mouth was full.

"Vampires and their darn liquid diets," Adam continued.

Willow's hand played with the collar of her shirt. "I know! When I eat, I feel like they imagine what my blood will taste like. Especially the ladies. They haven't been vamps very long."

Nessa nodded as she reached for her wine glass. "I think you're safe. I saw them at their worst, and they were pretty tame."

Adam raised a brow at her. "You keep telling yourself that."

Nessa's eyes got huge. "You mean, they'd…"

"They'd take on a dragon in a nanosecond if they were truly hungry."

"Our ladies?" Willow demanded, equally wide-eyed.

"Yep, and they'd use the same force if they felt you were threatened. I've been involved with the undead for twenty-five years, and they are fiercely loyal."

"This venison is fantastic!" Jude said, eager to steer the conversation away from vampires.

"What's that you're eating, Willow?"

"These are fried squash blossoms with ricotta cheese, wild mushroom risotto, and white asparagus. I've never seen such a range of vegetarian offerings anywhere. Leave it to our supernatural hosts to provide a decadent menu!"

Adam poured more wine into Jude's glass. "I'm sorry we interrupted your honeymoon with work, and worse yet, we stole time from you. Hopefully, you can return here when the strife is over and fully enjoy yourselves."

Nessa frowned. "There are those of the old school who would like to see me produce a clutch within the next six months, but under the circumstances, I'm unable to release my dragon. It simply can't happen until we're able to relocate."

Willow buttered her bread and followed Nessa's words with an uneasy look on her face. Adam, as usual, noticed. "What's on your mind, Willow?"

"This is going to sound crass, but as a zoologist, I have to ask, how does a dragon practice birth control?" The dragonfolk burst out laughing. Nessa's face flushed bright red. "Oh, honey, I'm sorry, you're so young, and you're on your honeymoon, and I'm just a scientist ruining the romance."

Jude got control of his laughter first. "Well, luckily, dragons don't reproduce in human form. If we stay human, there's no concern. Not until we shift."

Willow hung her head in embarrassment. "Gee, that's news I can use!"

Adam patted her thigh under the table. "But, wouldn't they be precious? Little dragons with Pegasus wings?" Adam's laughter was contagious, except for Willow. She was not amused.

"We'll talk about that later."

"Have you heard from anyone at Flight's End? How is the transition going?" Adam asked.

Nessa nodded. "The children have been the quickest to pick up the technology, but they're fighting the fact they're forbidden to shift. Of course,

Queen Petra acts like she can't do a thing, but when we aren't around she's using the tablet for card games, and she Skypes with her grandchildren in Alaska."

Adam's expression wilted. "That complete old fraud!"

Jude shook his head. "Not quite as helpless as she'd like us to think. Don't be surprised if she comes up with a list of possible habitation sites for you!"

The group laughed, and Adam ended the discussion. "I hope she does, it'll give her something to focus on besides me!"

* * * *

It was well after midnight when their group assembled in the living room of Adam's suite to begin what they called the Off the Rails Con. Computers, fax machines, scanners, and telephones were set up in an area now resembling NASA rather than a living room. The back wall was overtaken with a huge whiteboard detailing the steps and alternate plays for completing the public humiliation of Flynn Rail.

Adam got off his laptop and handed Cat a clipboard. "I weaseled his personal email and two contact numbers from the power company."

Cat looked up from the scanner. "Okay, I've uploaded the pictures. Shall we write the copy together? I'd love everyone's input." After an hour of meticulous thought, the group came up with a provocative email.

> *To: Flynn Rail*
>
> *Subject: I HAVE PROOF DRAGONS EXIST*
>
> *I'm putting my job on the line to write to you. My name is Carla Starr, and I'm an investigative reporter for Nature News Now, which you may know is the premier publication for nature preservation specialists. My editors refused to run this story, and yet, I know with my entire being, it is true. The reason I'm sure of my facts is because my college roommate, who is now a Ph.D. in zoology, brought me the story. I looked her in the eyes, she showed me many more photos and videos than the ones I've attached.*
>
> *I'm sending this news to you, because you've already run an article about a similar sighting, and you have photographic evidence. Your source was not a hoax and was not mistaken, nor is mine.*

Mr. Rail, this will blow the lid off the world of traditional biology and zoology. I would love to be the one who garners the fame for this story, but since my editors are a bunch of cowards, I'm sending it to you.

Put it under your byline. Contact me, and I'll put you at the site, and you can authenticate it yourself. What's important is the world receives this astounding information, not the inevitable fame that will greet the person who reveals it.

These photographs have been certified as unaltered by two independent experts. You have the opportunity for the story of the century. Dragons still exist.

Carla Starr.

Adam stood, satisfied. "I cannot wait to see his face when he takes the bait."

Matt removed tags and used sandpaper to rough up his nature-guide garb. "Yeah, wouldn't you love to be a bug on the wall?"

Adam's grin spread across his handsome face, and he sat at the computer, pressing the "enter" button. "I've created this cloning virus to evade the malware detectors. Once he opens this email, I'll be able to track everything he does on that computer, and we'll see his smiling face."

Willow snickered "I'm going to make his eyes roll back in his head with the rest of these pictures."

"I'm guessing by the day after tomorrow he'll be here in Chile, and it will be game on!" Adam said.

"I've found the perfect rundown shack for Matt to call home when Rail finds him." Rick crowed.

Anna pointed at the location photo. "The legitimately important thing is, you gave that poor family a fresh start in a completely furnished new home." Rick shrugged.

Cat moved behind Adam to gaze at the computer over his shoulder. "Once you're in Rail's computer, can we get info on that first dragon image? We have to discredit that, too."

Adam's fingers flew over the keyboard. "It won't matter, I'll have access to his cloud too."

Rick stood, hands in his pockets. "As soon as you get that information, Anna and I will head for the location of the photographer. We'll make him an offer he won't refuse."

Anna slid next to him. "I love my double O agent!" She winked at Matt.

* * * *

Adam rose and pulled Willow close, his hand on the back of her neck. His aqua eyes burned through her as he whispered, "A watched mark never responds. Do you want to play?"

"Seriously?" Willow looked around the full room and melted into his embrace.

"Seriously…" Adam nodded. "Okay folks, we've got some downtime. Why don't you all go about your business?"

Rick caught Anna's hand. "I think that's shifter-speak for 'get out'." Anna shook her head at her mate.

Once the room was empty, Adam and Willow went about setting the scene. Adam walked to the closet and returned with a hefty length of silk rope in his hands. "I brought this with me thinking we might need to fill the downtime with something interesting."

"Oh, your offer is interesting."

"Glad you approve." He assumed a commanding stance and his voice took on a new edge. "Go to the window and undress. Slowly." Sheer drapes covered the wall. Because of the high vampire occupancy, three forty-five in the morning ensured a high visibility experience.

Wishing to exceed her Master's command, Willow set about undressing to thrill. She slid the bench at the bottom of the bed over to the window. Sitting sideways, she slipped one ballet flat off one foot, then the other. She stood with her back to Adam and unbuckled her belt. It flew out of her belt loops with a whoosh. She turned her head over her shoulder and flung the belt at Adam's feet.

He leaned down to pick it up. "This could come in handy later. Continue."

Willow turned on the bench and sat with her knees spread. She licked her lips as her fingers opened each button of her crisp, green blouse. Grabbing each side of it, she flashed open the shirt to reveal her lacy bra. With coy modesty and flashing eyes, she alternated the side of the closed blouse, featuring one breast or the other. She stood abruptly, and when her arms went down by her sides, the blouse shimmied to the ground.

Adam felt himself quiver to life as she tempted him with more flesh. With one foot, she kicked the blouse aside, and then her hips swayed a slow figure eight. Adam heard the zipper lower tooth by tooth. His breath hitched as she bent over the bench and leaned on the window sill. Her body was a rhapsody, moving sensually in the silence of the room. Then, she bent at the waist, her perfect ass up, and the tight, straight-legged jeans began to descend. *That strap of thong matches her bra.*

Adam rubbed his now full-masted erection with a slow hand. He hid the enormous smile wanting to burst forth and kept his Dom demeanor.

Let her work for it. I do like what's hiding under the lace.

Willow sat on the bench and gracefully extracted one long, slim, leg after the other. She held the crush of jeans in front of her wide, spread knees and, when his gaze burned through them, she launched them at him.

"Stand on the bench and face the window. Our good friends outside want to see your beauty." Willow's cheeks flamed, but she obediently stood on the wide bench. "Think about how many people out there want to be as seductive as you are." Her hands began to caress her thighs, and she swayed to some unheard melody. Her hips dipped and rose as her hands slipped under her bra clasp, and she held out the end to her side and taunted him. Sliding one arm and then the other out of the straps, she made a half turn and shook the bra at him. At his nod, she tossed it casually.

"Show everyone your glorious breasts."

I'm going to make you come just working those tasty nipples.

Willow bit her bottom lip, but her hands lifted her breasts, as her thumbs danced over her tightening nipples. "Okay, those lucky watchers have seen enough of you. I want to see you dance."

Willow bent over and slid her hands into the sides of her thong, kicking them aside, she turned and threw her hands up in sensual victory.

"I want you to touch yourself. Tell me how you taste." Adam fought to loosen his jeans buttons, releasing his hard cock. He was delighted when Willow's eyes brightened at the sight of his dick.

That got your attention!

Willow popped a hip to the side as those long fingers dipped into her folds of flesh. The bright light made her juices glisten as her fingers moved to her mouth.

"Face the glass again and put your right foot on the windowsill." Following his command, she slid open the sheer drapes and then did his bidding. "I didn't give you permission to open the drapes." Willow froze. "But, I like it, so, we'll keep it." Willow relaxed. "Thrust those breasts onto the glass and touch yourself again." Three floors below, in the courtyard, there was a growing audience whistling and applauding her sex show. Willow touched herself again, and the crowd cheered her on in various languages. She hesitated in the act of bringing her fingers to her mouth.

Adam was abrupt. "No hesitation, sub. Follow my instructions."

Willow looked over her shoulder at him, those fabulous eyes wide. "I'm gathering quite a crowd down there. I'm afraid someone will call management."

"You let me worry about that. Turn around, bend over, and touch your toes. Hold that position, until I tell you otherwise." The crowd below wolf whistled. Obediently, she did as commanded. Adam slid the blackout drapes closed. The crowd "Aww'd" in disappointment. He stepped up behind her, and she startled when his tongue slipped over her wet lips. His hand held her to his mouth as his lips and tongue plundered her. He wondered, *is she this wet for me, or did her audience spur her on?* She fell back into his hands and mouth, her moans rising with his attention. Adam grinned, stepped away, and denied her orgasm.

"I told you to hold your position. Can't you follow directions, sub? Sit on the bench, spread your knees." Willow hurried to comply. Adam tied each delicate ankle to the front legs of the bench. Her swollen sex was fully exposed. "Lean back on your palms." He coiled the rope around her right wrist and below to the rear bench leg and then did the same to the other. Adam sat on the bed and slowly untied his shoes. Their gazes locked as he removed each sock.

A good sub would not be allowed to watch me undress, but I like those enormous brown eyes devouring me!

"That's right. Fuck me with your eyes." Her eyes went to slits. "Yeah, your mind is full of my hard cock slipping in and out of your tight pussy." She shivered at the comment. "I'm going to take off these clothes..." Adam unbuttoned his shirt and let it fall to the bed. He laid back, and his cock stood up from his open jeans. "I can feel your hot, wet tongue on my shaft, as my mouth covers your sultry pussy." He slid out of his tight jeans and his hands cupped his weighty sack. "You know the best things come to those who wait."

Willow whimpered.

"Oh, the more you beg, the longer it will take, but I do relish the begging for this." He grabbed his rigid cock in his other hand. "Breathe with me, Willow." His husky voice compelled her to join him. "Imagine my hands on you, my fingers caress your cheeks and stroke along your neck. I'm not going to touch those hungry breasts; my fingers are going to stroke your arms like a butterfly on a flower." His hands rested by his side as he sat up and began his verbal enticement. "I see your breathing is beginning to labor and your sex is florid and wet." His posture was as rigid as his cock. It bobbed as he spoke. "Tell me what your breasts are feeling."

"They feel full and lonely because your lips aren't on them…"

"I didn't ask what would please you. I asked what they are feeling. Describe the sensations to me without demands. You are *my* sub."

"They feel heavy and hot, and my nipples feel tender."

"Tell me what you taste when you eat my cock."

Their gazes burned for silent moments. She licked her lips, and he immediately saw her need. He carried a glass of cool water with a straw over to her and placed the straw between her pouting lips. His cock brushed her arm, and she startled with a sigh. She drew hard on the straw.

"That's right. Get your lips ready to use on me."

When the glass was empty, she pushed the straw out with her bright pink tongue. "You do know how to use that tongue, don't you, sub?"

"Give it to me and find out."

"Oh, but you think you've earned it already. The proper response was 'whatever pleases you, Sir'."

"My apologies, Sir."

"I asked you a question, what is *your* answer?"

"You have differing flavors, Sir. When we come in after a day outside, I taste a salty earthiness, like a black truffle." Adam nodded as he stroked his turgid erection. "When we've showered, and we play, your cock is sweet, and your come is slightly salty."

"Do you enjoy my taste?" Adam raised a brow as he held his cock within a foot of her mouth.

"I've enjoyed every experience of sucking you off."

"And I've developed a taste for your wet pussy. When you walk ahead of me, I see your thighs in those tight jeans, all I can think of is eating through the denim to get to you." Willow blinked as she squirmed under his gaze. Adam stepped closer, and his cock was thick and ruddy. The tip glistened and grew like ripe fruit, begging to be eaten. Her eyes riveted to the delicious sight. Willow leaned forward without invitation. "No, no. You may not touch me without permission. I believe I should have my taste of you, first." Willow gaped at him as she sank back, unconsciously pushing her sex forward.

Adam knelt, and his hands drew her even closer. His large hands settled on her inner thighs, as his thumbs peeled the petals of her wet sex back to reveal her glistening folds. Adam bit his lower lip and shook his head, admiring her beauty. "Wow. Look at you. That's the hungriest cunt I've ever seen. The perfect rosy shade of pink."

Willow groaned.

"How much do you want me to eat that pussy?"

Willow studied his stunning face, flushed with passion. She could almost feel his tongue parting her. She squirmed, unable to control herself. She gritted her teeth to keep from moaning. Adam chuckled. "Yes, I can see you're eager for me."

He dropped to his knees, his tongue delving into every eddy and path of her folds. He smiled and pulled away. "How responsive you are, but I'm not ready for you to come yet." His blonde head dipped as if he would begin his assault on her sex, but then it rose, and his cool aqua eyes sparkled. "I'm going to lick every fold of your pussy, but not your clit." He winked and began his torture. With his sure strokes, her back arched to shove her further into his hungry mouth. When she could feel the heat of his mouth on her clit, he retreated to the length of hollow between her thigh and her pussy. She was dogged in pursuit of his tongue, and he was as cagey in his withdrawal.

Adam saw the desperation in her beautiful eyes and took pity on her. "You're glowing and shaking. Can your orgasm be far behind?"

She whipped her head like a wild woman. He rose and guided his cock across her collarbone and down the center between her breasts. "The way I've tied you here, I can't get my hungry cock into your tight pussy. Should I untie you from the bench and tie you to the bed? Think carefully about your answer."

"If…it…would…please you, Sir," she stuttered, trying to harness her lust.

"Well said. I believe it would please me." Adam reached for the end of the silk rope and with one tug, the series of knots released. Willow ran her hands through her hair, sweaty spikes stood upright. She resembled a mighty warrior princess.

"On the bed, please lay on your stomach and wait for me." He watched her jaw clench, but she obeyed. "Very good." Adam laid down beside her and whispered into her ear. "I have just the place for you to sit." His strong fingers wiped across his lips. "I want your sex right here." His tongue lingered over his lips. Willow shook as she straddled him and moved up his body. The heat of his breath was almost enough to set off her anxious clit. Willow grasped the headboard as she tested just the right distance from his waiting lips. Adam raised his head and caught her clit between them. He hummed and let his tongue stroke her once. "That's one hard clit." Willow's head fell back as she arched deeper into his mouth. "That's right, give it to me." His hand caught her hips, and she fell into his grip. "I told you good things come to those who wait. I've waited long enough to make you come."

There were plaintive sighs and then she cried out. "Yes, yes, yes, if it would please you, Sir."

"It does please me." His voice was insistent. "Come for me. Now." His lips held her clit ransom only releasing it when he felt her body tense and shake. The fist of her pussy spasmed wildly, and Willow gritted her teeth with intensity and cried out. He felt her cream run, hungrily lapping it up and extending her orgasm.

In the following stark silence, when she began to sag against him in boneless exhaustion, he rolled out from under her. She fell to the bed; Adam slid a pillow under her hips. "It's time for the other kind of orgasm…"

Willow huffed out a breath and dropped to her forearms. Her glorious ass was there for his grasp. Teasingly, he dipped the head of his cock inside her and coated it with her cream. He let the hefty weight of it drop on the cleavage of her buttocks. Her breath hitched as her ass followed his heat. With a masterful stroke, Adam's cock nuzzled at her swollen sex. He chose the right moment to sheath himself fully within her. When their bodies were one, the heat fueled his long, deep strokes. The pleasing curve of his cock rubbed her just the right way and built another toe-curling orgasm. "Aren't you slippery tonight? I could stroke you like this for hours. How many times would you like to come again?"

Willow was speechless. Her fist pounded the sheets three times. "You'd like my cock to hit your g-spot how many more times?" Now, Willow nodded three times. "So, you think you can take it?"

She clutched the pillow before her and screamed, "Yes!"

He continued those maddeningly perfect strokes. "Yes, what?"

Willow groaned and gritted out. "Yes, Sir, please."

He grinned wickedly into the mirror over the headboard. "You should have said something."

My God, this woman is a sex bomb! He artfully held her at the precise angle and felt her heat back up, those reawakened nerves making her tremble beneath him. She bathed him within her tight silken fist.

I'm not going to make it all night at this rate. She's really got a hold on me!

Adam leaned over her back, and his lips laid a devil's line of kisses, she met his thrusts with insistent power.

Where is she getting this energy?

He whispered into her ear. "Ah! We're burning up this bed!"

"We're gonna burn down this resort." Their sex-sweated bodies slapped their rhythm to her next orgasm.

Adam's spine burned all the way to his root. As she quivered in his arms, his kisses made their way to her other ear. "Would I disappoint you if I only made you come twice this way?"

She replied with more insistent thrusts against his strokes. Her groans vibrated through her, strangling his self-control.

She is dismantling me, stroke by stroke.

He felt the orgasm rising from his root, forcing its way up his cock. He broadened and lengthened, just nudging her to a second orgasm. They came together, his hot explosion fighting for space within her. Her fist of a pussy caught him and milked him dry. Adam panted, and Willow mimicked his gasping breaths as they sank as one into the welcoming down duvet. It was a comforting embrace as he rolled them to their sides, his cock still within her. Adam's words were nearly breathless. "You really got a hold on me."

Willow could barely turn her head. "Yeah." And they slept.

10

The jet whisked Rick and Anna to Inverness, Scotland. The group decided it would be their jumping off spot in their search for the dragon photographer. Adam assured Rick he would call as soon as Rail opened the email and he could clone the con-man's computer. They were ninety percent sure the photographer was Scottish, and they had to start somewhere. The clock was ticking.

Once their jet lifted off, Rick and Anna kicked off their shoes and spooned on the sumptuous leather sofa. Rick combed his fingers through Anna's brilliant red hair.

"But it was so beautiful. How could you do that without asking me?" Rick's puppy dog eyes were pathetic. "It was your crowning glory…"

Anna looked over her shoulder at him. "What's the gist here, Fitz, I have to ask you before I cut twelve inches off my hair? It's still down to the middle of my back. Have I dashed your fantasy?"

"Well, you're certainly no longer Maid Marion.

Anna tapped her nail on his arm. "You know what happened to her?"

Rick shook his head. "Ya know, Cupcake, that event was poorly handled by the novelist."

Anna turned in his arms and levied a stern expression at her mate. "Fitz, have I ever asked you to grow a beard or mustache?"

"But…that's not the same! Your hair was…singularly you."

"Nice try, kiddo. When I was in Columbus, I looked like I was still in high school. I'm tired of looking like a teenager. You deserve a worldlier woman."

Trying to save face, he pitched, "It's still quite…nice." He caught up a hank of it and held it to his nose. "Though, I'm guessing one could be worldly and have Rapunzel-like locks."

"Fitz, first you had a thing for Maid Marion, now it's Rapunzel? Because of course, her tale was mis-told, too."

Rick rolled his eyes. "Don't be silly, she was a tart they stowed in a tower. What a nympho."

Anna's jaw dropped. "But they made a children's movie about her…"

"Ironic, isn't it? Nor was her hair a sixpence as beautiful as yours." Rick nuzzled her neck, moving a thick handful of hair to do so. "I've always loved the way your hair smells."

Anna sunk deeper into his embrace. "You know how I am when you do that. It's your secret weapon."

His lips skirted her ear. "If I ask sincerely, would you consider just waiting a few months—or years—before you cut it again?"

"I'll make a deal with you. If you grow a beard and mustache like the Holbein painting of you at the castle, I'll let my hair grow as long as you like it. You want me to look like my teenage self? I want you to look like yours."

"As long as I don't have to wear that ridiculous codpiece, it's a deal."

"Oh! I can't wait! I remember Mom ribbing Daddy when fall came and he began his beard for the cold weather. She'd run from him because the first week he was a porcupine." Anna giggled.

His smile was sublime. "Luckily, you still have two feet of hair left, I'll catch you."

Rick's phone rang. "Hiatt."

"Yeah!" It was Adam's happy voice. "Rail has gotten our little email, and he's an excited boy! It's Christmas in February!"

Rick winked at Anna and turned the phone on speaker. "Okay, Adam, we're waiting to hear whose arm we're going to twist."

"The IP address is located in a little town close to Loch Ness called

Lochend. The email attached is signed by Delilah McGillicuddy. I guess you've got a date with Delilah!"

"I have to know, what did Rail do when he read our email?" Anna asked.

"At first, he was just stunned, ya know? Then he pulled up the pictures and printed them and the email and called all these staffers into the room. They were all looking at everything, everybody getting whipped to a frenzy, it was like blood in the water. Those sharks were hungry, too! I expect Cat will get a call in less than an hour, once they've done some preliminary checks on the photos and her name. I did a whole web page for her; they should be duly impressed."

"Keep us posted, Boyo. If Ms. McGilicuddy is cooperative, we'll be back at Serenity tomorrow, we don't want to miss a minute of the live action."

Anna's phone pinged, and she said, "I just got Adam's email with Delilah's address."

* * * *

Cat and Matt were rousted from their rest early, since Adam expected her to receive Rail's call any time, now. Cat slumped in the desk chair, her arms folded under her breasts and her face showing a numb ennui. Matt stood in the kitchen opening, checking, and closing the cabinet doors. "Where do they keep the glasses in these kitchens?"

"I'd come in and show you, but Adam insists I stay right here in case the phone rings."

Matt came to the doorway. "Well, I could wait while you get us our breakfast." His hair stood in thirty different directions; his face adorned with a scruffy three-day growth. He wore gravity-defying red silk pajama bottoms. Leaning against the doorway, his one foot scratched at his standing leg.

"I say, standing like that, you look like a flamingo."

"P-shah! My pajamas are red. There are no red flamingos." Matt mindlessly scratched at his six pack and blinked awake. He studied Cat's face. "You need more rest, babe."

"We both do. These mortal hours are killing me."

Adam's bedroom door opened, and he and Willow appeared, freshly showered and bright-eyed. Willow dropped her cross-body bag on a living room chair. "Isn't it a beautiful morning? Did you see that sunrise?"

Matt's growl began deep in his chest, and he replied, "I do better howling at the moon."

Willow stopped to admire Matt in his roughest condition. "I've never seen you like this—all scruffy and such. Is that what vampires sleep in?"

Adam shook his head, and behind Willow's back, made a comical expression at Cat while Matt took a second to think. "Not really, but as a concession to you being new to the undead, I put on all these clothes." Matt snapped the elastic in his waistband.

Willow's face reddened. Cat waved her hand. "Willow, I told you, if you have any questions, just ask. But don't ask Matt. Matt's suffering from men's disease this morning. Would you mind finding us a couple of drinking glasses?"

Her phone rang, and they all hurried to her side. "Carla Starr," she answered brightly.

"Ms. Starr, this is Flynn Rail. You emailed me?"

Cat nodded vigorously and put the phone on speaker. "Yes, Mr. Rail. Did my email and pictures interest you?"

Adam spun his open laptop toward the group. They all witnessed Flynn Rail in plaid boxer shorts, scratching as he spoke to Cat. His voice was casual, bordering on indifferent. "Yes. I got the material, if it tests out, there may be interest." He stood gnawing his clenched fist.

Cat smirked. "I assure you; you'll find the photos real. I've talked with the guide who witnessed it. I encourage you to test everything and confirm it. Then, you need to get down here to Patagonia for a personal look."

Rail held on to the back of his office chair and danced foot to foot in excitement. "I'd be keen to check it out myself. The authentication will be complete by tonight. Where am I going?"

"There's a little town at the foot of the Andes called Puerto Natales. You'll fly first to Santiago, and from there to Puerto Natales. Our guide will hike you to the remote mountain. From there—assuming we can get him to take you in. Be prepared for rugged terrain and a primitive way of life."

While Cat spoke, Rail scratched his buttocks in contemplation and leaned over his monitor to bring up the photo of Carla Starr. When Cat's beautiful face appeared, he bolted upright and smiled devilishly. "Will you be going with me?" The room shook their heads, and Matt's eyes went opalescent.

Cat covered the phone receiver and winked. "Oh, hell no, I don't go into those places. Too dangerous. Our guide's last assistant didn't make it back. I wasn't kidding when I said, 'if we can get him to take you'. You may have to offer him a significant incentive."

Rail frowned, and the group held their breath. "Well, if the story's real, I'll make that back in an hour."

"There's someone else I want you to meet. She's the roommate I mentioned in my email. Her name is Wanda Jones." They watched Rail's enthusiasm flag at the name. "Wanda is a Ph.D. in zoology, as I said, and you can find a webpage about her work at WandaJonesPhD.edu." They watched him type, and his face brightened when Willow's smiling photo was on his monitor.

"Will she be there? Will I meet her?"

"We'll both be in Puerto Natales waiting to give you all the support we can."

"A guy couldn't ask for more." He made a beating-off gesture with his right hand.

Cat and Willow made disgusted expressions, while Matt's fang's dropped, and Adam's lips drew straight and tight. "It's nice to finally be appreciated, Mr. Rail."

"Oh, no, please, call me Flynn."

"Alright, Flynn. I'll meet you at the airport tomorrow evening around five o'clock local time. We'll go straight to meet our guide, his name is LaClaire. You can no doubt see his reviews on Yelp."

Adam smirked as he watched Rail bring up travel reviews on Frank LaClaire. He'd made sure the remarks were just this side of insulting. The photo of Matt was far less flattering than his passport photo. Rail bit his tongue. "This man looks deranged! You trust him?"

Cat winked at her mate. "With my life! He may not be pretty, but he has skills, and knows exactly where those dragons nest."

"I'll have to take your word on that." Rail sighed in resignation.

Cat stifled her laugh. "Alright, then, Flynn, Wanda, LaClaire and I will see you tomorrow evening, and by the following day, you'll be witnessing dragons for yourself!" Cat clicked off the call and looked around the room. "Can we go back to bed now?"

Adam grinned. "Absolutely, and you'll have the whole suite to yourselves until tomorrow afternoon because Willow and I are going to the campsite to prepare everything."

Matt and Cat nodded gratefully. Matt arched a brow at Adam. "Why did you pick me to be the tooth-sucking, front porch reject of a guide?"

Adam thought for a beat. "Well, everyone else was chosen for their talents and abilities. You got what was left."

"Asshole," Matt muttered as he followed Cat to their bedroom.

* * * *

Anna and Rick were still laughing at the face Rail made when he saw LaClaire's reviews on Yelp. Anna navigated while Rick drove. "It's kinda hard to tell, but, as clear as I can make out, we're headed to a lighthouse."

"Delilah gets more interesting by the minute!"

"Could this be? A fair maiden in a tower? Will she drop her lovely locks down for you to climb up and see her?" She bristled with sarcasm.

"One can only hope." Rick checked his smile in the rear-view mirror.

The GPS took them to the front door of the lighthouse. Rick straightened his black tie in the reflection of the window. He came around the car to open Anna's door. "This black suit has got to be the ugliest thing I've ever worn. I look like a bargain-rate mortician."

Anna shook her head. "But you pull it off. Who are we with, again?" She asked in subtones as she fussed, buttoning the black jacket.

"IFAW, International Fund for Animal Welfare." He knocked on the door, and they both donned their dark wrap-around sunglasses.

A sturdy-looking septuagenarian swung open the door. She wore a straw hat over wiry grey hair. Her face was a map of waterfront experience. Under one arm, a gnarled hand held an artists' paint box. Under the other, she held a camp seat. "And what are you doing here?"

She stared up into Rick's smiling face.

"I'm looking for Delilah McGillicuddy. Are you she?"

She dithered in response. "I…I…If I was?"

Rick bowed courteously and flashed fake credentials. "Ms. McGilicuddy, this is Agent Tubbs, and I'm Agent Crockett from the International Fund for Animal Welfare. We'd like to ask you some questions about the pictures you sent to Flynn Rail. Am I talking to the owner of those pictures?"

"Oh I, oh I, why, yes I did send pictures to that young man."

"I can see you're on your way out, may we interrupt your day for a few moments to speak about the plight of these endangered creatures."

"Oh, I don't have any money."

"No, ma'am, we're not fundraising. May we come in?"

"Where are my manners, yes, please do come in." She stood in the doorway and Rick, and Anna squeezed past the doughy woman to enter a cozy sitting area. "Would you like some tea?" She headed to the next room before they could answer. Her voice trilled. "Come into my kitchen. I don't bite. It's friendlier in the kitchen."

Anna and Rick shared a look and took in fifty years of maritime décor on the first floor of the lighthouse. The kitchen was overtaken by pots and pans and herbs and dried flowers hanging from the rafters. It smelled of cinnamon and rosemary. She gestured to an aluminum table and chairs with an aqua Formica top. The aqua vinyl seats whistled as they sat. Anna stifled a laugh.

Delilah poured water into the teapot to steep and turned to them. "What does my picture of Nessie have to do with endangered creatures?"

"This is top secret information, Ms. McGilicuddy, but since you have a picture, you're aware these creatures survive to this day." Delilah nodded emphatically. "Most people think Nessie is a myth, and that's what the IFAW wants them to think. I'm sure, you saw how beautiful Nessie is?"

"Oh, yes, quite beautiful! I wanted to paint her." She busied herself at the tea cart and pushed it over to the table.

Rick frowned. "The problem is, these animals are critically endangered. As far as we can tell, there are maybe four left alive on earth."

"That's too bad, isn't it?" Delilah asked, setting a plate of cookies before them.

"Yes, ma'am. And you see, having a picture published, simply endangers them further by creating would-be hunters." The three sat in silence while Delilah poured and mumbled to herself. She slid the teacups in front of her visitors.

"That Mr. Rail said he'd pay money for unusual creatures caught in pictures. So, I sent mine to him. I never got another word, and no money."

Rick nodded. "The IFAW would like to compensate you for your picture if you will give us the file."

The woman's face screwed up in confusion. "File? File? I only have it on this contraption of a phone my grandson gave me."

Rick leaned forward. "Who else has seen this photo?"

Delilah drew back at his interest. "Just that Mr. Rail and me. Caleb gave me the directions over the house phone while I sent the picture."

"Who else has seen it?" Rick slid closer to her.

Delilah moved her chair back, as she recollected. She held a conversation with herself as her hand seemed to draw diagrams. "Well." She halted, shook her head, and began again. She pointed a bony finger to Rick. "I'm here by myself, as you can see," She handed the phone to Rick from the pocket of her apron. "Here's the date. It's been two weeks now. There's loads of gossip around these parts about Nessie. Nobody here cares about a picture. We either see 'em, or we don't. We get the tourists—bothersome lot—whether there's a real photo or not. I would guess it would benefit us all if ye got rid of that photo. Seeing that Mr. Rail hasn't come across with his promise."

Rick held the phone. "How much did he promise you?"

Delilah leaned back and pulled her shoulders up. "He promised me three hundred pounds. It was enough for me to visit my sister in Edinburgh."

Rick gave her a compassionate smile. "If we were to offer you twice that, may we have this file?"

"Twice that? Today? In cash?" The woman was paying attention, reverently.

Anna opened her black briefcase a crack and grabbed out a banded stack of bills. "Yes, ma'am I have cash for you, right here." Anna held the stack. "We get the file, and you get the cash—on one condition."

Delilah looked seriously concerned for the first time. "And that is?"

Anna folded her hands over the cash. "Should you decide to paint Nessie, the IFAW would appreciate it if, when you are asked about the image, you say it's a creature you imagined from your childhood."

Rick nodded. "The fewer believers, the safer Nessie will be."

Delilah nodded emphatically. "Oh, I want to do everything I can to be sure Nessie is safe."

She looked perplexed. "How do you get this file thingy? You don't have to keep my phone, do you?"

Rick gave her a relaxed smile as he handed the phone back to her. "No, ma'am. Just put your thumb on the start button to open it, and I'll send the file to me." She did as he asked, and Rick deleted the file and emptied the recycle bin. He handed the phone back to Delilah after Anna gave her a sound stack of twenty-pound notes. Rick rose and concluded. "Thank you very much for keeping Nessie's secret, and hopefully, someday, there will be more of these beautiful creatures in our Lochs."

Delilah and Anna rose. "When I get to my sister's in Edinburgh, I'll have a pint on you two." She waved the money at them as they left her doorway.

Anna looked up at him while they walked to the car. "I want to be just like her when I grow up."

Rick laughed and opened her door. "She's a dear, that's for sure."

"I gave her a few hundred over. Is that okay?"

Rick settled into the driver's seat. "Sure, it's Adam's money."

* * * *

Before dusk, Adam surveyed the luggage trolley holding their camping supplies. Matt entered the living room scratching his head, half alert. Adam shook his head. "I didn't know vampires got jet lag."

Matt gave him a sour look. "I could fill a book about what you don't know about vampires."

Khuno, the guardian assigned to most North American visitors, appeared from the kitchen, carrying a filled canteen. He handed it to Adam with a smile and turned to Matt. "I hear your words are still building walls."

Matt ground his teeth. Cat ran up behind him. "Good evening, babe." She caught him from behind and hugged him around his waist.

Matt pulled her around to his side. "Look, our favorite guardian is here!" Cat pulled the hem of Matt's pajama top down to cover her panties.

"Hey, Khuno, obviously, we weren't expecting guests."

Khuno bowed a greeting. "Catherine, your last letter demonstrated how far you have come on your journey. It's inspiring to hear a fledgling is instrumental in helping another on her path."

Cat shrugged but beamed at his compliment. "Aw, thanks, Khuno."

Khuno gave her a deep bow of respect and raised his hand in blessing. "Well done, Catherine." She nodded and ate up his praise. Khuno turned to Adam. "Once you have assumed your animal forms, I will load the equipment on Dr. Greer's back and yours. I'll await you in the clearing, Dr. Lachlan." Khuno bowed his goodbye to Adam and Willow and then turned to Matt. He barely nodded his head. "Matthew."

Matt expected an 'atta boy,' but got nothing. He gave Khuno a thousand-yard stare and returned his nod. "Khuno."

Once the door closed, Adam shot a shocked look at Matt. "Boy, when you piss somebody off, it lasts a long time."

Matt poured his glass of A positive and lifted it in salute to Adam. "It's the Irish in me. I can hold a grudge forever." Matt downed the glass without stopping and plunked it on the counter.

Cat waved goodbye to Adam and Willow and embraced her mate. She ruffled his hair from around his face and kissed the cleft in his chin. "You're always a grouch when you get up." She hugged him and flattened her cheek to his chest. "Khuno really does like you, you know."

Matt stood stoically. "No, he doesn't."

"Yes, he does. He's just mirroring your vibration back to you." Cat smiled as she held onto his hips and looked into his sleepy eyes.

"Huh!" He said before he poured Cat her meal of the day and then leaned against the kitchen doorway, one hand on his hip. His demeanor was far friendlier with an empty suite. "Wanna go back to bed?"

"Sure." She looked at him from under her lashes as she drank.

He stalked her from the doorway and standing close, bumped her hip. "Wanna mirror my vibrations, now?"

* * * *

The crickets and early evening wildlife sang as the sun dropped behind the mountain. In the clearing, Adam and Willow stood in their shifted forms as Khuno packed the supplies onto their backs. Willow shrugged her shoulders and fluttered her wings, delighting in the feel of the ropes binding the camping gear to her.

Khuno showed her a length of rope hanging from Adam's pack. "Use your teeth and pull here, and that will release Adam's burden. Then he can shift and remove yours." Khuno stood back at the edge of the clearing and waved. "Be at peace."

* * * *

Adam arched his long neck and nodded to his right as he approached Mount Viejo, making a circle of their planned camping area. He saw the exact spot he wanted and dipped his wings to Willow while picturing the spot in his mind. She nodded regally and spiraled downward, coming in for her customary perfect landing. He followed.

* * * *

Willow's Pegasus grabbed at the rope with her teeth. The packs fell to the earth, and she stood back to watch him shift. In the setting sun, he was as golden as his dragon.

He is perfect!

He crouched to the backpack and removed two hooded robes, draping hers over the pack.

Even putting on a robe he's graceful. I wonder if his mortal self can hear all my foolish prattle?

He smirked as he approached her. "I don't know if I should be too quick to remove these ropes. I think you kinda like the feel of them." Willow bobbed her head several times and pawed the ground. "Maybe I should take the packs off, leave the ropes on, and make you take me for a ride?" Willow sent a mental picture of him being thrown off and impaled on a mountain peak. "Naughty, naughty. Now, I might just have to 'break' you!" He stared at her and laughed. "I don't even need words to understand that picture! Okay, let me untie these ropes, and then you can shift."

Once Willow returned to her mortal form, Adam held the robe for her to step into and hugged her against him. He whispered in her ear, "There's just something about you and ropes…"

Pulling the belt tight around her waist, she turned in his embrace and tucked her head under his chin. "What would you say, if I admitted I like *you* even more than the ropes?"

He stepped away from her and headed to the duffle holding his tent and busied himself laying out the poles and the ground cloth. Willow was crushed.

Well, I guess that was the wrong thing to say. He's driving me crazy with this on again-off again.

He worked silently, ignoring her. Willow began sorting her gear for the night.

One minute he wants to be close, then I say something, and he's off.

She flipped on the LED lantern and hung it from a tree limb while she worked, half-watching a pensive Adam. The romance flow chart began to formulate in Willow's head.

Kink is his business, so everything we've shared has been business. But, he's not wearing his wedding ring now, does that mean he's open to a new relationship? Well, maybe he's not open to a new relationship with me.

* * * *

Adam knelt, starting the fire. "With these breezes, your tent is going to be full of smoke," he said implacably.

Willow stood with her hands on her hips, eyes narrowed and huffed out an annoyed breath. "You're telling me now after I've already set up the tent?"

Adam dismissed her. "I thought you had enough experience in the field to know that."

"Listen, buddy, I'm sure I have far more experience camping than you do. I had my mind on other things."

"And this is my problem, why?" He didn't look up from his flint and steel.

"You arrogant son of a bitch!"

Adam's tone was flippant. "Oh, we've degenerated to name-calling?"

The spark lit the dry kindling. Willow stalked over to the fire and with the side of her foot, brushed enough moist dirt to extinguish the small flame. "Why are you being such an ass?" She leaned over the smoldering dirt.

Adam looked up at her with exaggerated patience. "At least my sleeping bag is rated to thirty below."

"I doubt that would thaw out your heart."

"What is your problem?"

Willow stomped over to her tent and amplified the difficulty in moving it with her own fury. "What is my problem? What is *your* problem? You're the one who doesn't communicate!"

"What? I excel at communication. When have I not communicated?"

"Ten minutes ago, when you were all manners and kindness helping me into my robe."

"Huh?"

"Huh? Huh? That's all you have to say? Is there a brain with a memory inside that head of yours, or does your skull just hold the roots of all that gorgeous hair?"

Adam straightened up and skewered her with a look. "Willow, what the hell are you so pissed off about?"

He followed her around as she un-staked the tent and dragged it by the ground cloth to a different location. He knew better than to jump in with help. She pulled the tent floor taunt and re-drove the stakes with a rubber mallet. Without giving him another look, she picked up her backpack and unzipped the tent fly. "Goodnight." She dropped her gear inside and zipped down the screen as well as the privacy flap.

Adam snickered. "Now, who's not communicating?"

Silence.

Adam thought for a moment. "I know you can hear me."

Silence.

"You know, this is a well-known dynamic. People in intense circumstances, bond and become artificially close. Sometimes, they even think they're in love, and after the situation concludes, they suddenly realize they don't really know each other…"

"Well, thank you, Dr. Freud."

"That answer is not helpful, and it's childish. I'm trying to point out that whatever feeling you may have for me, or I may have for you, could be temporary."

Willow unzipped the flaps but stayed inside the tent. "What feelings do you have for me?"

Adam crouched to look in her eyes. "I like you very much, Lolo. I think we have a lot in common. I think even our kink matches. And I also think, I don't know you very well yet, so I'm trying to build a relationship, naturally. We've been going at warp speed since we met, and I'm not sure that serves you or me."

Willow sat cross-legged in her tent's doorway. She looked deflated as if the anger drained her. "I've never met a man I was so attracted to that I jumped into bed with him on day three. But that's what happened to us. I never imagined I'd end up in the middle of this. I was going to get laid and get out of there. But it got complicated. And maybe we aren't made for each other. Maybe, the only reason we're together is to pull off this con and protect your people. Maybe the kink was down-time recreation for you. If that's true, it was my mistake for getting into bed with you."

Adam dropped down to sit cross-legged in front of her, recognizing she shared a visceral moment. "I can see this is a sensitive topic for you, and you feel exceptionally vulnerable. I want you to know, I don't want to take advantage of your vulnerability." He reached for her hand, and after some hesitation, she let him take it. "We have a lot of great chemistry. The sex, I think, is incendiary. Now, I think we need to know if we're truly compatible as friends. In any relationship, if you can't be friends, sex will only take you so far."

Willow's lips tightened, and her head tilted as she closed her eyes and drew in a deep breath. "So, we stay out of each other's beds? We put ourselves through this gauntlet of 'getting to know each other,' and then we see where everything lands?" Her tone did not sound hopeful.

Adam frowned and kissed her hand. "Don't see this as a rejection."

Willow took back her hand.

"There are many positive things about the two of us. We're finally able to show our shifter selves to another person in the mortal world. You've always felt like you didn't fit in, right?" Willow nodded slowly. "I do too when I'm with mortals. It's enormously important that you and I share shifting." He smiled, as he felt her body language relax. "I love your sense of humor; I love your intelligence and compassion. I want to see where our combined qualities take us when we're not in the middle of all this drama."

Willow snorted. "You think there's ever going to be a time when we're not in some kind of drama?"

Adam chuckled softly. "God, I hope so. Are you willing to take a little time and see?"

Willow's eyes suddenly became filled with suspicion. "Is this about you controlling our relationship? Are you…being a Dom?"

Adam reared back as if she'd physically struck him, his jaw dropped in surprise. He stood and gave a curt, "Goodnight."

Willow rose from the tent and shouted at his retreating back. "Judge, may I offer into evidence, the plaintiff seeks to control every aspect of a relationship, and is, therefore, exercising his Dom role in the real world!"

Smartass! Adam thought as he stalked to his tent, went inside, and zipped up the front.

11

The Grande Hotel at Puerto Natales was clean and comfortable. Cat plunked down cash, and the reception clerk was more than happy to register her under any name she desired. A little extra coin allowed her to keep her passport with her. "I have a friend joining me later today." She told the friendly desk clerk. "May I register for her as well?"

After her one piece of luggage was delivered to the room, she and Matt hailed a taxi to take them to the shack Rick arranged for his guide persona. Matt slid the key into the lock of a door that could not possibly stop an intruder. Even he grimaced at the conditions. Cat was horrified. "I don't think you should sit on any of the furniture."

Matt shook his head. "I don't intend to." He glanced around the scarcely furnished home. At least the table chairs are wood. We can probably sit at those safely."

"I don't think you should put your duffle bag on the floor, or the bed, or…"

Matt pointed. "There's a cantina across the street."

Cat shook her head. "And I am eternally grateful that I do not have to eat food there."

"Yeah," Matt agreed. "But, I'll wait there till I see you coming. I'll be in the house when you knock on the door, and we'll walk over to the cantina to talk with Rail. That way, nobody has to sit down in here."

"Good plan!" Cat agreed. "Let's go back to the hotel for the next few hours. Rick and Anna will be landing around three in the afternoon, and they'll join us. You'll need to conserve your energy." Cat winked at him.

* * * *

Adam peeled off five big bills and handed them to the shepherd with a smile and a nod. The shepherd's sons placed the skinned sheep's carcasses in the middle of the campsite. With a wave of hands and many smiles, the men went back down the mountain. Willow was intensely polite, as she'd been since they'd awoken. If he was honest, Adam was rigidly courteous, too. There was a certain comfort in the space they gave each other.

Adam pointed at their gear. "We need to set up the locator beacon, butcher these carcasses, and mess the campsite. Do you prefer a certain task?"

"I've studied anatomy, I can butcher the sheep. You do want blood along the campsite, right?" Willow got the ax and began her task.

Adam dug a hole and set the locator beacon inside it, hoping the larger forest animals would leave it alone. He tore the two tents and scattered articles of clothing and camping implements about.

The mindless tasks allowed his thoughts to wander into a pit, his relationship with Willow. He was glad their telepathy didn't transfer to their mortal forms. She struck a nerve last night when she accused him of trying to control their connection. Was he a control freak, and did he wreck his first chance at an equal relationship? *Do I not want to be bound to the same woman for hundreds of years? Do I have commitment issues?*

He took several pails with him to the rushing creek a few yards away and carried water back to the site. They staged it as if wild animals plundered the area.

* * * *

Willow efficiently butchered the sheep carcasses, not for eating, but to look as if huge beasts eviscerated human bone and tissue. She'd always found the smell of blood and entrails sickening. Her stomach heaved, but to be honest, she was already a bag of nerves, and her stomach was uneasy since last night.

I shouldn't have said the final bit, last night. He wants to get to know me? Well, this is me, when you go analytical.

She did regret the harshness, though, and this was probably the end of any possible romance with Adam Lachlan.

She staged the area with blood, bone, and flesh, critically surveying the site, hoping the remains looked at least somewhat human. They could always correctly point out whatever the dragon left would have been plundered by forest predators.

Adam startled her when he walked up behind her. "Looks good."

Willow walked back a distance and surveyed the entire scene. "Yeah, and I think some scorched earth and belongings will do the trick. It's about noon now, and my escort down the mountain should be here in a few. You should scorch this place and take off. I've got it from here."

Adam walked back to the creek and dropped his robe on the shore. His dragon emerged from the dense woods, and he broke several tree limbs in his wake. Once he saw Willow was ready with a pail of water, he reared back his great horned head and blew a precise stream of fire at each of the body parts. The smell of burnt animal flesh permeated the area. The torn tent caught a bit of his flame as he moved around the clearing and was quickly doused. Adam went Godzilla on the campsite, flattening cups, bowls, and cooking pans. The tent poles snapped, and the tents hung haphazardly. His claws ripped the sleeping bags, and everything any human touched bore signs of his savagery.

Willow held the last of the full water buckets, making sure all the flames were doused. "This is great!" She laughed. "Looks like Godzilla was here!" She dropped the bucket and waved. "I'll see you on the other side." She looked at the position of the sun and headed to her rendezvous point. For a few paces he hovered, then he saw the approaching Serenity jeep, and under his own wings, he flew back to the resort.

* * * *

When the prop plane circled and halted, Cat alighted from her heavy-duty SUV. The sun set an hour ago, and she spent the time waiting by boning up on all the bogus events Flynn Rail posted on his website. Her particular favorite was the Sasquatch search of 2015. There were endless positive reviews from the twelve stooges who paid twenty-eight thousand dollars a person for this seven-day trek.

She shook her head as the arrogant bastard exited the small plane. He was as tall as his photos showed him to be, but his face wore the dissipation of someone prone to burning his candle at both ends. "Mr. Rail. Over here!" Cat waved and felt a sour taste in her throat.

"Carla, my dear, pleased to meet you! You are far lovelier than your press photo shows." He moved in for an aggressive full body hug, and Cat made sure she held her ground. He'd never tried to hug a vampress.

"Thank you, Mr. Rail. We have a full evening for you before you bed down tonight." Cat said over her shoulder as she moved toward the black SUV.

"Is there somewhere I could eat real food?" Rail raised his supercilious nose as if he could sniff out a meal.

Cat unlocked the car and stepped in, knowing he was still shoving luggage in the back.

Oh, how I want to let my foot off the brake and let the car roll a foot or two out of his reach.

He slammed the rear hatch down and jumped into the front seat.

Cat slanted her eyes at him. "You may be more comfortable in the back."

Or at least I would be more comfortable if you were lashed on the roof like roadkill.

Rail preened in the visor mirror and declined. "Oh, but we have so much to talk about. I hate to make you take your eyes off the road."

I'm keeping my eye on you, buddy.

Cat keyed the ignition, and they left the smooth airport roads for the tiny village of Puerto Natales. "I believe there's an adequate Cantina across the street from Mr. LaClaire's…uh…house. First, we're going to swing by my hotel and pick up Dr. Jones. Unfortunately, if we want to catch LaClaire sober, we'll need to head to his place directly."

Rail sat back against the car door and ogled Cat full on. "I'm looking forward to meeting Dr. Jones, but I'm still not too sure about this LaClaire fellow. Maybe we should have another guide?"

Cat shook her head. "Oh, no. For one thing, he's the only one with the guts to go into that region. The other guides believe the mountain is haunted by devil creatures that protect the dragons. None of them will go there, and LaClaire is the one who actually knows where their lair is. He's peculiar but dependable."

"Didn't you say his last assistant *died* there?" Rail countered suspiciously.

"Yeah." Cat nonchalantly blew him off.

"Changing our focus for the moment, once we have our evidence, I'd like to have a big media announcement. Perhaps Santiago would be the appropriate place." He busied himself trying to get a phone signal. "My staff at home are all set to go with arranging it. Just one phone call and the media will be waiting for me at the airport hotel."

"What a great idea!" Cat complimented. "I knew you were the right man for this job!"

Rail feigned modesty. "Well, this is what I do best."

Cat swallowed sourly for the second time in thirty minutes.

"I've arranged a large suite at the best hotel in town. Perhaps you and Dr. Jones would honor me with a late dinner and drinks in the room?" He picked at unseen lint on his trousers.

Cat checked her watch. "Let's see how the evening plays out. Oh, here we are at my hotel. Dr. Jones should be down in a few minutes." Cat pulled the car up to the entrance and Willow waved, exiting the door. "And there she is now!"

The doorman opened the back door, and Willow stuck her head in first. "Mr. Rail, how nice to meet you." Willow stepped up and buckled in. "Hi, Carla. Good to see you again! I guess we're headed to LaClaire's home?"

Cat nodded and rolled her eyes while Rail drank in the ambiance of the hotel's neighborhood. The village declined as Cat drove. The SUV was the largest vehicle on the road, driving past donkey carts and motorbikes as the houses became smaller and progressively more ramshackle. The one Matt used looked as if it might collapse if the big bad wolf made one good blow.

Cat pulled up in front of the hovel and cheerfully announced, "We're here!" Rail, looking dubious, was the last to leave the SUV. Cat cautioned, "Everyone's wearing closed toe shoes, right?" Rail's eyebrows ascended into his hairline.

Willow couldn't resist piling it on. "Oh yeah, I wore my boots. I see you did too." Rail lifted his pant leg to reveal flashy loafers without socks. Willow glanced down. "Oh, that's too bad."

Cat knocked on the tin door, and there was no answer. Cat knocked again and called out, "The lunatic is on the grass."

They heard shuffling and movement behind the flimsy door. Footsteps came towards them. It was a gravely, country boy, redneck's cadence that replied. "The lunatic is in my head." Rail shivered and shook his head. As the door swung open, Matt Brenner's persona couldn't be further from his perpetually hip image. He'd stopped shaving a week ago and let his dark, luxurious hair hang lankly, unwashed, past his collar. Matt wore a plaid Woolrich jacket and flapped hunter's hat, the cuffs of his denims were stuffed into high top hiking boots. His ornate belt buckle declared he'd won first place at the Dubuque Big Time Bull Riding Championship. Cat stifled her laugh as the color drained from Rail's Las Vegas tan.

Matt thrust a grimy hand forward. "I'm damn pleased to make your acquaintance. It's not often I meet a man who sees things as they really are." Matt's other hand clamped on Rail's arm, and he shook it until the man was staggering.

Rail looked down at Matt and grimaced. "Certainly. Yes."

Matt stood back. "Where are my manners? There's ladies present, and I haven't offered y'all a seat or a beverage." He waved the three into his one room. The back wall was covered with photos, printed pages, and maps. The jumble of evidence was entirely in Spanish, and red yarn ran from articles to locations on the map. "I'll bet you want to see this stuff I've accumulated. You speak Spanish? Well, they speak a kind of Spanish, here. If you're educated to speak it, you won't understand them. Y'all have a seat!" Willow and Cat gravitated to the center of the room, not touching a thing for fear the walls would cave in.

Something in the corner skittered, and Rail shivered. Matt waved a dismissive hand. "Those spiders, they're good. They eat the bed bugs. Don't worry about them. Speakin' of eatin' y'all hungry?" He moved to a cooler and pulled out water bottles. "This is all I got unless we go to the Cantina."

* * * *

Rail spun on his heel and asked. "How close is it?"

Matt motioned toward the door. "Right across the street. This place has ever'thing I need."

Rail's gaze swept the computer on the eight-foot table. It was one of the early 1990s models featuring a large, cumbersome monitor. His mind did inventory on the number of external hard drives linked to the ancient computer. He followed the number of electric cords plugged into a single surge protector, hanging on a nail on the wall. There was a bare bulb hanging from a frayed cord in the middle of the room. Rail shook his head, and Matt did the same. "I tried hookin' ever'thing up to that one outlet? But it couldn't float enough power. The light kept dimmin'."

Rail shook his head and muttered to himself. "A miracle it didn't burn the place down." He turned to the women with a smile. "I'm sure you've explained to Mr. LaClaire that we'll need his computer, camera, and phone to transfer all his data."

"Oh…I…don't know 'bout that." Matt folded his arms over his chest. "That stuff is val'able. That's my bread and butter. Wha'd'ya gimme for it?"

"Of course, you should expect compensation, Mr. LaClaire. I'm prepared to offer you…" Rail took out a small spiral notebook, and a pen wrote and handed Matt a piece of paper with a dollar amount of one hundred and fifty dollars.

Matt looked affronted. "What's this?"

Rail looked down his nose. "It's the amount I'm willing to pay."

Matt shook his head emphatically. "I couldn't let go of this stuff for anything less than one seventy-five."

Rail smirked. "You drive a hard bargain, sir, but…" He nodded sagely. "You're worth it. One seventy-five, it is."

Matt spat in his hand and held it out. "Then we have a gentleman's agreement. I guess dinner's on me!" Matt held out his hand for the money. Rail stared at him and wiped his hand repeatedly against his trousers. "And the cash?" Matt prompted, satisfied only when Rail tight-fistedly counted out worn twenties. "I'll get 'cha change at the cantina." Matt pocketed the hundred and eighty dollars. "We better wait till we get back to load all this stuff, though. There can be some low-down thieves around here."

"I'm sure you're right, Mr. LaClaire. Does this cantina serve alcohol?"

"Sure does! Best Pisco in the country!"

Rail choked out his question. "What is Pisco?"

Matt slapped him on the back. "Well, it'll kick your ass! It's the local drink, and it's made from grapes. You wouldn't think a little grape could knock a big man down, but it sure as hell does!"

* * * *

Willow was relieved she'd worn boots and jeans. The cantina was marginally cleaner than the hovel they'd left. She certainly had no intention of eating here. She trusted the alcohol would disinfect the glasses.

Matt ushered them to a large round table. There was a candle in a wine bottle with years of wax dripping down the neck. Matt pulled out the chairs for the two ladies. Conspiratorially, he whispered. "Y'all ain't allergic to nothin' are ya? Ever'body eatin'?" Matt walked over to the window, smiled at the cook, and spoke rapidly in Spanish. He returned to the table with a large bowl of bread and crocks of butter and honey. He went back to the window and returned with four glasses. The doughy lady of the house put a liter of liquor on the table. Matt leaned over the table to Rail. "I've got twenty of your bucks says I can drink more of this than you."

Rail sniffed the bottle. "This is well liquor. Don't they have a call brand?"

"This is their traditional liquor, but their top shelf would be the Grande. They do serve the Grande."

"Frank, why don't you send this bottle back and get the Grande?" Willow's Mona Lisa smile lit the room.

"Miss Dr. Jones, you are pullin' out all the stops tonight. Just fer that, I'll pour you. You got the bar bill, right?" Willow nodded accommodatingly as Matt returned the plain bottle for one with a gloriously decorated gilt label. Willow and Cat held out their glasses. Matt poured generously into each glass, serving Rail last. He held up his glass in a toast. "Here's to good business and good partners!"

Willow's brows leapt upward; her face flushed. "Oh my, this is sweet, isn't it?"

Cat reached for a lime. "Flynn, may I call you Flynn? Would you like a lime?"

Flynn Rail grabbed at the fruit. "About how many of these do you drink a night, Frank?"

Matt chugged the second glass and wiped his mouth with the back of his hand. "Who can remember?" And then he lowered his voice. "But I can remember dragons!"

Willow reached for anything to get the taste out of her mouth. She broke off a piece of bread and smothered it with honey, knowing it had antiseptic properties. She looked at Matt. "You know, Frank, Mr. Rail, here, wants to see the dragons, himself. You're the only man I know brave enough to take him there."

Matt scratched his stomach. "After what they did to Lenny? Aw, hell, no! No way I'm going up that mountain. Not for a million dollars!"

Rail's expression turned sly. "How about three hundred dollars?"

Matt shook his head vigorously. "Do you know what they did to Lenny? They tore him apart and burned him and et him! Why would you want to risk *that*?"

"Because it's worth the risk to show the world a rare creature as powerful as this." Rail declared.

Matt was adamant. "You better find yourself another boy. I don't know any weapon you can use against 'em. No way to protect ourselves. They can smell ya, coming up the hill, and they've already decided they don't like people. It's sewercide."

Rail pursed his lips. "Would one thousand dollars cash make it less suicidal?"

Matt hesitated as he poured more liquor into both their glasses. He arched a brow to Cat before he drank. Cat patted his thigh under the table. "Maybe I just gotta get liquored up to do this." He shook his shaggy head and downed another glass of Grande Pisco. He pointed the glass at Rail and held out his hand. "Where's the money?"

Rail nodded and patted his breast pocket. "Oh, my money is in my suitcase."

"Then you need to hoof it out to that suitcase." Matt downed another mouthful. "Without that cash, I'm not leaving this table."

"You drive a hard bargain, Frank." Rail frowned, stood, and reached into his trouser pocket. He peeled ten one-hundred-dollar bills off a fat clip.

Matt rolled the bills and shoved them in his boot. "Don't let what happened to Lenny happen to you!"

Rail sat and turned to Willow. "How do we explain these huge, previously unknown creatures suddenly showing up in Chile?"

Willow looked pensive. "I believe they're both water and air creatures."

Rail leaned into her excitedly. "May I quote you on this? Are you willing to be our expert?"

Willow leaned away from his leer. "Certainly."

Matt stood. "Well, I'll drink to that!" He hoisted his glass, and the women followed, urging Rail to consume more and more.

By the time the empanadas were brought to the table, Rail consumed several glasses of the eighty-six-proof brandy. Matt did his best to slur his speech and lean on one hand, looking at Rail through his thick eyelashes. This stuff wasn't budging his metabolism one bit. Willow kept switching glasses with Cat. The rest of the Cantina emptied as employees wiped down tables and Rail's face finally fell in his bowl of rice.

Willow grabbed a handful of over-gelled hair and lifted his head from the bowl. His eyes did not open. "Cat, Matt, do you hear a heartbeat?"

Matt spoke clearly. "You can't kill him. He's too mean to die." Matt stood and threw the six-foot four man over his shoulder. "Into the SUV?"

"Yep!" Willow nodded, paid the bill, and they left.

Matt dumped the unconscious man into the back seat. "I'm gonna take off before he has a chance to come to. Here are the keys to my car. Tell Rick and Anna to meet us at the end of the road at dawn."

* * * *

Adam grinned, watching the closed-circuit feed as Matt, Cat, and Willow duped the hapless Rail. The earbuds and button cams worked perfectly, and while they were all together, there was no reason to use his microphone. With Matt gone, he wanted the women out of that sketchy part of town. "Okay, ladies, get in Matt's car and get out of that neighborhood. Rick and Anna are at the hotel. Willow, you're probably ready for some room service. What do you want for dinner? I'll call…"

Willow shook her head. "I'll figure out my own dinner." Cat gave her a curious glance.

Her last response was a little too sharp, he thought. "Your choice." He paused a moment. "Anything else I can do for you ladies before I sign off to cover Matt?"

Willow keyed the ignition. "We're good."

Adam punched up Matt's monitor and spoke into his earpiece. "You frisked that guy for weapons before you took off, right?"

Matt eyed Rail's slumped body in the back seat. "Who used to be the detective?"

* * * *

The forest was awakening. Birds twittered and chirped flying in great swoops. The morning mist hung heavy while the sun crested the mountain range. The air was fresh with the scent of rich earth and exotic foliage. Matt leaned against the driver's door with his long legs spread into the front passenger's seat. He enjoyed watching the deer lick last night's rainfall from the leaves and gullies around the SUV. He hadn't camped out in over a hundred years, and he found this was an intriguing part of the world. He'd never convince Cat to live in a tent for a weekend. His mate 'required a bathroom' preferably one with a rain shower and pulsing jets. Periodically, Matt watched Rail's sleeping body as it slid in its drunken stupor.

I hope he doesn't have alcohol poisoning. That'd solve the problem, but it wouldn't be nearly as much fun.

Rail made several embarrassing sounds as he slept.

One of the benefits of vampirism is I no longer snore, and neither does Cat.

Rail, on the other hand, possessed the synchronized talent of passing gas in rhythm with his snoring.

During the last six hours, Matt picked Rail's pockets. He cloned Rail's iPhone and used Rail's sleeping thumb to gain access and change a few of its settings. Now, anything Rail did with this phone was copied to their computers. His wallet was a Gucci knockoff, the type sidewalk merchants sold unsuspecting tourists. It held a number of credit cards, each with a different name, the metal card was, in fact, issued to Flynn B. Rail, but it expired last month.

Why would anyone carry an expired credit card?

Receipts from a local home repair store showed he purchased lengths of chain, rope, clothespins, and fasteners.

Oh my, he gets his kink-on budget style.

The most telling item was a loyalty card from a place in Pahrump called The Sittin' Chicken. Rail's card was punched for nine visits. Just one more visit and, the card proclaimed, he could get one golden shower or a service to be chosen from the variety column.

Oh good, he has a reason to live.

The Nevada driver's license was his photo but was issued to Millard F. Railiski.

Really, man? No wonder he changed his name!

Matt replaced each item exactly where he found it and swallowed the last of his smuggled travel mug of A positive when Rick and Anna arrived in a nondescript car that screamed government issue. Matt met them at their car and leaned into Rick's window. Rick pulled back and made a face. "I see you're a fan of The Method School of acting. Could you stand down-wind?" Rick rolled the window partially up.

Matt shrugged. "If you're gonna do something, do it right. You could've played this role."

Anna leaned forward. "Not if I have any say in it!"

Rick looked around. "Where is he?"

"The pigeon is in the SUV's back seat."

Rick shook his head. "That's a deposit I won't get back. They'll never get the smell out. Did you roofie him?"

Matt crossed his arms over his chest and grinned. "That damn Pisco is Chile's secret weapon. Just ten jiggers of that stuff verges on alcohol poisoning. But he's got a good heart rate. As soon as we're ready I'll be able to roust him."

Rick suggested, "Perhaps we should wake him in the middle of a fight."

Matt nodded and walked back to the SUV. He thumped the back of Rail's head until he got a response. Just as Rail was coming around, Rick knocked on the window, Anna by his side. The two stood in their black suits, topped off with the obligatory mirrored wrap-around shades.

When Rail lifted his head and blinked bleary eyes, they started the "argument."

Matt barked "I don't see what you have to do with this! I'm just takin' my friend up the mountain to do a little bird watchin'."

Rick's lips turned down. "We know what 'birds' you're watching, Mr. LaClaire. I would think your latest camping disaster would discourage you from roaming that mountain."

Matt challenged Rick. "Who do you think you are, to restrict me?"

Rick flashed bogus credentials. "International Fund for Animal Welfare."

"What's going on?" Rail's fog cleared.

Matt gestured toward Rick. "This stuffed shirt says we can't walk up the mountain."

Rail looked guilty as he dragged his hand through his hair and slid toward the driver's side of the car. He opened the door, and Rick pulled a Glock out of his shoulder holster.

"Show me your hands!" he commanded in his best SWAT team voice—Anna followed suit.

Rail froze and stuck out both hands. "Take it easy! We're not criminals, I just want to talk. A simple conversation."

Anna lowered her voice an octave. "Alright, Sir. Step away from the vehicle, slowly. Keep your hands where I can see them."

Matt folded his arms over his chest and dropped his head. Rick shot him an exasperated glance as he stepped into Rail's personal space. "You have identification, Sir?"

Rail slowly pulled his wallet from his breast pocket. "I'm a member of the press. I represent Hi Hopes Media, LLC. You wouldn't want to restrict a member of the press from a story without an explanation, would you?"

Rick spun Rail against the car and frisked him none too gently, while Anna stepped up and spoke forcefully. "Sir, we support the implementation of international agreements in part through effective enforcement of wildlife regulations, training of anti-poaching rangers, customs agents and wildlife law enforcement officers, Sir!"

All three men stared at her for a moment. At last, Matt found his tongue. "It don't matter if you're King Kong's nursemaid! This is public property. And we are the public."

Rick let Rail relax against the car. "We can get a court order to keep you off this mountain."

Matt squinted his eyes in defiance. "You go ahead and do that. I'd like to see you explain to a court why you're keepin' camera toten' folks off public land. We got no weapons as you can plainly see!"

In a stage whisper, Anna asked Rick, "Sir, do you think this rube could be—a dragon hunter?"

Rick's jaw dropped, and he made a quarter turn away from Matt and Rail. "That was a rookie move, to mention those rare and impossible-to-see creatures. Put yourself on report for that comment!"

Anna's chin dropped in shame as she stood at parade rest. "Yes, Sir."

Rick turned back to Matt and Rail. "Expect me to come back and personally remove you from this mountain…if you're still alive!"

Rick and Anna nodded a curt goodbye and got back into the sedan. He squealed the tires in mock frustration as he headed back down the road.

Rail turned to Matt. "They know damn well there are dragons here!" Matt nodded. Rail stepped away and over his shoulder said, "After that, I gotta see a man about a horse."

* * * *

Adam sat at the monitoring station. "You guys are having too much fun!"

"Fun? This is deep cover work, buddy!" Matt watched for Rail's return.

Adam scoffed. "Oh, yeah, right. Listen, I'm gonna turn this show over to Willow for now. Willow are you on?"

Willow sat in front of her monitors. "I hear ya."

"I have to fly over to the volcano and get ready to show Rail what a dragon can do."

"Give us two hours," Matt whispered as Rail approached.

"See you there." Adam signed off.

* * * *

Matt grabbed a backpack and a machete. "I hope you brought other gear. Those shoes don't look like hikers."

Rail looked down at his travel clothes. "Of course, I have hiking gear! I expected to be at my hotel last night. What the hell happened?"

"Looks like you can't hold your Pisco." Matt jabbed him with his elbow. "I told you it'd give you an ass-kickin'."

Rail looked indignant and more than a little nauseated. "How is it that you're awake, and where the devil are we?"

Matt puffed out his chest. "Drink enough of it, and you can kick its ass. And we're at the end of the road to the mountain. We gotta hoof it from here. The campsite is about two hours away." He pointed with his machete. "Straight uphill."

Rail groaned as he dug through his luggage and stripped to put on safari gear. Matt ground back a guffaw when Rail appeared in khaki, down to a pith helmet with mosquito netting. Rail looked at the fast-flowing stream nearby. "I'd like to brush my teeth."

Matt shook his head vigorously. "Not in that stream! You drop your hand in that, you could pull back a bloody stump! There's piranhas in there, and there's nothin' funny about'em. Besides, you'd be the dragon's dessert, they love peppermint!"

Rail stuffed his kit back in the SUV. "Is there any place in this Godforsaken forest that isn't dangerous?"

Matt drew his thumb over his chin in thought. "Nope." He trudged off, deliberately leaving Rail and the beaten path. His machete moved in great swooping chops as Rail stumbled to catch up.

* * * *

After a two-hour trudge up the mountain, Flynn was visibly winded at the edge of the campsite. When a piercing feminine scream, generated by their loudspeaker, electrified the air, Rail dropped to his knees. Matt tensed and looked over at him. "I hate tourist season." He gestured in the direction of the scream. "They come up here, and they're never seen again."

Rail gawked at the carnage. "Shouldn't we call for help…"

Matt struck a questioning pose. "Who ya gonna call?"

Rail threw his hands up. "Those people who stopped us. He had a gun."

Matt pulled his furry hat off his head and scratched at impossibly filthy hair. "You call that a gun? Hell, that gun couldn't stop a puma without emptyin' the clip, much less stop a dragon."

"Well, should we…"

Matt chopped the air in the destroyed campsite. "You wanna play hero and get yourself eaten like Lenny," he pointed the machete to bones and scraps of sheep carcass, "you go right ahead, but don't be lookin' for backup from me. I intend to live through this last go-round with dragons."

"What do you mean, last?"

"I mean, there are plenty of other mountains here that don't have dragons. Folks can visit them. So's, if you're lookin' for a close encounter, don't expect me to save your ass!"

Rail was dumbstruck. "But you're the guide!"

Matt continued to swing the machete aimlessly. "I'm your guide, not hers! If I'd 'a been hers, she wouldna got within flaming range of those dragons!"

The sound of trees being toppled and crushed drew closer. Rail's face paled. Matt shook his head. "You hear that? It's gettin' closer, so's unless you wanna be toe jam, we gotta hide!"

The final scream was cut short with an animal growl.

Matt pulled Rail into the frigid, rushing stream. "They can't smell you if you're in the water."

Rail looked around anxiously. "What about piranhas?"

"You play, you takes your chances. You could live with stumps, but if that dragon eats you? Just look what they did to poor Lenny!" He lowered his head as if in a moment of prayer, then paused, and looked contemplative. "Maybe it wasn't such a good idea to come back to the old campsite." Matt scratched at his chest. "You reckon dragons got memories? Goldfish only have a two-second memory. That's why they keep swimmin' around, all happy and stuff."

* * * *

Willow threw Cat a wry look. "He could do stand up."

Cat smiled proudly, "He's in character. You know, he was the LAPD's youngest detective in his day. He had quite a reputation for stings. You should see his impression of Rick. Shh, don't tell Anna."

Willow rolled up to the mic. "Adam, our stooge is primed, let's rock and roll!"

The entire group heard Adam's reply. "Have we got a pool going on how soon Rail pisses himself? I'm taking three seconds!"

Willow looked at Rail shivering up to his thighs in the stream. "He looks pretty cold, maybe you should go in flaming." His last communication was a long chuckle.

* * * *

Matt hunkered down, his vampire metabolism enjoying the chilled water. He smacked Rail on the head. "Can you hear it?"

Rail winced. "Hear what?"

Matt whispered. "Listen for the wings. They swoop real loud. I heard tell that's the last thing you hear, before, you know…"

Rail lost patience. "Well then, shut up!"

Matt looked away and muttered. "There's no need to be so damn rude!"

Adam flew low, following the stream, flaming a narrow swath of fire as he went, careful not to set the forest ablaze. His eyes met Rail's, and he zeroed in.

"It's looking at me! Oh my God! What should I do? What should I do?"

Matt crouched low and backed away. "Getting' hot here! Good luck!" Matt took off at vamp speed, leaving Rail to face his fantasy.

* * * *

Adam watched the fear envelope Rail. He'd never actually engendered that reaction before. *This is kind of fun.*

He watched Matt run off, leaving Rail hip-deep in icy water. Adam swept his great leathery wings back and hovered over the man. His powerful posture as a humongous airborne threat gave him the adrenaline to see Rail fall backward in the water. Once Rail went under the rushing current, Adam swiftly beat his wings to circle and obscure himself behind the tree line. His flight sound was more menacing than a squad of helicopters over a battlefield. Adam listened for Rail's plaintiff cries as he circled overhead. He followed the sounds of Matt's screams. If this was going to make the right impact, Adam had to pick Matt up and carry him away with the greatest possible terror.

Hmm. Should I pick him up in my mouth and give him a shake, or should I carry him off in my terrible claws? Decisions…

In the end, Adam decided the mouth was far more fear-inducing.

Okay, you big, bad vampire, get ready for dragon breath.

He swept in, his mighty tail taking out trees, causing leaves to swirl in fierce eddies, and forest life to scatter to the four winds. Adam's dragon eyes allowed him a great view of Flynn Rail, the cowering tourist. Adam caught the tail of Matt's thick coat, and he prayed the ugly thing was buttoned well. Actually, Matt's expression wasn't far from Rail's. Adam heard him babbling about 'take it easy'. Once Adam flew to a clearing within the crater, he gently set him on his feet. Matt's feet hit the ground, and he quickly dropped his coat and hat.

"Good, God, do you slobber like that all the time? That is gross."

Adam's dragon tilted his head and yawned. The sound was triumphant, just enough to convince Rail he'd consumed Matt. Matt held out a cautioning hand.

"Hold on buddy." First, Matt broke a bag of blood over the coat. "What a waste of A positive!" And then, he hooked the bloody, slobbered-on coat on Adam's lower fangs. "We need to have proof of death." With a confirming nod, Adam ascended to deliver the final blow.

Rail managed to get himself out of the creek and onto the bridle path and was heading down the mountain as fast as his terrified legs could carry him. It was a simple matter for Adam to fly low over him and swipe at the petrified man with his claws, taking care to miss every time. Finally, he let Matt's bloody coat drop directly in front of Flynn, as he emerged from the thick forest. With a deafening cry, he pulled up and let the breathless man escape.

Adam shifted and hung behind in the thick foliage to watch Rail beat on the car doors seeking entry. In a moment of clarity, Rail tracked back to the bloody coat and squeamishly shook the car keys out of the pocket. Like a man approaching the pearly gates, he ran, unlocked the car, and locked himself inside. He jammed the key into the ignition, and the wheels spun as he put it in reverse and got the hell out of Dodge.

Adam swallowed his satisfaction and shifted back to find Matt and fly them both back to Serenity.

12

Adam circled the helipad one extra time, for the fun of it. Matt, perched on the dragon's neck, cheerfully waved to a stunned pilot and his passengers as they took off. Their startled faces gave Adam a chuckle. He zeroed in on his target and landed as softly as a dragonfly on a flower.

Matt patted his neck affectionately, climbing down one powerful leg. "That was a gas! We gotta do that again!"

Adam shifted, and laughing, waved to someone over Matt's shoulder. "I'll tell you what, help me relocate the clans, and I'll take you flying whenever you like!"

"That's a deal!" Matt turned and bumped directly into Khuno, who was approaching with a robe for Adam. "Hey! You're everywhere these days, Khuno."

Khuno bowed. "I trust your venture was successful, gentlemen?"

"It was aces, my man, but we're not done yet."

"Perhaps when this is over, you would enjoy our hydrotherapy spa and a massage." Khuno walked alongside them as they headed back to the suite.

Matt nodded, and Adam considered what fun he and Willow might have in a hydrotherapy pool if she was still talking to him.

Matt looked down at his attire. "I gotta get out of these clothes. I pray the altitude is too high for fleas!"

Adam scratched his neck. "Please tell me you didn't leave any critters with me!"

"I'll leave orders for the standby helicopter to be brought to the helipad for you. You two have an easy time in the de-lousing room."

Matt looked alarmed. "You have one of those? I was joking!"

Khuno's placid face was impossible to read. "If I told you every service we have available, you would be incredulous."

Matt nodded at Adam and Khuno. "Color me incredulous! And probably grateful." He scratched at his back.

Once inside, Khuno waived his customary blessing gesture and headed for the lecture hall. Matt and Adam hesitated in front of their suite's door. Adam pointed to Matt. "You might want to drop those clothes out here in case you brought something other than success home with you. I'll go inside and grab a laundry bag and toss it to you."

"I could use a robe."

Adam shook his head. "Not until you've showered and washed your hair." Adam closed the door on Matt.

Other guests walked by, and their vampire senses were assaulted. He nodded at a few and tried to explain. "It was for a good cause." They scurried past him. He hollered at their retreating forms. "I lost a bet!"

* * * *

Willow stretched in front of the closed-circuit monitor processing the feed from the SUV. They could see Rail, dripping wet, terrified, but still in sleazeball mode, calling his crew on the satellite phone.

"Jonah! Get the media set up!"

Jonah, Rail's executive assistant, was a dancer in the Down Below Revenue until he herniated himself lifting a zaftig bride-to-be. He found little interest in Rail's endeavors, except for his weekly paycheck. His passion was costume design, and this job would do until he could get an internship with Viva Vegas. Even the most outrageous claims left him flat, and he'd decided months ago the real drama queen was Flynn Rail.

"Media? Yeah, okay." Rail could hear him sucking on an energy drink all the way to Chile.

"Jonah! Jonah, I'm lucky to be alive!"

"Yeah?"

"You don't understand, the dragon ate him!"

Jonah's bored voice replied. "Boss, there no such thing as dragons who eat anybody."

Rail pushed his soaking hair out of his face. "Oh, yes, there are. Not only are there dragons, but there are piranhas in the creeks, and the dragons breathe fire!"

"Are you on Acid? Cuz it sounds like you are trippin', girlfriend!"

"I am stone cold sober! In fact, I'm freezing. I nearly drowned in that damn piranha-infested creek, and the dragon flew off with the guide!" Rail heard the screech of his desk chair. "Are you sitting in my chair?"

"Me? In your chair? No sir! Who again did you want me to call?"

Rail sighed heavily. "I gave you the list before I left. What did you do with the list?"

"Oh, that list…I used it for…I think that got filed with your itinerary."

Rail ground his teeth. "Find the list and get them to the Grand Ambiance Hotel in Santiago today at five."

"The Ambulance Hotel in Chile?"

"No!" Rail blustered. "The Grand Ambiance Hotel in Santiago."

"Got it, boss. Sure thing."

* * * *

"If I tried to write this kind of character, people wouldn't believe anyone could be that stupid!" Cat shook her head watching Rail's exchange.

Willow nodded in agreement. "You can't make this stuff up!"

Anna focused on the practical. "Where's he headed? Here? Santiago?"

Tapping the keyboard, Willow brought up a map. "The SUV is on the road to Santiago. We'd better get dressed."

"Does this say journalist?" Cat walked to the portable clothing rack and pulled out an attractive dress.

Anna nodded. "It's fine. I don't think he'd notice anything you were wearing unless you were naked."

"Fat chance on that! This con work is tedious. I have no idea how Rail has the energy to constantly bilk people."

Willow stood and chose her clothing for the press conference. "Well, we're doing it for the greater good, and he's doing it for the greater paycheck.

I guess he has about a hundred thousand more reasons to keep up the pace. Plus, he's a narcissist."

Cat's cell phone trilled. It prompted the recorder in the computer to begin. "Yes."

"LaClaire is dead!"

Cat watched Rail's face on the monitor. "No!"

"Yes! And I barely escaped with my life! I could hear that horrible beast tearing him apart! The screams! That was the only reason I was able to get away."

Cat winked at the other women. "Too bad you already paid LaClaire."

Rail calmed at the thought. "I should have checked his coat more closely. I was utterly terrorized; I didn't realize that!"

Cat slipped into her dress. "I wonder if he had any family?"

Rail dismissed the thought. "Well if he did, they're about to hear about his grisly demise on national news!"

Cat smiled at Willow and feigned interest. "Oh? You're planning an interview?"

He laughed manically. "Interview, hell! I have a news conference set up for five o'clock in Santiago. You and Dr. Jones will be my witnesses. And I have footage to back it up!"

Willow zipped the back of Cat's dress. "I have a pilot friend who can get us there to meet you."

Rail scratched at his back and belly through his wet clothes. "I've got the SUV, and I'll keep it to drive down if that's okay since all my bags are in it. We'll meet at the Grand Ambiance Hotel Ballroom."

Cat crooned sweetly, "Oh, perfect! We'll see you there!" She clicked off the call. Anna gestured a noose around his neck.

Willow knocked on each of the bedroom doors. "Hey guys, you ready to roll? We've got our date with destiny at five P.M.!"

Adam entered the hotel suite showered, shaved and deliciously handsome in a navy suit. Rick emerged from his room in his familial tartan trews and his deep blue velvet jacket.

Adam circled him scrutinizing his grooming. "This is a new look for you, isn't it? Did you forget your razor?"

Anna burst into the room, her hair loose and flowing. "He made a deal. He grows a beard and mustache, and I let my hair grow again."

Adam looked at her luscious long red hair and squelched a grin. "Seriously? I think that beard's gonna come in bright red."

Anna put her hands on her hips. "And what's wrong with that?" She pointed to her own red hair and rolled her eyes and then fell into Rick's open arms. "I like it." She kissed the dimple on Rick's cheek.

He winked. "And that's the important part."

Matt made his entrance, scratching like a hound. He looked repeatedly over his shoulder and down the V-neck of his black cashmere sweater.

Rick shook his head. "What are you looking for, dear boy?"

Matt ran both hands through his dark curls. "Do bugs love vampire blood, or what?"

Rick separated a patch of Matt's hair and inspected him. "The altitude is far too high for bugs. There's not a critter there. It's all in your head."

Matt was ruffled. "I'm going to have to shave every bit of hair off my body to get rid of this."

"No!" Cat cried. "Listen to Rick. He's right, babe! Nothing is crawling on you." She caught his busy hand and kissed the back of it. "You've showered and shaved. Just to be safe, you even took that treatment back at Serenity. It's all in your head, honey." Cat attempted to keep Matt from scratching. "The itching is probably coming from skin dryness from the treatment. Just don't think about it."

Matt rolled his eyes and imitated Cat. "Just don't think about it! Good God, that's all I can think about!"

Rick brought him a tall tumbler of Everclear and O positive. Anna stuck her hand between the men. "You can't give our pilot liquor. It's twelve hours from bottle to throttle."

Rick looked at the tall tumbler. He took a sip. "Well then, each of us takes a sip or two, and then Matt's whining won't bother us."

Matt posed hands on hips. "Thanks a lot, old man, good to know you have my back."

Rick toasted him with the alcohol and passed it to Anna. "Anything I can do, just let me know."

* * * *

Matt landed the helicopter neatly, the concentration to fly a helicopter freeing him of his bug obsession. They headed to their assigned locations nearly giddy with expectation. Adam, Willow, and Cat headed directly to the ballroom. They were pleasantly surprised the auditorium seating was nearly at capacity, with international media milling with a loud buzz.

Cat assessed the networks and top news personalities present. "Oh, these are the heavy hitters of the news world."

Adam peered over the top of the crowd. "The better to knock him down."

Willow glanced at the six seats reserved in the front row. "Are those our seats?" She grinned sweetly. "Where are the others hiding?"

Cat nodded toward the doors behind the pipe and drape stage. "They'll arrive once he's mid-meltdown. Adam, how did the editing go on his video?"

Adam smiled like a mischievous little boy. "I don't want to ruin the surprise, but, this is some of my best work."

Willow tilted a look up at the cantankerous hunk. "I'm sorry we don't have popcorn for this!"

Flynn Rail whistled for them from the partially open hallway door. Cat and Willow cringed.

"What a douche." Adam shook his head in disgust.

Cat assumed a placid expression and led the trio to their mark.

Rail, dressed in yachting wear, was a sight! From his pristine leather shoes, white trousers, and navy-blue double-breasted blazer, to the burgundy ascot and white officer's cap, he personified the Captain of the Love Boat.

Adam muttered out the side of his mouth. "What the hell is he wearing?"

Willow's lips never moved as she spoke. "We couldn't have dressed him better. He looks like a psycho before we even get started."

Cat led the trio to Rail and caught his extended hand in both of hers. "Are you ready to show the world who you really are?"

"This, Ms. Starr, has been a long time coming!" Rail enthused. And then his joy flipped to suspicion. "Who is he?" Their mark was used to being the tallest man in any room. Adam's six-foot-six was just enough to intimidate the hell out of the perpetually insecure narcissist. Rail couldn't compete with Adam's broad shoulders, slim hips and larger than life golden perfection.

"Oh! Let me introduce you to…the number one stringer from Now Press, and a particular friend of mine."

Rail's lips turned downward. "Oh, really?" He thrust his hand into Adam's personal space and was forced to look upward to Adam's stunning aqua eyes. "I didn't catch your name."

Adam cut the handshake short and peered down at Rail. "I didn't throw it." The air was thick with testosterone until Adam relented. "I'm Arthur Buchwald."

"Isn't he dead?" Rail's face twisted.

"My parents were big fans of the reporter."

Rail's real attention was on the stage crew who were checking the podium. He glanced at his watch. "Which one of you lovely ladies would like the honor of introducing me?"

Willow rolled her eyes behind Rail's back and stepped forward. "I'm embarrassed to say this will make my reputation, so, if you don't mind me reflecting in a little bit of your glory, I'd be happy to introduce you." Adam pressed his lips into a thin line.

Rail caught her elbow and pulled her toward the stage steps. "The pleasure will be all mine, my dear."

Au contraire, the pleasure is about to be ours, Adam mused.

Willow stepped up to the microphone and the room hushed. "Members of the press esteemed colleagues, ladies and gentlemen, please let me introduce Flynn Rail of Hi Hopes Media. I understand he has some startling revelations for us today."

Rail stepped up to the podium, and the crowd chattered softly. "Ladies and gentlemen, some of you may have seen my website's posting last month about the Loch Ness Monster." The crowd groaned. He raised a calming hand. "Now, I know there has been a lot of doubt and speculation about the authenticity of that picture. I'm here to tell you, Nessie is a dragon, and she is not the only one of her species." Chuckles traveled in a wave from back to front and increased in volume. "Oh, you laugh now, but you'll see the photographic and video proof, authenticated by one of the rising stars of zoology, Dr. Wanda Jones." The crowd was momentarily stunned by his citing such a credential. "When a concerned member of the press first contacted me, it was my good fortune to make the acquaintance of Dr. Jones and Carla Starr. I will now present my proof that dragons live among us."

The lights dimmed, and he hit the play button on his laptop. His back was to the huge screen above him. Instead of the screams and thrashing Rail expected, the classical music, Call to the Cows played melodiously over scenes of the Chilean forest at daybreak. Mist hung as the wings of hummingbirds beat a pleasant staccato.

The scene shifted to a patio, set with a grill and cooler. The camera zoomed in on a young couple in love. Clad in terry robes, they embraced, and the crowd's murmur grew to outright protest. The couple went back into their room and in a split second, returned in plushie dragon costumes. They rolled around on the double chaise as intimately as two bulky, fluffy would-be dragons could. They struggled to their feet and with Puff the Magic Dragon playing over the scene, the larger dragon began grilling dinner and drinking beer. The more petite dragon brought out a Jell-O mold and sat it on the table, waving enthusiastically to the camera as if in a home movie.

The crowd hooted and laughed, and Rail turned to the screen in shock. He hit the stop button impotently as the video continued unimpeded. The next scenes were photos of his Las Vegas headquarters; obviously, an abandoned motel in a rundown industrial area, accompanied by a voice-over of Rail berating his employees. "This is Vegas, baby! If we don't fleece them, someone else will bleed 'em dry!"

Rail panicked, frantically pressing every button to stop the reveal. His ex-wife's voice joked "Honey he owes everybody money… Sky Hi Hopes, LLC…he's living above his racket…in Vegas."

Rail picked up the laptop and slammed it on the ground in front of the stage. "Turn on the lights! Stop this! Carla! Dr. Jones!" The lights came up as Rick, Anna and Matt strolled in to take their seats in the front row. Rail pointed hysterically at Matt. "You're dead! I saw the dragon carry you off! I had to go through your bloody coat to get the car keys." Matt looked at him as if he were mad, shrugged, and shook his head.

Rail continued his rant. "Dr. Jones, tell them I'm not lying."

Willow stepped up to the podium. "I'm sure Mr. Rail believes he's telling the truth." She looked sorrowful. "I believe he's having a mental breakdown."

Cat nodded agreement and stepped forward. "I concur. I think he needs medication and observation. This behavior should not lead to ridicule, but rather to compassion and treatment. We all understand the lure of drug experimentation…"

Rail gaped at them. "What do you mean? You contacted me!" Cat shook her head. He pointed wildly at Rick and Anna. "Ask them! They had sunglasses and badges… and guns! They tried to stop me from seeing the dragons." Sitting in the front row, steno pads and pens in hand, like all the rest of the reporters, Rick and Anna turned bewildered faces to the crowd and shook their heads.

Adam opened the ballroom door, and two gentlemen from the local police stepped up, showed Adam papers, and he directed them to the stage. Rail saw the approaching men and actually thought he could hide behind the statuesque Willow. Adam put a hasty end to that and escorted Rail bodily to the police.

A plainclothes officer strode to the podium. "As a legal representative of Chile, let me assure you there are no dragons, no one has been carried off and murdered. We believe once this criminal," he glared at Rail, "has been processed by Interpol, all of this will be revealed as an elaborate hoax."

Rail's voice rose above the detective's calm announcement. "It's all them! They did this to me! Dragons exist! They fly! They flame! They kill…"

* * * *

Adam watched with satisfaction as Rail was dragged away to a squad car by the Chilean police. "Uh…if you could please check his pockets for the keys to my car? He 'borrowed' it to drive here." Adam said to one of the officers in perfect Spanish and was soon given the keys to the SUV.

He jogged back to the group who were gathered around the helicopter and anxious to escape reporters in search of more of the story. "Okay, somebody has to drive this beast back to the airport, who's the lucky driver?" He dangled the keys in the air like bait.

Matt puffed out his chest. "I've got the chopper and eleven-hundred and eighty dollars in cash." He turned and all but ran from a long, bumpy ride. Rick looked at Anna and then Willow. Anna made a quick shake of her head and caught her mate by the elbow.

"Come on, Fitz, let's give Adam and Willow some space." Rick made a wry face and followed her.

Adam looked around. "Don't feel obligated to ride back with me…"

"If you don't want me to ride along…" Willow looked at her watch.

"I'd welcome the company. It's a slow and bumpy ride, but once I turn the car in, we can fly."

* * * *

Two weeks ago, we couldn't keep our hands off each other, Willow thought. They'd spent more than twenty-four hours straight between the sheets.

I could barely stay hydrated, now he wants to turn in the car and fly back to Serenity. What did I do?

"It's been a long day; it might feel good to stretch my wings." She climbed into the front seat and pushed the seat back to stretch out for the ride. This position afforded her a clear view of Adam's profile. She needed to get her bearings.

Our conversations used to be so easy, sometimes even light, and stress-free. Now, I feel as if I'm extracting deep thoughts. If we can't make conversation, he's right, we won't make it as a couple.

She leaned back and buckled in. They got on the road.

"You wanna find some music?" Adam gestured to the radio. Willow dialed from one end to the other. The languages were all foreign to her, and the stations were either religious or local folk music. She dug in her purse and pulled out her iPhone, plugged it in, and chose her concentration playlist.

"I hope you don't mind classical. I have this or my workout playlist." Willow laid back. Adam waited for the music; Debussy began. "What's your workout playlist?"

Willow flipped the lists and Korn bellowed back to them.

"Twisted Transistor." Willow was unfazed.

Adam gestured in the dark. "Debussy's good."

Willow flipped back to the original song. "What kind of music do you listen to when you want to relax?"

She watched Adam's head move as he maneuvered the twisting roads. "Gershwin, ah, *Rachmaninov…*"

"Sorry about not having any of that. I probably should be better prepared."

"How do you prepare for easy listening? You're just listening… Sinatra's easy…"

"I guess our tastes are a bit diverse."

"I've been in this world for two hundred years; we're bound to be different. I could probably use some updating. But, how do you work out to that?"

Willow laughed out loud. "When I work out, this music energizes me. I work off a lot of frustration and anger."

"Interesting, tell me what you're angry about." His eyes stayed on the treacherous road, but he leaned attentively toward her.

"Sorry, Doc. When I get angry, I'll let you know."

"Are you aware that you do that?"

"Do what?"

"Whenever I get marginally deeper than superficial, you put me off. What don't you want to tell me, Willow?"

What am I afraid to tell you? It was great to get to know another shifter, but when I spoke my mind, I got therapy talk. So, you can keep your therapy talk, and I'll keep my mouth shut.

"We've met through some unusual circumstances. I generally like to get to know people by the way we experience things together."

"Experiences are great, they tell us a lot about each other, but they're not feelings. And to really know another person, you have to share feelings."

"Well, that's great. Share."

"Okay, I'll share a feeling…hum. I feel uncertain about you right now. I feel a distance growing between us. But I've been trying to bring us closer, and that simply seems to create more distance. I'm feeling pretty frustrated."

His words were like a smack in the shoulder, she turned and put her hand out on the dashboard. "When you have a project, your directions and your communication is spot on. You're a joy to work with. When we have a personal conversation, it comes out like therapy. It's your way of maintaining control."

"You may be right. I understand that's what you feel. I am trying to get to know you. And I feel that you don't really want me to do that. And I'm wondering why?"

Willow closed her eyes and shook her head. Adam's eyes riveted on the twisting switchback road. "This is not the right conversation to have when you're trying to keep this beast on the road." Willow straightened back around and reclined her seat.

Or, ever, right, Willow?

* * * *

Adam was frankly mystified. He was notorious for getting under defenses both as a therapist and as a Dom. He knew she grew up feeling like a freak and she dealt with her differences by stepping outside sexual norms. She entered an intimate world where everyone was a freak, and she felt included. It was obvious to him that sharing her feelings led to pain in the past. If he couldn't gain her trust, they would have nothing.

Soon, the only sound was her deep, even breathing. She was asleep. He flipped off the music, its calm was irritating. Eventually, even miserable car rides end, and he pulled up to the Puerto Natales airport. The sudden lights roused Willow.

Adam folded the rental papers into his pants pocket. "Do you want to get something to eat first, or just fly back?"

"It won't take us long to fly back, I can get room service. Unless you need a break?"

His voice was flat. "I think flying will clear my head."

"I need to get some water…" Willow exited the car and headed inside.

* * * *

In the privacy of the bathroom, Willow dug for her phone, finding the voicemail intriguing. "Dr. Greer, this is Khuno, about the subject of other Pegasus shifters. You may be interested to know, I have located a clan in Kentucky, who I believe may be related to you. When you get back to Serenity, I'll have follow-up information. Call me when you return."

Willow clutched the telephone and closed her eyes.

This is a Godsend. I don't know what's waiting for me, but I'm not alone.

She stepped into the gift shop and found a long-handled canvas bag. She bought two and walked outside to look for Adam. "We've been thinking about nothing but Flynn Rail, and we forgot to make a plan for our clothes." She tore the price tag off the bag and held it out to Adam.

"We did, didn't we?" Adam looked up into the starry sky and nodded at the golf course. "We can undress in that copse of trees and take off from there. Do you think this thing will fit around my neck?"

"Seriously? You can fly like the Queen with her purse on her arm." Willow took off for the darkness and began undressing and folding everything to fit into the bag. "If shifters are so damned evolved, how come we don't have pouches like kangaroos?"

Adam silently undressed and waited for her. "If we stay close to the treetops we'll avoid radar and small aircraft."

"Too bad we couldn't have buzzed Matt." They each shifted and were airborne in a matter of seconds.

* * * *

Their flight was void of telepathic conversation. Adam flew before her, keeping her feathery silhouette in his peripheral vision. As his broad wings swept with ease, he kept a pace her smaller Pegasus could maintain. In their previous flights, Adam was exhilarated at the freedom, as well as anticipating being skin to skin later. Those flights where their foreplay. Shielding his thoughts from her, his mind juggled their problematic relationship.

* * * *

Serenity came alive around midnight. Adam and Willow landed and dressed before they came out of the tree line. Although Adam's stride was almost twice hers, she clipped along at a trot toward the reception center.

"Which way are you headed?" Adam waved at her.

"Oh, I'm sorry. I'm preoccupied tonight. I need to meet with Khuno." She was impatient, bobbing from foot to foot.

"Oh, okay. Ah, I'll meet you back at the suite?"

"Yeah, yeah, sure. I don't know how long I'll be, don't wait up for me."

"What's going on?"

"I'm not sure, myself, yet. I'll let you know when I find out."

"Yeah." He gave her a slanted glance. "Okay."

Willow waved awkwardly and jogged toward the illuminated rotunda.

* * * *

The reception center was a marvel of UV protected stained glass, polished tropical walnut, and warm shades of marble. There was a low song of voices as Willow pulled the massive wood door open. It glided effortlessly and invited visitors to acclimate to the tranquility of the resort. Khuno's office was down the right corridor. For a moment, Willow stood under the complex leaded-glass rotunda and marveled at how vampires created the illusion of noon at midnight. Remembering why she was there, she snapped out of her reverie and headed down the hall.

Knocking quietly on the partially open door, she waited for a response.

"Enter." Khuno stood behind his wide slab of a desk.

Willow approached him and extended her hand. He came around the desk and embraced her, making an effort to look her directly in her eyes.

"I feel your excitement at my discovery."

"I am excited! This has been my life's quest. I can't thank you enough for finding them! Have you reached out to them?"

"No, I wouldn't do that before we discussed it. Let me show you everything. Have a seat. May I offer you tea, have you eaten?"

"Tea would be lovely, I'm too excited to eat."

Khuno turned on a large monitor and gave her the remote. "Keep pressing forward as you view the slides." He turned to a tea cart and prepared fragrant cups for each of them. As she ate up the images of a rural, mountainous region in Kentucky, her gaze danced from point to point.

"How did you find them? I'm in education and never found a clue."

"It's rather easy when our center deals in all facets of the paranormal. Through the ages, each segment has sought a place of solace and contemplation. Eventually, all come to Serenity."

Willow held the warm pottery mug in her hands and looked for familiar features on the faces of the residents. Who might be her cousins or aunts and uncles?

"How many of them are there?"

"The last count we have, from the paranormal census of 2000, was roughly one hundred Pegasus shifters. They're not as prevalent as Lycans or Were-cats."

"Are they anywhere else in the world? I don't remember my adopted parents saying my family was from Kentucky. A Roanoke family adopted me after other blood relatives couldn't be located."

Khuno handed her an annotated map. "There are other Pegasus shifters in Austria, South Africa, Greece, and Egypt. I'm sure there are smaller pockets in other areas, but these are population centers who interact with other paranormals."

"I'm blown away! I guess I need to book a flight and a rental car and prepare to be amazed."

"Perhaps you'd like to send an email to this address." He slid her a list of information points. "They own the mountain and the mining company on the land. The fences keep interlopers out of their business. Their CEO is Olympia Steed, her contact info is here. I've forwarded copies of this to the email you listed when you checked in. Your destination would be Harlan County, Kentucky."

Willow's cheeks warmed—her mind moved a mile a minute. "I'll need to fly back to Florida and settle some things and then drive up."

"Are there any introductions you would want me to make? This is a closed community."

Willow laughed. "I should have known that. Certainly, please do that for me. Even send them a photo of me." She pulled out her phone. "Let's take a photo together under the Serenity sign. That should lend some credence."

Once Khuno packed all his data into the portfolio, Willow clutched it to her chest and hugged him with her free arm. "I'll keep in touch and let you know the fruits of your labor."

"That, Dr. Greer, will be most rewarding. Go in safety. Never part without loving words to think of during your absence, it maybe you will not meet again in this life."

"I'm sure in the next life, you will be exactly where I need you, thank-you, Khuno."

* * * *

Willow felt airborne! She grinned all the way to the suite's door. Slipping the keycard into the lock, she clutched at the emotions colliding within her. Adam fascinated her, she was past what Anna called 'crushing' on the dragon shifter, and these four vampires invested their faith in her news about Flynn Rail. Whether it was in support of Adam or belief of her veracity, she came to a comfortable place with her new friends.

The door opened on a jubilant celebration. The gals were relaxing on the butter soft leather couch in their bare feet, fashionable pumps cast aside. The large screen television showed Rick and Matt's personas caught in the path of a savage dragon. The star of the show, Adam held a tall tumbler as he lounged in every inch of the leather club chair. It bobbed and swiveled with his anxious energy. Vampire hearing being what it was, the four turned to Willow in the brightly lit entry.

"Everything okay?" Cat leaned over the side of the sofa with careful curiosity.

Willow nodded and waved. "Khuno had some great news, so yes, it should be okay very soon."

Rick grabbed the TV remote and switched off the "show". "From the looks of that portfolio, it seems like there's plenty to consider. Anything legal you need to be interpreted; Adam here was an attorney many years ago." Rick, ever the host, moved to the bar and made one of the fizzy, soda-water mocktails she liked. "We were just making fun of Matt's performance as a country bumpkin, so I'll wager he'd love for you share your good news."

Willow accepted the drink and sat in the empty club chair across from Adam. She felt the room's eyes and ears waiting. "Khuno located several Pegasus shifter clans. From the information I gave him, he identified a herd in Harlan County, Kentucky." Adam transformed from a relaxed manspread to an upright posture, leaning toward Willow. "He's forwarding a photo of the two of us, and they'll see I'm on the level." Willow took a long draw on the drink. The silence was deafening.

She saw the four of them exchange looks with Adam. "When are you leaving?" His words were delivered hesitantly and low.

Willow relaxed back into the chair. "I have to arrange a flight through Atlanta to the Gainesville regional airport. I rent a garage apartment from another professor; I'll check in with him before I drive up to Kentucky." Thoughts raced through her mind. It would probably be a crowded commercial flight and then something older and smaller from Atlanta to

Gainesville. She stared into the bubbles in the tall glass. Her five friends talked excitedly, but she was simmering, and their words were a babble. Adam touched her knee, and she jumped. "Oh, cripes, I'm sorry, Adam."

Rick leaned against the credenza, taking everything in. "Nonsense about the flights. Let me fly you to the regional airport. You've just exhausted yourself on our little conspiracy project. You deserve rest and a direct flight."

Willow shook her head and raised a hand. "That's too much, seriously." Anna and Cat launched simultaneous reassurances.

"Willow, there's no stopping Rick when he sets his heart on it. How soon do you need to leave?"

* * * *

Adam's heart lurched at her news. In the distant recesses of his mind and soul, he saw this coming, but his heart bet against it.

"Well, if you folks are all leaving tomorrow it would throw a kink in your plans. I do have the money for the flight." Willow sat up straight. "All of you have been incredibly welcoming, I can't impose further on your generosity."

Rick insisted. "We're not actually leaving until the day after tomorrow. We need a little rest, too, my jet has plenty of time to take you to Gainesville. It's settled. That's what's happening." He reached for her glass. "You deserve a refill. Wheels up at dawn okay for you?"

Adam hoped his glare at Rick said dawn was too soon, but it flew right over the effusive vampire's head.

Cat jumped up to lend a hand. "If you want, I can pack your fancy clothes in my luggage, and you'll have them when you come back to Scotland."

Adam nodded agreement, hiding the movement by bobbing the club chair.

"That's just another thoroughly kind thing you've done for me, Cat. Thanks."

That's a point for my side. Our coming together took so long, why is your good-bye so brief?

He wanted to hold her, wanted to convince her to make the trip back to Scotland with him, while he handled the dragonfolk's immigration to Mount Viejo. Then he could go to Kentucky with her. "Why don't you sit a moment, have something to eat and even have a glass of wine? Relax…"

"Relax? I can't relax! I'm so excited. This is the best news I've ever been given. I'm not a freak, there are others of my kind. I'd fly there myself, right now, if I could."

Anna pulled the salad from the refrigerator. "This has been waiting for you. You need to eat. Then, we'll help you pack. You've got several hours. You haven't eaten all day."

Adam clenched back his words.

Several hours? No, we do not have several hours. We have precious few.

Anna placed the salad on the dinner table, and Adam rose and pulled out the chair. "Have a seat, and don't rush your meal." He poured her a glass of wine and set a water glass next to it. "There's fettuccini, I can heat it up for you." Willow shook her head. "I ordered you a piece of peanut butter pie. I remembered how much you liked it."

Adam watched her unfocused gaze, knowing she was miles away, with her new discovery, and handling their interactions by rote. Adam bent and kissed her cheek, and she smiled up at him fondly. "You enjoy your dinner, and then I'll help you pack."

Cat and Anna exchanged a guilty glance with him.

* * * *

Willow laid her small suitcase and backpack on the bed, ready to fill them with sensible clothes and toiletries.

Adam held up a designer dress he'd ordered online. "I was gonna surprise you with this. I thought maybe we'd have a little time to relax together and go to dinner…"

"Wow, that's really beautiful. I love that color. I'm sorry I didn't get to wear it, but I don't think I'll need a designer dress at a horse farm in Kentucky."

Adam lowered the dress, and his look was serious. "So, are you ever coming back to me?"

Willow was floored.

Who are you, and what have you done with Adam the brusque?

"I thought we were just friends…"

"Is that what you want?"

"What do *you* want?"

"I hear you saying you're more interested in forming a relationship with the Pegasus community, than continuing a relationship with me."

"We have a relationship, now? When did that happen? I didn't get the memo. The last I knew, I told you I liked you better than the kink, and you freaked out. That's the last news you shared about a 'relationship'."

"Willow…"

Willow pushed past him, a load of suits and dresses in her arms. "Excuse me, I need to give these to Cat."

Adam blocked the doorway. "Willow, obviously I hurt you, I'm sorry. Haven't I told you for days that I want to get to know you? What more can I do to express my interest?"

Willow's heart sank, and she decided this was the time in the "relationship" to speak her mind. "Look, I tell you I love you, and you want to 'get to know me'. That's never worked for me, Adam. And I'm tired of the rejection. I want someone who wants me, without stipulations. Obviously, that's not you."

"What are you talking about?" His face turned bright pink, and his aqua eyes blazed. "Haven't I just said I want you? You've entered into all these romantic entanglements only to be disappointed because you couldn't show who you really are. And now, when you can show your true self, you want me to come across with hearts and flowers. Except, that's not who I am. I've been hurt too. We're intelligent people, who could build a solid relationship. You've ignited a place inside me. Yeah, we know the sex is fantastic, and it probably shouldn't have happened as fast as it did, but it was part of our instant attraction. BDSM is not life. It's a lifestyle, not where I want to build a lasting relationship.

Willow shook her head. "No, what's happening is, I've discovered I love you, BDSM or not, and you don't feel the same for me. Okay, let's part as friends, can we agree on that?"

Adam clenched his fists in frustration. "No! You have to understand, some people's feelings grow slowly, and you're not the only person in this relationship. This isn't all about you. It's about us."

Willow pushed past him. "No, I don't think it is. It's about the fact that we are on the wrong foot, and I don't think we're ever going to step in time. Maybe I'll learn love is easier found with my own kind."

"If they're like my kind, you'll be pressed to marry a man who has nothing in common with you personally. You'll be directed to live a life of duty, not passion or romance…" But he was talking to her back.

In the living room, Cat and Anna jumped and looked as if they wished they were anywhere but here.

"These are dresses and things, if you see something you like, just wear them." Willow handed the hangers to Cat.

"Well, you may need them when you come back…"

"If I come back," Willow said sadly.

Cat reached out a hand. "Willow…"

Willow brushed at the tears she could no longer control, and took off for her bathroom, turning on the shower and locking the door. By the time she came out, Adam was gone.

13

Willow didn't sleep before she got on Rick's company jet. Enroute, her mind excruciatingly looped her last conversation with Adam. He hadn't seen her off at the small airport, though she was certain he was there somewhere. She could feel his eyes on her.

And isn't that just more proof? I love him, he's uncertain about me, and I've been through this scenario way too many times.

She was certain it was real love, and that meant he possessed the power not only to hurt her but destroy her. She was not giving that power to anyone. Never again. She sighed and brushed away insistent tears. She would get over this interlude. Better to take the lesser pain now, than hang around for devastation later.

* * * *

Adam glided in for a perfect landing at Mount Viejo. Rick warned dragon flight over Chile might be dangerous, since it was a topic of conversation on the international news, but Adam was willing to take the chance. He needed to think and strategize. Recently, he rediscovered flight gave him clarity, and he was careful to stay out of sight.

He scanned the dormant volcano's topography. There were perfect areas for herding, tanning, caves for stabling, this area would be ideal. Yes, he would take care of his people. Two hundred years ago, he'd screwed up in a major way, leaving a vulnerable girl to face disgrace on her own. He'd alienated his clan, not to mention his family. He felt responsible for making things right now, and nothing was more important than his duty. All the attention Flynn Rail focused on dragons would be eclipsed within a week. In a month, at the latest, the two Scottish clans would be relocated. *And what about me? What's my destiny?*

He'd found this great woman, another shifter, who was beautiful, sexy, intelligent, educated, inquisitive, she flew, she shared his kink, she was in just about every way, his perfect mate. What the hell happened? Was it a look, was it a phrase, was it his body language? What the hell made her issue an ultimatum and take off? *Talk about topping from the bottom!* Willow Greer took ultimate control and now…*can I allow that?* She was the most contrary female he'd ever encountered. *She says she's a submissive, are you fucking kidding me?* She was bordering on shrewish! What does a man do if he's in love with a woman like that?

* * * *

Willow knocked on her landlord's door. The professorial-looking man's lips turned down. "I got your email. It's rash to believe that family would demand your resignation from the university. Won't you consider a leave?" He held the door open in invitation.

"Thanks, Randall, but my life has taken a new direction. I appreciate you keeping the car running while I was away. Here are the keys to the apartment. I left everything. It could be rented as furnished if they like starving-professor decor."

Randall took the keys from her and offered a hug. "You have my email. Keep in touch. Bettina and I are sorry to lose you. There's no need for this month's rent, we'll take the furnishings in lieu of that. And, despite what you think, you've made an attractive home there."

"I'm shoving off. I'll raise a flare when I stop, and I will keep in touch."

* * * *

The interstate highway was a cacophony of billboards advertising fresh squeezed orange juice or bagged pecans. The southernmost tree line was coming alive from its winter doldrums. Her car tooled along on cruise control set to one mile per hour under the speed limit. She wasn't going to waste money or time getting pulled over. She lived without blood family for thirty years, she could be patient when her goal was eleven hours away.

By the time she was outside Warner Robbins, Georgia, she realized she didn't have a bit of food, and her water bottle was empty. A stop for gas and a bag of road food would carry her to Marietta for the night. She played every CD in the car. The radio stations crackled and spit back ads for year-end deals on trucks. The bag of snacks offered a carbohydrate coma the extra-large coffee couldn't fend off.

Checking into a seemingly safe roadside motel, she parked her car in front of her room. Willow showered and lay on the stiff mattress. Her cell phone's silence mocked her. Who did she expect to call? Anna and Cat were probably back in Ireland by now. She'd had no contact from her possible relatives in Kentucky. Rick and Matt were undoubtedly playing Dungeon Masters.

If only she had met those two a year ago! Their mates were insufferably happy and in love. Those men doted on their every blink of need. Why couldn't she find a man like that, who was also a shifter? Maybe he was waiting for her in Kentucky. She checked her cell phone, again. Nothing.

* * * *

Her anticipation escalated as the Black Mountain compound drew closer. Once she was on Black Mountain Ridge Road, aggressive signage warned trespassers to "turn around." Reinforcing their demands that interlopers keep out, were fisheye cameras spaced every fifty feet on the high chain link fence. Khuno's directions got her to a guard gate for the mining company.

Willow slowed and rolled down her window when a terrifically built young woman with the face of an angel waved her muscled arm at her. Her fatigues were skin tight, and her thighs carried twin holsters. "Please state your business and present your government identification." The blonde stood intimidatingly at Willow's car window. Her outstretched hand waited while Willow dug for her wallet. "I'm family. I sent an email to Olympia Steed forty-eight hours ago. I'm expected." She placed the driver's license in the guard's hand.

The guard examined the license for signs of tampering. "Yes, Dr. Greer, we've been expecting you. Stay on this road, do not venture off the asphalt."

The gate rose, and Willow pocketed her license in her shirt, leery she would have to show it again. The trees rose majestically, wild, and untrimmed. She rejoiced in the fragrance of the grasses and plants. Everything smelled delicious. She envied the grazing horses in the pastures fragrant with clover.

The road circled as it climbed the mountain. Street signs directed drivers to paddocks or barns or arenas named in honor of Greek gods.

The sun's rays danced on the pond in front of the large painted brick mansion perched on the side of the mountain. She blinked and thought for a second she was in Washington, D.C. at a miniature White House. She stopped under the portico as a man approached her car. He was strikingly handsome and wore casual riding gear. A blinding white polo shirt contrasted with his rich and well-earned tan. Perfectly cut, but tousled indigo black hair nudged his collar, and he sported stubble on his chiseled chin. It was impossible to ignore the long, coal-hued eyelashes framing his challenging coffee eyes.

"Dr. Greer, I'm Bradley Dale. Ms. Steed will meet you around back in the garden. You can leave your keys in the console, no one will bother your car." His stance was militant, his posture born of duty and authority.

Willow glanced around, feeling a sudden chill in the air. "Thank you, Mr. Dale. Should I follow you?"

He opened the door and extended his hand to help her out. "Please, leave your purse in the car. I'll escort you."

Bradley stood, blocking her exit until she slid the purse on the floor. Willow nodded and exited her car. She followed him around the building, through an ornamental garden full of life-sized statues of the gods. The boxwoods were trimmed in obsessively square increments besides the concrete walk. When they turned the back corner of the house, Willow saw a gathering of almost one hundred people. They were seated in folding chairs as if waiting for something to begin. Under a massive pergola, covered in honeysuckle, sat an imposing beauty of a woman, her golden hair swept back into a severe ponytail, except for a sweep of bangs caught behind one ear. Her bone structure was classic, her profile a model of perfect proportions.

Willow followed Bradley to stand before Olympia Steed. Her gaze scanned the variety of guests in the audience. Young children sat around their mothers, toward the middle. The young men in the group were randomly interspersed throughout the crowd. There was a lone older man, buff, erect, distinguished beard, and mustache adorning his handsome face, with the ever-present huge brown eyes like her own. Clearly, this man was the Alpha stallion and mate to most of the women here, including Olympia.

Willow knew enough about the culture of horses to know stallions are protectors of the herd, especially protectors of their mares from challenges offered by other stallions. However, it is the Alpha female and her Beta female helpers who actually run the herd. They decide who stays and who goes, where the herd will eat and drink and when they will move to safer lands. It fascinated her to see the Pegasus society structured in a similar way.

Olympia Steed was clearly the Alpha female, and Willow split away from Bradley to walk up the platform steps and confront her directly. She paused a respectful distance from Olympia and extended her hand. "Ms. Steed, I'm Willow Greer. I believe Khuno Maldonado wrote to you about me."

"Dr. Greer," Olympia replied smoothly. "We were informed of your coming. We have a tradition here at Black Mountain. We feel all the talk in the world is surpassed by one demonstration. Please remove your clothes and shift for us."

Willow glanced around in self-conscious confusion. "Take off my clothes in front of all these people?" There were twitterings and derisive snorts from the crowd.

A small boy wiggled in his mother's lap and looked up to her. "Mama, she doesn't know how to take off her clothes."

Willow's face flamed, and she stripped with a grim, emotionless expression. She drew in a deep breath and shifted, longing for the cover of her magnificent black and white coat. Within seconds there were awed, indrawn breaths from the crowd, and by the time her black-tipped wings manifested, the crowd transformed. She found all of them shifted and down on one knee.

This is a peculiar reception.

She glanced toward Olympia, who's Pegasus was a dark palomino with a white mane and tail. She was stunning, and like all the others, including the Alpha stallion, had taken a knee.

Willow spoke telepathically. "Um…is this your usual greeting for new herd members?"

Olympia's telepathic reply was amused. "Not exactly. Will you fly with us, your Majesty?"

Willow was nonplussed. "I…uh…I'm happy to fly with you…" her voice trailed off.

Olympia launched herself into the air, followed by the Alpha stallion. "Grace your people with a demonstration of your finest flight."

Willow mentally shrugged and decided to replicate her favorite aerobatics, those she enjoyed with Adam at Flight's End. Little by little, the audience members joined her in the air, and she particularly enjoyed teasing the yearlings as she performed an eight-point roll. The herd glided together as one. She decided to touch down in the polo field, which would give everyone a level and spacious place to land.

Throwing her self-consciousness to the winds, Willow shifted and waited as Olympia and her mate did the same. Olympia gestured to the dynamic man beside her. "Your majesty, may I introduce our Alpha stallion, Iago Caballo."

In his human form, he took a knee and bowed his head. "Majesty."

"Why are you all saying that?" Willow demanded.

One by one the shifters landed and encircled them. Olympia cocked her head and searched Willow's eyes for veracity. "Because, it is clear from your markings, your family is royal. From your movements in flight, it's evident you are the daughter of our lost queen, Summer Destry."

Willow's eyes grew even larger. "When did you lose your queen?"

Olympia shook her head. "Majesty, may we fly home, where we can be comfortable, and we will show you an account of your family's history?"

Willow nodded and shifted in seconds. Her mind sped.

This is what Khuno shared, he believed I was one of them. Should I even be thinking? Can they hear me?

She listened for telepathic conversation and heard none. Before she could form another thought, she made her landing and reclaimed her clothes. She looked up from buckling her belt to find her "subjects" all on bended knee once again.

She blushed and turned to Olympia. "Please get up and ask them to stop doing that."

Olympia cocked her head. "Majesty?"

Willow shook her head and waved her hands. "Please, tell everyone to stop bowing, and while we're at it, please stop calling me that! I can easily discern respect by your demeanor, and I'm much more comfortable with you using my given name. It's Willow, or if you want to be formal, I'm Dr. Greer."

Olympia bowed her head. "As you wish, Ma…" Willow slanted her a look, "Willow."

* * * *

"When one hundred and ninety-nine people travel over nine thousand miles, they need only their most precious belongings. Each of you needs to be ready to roll when my friend's aircraft has clearance to leave." Adam's tall body leaned over the conference table. He was tired. His flat palms held up his fatigued torso, as he repeated his instruction twice.

Okay, I've covered that. By the time they get there, the prefab homes should be up and ready for habitation. I've covered that food is being delivered, I've even covered that season-appropriate clothing will be waiting.

Adam winced at the hand waving from the back row.

"Our food stock comes from the loch and herds. What will we eat?" The man nervously rolled his soft cap in his hands.

Another voice cried out. "Is the water fresh?"

Jude stood next to Adam and picked up the answer. "There's nae danger of you going thirsty or hungry. Adam's found us quality fishing in the area. The water is crisp and cold and fresh." Jude pressed a hand on Adam's shoulder indicating he could be seated. "I have a presentation that will outline the opportunities for us. You'll remember we mentioned living off the grid, and having more comforts than ever, here in Scotland."

The room buzzed with incredulity. Jude waved a hand. "As your King, would I take you someplace I hadn't been? Nessa and I have slides from our short honeymoon, and you can see the bounty we've been given."

Adam rested his head on his palm as he slanted a look at the screen, and Jude described the site to his subjects. The buzz in the room turned to murmurs of excitement and gratitude as the people realized they were actually moving to the land of milk and honey.

Adam stood again. "Now, to make this all work efficiently, we'll take laborers and builders first. That should take about two weeks. Next, we'll move all able-bodied men. That should take one week. Finally, the women, children and the infirm. So, my friends, within six weeks at the latest, you will be relocated to a place beautiful beyond your wildest dreams. Beautiful enough to warrant leaving your homeland and the dangers inherent here."

The pessimistic school teacher stood. "You'd better send some women with those able-bodied men if you want to have the place ready for women and children."

Adam grinned. "You might be right, Miss Ferguson, maybe we should amend that to say all able-bodied men and any childless women who care to join them. Jude will be coming with the first wave, and Nessa will stay here until the last have boarded."

Adam scrubbed at his face, numb with fatigue. "I'm jet-lagged. If you'll excuse me, I'll go to the Queen's house and get some sleep. I'll be happy to address anyone's concerns, one on one, when I awaken. I'll be here in the days it takes us to sort out what to take and what to leave. I have to tell you, almost anything you can think of as a necessity will be provided new and in perfect shape there, so be sparing in what you decide to take with you."

Tonight, the Queen's home was his refuge. His mind boggled with all the telepathic questions bombarding him. He'd begun by shielding that portion of his mind, but his fatigue cracked the barrier, and he was reduced to a raw nerve. He saw himself in the foyer mirror and stuck out his tongue.

You're lookin' scruffy, lad.

He relished the total silence. When had he last had silence?

My last silence was sitting in a non-descript car at the airport as she dragged her carry-on behind her.

He made his way back to the bedroom and saw the duvet turned down and a soft woolen robe across the foot of the bed. He made for the utilitarian bathroom and was relieved the shower stall was king size. He wearily dropped his clothes where he stood and turned the shower hard and hot as possible. This evening he did well to lean against the wall; however, his thoughts weighed on him, and he slid to the floor.

The cold tiles felt raw on his ass but were a comfort on his tired feet as he walked them up the wall. He lay back and thought of the last shower he shared with Willow, wishing she was here now to give her loving emotional support. He felt as if he'd suddenly lost a body part without her, and damned if he knew how to get his stubborn woman back! It was too much effort to consider it now. He washed the critical areas of his body, toweled off and headed for what he remembered was a lumpy, feather bed. To his surprise, he found the feathers replaced by memory foam.

Oh my God! This feels so good! I'm going to sleep well. It was his last conscious thought, or so he hoped. What began as a reminiscence of meeting Willow, became a repetitious nightmare. At each junction of their meeting, his end of the conversations grew more contentious. The right combination of words eluded him, and he dug a deeper grave each time he spoke. His dreams were a complex and dispiriting flow of romantic failure.

Waking, he was more exhausted than when he fell onto the crisp, clean sheets. This morning, they were nearly twisted off the bed, and in his cold sweat, they stuck to him. The clock said he'd slept twelve hours, but he felt as if he'd worked hard labor.

* * * *

"Your parents were charged with retrieving a central piece of our folklore, an illuminated family tree from the nineteenth century," Olympia spoke reverently as she prepared fresh fruit from the garden. "Your father wanted to confirm your mother's lineage. There was a division within the herd, and it was your father's wish that Summer is seen as the rightful Queen."

"My Mother was on the throne, yet it sounds as if someone was challenging her?" Willow accepted the plate of fruit and bread and placed it on the carved coffee table before her. She was hungrier for the truth than for food.

"Your father was the alpha stallion, promised to Summer. Directly after she ascended to the throne, there was a challenge, it was inflammatory, but merely innuendo. Your father felt he could further secure her crown with the document."

"The certificate was part of an art collection in Williamsburg, Virginia. They were driving to retrieve it. The document was collected from the museum. When your parent's van was consumed by fire, it was lost.

They believed your small body was burned. It was weeks before we heard the news. I was a child; I remember the mourning period. We did not fly for three months, a month for each of your souls." Olympia's head bowed at her narration.

Willow found herself nibbling on the berries as she fought to find her earliest memories. "I was raised by a Roanoke family. Their older children said I was bought from a roadside fruit stand and my Daddy would correct them. He claimed I was brought by the Easter bunny."

"Your parents were killed on Holy Thursday." Olympia reached for a thick album. "These are family photos from your Mother's side. Your Father immigrated from our Greek herd to strengthen the bloodline, Leonides Megalos was known to us as Leon. Your coloring is your father's, he was a magnificent Pegasus. There are a few photos in the last few pages of the two of them, with you."

Olympia stood and bowed slightly. "I apologize, your Majesty. Customs die hard, and we are in awe of your arrival. I'll leave you with these albums too, they are clearly marked, and should you need any of us, my daughter, Lily, will answer your call." The statuesque blonde retreated from Willow, all the way to the large double doors that she pulled closed in front of her.

Willow slowly flipped through the pages. Her Mother was slim and spritely with butterscotch color hair. Her expressive brown eyes dominated her heart-shaped face. The most fetching image was a candid photo of Summer being hugged by both *her* mother and perhaps an aunt? Both older women were totally focused on the fresh-faced preteen in a dreamy linen dress, wearing flowers woven into her braided hair. In an ornate hand were the words: First Shift Celebration.

Oh, what a life to be celebrated! I spent my first shift awkwardly wondering when or if it could happen again at any moment. Am I prepared to see every benchmark of my mother's life celebrated where I clumsily thundered through?

Willow's reverie was broken by chimes. The double doors opened and Bradley, *his name was Bradley, right?* Stood in the doorway, his originally officious and cold manner replaced by something like charm. Now, a smile creased his expressive brown eyes, and his posture softened. "Dr. Greer, there will be a dinner in honor of your arrival. I was given the honor of escorting you to your quarters. We took the liberty of moving your luggage into your closet and have parked your car in the garage."

Willow snapped to attention at his new warmth, he was almost engaging. Once she reached him, he extended his elbow for her hand.

I'll bet you got your merit badge for escorting women across the street, too.

She couldn't think of anything to say; she was in a personal whirlwind. In a wing off the center hallway, Bradley used the single key on a ring she hadn't noticed he carried in his hand. The double doors opened on a simple, but elegant sitting room with multi-paned windows overlooking a rose garden. "We can make meals available for you here." He slid pocket doors open on a similarly designed dining room with a table for twelve. "There is a small kitchen for your personal use, behind that door." He pointed to the left with his entire hand, thumb tucked into his palm, military style. "Your dressing room is this way, also a bathroom and your bedroom." Bradley whisked her through the rooms, stopping in the center of the bedroom. She turned in a circle and took in the comfortable furniture with clean lines, completely different from the exterior architecture. French doors opened onto a walled flagstone patio.

"What are those doors?" She gestured to double doors on the opposite side of the bedroom.

"Those are your consort's quarters," Bradley whispered with a soft smile. He stood with his hands clasped behind his back. He was tall, taller than she'd thought when he cornered her in her car. His charm was in his smile, those brilliant white teeth dazzling her as his ebony eyelashes nearly fanned her. His riding gear emphasized his athletic prowess, right down to his well-developed forearms.

"Consort? Do you know who it is? Would it be the alpha stallion I met in the garden?" After all the empty sexual relationships she initiated when she was a shifter alone in the mortal world, she shuddered at the thought of sex for the sake of procreation alone. Iago Caballo was a striking man, the sort of gentleman used to advertise fine British motorcars or bespoke clothing, but she was not drawn to him. He was no Adam Lachlan. The thought of sharing the king-size bed with him made her wish they could shift into their Pegasus states and have it over in seconds…but then she'd spend long months as a pregnant Pegasus.

"Did something strike you funny?" Bradley inquired, his ready smile about to break at the corners of his handsome lips. Willow walked the perimeter of the room scrutinizing the oil paintings and graceful art tastefully placed among old books on dark wood shelves. Subtle down lighting enhanced the small copy of *Renown holding back Pegasus* by Eugène Lequesne. Willow reached out to touch the bronze, remembering she bought a small plaster of the same, in the Musée d'Orsay after seeing it on the southwest corner of the roof of the Palais Garnier, in Paris.

"I'm still trying to get used to all this."

Bradley nodded, opened the door, and held it for her. "Whereas your chambers have north garden access, your consort will have east garden access. Both gardens are walled and connect, should you desire to shift and fly together. I'm told it's quite exhilarating to fly with your lover…"

Had a looker like Bradley never experienced a love match? Willow's head snapped up at the thought. *Was Adam right?*

The sun was an orange semicircle resting on the peaks of Black Mountain when Bradley waved her to join him where the meeting began this morning. White chairs were gathered around tables, set for dinner. A string quartet practiced their program under the pergola. Informal beds of German chamomile, bee balm and yarrow offered up their tasty flowers.

Do the Pegasus shifters enjoy the taste as well as the scents?

"Dr. Greer, now that you've toured your wing of the home, you have about ninety minutes before our meal. You may want to rest and prepare for the evening." Bradley stood shoulder to shoulder with her, his gaze following Willow's.

"I get the hint this evening is going to go on for a while, right?" Willow dug her hands deep into her jeans. The rolling vista before her was magical, fascinating, and curiously inviting.

"It may, I hope it doesn't disappoint." Bradley nodded, and she felt his appraising gaze.

"You've convinced me, I think I'll check out that soaking tub." When Willow began to retreat, she felt the scrutiny of the staff.

* * * *

Willow entered the orderly walk-in closet and found her purse. Finding her phone, she pressed the home button. The phone was dead. She fumbled for the charging cord and carried it into the spacious marble bathroom. She opened and closed doors finding personal care items, lotions, shampoo, cotton squares, and perfumes. Heavenly perfumes, labeled with the same cursive script in the photo album, listing the essential oils in the compounded scents. Drawing the curtains in the bedroom and locking the double doors, Willow began undressing and walking freely in her "quarters". A silk robe hung on a padded hanger over a pair of memory foam slippers. Before she stepped into the sumptuous shower stall, she checked her phone. It was charging, but service wasn't evident.

Scrubbing away the road weariness, she shampooed her growing hair. It was twice as long as it was four weeks ago. Her muscles thanked her for finding the pulsing jets, they beat away the tension in her shoulders.

What is he doing right now? If it's five-fifteen in Kentucky, what time is it in Scotland or Chile? Where would he be? It's a moot point, I haven't seen one computer, and my phone is only good for snapping photos. Yeesh.

As Willow soaped her back, she thought about her siblings outside Roanoke. Her adoptive parents were long buried, and her oldest sister occupied the Shawsville home where the good Highway Patrolman lived with his wife and five children.

We were mutts. All of us cobbled together through family court when a child became too cumbersome. Daddy said the Easter Bunny brought me, and I finally believe him. Does Ivy, my spinster sister, have the backpack that came with me? Is there a rolled document shoved into it? I guess curiosity goes dormant when a toddler is brought home in the wee, small hours of the morning.

Solar-powered lights illuminated the garden. Night blooming white flowers opened as the moon rose over the peaks. Willow found a loose natural linen shift and angora shawl in the closet. It was more comfortable than jeans, or her usual chino slacks hugging her hips. Opening the French doors, she stepped into her consort's garden to make her way to the gathering.

* * * *

Adam forced himself to do yoga. Hopefully, the habit would bring him back to the place he needed to be. At Cat-Cow he remembered kneeling over Willow's hips as they bucked and stroked to sacred completion. From Downward Dog to Warrior One and Warrior Two, his desire to see her moving with him in unison clutched at his heart. It was all he could do to hold his poses, whether it was the Extended Side Angle Pose, or God help him, with the Tree Pose. When her face danced in front of his eyes, he squinted them shut only to hear her lilting laugh or her deep breathing. Distracted, he shook out his arms and legs and reached for his cell phone. Was she five or six hours behind him? He put the phone back down and went to shave.

With everything you're doing today, why shave?

His haggard face frowned, and he agreed. He dressed and jogged his way to the meeting hall where the combined clans gathered for their meals. Adam cocked his head toward the group, other than the sounds of utensils and low conversation it was… silent.

Yes!

There was no cacophonous chatter pushing into his brain.

Jude came around the corner with two cups of coffee. "Hey, good morning. How was that mattress? It was one of the things I stood my ground on." His expression was rested and his tone friendly. "Also, listen to this…" Jude motioned to the room. "I put my foot down last night after Nessa left the room, and I think I got 'em by their throats. I haven't heard any telepathic complaining. Sure, she has to be kind and rule benevolently, but I can be downright irascible. You looked rough last night when you left." Jude looked over his shoulder at Nessa and then back to Adam. "If you don't have a seat, join us."

Adam carried his plate to the back row where the royal table dined in relative splendor as opposed to the common members of the herd. He recognized the table he planed and finished as a gift to his mother when he reached puberty. The Queen Mothers sat at the sole table with individual chairs, all the other tables were roughhewn with bench seating. His regal mother, Petra, appeared in deep conversation with Nessa's mother, Zora. The two were not finding it easy to relinquish the reins of their kingdoms. The role of Queen Mother didn't appeal to either of them. Adam balanced his wooden plate in one hand as he pulled out a highly polished chair with the other. "Good morning," he murmured, his voice froggy.

Petra pinned back her shoulders and held her head upright. Chin out. "I'll thank you for greeting us properly with a bow and appropriate title."

"Sorry." Adam bowed from the waist to both women. He couldn't help sliding in a jibe against her haughtiness. "Queen Mother Petra, Queen Mother Zora, good morning."

Zora raised a gentle hand and nodded. Petra screwed up her face in agitation and admonished. "Never forget who I am." She inclined her head regally. "We give you leave to sit."

Adam bobbed his head in their direction and went to the next table to sit with Nessa and Jude, among the commoners. Nessa raised a brow as he sat. "I see you've been corrected by the protocol patrol."

"You don't have to hit me twice with a rolled-up newspaper. I fear they will lose more and more protocol when the freedoms of Chile sink in. This will be such a revolutionary change for the people."

Jude took a bite of the hearty oatmeal, always the staple breakfast of the clans. "Is your lovely Willow coordinating things in Chile?"

Adam's fair brow furrowed, and he let out a gusty, way-too-revealing sigh. "No, one of the guardians at Serenity found a herd of Pegasus shifters in Kentucky. He thought they might be relatives of hers. She's there now. Should be about midnight her time."

Jude and Nessa shared a glance, and she offered, "It will feel like a long time until she returns."

Adam put down his utensil, and his hands rubbed his thighs. His thousand-mile stare spoke for him.

* * * *

Willow approached Olympia, Iago, and Bradley. They bowed their heads, and she waved it off. "Honestly, stop that!" She grimaced and shook her head. "Good evening to each of you."

"How was your tour?" Olympia smiled at Bradley.

"The quarters are lovely. Ah, Bradley, you kept that key you used to open my quarters. Is it mine?" The trio bounced a glance between them as Bradley dug into the back pocket of his chinos and held up the key ring. Willow reached for it and slid it into her pocket. "What's on board for tonight?"

Iago gestured toward the many tables set for dinner and the people filing in to be seated at them. "As much as I'd like to tell you this banquet is entirely in your honor, I have to confess this is the quarterly State of the Herd presentation, and the judgments of disputes."

Olympia joined in. "Actually, this is fortuitous, since it will give you the opportunity to hear the most current status of our herd."

Willow smiled shyly. *Great.* She began her stroll through the tables looking at the place settings and floral arrangements. Bradley was always a half-step behind her and to her left.

Wonderful, I have a shadow. This is just creepy.

She played with the key in her pocket to help soothe her jangled nerves. "Is there something you need from me, Bradley? I'm perfectly able to walk on my own."

"Watching you see all of this for the first time, gives me a new appreciation for what we have." Bradley's voice was soft and caressing. "Besides, you're absolutely a vision to watch."

Eww.

"That's kind of you. Maybe you'd like to watch from afar." Willow turned to greet one of her subjects and admire the family's stair-step children.

Bradley bowed humbly and gave her space.

* * * *

After a truly delicious vegetarian dinner, when all the plates were cleared away, and after the string quartet finished their performance, Olympia stood at a lectern to begin the State of the Herd meeting.

"Majesty," one department after another bowed to Willow and used her royal assignation. A woman in a blue business suit with practical shoes and a sensible haircut began. "I'm pleased to report, Black Mountain Coal, Inc. has now been reduced to one-half capacity. We have made progress with our retraining efforts, and most miners have expressed the desire to work with us in maintaining our wind turbines and solar power."

A tall man with salt and pepper hair took the floor. "Your Majesty, our trotters are doing particularly well on the track. Most importantly, the horses are healthy." His expression darkened. "Our herd's births have declined for the seventh consecutive quarter. Some of this is due to a decline in fertility. Unfortunately, some are also due to miscarriages and stillbirths. This indicates a lack of diversity in the gene pool."

Willow turned surreptitiously to Olympia and whispered, "Who is he?"

"Our vet and herd doctor," Olympia whispered back.

Willow finally felt a sense of worth as she listened. Gene pools and migration was something she understood professionally from her zoology studies. Perhaps she could help.

The tall man continued his report when she turned back. "I fear without an influx of new blood; our herd will dwindle and die within two generations. To survive, we must reach out to other herds and make our community so enticing that others are anxious to relocate to our beautiful setting."

"Majesty." A tall woman, who looked about fifty, and was therefore probably in her hundreds, stood next. "The balance sheet for the herd is up, slightly. Our intake exceeded our output by five percent last quarter and assuming our investments stay strong, we are in a livable position financially."

Willow realized in short order being the Queen was far more than a figurehead. If she accepted the role, she would be the CEO. The lives of the

Black Mountain Pegasus Herd would be in her hands. The enormity of it was overwhelming. It was a long way from being an educator and researcher. Politics never appealed to her. She sighed, not at all sure this was the life she wanted.

After the reports ended, Willow longed for her bed. Olympia stepped to the lectern again and announced, "In honor of Queen Willow's return to the herd, royal judgment of disputes will be handled by her this evening."

What?

Willow stood uncertainly, feeling as if she'd been blindsided and wondering if this was more a snare to show her incompetence than the honor Olympia announced it to be. She gathered herself and walked woodenly to the podium.

"Please bring your complaint before me," she commanded, in what she hoped was a confident voice.

"Majesty." A group of startlingly pretty, young women, who looked to be in their late teens, stood in opposition to a tall, slender, athletic woman with a shock of silver streaks highlighting her ebony hair. This woman was lovely in a mature way, as opposed to the youthful beauty of her rivals.

The young spokeswoman of the group stepped up. "Majesty, this woman, Elly, has been the alpha mare of our small herd for hundreds of years. She's becoming unable to breed. Her last foal was twenty-five years ago. She's stuck in the past, ordering us all around as if we're her servants. Telling us how to raise our young. Holding sway in decisions with our stallion. We believe it is high time she went to live at the crone's quarters."

Willow squelched a smile. "I see. That's quite a list of complaints." She supposed everyone expected her to question Elly. Instead, she looked into the audience. I'd like to speak to the stallion of this little family, please.

A man with a strong nose and chin, with broad, muscled shoulders and tall, sturdy legs stood and walked forward. His brown hair was neatly groomed as was his closely trimmed beard. When he spoke, his voice had a silken, gravel quality. Looking at him, it was immediately obvious to Willow why the young women were vying for his sole attention.

She nodded her head to him. "Your name, please?"

"Galen, Majesty."

"Galen," she echoed. "What have you to say about this dispute?"

"I try to stay out of the women's fray." He shuffled his feet. "I've found any suggestions I make, blow back on me. There's more of them than there is of me."

"I understand that. Do you understand what you would be losing if Elly was sent to the crone's quarters?"

"I do, Majesty."

"And what is your feeling about that?"

"Majesty, Elly has been the backbone of our family since our first breeding. She was my first mare, my first love, and she has always managed our household with wisdom and fairness. I rely on her counsel, and I know she guides the younger mares with grace. I would be devastated to lose her." He turned and smiled at a tearful Elly.

Willow nodded. "Well said, Galen." She looked at Elly. "Elly, how do you feel about the testimony you've heard tonight? Do you desire retirement? Are you able to continue in the role of the alpha mare?"

Elly brushed the tears from her cheeks and stepped to take Galen's hand. "Yes, Majesty. I am able to continue. I've thought our homestead needs renovation for some time. I believe some good honest work, where chatter and gossip are at a minimum, will be beneficial for all the members of our household. When it's time for me to retire, I'll be the first to ask, but that time is at least one hundred years away. Perhaps the mares of the herd who, like me, are more mature, should have meals together once a month to discuss how to transition the omega mares into more prominent roles as they mature."

Willow's smile was broad. "I see Galen's assessment of your wisdom is warranted, Elly." She spoke to the crowd in general. "It is my finding that Elly is an active and necessary member of this herd, and as its alpha mare, deserves all the respect due her. I do not agree that she should be retired, and I furthermore order the omega mares of the household to submit to her tutelage." She turned to Galen. "I do not expect another visit from your omega mares when you should handle your herd's business. Though stallions rely on the alpha mares to do much of the policing, you are still the protector of the herd. In this setting, where there are few predators, you must also protect from internal predators."

Galen looked abashed. "Yes, Majesty."

Elly and the omega mares wisely held their peace.

Willow glanced at her watch. "My friends, the hour is late. If there are more disputes to come before me, I ask that we adjourn until tomorrow morning, when I've rested and can make the best decisions. Until then, let me thank you for your warm welcome, and I hope to get to know each of you personally in the future."

Bradley stepped forward and offered his arm to lead her from the meeting place and back to her quarters. Her departure was greeted by increasingly loud murmurs from the crowd.

* * * *

Once in her sitting room, she dropped into a chair and slid out of her shoes. Bradley handed her a tall iced glass of something green.

Willow stared at the glass as if it were a snake. She sniffed it. "What is this?"

"It's wheat grass, Dr. Greer."

She handed it back to him. "Don't you have anything stronger? Feel free to have this yourself."

He bowed slightly. "I may have something you'll like…"

He's gonna come back with some kind of tea that tastes like the underside of a lawnmower.

Instead, he returned with an iced grape soda on a tray and presented it with a bow.

"Now we're talking!" He hovered over her. She looked up at his handsome face. "Why are you standing over me?"

"Dr. Greer, it is not permissible to sit in the presence of the Queen unless invited. And, I am here to serve you."

"Oh, this is killing me. Look, Bradley, I give you leave to sit or stand or do jumping jacks or anything else you desire in my presence from now until the end of time, okay?"

Bradley looked appalled to the point that Willow had the rebellious urge to tell him to change his face lest it freeze that way. "Majesty, that would be a most egregious violation of etiquette." He explained pursing his lips.

Well, isn't he a doll baby when he does that?

Willow shrugged. "There are gonna be a lot of etiquette changes around here if I decide to stay." That announcement visibly took him aback. "Starting with, I don't know, do I have to make some kind of decree to say, do not call me Majesty? To call me Willow or Dr. Greer? This is not the dark ages. I don't want all this silly formality."

The man actually caught his breath at her pronouncement. "This would change our society." He gasped. "It could lead to social anarchy…"

"If you want me for a queen, you're gonna have to risk it." She sighed and took a sip of her soda, realizing he wouldn't leave unless she dismissed him. "I'm tired, Bradley. I'll see you in the morning. Please, let me sleep until I wake on my own. This has been a stressful few days, and I need to recharge."

"I'll let the petitioners know, Dr. Greer."

Willow felt guilty, but she'd been in several different time zones and a world of turmoil in less than a week. If she was to settle disputes wisely, she needed rest. "I have no idea how long I'll sleep. It will be my luck to wake with the sunrise, but I'll come out when I'm ready."

Bradley stood, bowed slightly, and with a "sleep well," and left the room.

14

Adam was relieved beyond measure to get out from under his mother's reproachful gaze. If she lived to be four thousand, she'd never admit this change was necessary and beneficial to the clans. Thankfully, Nessa and Jude seemed to have a good handle on things, and as the duly elected leaders of the clan, didn't have to take the same grumbling he was subjected to.

Seventeen hours in a C-130, with farm equipment and backhoes, wasn't conducive to rest. Adam, Matt, and Jude used the time for planning the first phase. Foundations needed to be dug, and concrete poured, fields needed to be designated, cultivated, and fenced. Pasture land had to be checked for hazards and fencing, and they had ten days to do it all. Modular housing would be flown in and placed by helicopters, which was a help, but there was still a great deal of city planning and construction to do. With the limited modern skills of the dragonfolk, Adam was not quite sure how to go about it all

It was unbelievable a phone signal was able to penetrate time, space, and a C-130, but it did. "Lachlan." He answered tersely, desperately wishing for more leg room in his cramped seat.

"Hi, Dumdum. Where are you?" His sister Izzy was irrepressible.

"What do you want?"

"I'm buying sheep. When can we transport them?"

"We don't even have fencing yet. I'm gonna say, six weeks from now. Sheep are nice. What we really need is something like a city engineer who can help us establish a colony of two hundred off the grid. Where do you advertise for somebody like that, willing to keep the project off their resume?"

Izzy was quiet for a moment and then began hesitantly. "I have a submissive who happens to be a civil engineer. I know they're between projects at the moment, and I believe if I asked to keep this on the down low, that would be okay. As long as we pay well, of course."

Adam sat forward eagerly. "At this point, I'm going to stop just short of saying he can name his price. I'll be incommunicado in a few hours after we land until we can get some towers up. Please, make the pitch, sign the contract, and I'll arrange with Rick to have a jet standing by as soon as your guy is ready."

"Sure, bro. Rely on me. I'll handle everything."

"You're the best, Iz, we surely need this help."

"Oh, you're gonna get it. It's my pleasure."

Matt looked up from his catalog of water purifiers. "What's up?"

Adam wore a Cheshire cat grin. "I think within the next three days; we'll have a city planner."

* * * *

The cold morning light filtered through the sheers in Willow's bedroom. The sun was slow to wake her. For a moment, she thought she felt Adam's long, muscled body next to hers, but it was a firm pillow she wrapped her arms around to go to sleep. His scent was so musky and male. She wrapped her arms around the pillow and tried to remember exactly how he smelled. She'd lost count of the times she'd checked her phone to see if he'd tried to call. Tower strength was iffy at best on the mountain. Mail delivery was regular, but she received nothing.

She'd mailed a letter to the girls in Ireland, asking how they were settling in, and how the stable animals were doing, but she'd heard nothing in reply. How long does international mail take? *Am I an email and texting junkie?* Now, every time she thought of Adam, a dull ache started in her heart. That terrible, desolate, sinking feeling she would never be happy again if she was forced to live without him.

What could she do? Running after him certainly wouldn't help the situation. Maybe, if she could go down to the coal mining office, she could get a call through to Cat or Anna and try to find out what was going on. She'd made a decree early last week to have phone and Wi-Fi towers installed around the settlement, but it took time, and with each passing day, she drifted further away from Adam.

* * * *

Andy, the grizzled trainer of the herd's horses, clicked the stopwatch and glanced at the trotter's time. He shook his head and looked at Willow. "He's off another tenth of a second today. That's the third day in a row he's lost time. I wish I knew the problem; I've checked him over forelock to fetlock, and I'm damned if I know why.

Willow stood and ran down the bleacher steps. "Let me talk to him. Maybe he knows something we don't."

Andy was stunned. "Talk to him?"

Willow approached as they were taking the light racing cart off and unharnessing the colt. He was a sweet thing, and easy to talk with. He showed her pictures of himself feeling weak, coughing in the field, and sometimes at night, shivering. "I'm sorry, Pickles, we're gonna help that right away, and we'll give you a couple days off to start feeling better."

Andy limped up to them, bow legs moving arthritically. "What'd he say?"

"I think he may have a selenium deficiency. He's feeling weak and run down. I think we should have the vet see him and draw some blood to be sure. Adding a little selenium to his diet would be a good idea, and let's give him some pasture time, while he rebuilds his strength."

Quizzical stares from the old trainer and his grooms followed her as she led the horse away to walk. "Uh…" Andy jogged a little to catch up to her. "How can you talk to him?"

Willow stopped and turned, amazed. "You mean you can't?"

"No. I've never heard of anyone who could talk to animals in their human form, precious few can even talk to horses while in Pegasus form."

Willow tilted her head and considered. "I've always been able to talk to animals. Any animal from my cat to a bald eagle. I thought all Pegasi could."

Andy shook his head. "That's quite an ability. You need to tell…well hell, I guess you're the queen…but you need to tell Olympia or the vet or somebody. You have any idea how much this could help our herds?"

"I'm sorry, I thought all of you could do it."

"No, ma'am! Eric!" He waved the groom over, "You walk Pickles here, give him a good comfortable rub down and put him in his stall for now. I'm sending the vet over to check him out."

Willow waved goodbye and said, "I'll stop by the vet's office and ask him to come to see Pickles. I have some questions for him anyway."

Dr. Frasier's office was located upwind of the main stable, and in the context of the herd, functioned not only as a vet to the racehorses but also as the local doctor. The office was always jammed, but being queen afforded her some clout, and Willow was ushered into his private office without delay.

The tall, salt and pepper vet with kind, regular features, greeted her warmly. "Your ma…"

"Stop that! It's Willow."

He grinned and rubbed at the bridge of his nose. "Old habits die hard. How can I help you, Willow?"

"First, you can talk to animals, right?"

He stared at her a long moment. "No." A quick frown creased his forehead. "Can you?"

"Will you think I'm crazy if I say yes?"

He paused a little too long. "That depends, I'd ask for proof, I think."

She motioned him forward. "Okay, let's see your patients together. I'll tell you what they say. You tell me if I'm right."

It took three appointments, in which Willow was dead-on accurate, to convince him.

He massaged the dog's back in the area he'd told Willow was sore and looked up at his queen. "Could your mom or dad talk to animals?"

Willow's smile was sad. "No idea. I was a baby in an infant seat when the accident occurred. I only remember my adoptive parents. I just know I've been able to talk to animals ever since I can remember. I thought older members of the herd might know. I thought everybody could do it."

"No, we are telepathic with each other when we're in Pegasus form, but not with other animals, and for sure not in human form."

There was a discreet knock on the treatment room door, and the Doctor opened it to find Olympia, Iago, and Bradley. Willow was unhesitatingly alarmed. "Is something wrong?"

Olympia stepped forward. "No, dear, just something we need to talk with you about, right away."

The kindly doctor gestured down the hall. "Go ahead and use my office, it's private." Willow followed and waved goodbye to the doctor.

The office walls bore the standard diplomas and certificates lost among the dozens of framed photos of babies he'd delivered, winning racehorses and jumpers. A framed photo of his family stood on the desk that filled up the floor space. Two comfortable chairs were pushed closer, and a rolling stool occupied the corner. Olympia gestured Willow into the chair behind the desk. Willow looked around uncertainly and asked. "What's going on?"

Olympia was forthright. "It's come to our attention you are in season."

"I'm in what season?"

"You're ovulating, dear."

"What? How can you know that? I don't even know that." She thought back to her last period and counted forward. "Although, that might be true, how did you know that?"

Bradley rolled forward on the stool. "It's the scent, it's unmistakable." His nostrils flared, and his brow rose knowingly.

Willow spun half-way around in the chair and took a whiff of her clothes. "I don't smell anything."

Bradley's lips curled. "I do."

Well, this is too personal for comfort... "Look, I appreciate your interest in my well-being, I guess. But this seems a little invasive, and I'm not sure why…" Willow pointed to the three shifters, "the four of us are discussing it."

Iago's eyes smiled before his lips; the mature gentleman stroked his mustache. "Customarily, as your consort, Bradley would discuss this matter with you alone." He gave Bradley a fleeting, derogatory glance. "But he seemed disinclined to have the conversation with you, so we're here on behalf of the herd."

Olympia sat further forward on her chair. "It's our custom to officially recognize the Queen's consort before her first season. We also have a formal ceremony celebrating your first coupling."

Willow raised her hands. "Whoa, whoa, whoa! When were you going to tell me this? I've been here a week, and all I knew was that the consort's bedroom adjoined mine. Who just decided Bradley would be my mate? I don't have any say in the matter?" Bradley abruptly stood at her tone, bristling affront. "No offense, Brad."

"My lineage is as royal as yours. My children are born strong and healthy. The women of my herd have amorously vied for my attention." He turned to Olympia. "Was I brought here to be insulted?"

You can't compete with a dragon, simply not possible.

"I recognize all of this is situation normal to all of you. I walked into this community thinking I was a freak. Until I was told about the herds of Pegasus shifters, I thought I was alone. You know there's no handbook on my nightstand that says how the queen is mated. You didn't cover that." Willow spun the chair away from them. The room was silent, and her voice was soft and slow. "If I choose to stay," Willow turned back around to face them. "I will select my own mate." Bradley sat down heavily on the stool. "I do understand your good intentions to continue the breed; however, I'm not a broodmare. In my life, I was an educator and a researcher. I chose my male companions on attraction, not pedigree." Willow turned the chair in Bradley's direction. "You have wonderful qualities, and you've been very attentive, but you cannot honestly say you're in love with me. We barely know each other." The irony of her words echoing Adam's was not lost on her.

Bradley rose and leaned over the desk, the chords and veins of his arms stood out against his tan skin. Black chest hair peeked out of his tailored shirt. "Give me a chance, Willow. I promise I won't bring you any more wheatgrass." His cute smile accentuated his point, and he gave her a little wink. It was the first time she felt he made an effort to talk to her and not the queen.

Maybe…maybe if he relaxes and we're together…I'll find something I didn't see before.

****

Iago folded muscular arms over his chest, his lips twitched under his salt and pepper mustache, and he announced to the room in general. "This is a good beginning." He stood and placed a fatherly hand on Bradley's broad shoulder. "Remember, son, Willow is a queen, but she's a woman first. Woo, the woman, win the queen."

Bradley blinked at him, and Iago felt the tentacles of doubt upon him. Their Queen was a submissive, but she would only submit to an alpha male. It was yet to be seen if Bradley could fulfill that role for her. He extended his hand to Olympia, and for the first time ever, gave her an order. "Come, Olympia, let's give these young people some privacy."

* * * *

Bradley beckoned Willow, and she took the hint. Wordlessly, her intended consort led her out of the building toward a brightly painted Gator utility vehicle. The hood bore the ornate logo of the racing stables. Iago and Olympia sped away on their own cart. When Bradley turned up the hill towards the white house, Iago and Olympia were nowhere in sight.

"You must understand how intrusive that meeting was." Willow declared, her face still red. "You may have been raised to believe these discussions are situation normal, but I wasn't." They rode in silence for a few yards.

"I can see it disturbs you." Brad's gaze left the path to search her face. "I don't know if we met in the real world if I'm the type of guy who turns you on." The crickets were deafening.

Perhaps a year ago... Willow thought.

"They see us as stock that will improve the herd." Bradley defended reasonably.

Willow's hands flew to her ears. "I don't want to hear that doctrine. I need some time to absorb all this."

Brad nodded and drove a bit slower. "How would you feel about joining me for a picnic, tomorrow? There's a bucolic stream I visit when I need some 'me' time. I could pack a lunch, and we could go there and have some 'us' time." He turned to her. "I'll even give you the keys. If you don't trust me, you can leave me in the woods."

Baby steps, she thought. "Sounds okay to me. I hope I can spend the rest of today alone. Please, instruct the community I need this time without interruption."

* * * *

Looking down at the couple below them, Iago observed Willow's body language was defensive, and Brad seemed defeated. She jumped off the slowing cart and trotted to her garden gate. Brad sat a moment with his head down and then goosed the pedal, leaving a cloud of dust as he headed away.

Iago frowned heavily and turned to Olympia. "This isn't good. There's no attraction between them."

Olympia huffed. "It's her duty."

"Not in her mind. She will never accept duty over romance."

* * * *

Willow's morning was brighter. She and Brad were more relaxed as he spread out the checkered tablecloth and basket in a field of clover next to the stream. "They don't drink here, do they?" Willow poked through the basket of food.

"No, none of us grew up with it, and with our insulation from the regulars, as we call them, we've avoided it." Bradley opened a grape soda and offered it to her. She nodded and took it from him. Their fingertips grazed, but there was no spark.

Not a bit.

He uncovered a tray of fruit and cheeses and offered her first choice. *Do we talk about family? The queen's duties?* He stretched his long, handsomely muscled body along the other side of the tablecloth. From the bottom of his well-made boots to the top of his wavy ebony hair, he could have sold luxury cars or estate homes.

He is beautiful. A beautiful, beautiful man.

While she picked at the food, she felt him scrutinize her choices. *Are these supposed to be the silent pathways of the heart?* Leaning on his elbow, Bradley tossed a shiny apple repeatedly. The sun was warm, and the leaves played a pastoral melody.

Wistfully, Willow held out grapes. "Why do people want to talk to each other when silence is so..."

"Relaxing? Comfortable?" He dropped the apple, accepted the deep purple fruit, and began snapping them off their stems. He popped one between his rich lips and pushed it into his cheek. His lips moved sensually as he chewed the grape. He swallowed and repeated the act over and over until he tossed the empty stem onto his napkin.

No lust. No visualizing him nibbling on me.

"Yeah. I wish we came with fact sheets; you know...The things people want to find out about other people." Her smile was lazy, about as languid as her presence at this picnic.

"From what you've said, you weren't aware of other shifters. What do you want to know?"

So, he puts me in the position of asking him questions. Does he want to know anything about me? With all those good looks, could he be vain? What can I ever know about him beyond what I see? See, was the safest word.

"Tell me something that perhaps only I will ever know about you, Bradley."

What will you give me to remember you by?

He stared to their left, focused on a bird picking at the ground, and frowned as if absorbed.

Is he trying to phrase everything to make as good an impression as possible? Does he think I will be content with small offerings, or will he exert himself to seem unique?

"I have a twin. My brother was sent to the Austrian herd. I haven't seen him since we were three hundred years old." He drew a long drink on his grape soda and admitted, "It's not public knowledge, I arrived here just before the New Year. Few people know me here. What about you?"

Ah, turnabout is fair play.

"I...I... actually... Within my supernatural world, I know a community of dragon shifters and four vampires."

His smile was reticent. "I remember my mother...she was loving, I was raised by a fastidious herd. They knew Jacob, and I would be alpha stallions, and that was drilled into us." He sat up and crossed his long legs.

Adam's legs are longer.

Bradley's trousers rose, and she saw the black hair on his tanned legs between his socks and trouser hem.

Adam's leg hair is golden, like his thick eyelashes.

"You were raised with a strong sense of destiny, but you don't seem spoiled. You seem to be a fine person." Willow spread lemon curd on a blueberry scone.

Am I killing time? Is he trying to make time?

He sat up but didn't make a move across the tablecloth. "Do you have any hobbies?"

He's not very stimulating...how many mares have thought that?

"I'm a sculptor, it's a hobby. Most of it I give to my mares, sort of a courting ritual."

"I'm an equestrian. I used to show a lot, but work interfered."

"Ironic, isn't it? You're a Ph.D., right." He aimed his forefinger at her like a pistol. "That's the Dr. Greer you specified if we wished to be formal."

Oh, you're deep. He's running on flattery. She needed to open herself to her Dom. She needed to be desired, taken and owned…but not by Bradley.

The meal ended, punctuated with them dodging anything of a sexual nature. Bradley inhaled deeply when the breeze picked up and the sun ducked behind a cloud.

He fell on his back and looked over at her. "If you only knew how your Pegasus calls mine. I'm intoxicated." He rolled onto his stomach. "It's all I can do to stay on this side of the tablecloth."

Poor honey. I can only imagine what he's scenting.

"I don't want to make you uncomfortable. That's gotta be hard—no pun intended."

Brad balanced his chin on his hand and shot her a rueful look. "I respect that, and your feelings. What a waste of a beautiful day. It would feel invigorating out here." He pounded the clover and shook his head. Willow took the cue to rise, gather up their empty bottles and paper waste. "So, is this our first date?" Bradley asked as he sat up awkwardly, shielding his obvious response to her allure. He rolled up the tablecloth and pressed it into the empty picnic basket. They stood, shoulder to shoulder, his admiration shining on her. He let her precede him to the cart, and as she passed, he dropped his nose to her neck.

Willow started and stepped out of range. "How many first dates have you been on?" she yelped.

"They've kinda kept me a monk since I've been here…"

Willow stepped further away and took in the sky over the mountain range. "You mentioned your mares and your children." Her tone was wary.

Brad seemed to get her message. "The aim was finding the right royal for me. But back in Greece, let's just say, I led an active nightlife." They resumed their walk.

"You were just a regular tall, dark, and handsome!"

"Well, there are a lot of them in Greece." He laughed.

He put everything in the back of the Gator and reached out for the keys.

Willow sat on the bench seat and handed them over. "Ah…yes, you gave these to me in case of flagrant misbehavior." He smirked, keyed the ignition, and drew a long breath. Before Willow could move, he leaned in and stole a kiss. Bradley's lips were warm, strong, but not presumptuous. It only lasted long enough to brand his interest. Not long enough for even her lips to react. She caught his aftershave, tarragon, musk and sage and the scent of his clean ebony hair. She turned, stunned, and grasped the front dash.

No heat. And strangely, Willow was a little disappointed. Her life would certainly be easier if she felt some desire for the handsome man beside her, but there was none.

"Audentes Fortuna iuvat," he murmured as he turned the Gator around and headed to her residence.

"Fortune favors the bold." Willow shook her head and laughed deep in her throat. "Okay, here's one for you… In dubio abstine."

He frowned and goosed the gas pedal. "My Latin is rusty, but I hear something about abstinence…" He steered the wagon rapidly over the rutted road.

"When in doubt, abstain." She tucked her chin and folded her arms over her chest.

"Right…" He was silent the rest of the way home, as was Willow, but her mind moved at warp speed.

* * * *

Delivering their new employee, Matt brought the chopper in for a landing, a wry smile on his handsome face. "Now I'm curious, Adam's sister, Isadora is a Domme?" Matt removed his headset and ran a hand through his hair. "That's a rich piece of news. Adam never mentioned that."

"I didn't mean to spill the beans. I figure I can be upfront about my kink. It looks like everyone here is related to the Consort Group." Brett finger combed Nordic-blonde hair straight back and raised the hood on the windproof anorak. "Mum's the word on the worksite, though, okay?"

Matt nodded with a smirk. "I have a feeling there will be a lot of other words today." He gestured to a trailer. "Adam is over in the contractor's trailer. Would you let him know I'm going to tie this baby down for the night, and I'll be over directly?"

Brett Lindquist was a dragon shifter from a minute clan in northern Norway. Living with the extreme weather within a clan environment, taught Brett at an early age to learn a profession and get the hell out of the frozen north. Dressed for travel in trekking boots, zip-off softshell pants, and a vivid blue jacket hugging an athletic frame, the Civil Engineer made long graceful strides to the enclave. With a stomp of both feet and a knock, she waited. Adam threw open the door and filled the doorframe with his physique.

As the new employee dropped the hood on the bright blue anorak, Adam's greeting died on his lips. His jaw dropped.

Brett removed supple leather gloves and extended a well-manicured hand. "Hallo, I'm Brett Lindquist."

Adam blurted, "You're a woman!"

"I know that. I'm also a civil engineer with experience in off-grid planning, collection, and management of water, and I've handled much larger municipal infrastructure projects. My last green project was for a village of five hundred in Denmark, I can get the references if you like. May I come in?"

Adam re-gathered his wits. "Oh, of course. I'm sorry, I wasn't trying to be rude. It's fine that you're a woman. Izzy just didn't mention that." His teeth gritted. "She's such a prankster. We're grateful to have your advice."

"I'm happy there was a time in my schedule."

"C'mon over by the heater. You drink coffee? Are you hungry?"

Brett rubbed her hands together. "Don't worry about me, I'm used to the cold. Some coffee would be great. I see you're in the beginning stages of clearing land and pouring foundations. How many workers do you have?"

"I have thirty men from our clan, and there are also some men from the modular building company. I'm afraid you're the only woman, I hope you're okay with that."

She removed her anorak, exposing a silk-knit, crew neck top revealing every inch of her insanely sculpted, womanly body. Adam swallowed. Hard. "I'm fine as long as you don't expect me to cook and clean for everyone." She joked. "Actually, I'm used to being the only woman, because I'm typically in on the ground floor of projects, and I need to be on site to do that."

She turned, folded her jacket, and laid it on top of the backpack. As she bent at the waist, her khaki pants hugged every curve of her exquisite heart-shaped ass and toned thighs. Adam swallowed again, grateful when Matt burst through the door.

Matt stopped on the top step; head tilted as he watched Brett stuff the jacket into her gear. He flashed Adam a huge grin. "Looks like I got here just in time!"

Adam shook himself. "What do you mean?"

Matt pointed at the workers, shovels in hand. "It looks like they were about to dig in…" He trailed off, watching Brett hunt for something in her bag. Adam couldn't blame him; they could see every muscle responding to her movement. "You know, the drain tiles…" He trailed off again, tilting his head to the other side, as the men watched her squat to dig through her duffle bag.

"If there's anything you need, we have all the tools and equipment…" Adam began.

"Here it 'tis!" Brett said in her lilting Scandinavian accent. "I need my tablet." She straightened up, and her voluptuous breasts jostled into place.

Both men swallowed hard, and a pie-eyed smile passed between them. Adam found his voice. "I hate to put you to work the second you arrive, but I don't want the men to waste time digging unless you approve the plan."

Brett seemed oblivious to the disturbance in the force. "Right. No problem, I was looking for my tablet because I have the topographic map already loaded. That will show us proper placement. Let me get my jacket on, and we'll take a look."

Matt and Adam preceded her out of the trailer. Adam watched the reaction of the men to the stunning blonde. "I think we'll have you bunk here in the construction trailer. It's warmer, and it has a lock…"

* * * *

The Gator pulled up to the entrance of Willow's quarters. "Come in with me, Brad, may I call you Brad?" He smiled and nodded. "I think it's time for you to move into the Consort suite."

Brad's grin grew, and he aimed for more of his previous moves. Willow put a finger on his lips. "No. It's not for that. We have work to do."

Brad, confused, followed her anyway. She opened the door between the two suites. "Sit. Let's talk."

"You were quiet all the way home. What's going on in that mind of yours?"

"Have you ever been in love?"

Brad frowned. "I don't know if it's love. Maybe it's just infatuation…"

Willow searched his face. "What's her name?" She was fairly certain he wasn't going to say her name.

"Diana. She's a Greek Pegasus, a first cousin to you from your father's side, so she's royal." His eyes and voice turned wistful. "She's beautiful and graceful and kind. She has this incredible dark wavy hair, and in her Pegasus, where we're mostly paints, she's Appaloosa. She has this great sense of humor and a musical laugh…"

Willow frowned. "Why isn't she your alpha mare? Clearly, you have feelings for her."

Bradley sighed. "You must have figured out by now that royal matches are arranged, not romantic. I imagine when she reaches majority she'll be matched with Jacob, my twin. So, it's best for me to live my role and not dwell on my childish heart."

"I believe that's terrible. We may have Pegasus forms dwelling within us, but, to fashion what should be primarily human lives around breeding patterns and bloodlines is absurd, in this day and age. No wonder there are few vital Pegasus herds left. I'm doing something about this immediately."

"What? You want to change the tradition of thousands of years?"

"You bet your ass I do. If I'm queen, then I have the authority, and there will be changes made."

Bradley leaned back, an appalled look on his handsome face. "What do you plan to do?"

"Can I be absolutely straight with you? You're not gonna spill to Olympia and Iago, are you?"

"As long as you're not planning to hurt anyone, I'm with you."

"Far from hurting anyone, I plan to bring this herd into the twenty-first century. The others around the world can follow or do what they like, but the Black Mountain Herd is about to break the mold, starting with this ridiculous, archaic breeding system."

"But you're the queen…"

Willow pulled her chair close to his. "Brad, I have no intention of staying here and ruling this herd because of some accident of birth."

Brad leaned back in the club chair and threw up his hands. "Then, what are you gonna do?"

She stood and began to pace. "You could call it the queen, or you could call it the president or the CEO. One thing's for sure, whoever heads this herd should be versed in business and perhaps in politics. It's obvious to me that I don't have those qualifications. If I were running things, I'd suggest the herd be modeled after a city government."

There was a knock on the door. Lily stuck her head in. "Do you require anything, Dr. Greer?" Lily asked, a fetching combination of Olympia and Iago, tasked with waiting on the Queen, and perhaps, spying on the Queen?

"Yes, thank you, Lily. When dinner comes, please send two to my quarters. Mr. Dale and I will be dining privately tonight."

"Yes, ma'am." Lily agreed happily; her teenaged heart obviously aflutter with images of romance.

Brad grinned ironically. "You know that will set the herd tongues wagging!"

Willow threw back her head and looked at the ceiling, letting out a hearty chuckle. "I suppose it will, but this idea of noblesse oblige is outdated. We are not special, and everyone else are not serfs. Royalty or not, people should be pairing off for love, or whatever else floats their boat. It should not be based on bloodlines." She turned to Brad. "You should be paired with Diana, assuming she agrees."

"What about you?" He prompted. "Have you ever been in love?"

Her head dropped, and then she looked pensively into the garden. "Yes."

"You don't look glad about it."

"It didn't work out quite the way I thought it would."

"Why not? Is he blind? Is he oblivious?"

Willow sighed and sat in her abandoned chair. "No, neither. I guess he's just not the commitment type."

"Why don't you tell me about it?"

A shrug was all she could muster. "The brutal truth is, I admitted I had feelings for him, and he told me we hadn't known each other long enough."

Brad leaned forward, elbows on his knees, hands clasped between his legs. "You said just that to me, yesterday. How long did you know each other?"

"About three weeks."

"Three weeks, and you told him you loved him?"

She gave the ghost of a smile. "No, I believe my exact words were, 'I think I like you more than the ropes.'"

Brad's brows nearly disappeared into the locks of hair falling over his forehead. "Really?" He regathered his wits. "And that's when he said you didn't know each other well enough?"

"Well, he said we'd been in an intense situation since we'd met, which was true." She sighed, remembering. "And then he said it's common for people who are in such situations to confuse the intensity for love." She sighed again, and her words drew out slowly. "And that's when he said he wanted us to get to know each other under more normal circumstances." She paused. "He said he liked me very much."

Brad's gaze bore into hers. "Do you trust him?"

Willow was silent a long time, considering his question. She answered truthfully. "I don't know if I have much trust in any man."

Brad shook his head. "I don't know how to advise you, except to say what he actually said—about this intense situation…" Brad grimaced. "That I gather included ropes—was not a good time to quantify your feelings. It seems to me, this whole thing hinges on whether you feel he's trustworthy. Are you willing to trust him enough to wait and see?"

"We're not in the intense situation anymore. I don't see him here, do you?"

"Does he know where you are?"

Willow's mouth snapped shut with the sudden realization unless he learned it from Khuno, Adam didn't know where she was. In fact, now that she thought about it, she hadn't gotten any kind of response from her letters to Cat and Anna. It was more than a week.

Brad's penetrating look continued. "I'm gathering from your expression; he may not know where you are."

Willow nodded with horror. "Yeah."

"It's none of my business, but if I were in love with someone, I'd at least let them know where I was…"

* * * *

Cat, with Rick and Anna leaning over her shoulder, enjoyed Matt's virtual tour of the progress the builders were making at Mount Viejo. "The foundations have been laid to Brett's specs. Again, Brett is our city planner. There she is!" Matt focused the lens on tight leggings covering the lower half of a curvaceous body. "Wave to everyone, Brett!" The blonde abruptly uprighted herself, revealing her flushed complexion and a sweat-stained tank top. Dark half-moons collected under her generous breasts. Her wave created a sensual wiggle sending shock waves throughout her voluptuous body.

Rick leaned forward, mesmerized. "God's nightgown!" he breathed.

Anna pushed Rick back and leaned forward. "Did you see those jugs jiggling?"

Rick strove to be reasonable. "Well, once you get them going, it's kinda hard to stop…"

Cat's eyes narrowed. "Not in front of my husband!"

Anna patted her shoulder. "Don't worry, honey, he only has eyes for you."

Cat gave her an incredulous look. "He's still a man! She'd tempt the blind! Look at Rick!"

"She's got great equipment!" Rick agreed. "What are her credentials?"

Anna looked up. "I don't know exactly, but from here, I'd say 38/24/34."

"Man!" Rick agreed, awestruck. "Is she on my payroll?"

Anna gave him a withering glance. "She's on the Clan's payroll. And she needs to do her work and get out of there. Where's Willow? Adam's the one I'm worried about. No eligible man should be left alone with that…that…"

"Woman?" Cat suggested.

"I was going for a man-eater, but okay, woman," Anna replied.

"I sure hope Willow has written to him…"

* * * *

Adam's hand was on the doorknob when it struck him.

Oh my God, Brett is in there.

It was too early in the morning, and he was half-asleep. He knocked softly.

Maybe she's not even up yet. The sun has barely risen.

He heard music and footsteps just before the door swung open to reveal Brett wrapped in one of his bath sheets.

"Good morning! I was about to step into the shower. Do you need something?"

Adam tried not to gawk. "Uh…you really shouldn't answer the door without asking who's there. Especially, dressed like…uh…that…"

Her smile was sly. "Adam, are you sure you're a Master Dom?"

He used every bit of discipline inside him to look into her green eyes and nowhere else. "Yes, Brett, I'm sure I'm a Master Dom, and I'm saying this because you are the only woman in a gang of extremely horny, lonely men, and I don't want any fights or unpleasant repercussions."

She inclined her head in acknowledgment. "What did you need?"

"I left my toiletries and razor here last night. I need them."

"Of course!" She motioned him into the trailer. "Get whatever you need."

Adam forced himself to walk to the bathroom. He wanted to get what he needed and get the hell out.

Why in the world didn't I just ask Matt to let me borrow his stuff?

He shut the bathroom door to access the shelf in the cramped bath, stood before the tiny sink and tossed his travel-sized toiletries into the shaving bag.

His hands fumbled as the door bounced off his rump and Brett stepped in. She wiggled behind him to step into the corner shower. He leaned over the sink to allow her to pass, realizing with chagrin, he was half-mast already. Brett popped the frosted acrylic shower door closed and turned on the water with a breathy scream. "It's cold!"

"Yeah, sorry, no hot water."

She tossed her damp towel over the top of the door. "Then I will be quick."

"Me too. See ya later!" He was out the door before she could turn off the flow of water.

Matt was in the communal bathhouse when Adam stomped in. Matt turned at the sink, where he'd just lathered up. Adam dropped his jeans and headed for the shower; his hard-on impossible to ignore. Matt nodded at it. "Morning."

"That's not for you."

"Really, who is it for?"

"No one!" Adam growled. "Don't vampires get morning wood?"

"Not once we're off the slab." Matt looked at the shaving kit Adam dumped in the sink. "I thought you left that in your trailer last night. Isn't that what you said?"

"I just ran over and picked it up," Adam said with careful neutrality.

"I see." Matt spread the toothpaste on his brush and dropped his fangs. "The cold shower feels great in the morning."

"Yeah. I'm looking forward to it."

"Uh huh. Heard anything from Willow?"

Adam stepped into the shower and turned on the spray. He was sure, with Matt's vampire hearing, he would catch his muffled. "Fuck you!"

The frigid cold of the shower, connected to the glacier runoff, was daunting.

She wants you, Lachlan, she wants you bad! Why not? I'm an adult! What am I, a saint? I mean, Willow's the one who left. Why should I suffer?

You don't even know this woman, his conscience argued. She's just a piece of ass.

A great piece of ass. A submissive piece of ass. A spectacular piece of submissive ass!

Yeah, but you've done that before, and you know the way you feel the next day. Besides, you're leading a whole gang of men up here. You think they're gonna stand for you getting some and them not? Be the leader.

That's true. I am the leader. I need to be disciplined. I am a Dom. I'm a Master *Dom!*

What about Willow? An affair would be the death blow.

Yeah, she has no trust in men as it is, it would put a nail in the coffin. Now that Brett's got all the pictures and drawings sketched out, can't we send her to Serenity and let her work remotely? We can always bring her back on site if we need to.

Now you're thinking like Willow's lover!

That's easy for you to say, where is Willow to love?

Adam barely rinsed off the soap bubbles when he slammed off the water and dug his cell out of his jeans on the floor.

Matt, brushing his hair, cast a glance at Adam's frenzy. "I'll leave if you need to make a call."

Adam never answered, slung a towel around his hips and stalked out to his truck.

"Khuno, this is Adam Lachlan. I need the phone number of the place you sent Willow Greer."

There was a long pause. "Good Morning, Dr. Lachlan. How does this magnificent day find you?"

"Yeah, Khuno, it finds me anxious, it finds me frustrated, but mostly I'm in the dark. I need to contact Willow."

"Yes, Dr. Greer."

"Please, give me the phone number of her herd."

"I could contact them and have them call you…"

"Khuno, have you ever done any matchmaking?"

"I guide people to find the love within themselves and share it."

"Nope, you've never done any matchmaking. Sometimes when people in love fight, they do stupid things."

"Yes."

"I need to undo something stupid. You'd approve of that. I need her phone number."

15

Matt grabbed up the Consort SAT phone and headed for privacy. The phone rang twice before Rick picked it up. "Hey, Dear Boy! How's South America?"

Matt's voice rose. "It's getting hot down here. Have you seen Brett? Don't tell me what the women think."

"As a matter of fact, the women are right beside me, and you're…on speakerphone."

"Sure… Great…" Matt muttered. "Where the devil is Willow? Adam is a crazy man. You could slice the hormones with a machete."

Anna sniffed. "I'm sure Brett is egging that on. Did you see the way she's dressed? Of course, you did, you're a man!"

"Now, Cupcake." Rick patted her shoulder. "But returning to your Adam conundrum…"

Matt interrupted crossly. "She's not helping matters, that's for sure. We don't need any more drama down here."

"You know, I've been concerned about Willow." Cat cut in with solid reason. "We got one postcard before she entered the shifter community. What have they done with her? No calls and her phone isn't answering. All we know is, her address is in care of the Black Mountain Coal Company…"

Her mate chuckled. "And you want to swoop in and bring her out whether she's happy or not! She could be deliriously happy with her people."

"While Adam is delirious with pain?" Cat rebutted. "What's a vampire to do? Some friend you are!"

Matt's pained voice appealed to Rick. "Say something!"

"Well…" Rick hesitated. "A little interference could be arranged…"

* * * *

Khuno was the ultimate diplomat, Adam thought. He could refuse to give information all the while sounding like the most reasonable and helpful of men. Adam wanted to throttle him; he actually began to have some sympathy for Matt's conflict with the man. *Maybe Khuno only likes women?* Whatever Adam realized he was on his own.

He drew on his jeans over his last clean pair of boxer briefs.

Last pair of clean socks? I gotta get outta here.

Maybe Anna and Cat knew where she was? He drew his fleece vest over his flannel shirt and left the tent. He pivoted directly into Brett.

Jesus Christ, what is she almost wearing?

Her jeans were spray-painted on her long legs. Her cobalt blue down vest framed a thermal Henley unbuttoned down the front.

Did Mother Nature make those things sit up like that, or has she gotten surgical assistance?

She wasn't wearing a bra.

If she keeps parading like this, the crew will draw numbers to wait on her hand and foot, or worse. Time to say goodbye!

"Brett. Do you need me?" He rumbled, his voice low and dominant.

She stepped back, allowing him a full view of her stature. One booted foot posed at an angle to the other. A hip cocked upward as she stretched her long, toned arms up and bent her elbow to stroke at the back of her neck. It shifted the placket in her open shirt and riveted Adam's attention. "Yes, um, Adam. I was drawing on my body lotion when I saw you left your razor blades on the sink. I thought you would need them. Do you want me to put them in your tent?" She started to duck under the flap.

Adam caught her elbow and drew her back so quickly, she looked stunned. "I'll take them, please." He held out his hand. "I've been going over the plans, and I believe you've done such an excellent job, the crew can take it from here. I need you to return to Serenity, where we have a week's retreat reserved for you as a bonus. If we have any questions in the interim, you'll be nearby to answer. Your helicopter leaves in thirty minutes."

Brett pouted. "But, we didn't even get to know each other…"

Adam sunk his thumbs into his belt and levied a dominant stare her way. "I'm your boss. I know you did a great job. And most importantly for you, I know enough to cut your checks."

The mega-pout came out. "But you don't know me as a woman, and I want to know you as a man…"

Adam squared himself with her, Master Dominant bristling. "Look, Brett, I don't know what Izzie told you about me, and I'm not trying to hurt your feelings. You need to understand I'm not interested in a Dom/sub relationship with you. I have a woman in my life who I love, I'm not interested in anyone else. Your work here is done, go have a nice retreat, and go on from there. We'll call if we need you. Any questions?"

Brett looked as if he'd thrown ice water in her face, and he could imagine she'd not experienced many refusals in her life. Her eyes immediately cast downward; her lips followed. "Yes, Dr. Lachlan. I'll be ready."

Adam stepped around her and looked back. "Zip that vest up. This is a work site, not a Dungeon."

The empowered Dominant tromped the work site seeking Matt. There he was, in the shade, pondering the plan stretched out on a board balanced on two saw horses. "Hey, Sky King, I need you to move a mountain of a woman over to Serenity."

"Seriously? Now? She's the only entertainment we have!"

Adam shook his head. "I'm tellin' Cat!"

Matt threw up his hands, looked aside and then back to Adam. "She already knows. I sent Rick a gag reel of Brett's smooth moves last night. He was amused. The ladies… not so much. Sure, I'll wrap this up now, and go directly over to start my preflight. Anything you want me to bring back?"

Adam scowled. "A crate of single malt, not the cheap stuff, and Khuno's head."

Matt rolled up the plans and chuckled. "Hey, Sparky, now you're talking."

"And, oh yeah, I need clean boxer briefs and socks. They should be in my suite…"

Adam watched Matt's face twist. "I'm not going through your drawers! Eew! I'll have a crate of assorted sizes sent out. The crew could stand a change." Matt tapped his nose. "Damn vampire sense of smell."

* * * *

Two A.M. Willow stared at the digital clock mocking her. The darkness on Black Mountain was pervasive when it was lights out in the compound. She changed positions again and sighed. Kicking off the down duvet, she pounded the pillow. She thought about the morning she made Adam pound the bed with passion. Oh, crap! She fucked up. The one time the guy wasn't a snake trying to slither out of her life with lies, she'd run from him. All those other times… all the other bastards who didn't deserve her trust… she'd squandered it. This time…oh, God…

The hot tears were unstoppable. There was nothing as heartbreaking, she thought, as losing the one you love because of your own stupidity. Was it stupidity, or impatience, or insecurity?

I have a laundry list of screw-ups. Why should he ever want to see me again? Why should he look for me?

It hurt, damn bad, and she was scared. The sobs broke out over her attempts to stifle them. She gritted her teeth, pulled her pillow over her face, but was helpless to stop. Now, she was twisted in the sheets. Her nightgown wadded around her hips. She sat up, feeling strangled, and then slammed the clock down to obscure the time. Her sobs rolled out of her into loud cries. Through her loudest sobs, she heard a gentle knock from Brad's side of the door.

"Willow, are you okay?" His gentle voice solicited.

"No! I'm miserable!"

"May I come in?"

Willow looked around the room and pulled down the hem of her gown. "Sure. We can be miserable together."

He walked through the door wearing pajamas made from the same royal purple fabric as her gown. "Maybe we can cheer each other up."

Willow blew her nose into a tissue. "We could laugh at the pajamas. Dear God! Were they gonna dress us in matching outfits forever?"

Brad looked at her deep purple gown and shrugged. "They have a whole royal theme going. I see it, now." He cautiously approached the large bed.

"You've been wrestling with serious heartache in here." He gestured to the tortured linens. He sat next to her and pulled the duvet up toward her. "May I get you some milk or perhaps a chamomile tea?"

"I've never been a drinking woman, but tonight I would have started. I'd like a stiff drink."

Brad put his arm around her, and she let her head drop on his shoulder. "This sounds like a problem bigger than any glass or bottle could cure."

His comfort unleashed the dam. "I'm so stupid!"

"You're not stupid, you made a mistake, maybe even a few of them. In your heart, you have the answer. You've told me countless things about yourself. I know the answer is in there." The suite door opened, and Olympia trotted to the bedroom doorway. Brad jerked his head at her. "How dare you come into the Queen's bedchamber uninvited!" Olympia gaped at him. "We give you leave to depart. Now." Olympia stepped back ingratiatingly, and once out of sight, Willow heard her run and close the suite door behind her.

Willow chuckled through her tears. "Guess you told her!" Brad truly was a dear. His coal black hair askew, and his large chocolate eyes full of sleep melted the part of her heart that should have loved him.

He hugged her tighter for a moment. "I do know my role."

Even if you can't exercise it fully.

"Talk. Tell me what you think you need to do." Brad urged.

"I need to make up with Adam. I need to tell him I know I was wrong. I don't know how that will end, but I know I don't belong here. I have no desire to rule anybody, hell, I can barely rule myself." Brad was mute. "I've been here two weeks, and I haven't received a letter or a call. I feel so alone. I feel stranded."

Brad was quiet a long time. "Do you think you should have mail or a call?"

"Yes. At the least, I should have mail from the University, my final paycheck, my forwarded mail from my apartment. And, I'm sure my friends in Ireland would have called me after they got my postcard."

"I hate to suspect this, but, I wonder if they would dare cut off your incoming communication? We know why you haven't received any cell calls." Willow stared at him in disbelief. "Do you feel you're being held here, against your will?"

Willow's eyes dropped to her lap. "I already asked if I could trust you, and you said as long as no one was hurt you'd keep my confidences. They aren't holding me, but they aren't giving me much rein."

"As your consort and confidant, I've held your secrets. I wouldn't suggest we bolt down to the mining office, but I may recommend we go out to shop for rings." Willow looked at him in dawning understanding. "They won't keep us from that." Brad stroked her left hand and kissed the top of her head. "I have a car, but I'm thinking you'll want yours. We'll dress nicely and join the community for breakfast. No one will know the difference."

Willow drew in a deep breath, shaken by her tumultuous weeks. "Thank you, Brad." She was quiet for a moment. "You know, you should be the one running things here."

"We're a matriarchy."

"Then pick a mare you love, and trust, and be the power behind the throne. Accept that it's a new world, and the leader should be whoever is most forward thinking and qualified, male or female."

Brad smiled. "Well, that's something to consider, but for now, let's hope this place isn't bugged and let's get you out of here."

"I'll have my game face on come sunrise."

"That's my queen. Try to get a little sleep." Brad fell out of their embrace and covered her with the duvet. He strode silently back to his bedroom and closed the door quietly.

Willow considered what things she would want to take with her. She went to the photo album and carefully peeled the corner tabs holding the photo of her with her mom and dad. She slid it into her passport case and laid it with her purse.

* * * *

Breakfast was uneventful. Willow didn't know exactly what she thought would happen when they announced they were going into town to look for rings. All it took was a few imperious words from Brad to halt any objections. It might be an irrational fear, but she tucked her passport into her cargo pants pocket instead of her purse. She was sure even the most diligent guard wouldn't dare to lay hands on the Queen. But there were no purse or body checks, or even many objections. Olympia's narrowed gaze followed them the entire morning.

Before they bowed to their subjects in the dining room, Willow made a small point to speak with Olympia casually.

"Have you been sleeping well, Willow?" The older woman asked.

"I must be getting used to the mattress. The night before last I don't even remember my head hitting the pillow." Olympia nodded with satisfaction. Willow continued. "Brad wants to drive my car. Where are those keys?"

Iago raised a brow and sent Lily off. By the time Brad finished his juice, the teen returned with the key ring. Brad wrapped Willow's hand in his, and they waved goodbye.

Once in the garage, Willow shone her pocket flashlight under the bumpers of her car. She opened the hood and did everything television private eyes do when searching for a tracking device. Nothing. The mileage even matched what she remembered. She handed the keys to Brad and sighed with relief.

As Brad steered the car down the rutted road, he checked the rear-view mirror. "The coal company receives our mail. If you have undelivered mail, it will be there. Let's head to that office, first. Stay in the car, keep the motor running, if I'm not out in fifteen minutes, drive. Fast. The closest international airport is in Cincinnati."

Willow's brow furrowed. This was approaching cloak and dagger. "Do you think they're after us?"

Brad looked over his shoulder. "Not yet. But if they dilly dally giving me your mail, that might mean they're reporting to someone." He shook his head. "I honestly don't know what they're capable of. A Queen has never abdicated."

* * * *

While Brad was out of the car, Willow dug for her phone charger and absentmindedly organized the change and junk in the console. One song, an advertisement for horse chow, played merrily, then a fairly long song began its drum solo. She heard a door slam, and she peeked out from under the baseball cap she'd pulled from the back seat.

Brad ran, jerked open her door and tossed a bag into her lap. "They weren't even in the office. I used my key. You have a bundle here. Even one small box." He slid into the driver's seat and put the car in gear. Dust clouded their getaway. "Next stop, Cincinnati."

Willow fretted. "How are we doing for gas?"

"No worries."

Willow dumped the mail at her feet. A slender box landed, and the postmark thrilled her. She peeled back the tape and found a SAT phone and a small stack of fifty-dollar bills. *Rick, you think of everything.* She flipped on the switch, and the contacts list contained a few important numbers. She read the note carefully. His handwriting was old world impeccable.

> *Thought you might need communication. Stop. Matt is voting you're deliriously happy. Stop. The ladies are voting you're deliriously unhappy. Stop. Adam is miserable in Chile. Stop. As usual, I was the one to get this done. Stop. See you in Ireland ASAP. Stop.*

Willow giggled at the telegram wording and fanned the pack of fifties with her thumb.

Brad spied on her responses to the mail when he could take his eyes from the road. "Everything okay?"

"I think it will be." She paused for a moment. "Listen, Brad, do you have money of your own? I mean, money that isn't held communally by the herd?"

"I've never needed my own money."

They continued in silence, flipping the channels for better reception, and making small talk.

* * * *

By noon, Willow saw the airport. "We need to stop at a bank."

"I have cash."

"No, I've thought about this since our picnic. There's something I need to have notarized." Willow withdrew a notebook and tore out the carefully written order.

"You're really doing it." Brad's smile grew across his handsome face as he pulled off the interstate toward a bank.

"Wait here. I'll just be a minute."

The Notary didn't blink when she set her seal and signed off on the letter of succession. Willow gave the woman five dollars discreetly. "You get a lot of succession directives here?"

The experienced Notary smiled and put her book away. "The Society for Medieval Role Play has worn me out. Every year somebody doesn't want to do something. Are you from the House of Dragons or the House of Roses?"

Willow curtsied. "I'm looking to join the House of Dragons. It's just no fun being a Pegasus anymore."

That woman is going to be searching for the House of Pegasus members for the rest of her career.

Willow returned to the car with a manila envelope. "Next stop, I'm buying lunch."

The Wheelbarrow advertised itself as vegan-friendly, they parked, and Willow clutched the precious envelope. "May we have a booth in the back?" she asked the hostess.

They found themselves fairly alone, even in the lunch rush. She slid the envelope to Brad. "Here is my decree ending arranged marriages. This second form is the letter of succession. I've named you as king." Brad carefully read the first paragraph and the color drained from his face. "You don't have to do it if you don't want to. But, I think you're the man for the job."

"I'm speechless. Do you think I'll have a mutiny on my hands?"

"If you do, that opens the way for democratic elections. I think it's a win-win. But it's up to you."

Brad drew his fingers through his hair and sucked in a breath. He stared blindly at the papers. "You only have money held communally. That's no way to live." She slid a letter-sized white envelope across the table. "I'm giving this to you. You need it more than I do."

"Freedom *and* money?" Brad stalled. "It's all daunting, but I'll give it my best."

"Just in case there really is a mutiny, and you need to get back to Greece, it's here." She winked at him. "But if I were you, I'd hold things together and use that money to send for Diana." Willow slid a second envelope over. "I've signed my car over to you. It's a clear title, and you just have to say how much you paid for it to get it changed. You paid me one dollar, got it?"

Within the hour, Brad pulled into the departing flight's lane. He ran around the car to open her door and embrace her. Brad finger-combed her wild chocolate curls and gave her his best crooked grin. "You're the finest woman I've never loved." He gave her a brotherly hug.

She ran a light palm down the side of his square jaw. "You're the first man I've ever trusted. You've never let me down. Thank you." She rested her head on his chest and once more, there was absolutely no spark.

He ran back to the driver's door before airport security yelled at him a second time. "I'll be waiting for your letters."

16

Willow saw her reflection in the airport glass and shivered. *Yikes! I need help!*

A cab delivered her to the closest department store. It wouldn't be like shopping at Erne Castle, but she'd pick up a few things to get her to Ireland. She hoped Anna and Cat preserved her few nice clothes. Certainly, the St. John knit was irreplaceable. With her new carry-on and clothes, the next stop was a moderate hotel near the airport.

She sat in the steaming water with the scent of lavender and chamomile to soothe her jangled nerves, pressed Rick's number and put the phone on speaker while she luxuriated. It rang twice.

"Dr. Greer. Is this Willow in the flesh?" Rick teased.

She looked at her florid skin. "In fact, it is. Thank you, Rick! You think of everything."

"Well, I'm experienced in rapid extractions. If your cash isn't enough to get you out of a scrape, you generally just need more cash."

Willow boggled at his philosophy. "True. Very true."

"Where are you now? Have you called Adam? When can we expect you?"

"Slow down, Grand Inquisitor, I just got your phone today. I'm flying from Cincinnati into Dublin and will arrive around five in the morning. Is that too early for the car to pick me up?"

"Ah, I'm acquainted with that airport. Not too early at all, you're on vampire time, now." He paused. "And…about Adam?"

"Are you asking if I've talked to him?" She wrung out the washcloth and hid her face.

"That is what we do with satellite phones."

There was a long pause and it dawned on her Rick would wait forever. *Vampires have that kind of time...*

She grimaced and lay back in the bubbles. "I haven't had the nerve, yet. It took every bit of courage when Brad—and I'll tell you about him later— tricked the herd into letting us go shopping. It was about five hours to get here, and I had to do some paperwork. You are talking to the abdicated Queen of the Black Mountain Pegasus Herd."

Rick affected a snooty British accent. "I know just how you feel, welcome to the club! You're still royalty to us!"

"Once I cut my consort loose and gave him my car, I picked up enough clothes to get me home."

"You're calling us home? Wonderful! We've missed you. The animals won't hold a civil conversation with any of us. And that little General fellow is driving everyone mad, especially Player. What a little terror he is! And Adam?"

"Oh, you're persistent! I don't know, okay? It's easy enough to miscommunicate face to face. How do I rectify my list of errors over a phone?"

"Oh, dear girl, I believe you're over thinking this. How about you try— and I know this will sting—it does every time I have to say it—I was wrong. I'm sorry. Please forgive me. Come home'."

"What? You've been wrong before?"

"Why do you think I'm familiar with the Cincinnati airport? That's a story for another time."

"I've got time. The bath water is nice and warm."

"Well, I don't. I have a pressing matter in the Dungeon. Will you take a raincheck?"

"Okay." She sighed disappointedly. "I'll see you in the morning."

Willow stayed in the tub until the water cooled. All the time she stared at the phone, expecting it to ring. Wondering if she could answer it.

What if he doesn't forgive me? What if I've ruined everything? I don't think I could take his rejection.

* * * *

Adam hated sheep. It was rare for him to hate any animal, but sheep were stupid and mean when you got in their way. He thanked God for herding dogs keeping them on the dirt path as they headed up the mountain. Talk about mass confusion! He'd take cattle any day!

The SAT phone could not have rung at a more inconvenient time. "Whaddaya want?" he barked.

"I have a special delivery arriving for you at Erne Castle," Rick announced gaily.

Adam signaled to the herd driver on his left. "Get that bunch out of the trees. Damn it! I know you've herded sheep before! No different here than in the Northern Hemisphere!"

"Dear boy! Have I caught you at an inconvenient moment?"

"Ya think? Any deliveries to me need to be here in Chile!"

"Erm. I disagree, Sparky. This one requires special handling."

"You! You! Wake up, you're about to be stampeded!"

Rick actually sounded sympathetic. "There's a reason they let dogs herd sheep."

Adam sighed with relief when they got the last ewe past a precipitous drop-off on the path. He slowed and sat on a boulder to talk with Rick. "Now, what the hell are you talking about?"

"Willow's brush with her people was not what she expected. After making her escape today, she's on her way back to us."

Adam stood abruptly. "Escape? Is she alright?"

"She sounded fine. Evidently, she walked into more than she expected, but we'll get the full story when she arrives at five tomorrow morning." He paused. "When are you coming home?"

Adam took his time replying. He watched the sheep disappear over a hilltop. "Well, the second wave of immigrants have arrived. Within two weeks, we'll have the last of them. Everything's set up. With no hitches, then my job is done."

Rick sounded reticent. "So…are you coming back to Ireland? Going to L.A.? Of course, you can go wherever you want under the Consort umbrella. What's your plan?"

Adam was exasperated. "Do I have to have a plan right this minute? I wasn't expecting a call like this. I don't know!" He gusted an exhalation and sighed into the receiver.

"Dear Boy," and Adam knew he must be in trouble if Rick used that tone. "I believe you're over thinking this. How about you try—and I know this will sting—it does every time I have to say it—I was wrong. I'm sorry. Please, forgive me.'"

Adam chuckled. "You think that will do it?"

"Park your Ph.D. at the door. Lead with your heart. Well, I can hear you're busy. I'll let you go. Will you ask Matt to ring me up?"

"Sure, cuz I work for you…"

"That's right! Good day!"

* * * *

Matt jogged back to the tent with the case of single malt on one shoulder and a huge duffle of socks and underwear. "Hey, Sparky, we gonna share the whiskey with the men?" Adam lifted rheumy eyes to Matt as he rubbed at his sore feet. Matt stopped dead. "Yikes, what happened to you?"

"I herded sheep up a mountain road from the back. I don't recommend it."

"Ooh. And are all our little sheep in their little pasture?" Matt gibed.

Adam stood and stretched. "I don't really care. Is that whiskey? You got the single malt, right?"

"Are you planning on sharing?"

"I suppose I have to." He considered. "I'm thinking, a new pair of underwear and socks, and one shot each. The rest is ours."

* * * *

"And how was that plane ride?" Rick was standing at the curb for arriving flights.

"Wow! I got the boss to pick me up! I'll tell you all about it, but you owe me a story."

Rick's hands were clasped behind him as he nodded and winced. "You have a memory like an elephant!" He held open the passenger door. "Don't move from this seat, you'll want to hear everything about Cincinnati in the snow." He climbed into the car and keyed the ignition.

"I'm waiting…"

"On further reflection, Cupcake is a far better story-teller. She has the color commentary on me down to performance art."

"Oh, I may have to ply her with chocolate flavored Pegasus blood."

"Excellent! Now, let's talk business." This was the first time she heard Rick's "boss voice". Willow sat up a little taller.

It's time to lip-sync for my life, baby!

"You made yourself indispensable with that talking to animals thing. This is the only Consort site with animals of any kind, and obviously, we need someone to manage them. We couldn't think of anyone better suited to it than you, but, you've been an academic all your professional career. Are you even interested in this kind of change?"

"Tell me more. Where does a single woman live around here?" She bit her lip.

Did I just admit I'm gonna be alone?

"A person of that description, working as the stable manager, would have their housing provided on site."

Willow closed her eyes and imagined a studio apartment above the barn. Well, she lived in a studio over a garage in Gainesville, and it was all she needed. "Would the stable manager have access to the resort amenities?"

Rick slanted a look at her, and his smile rose wickedly. "Oh, my, yes, the butterfly room is yours whenever you like." There was silence for a beat. "And… the Dungeon. How does that strike you? Notice I worked in a little pun about impact play?"

This is essentially a job interview, and he's discussing impact play! How can I keep a straight face?

"Do you want me to sign a contract?"

"If that makes you feel more secure, I can do that. It won't be in blood. Seriously, I've run the numbers on comparable positions, and with your talents, I added in another thirty-five percent, along with a resort vehicle and of course the estate manager's cottage."

"How could I say no?"

"I don't like people who tell me no, I've avoided that all my life."

I can't even imagine anyone saying no to Rick Hiatt, except Anna.

"Well, then, I say yes. Yes, please. I would love that!"

The road turned bumpy, closer to the castle, and when Rick drove through the gates, Willow saw construction workers carrying sheetrock and flooring into a charming, stone cottage. Of course, the term cottage was quaint if you considered the two-car garage and the four-foot stone fence around the sizeable home. She could see at least two stories with heavy leaded-glass windows, and the roof freshly re-slated. An arbored gate was thick with dormant climbing roses. She wondered what color they were.

"We'll come down later when we aren't in their way. The ladies have some fabrics and paint chips they want you to see." Rick slowed the car.

Willow braced herself on the dashboard. "This is the cottage?" She huffed out a breath. "Yeah! Sure!"

Rick continued on to the hotel entrance. "Until the cottage is ready, you'll have a one-bedroom suite in the main castle. You'll be able to cook or use the restaurant, fielder's choice. I expect you'd like a hot shower, some breakfast, and a nap." He rushed around to her door.

"What service!"

"Go on in and get your key card. I'll have your bag sent up." He looked at his watch. "Why don't you give us a call when you wake up?"

Willow stood on her toes and kissed Rick on the cheek. "Thank you, Mr. Hiatt."

Rick grinned. "That's what I like. Respect."

* * * *

Willow startled in the bed. She thought she heard Adam in the bathroom. It was twilight, and the shadows were long. "Adam?" Silence. She patted the bed to feel for warmth. She was alone. The clock on the nightstand said four thirty-four.

This is my first restful sleep since I was here last. I must have been dreaming to think Adam was here. I understand why he found it easy to make a life within a vampire community. I feel more welcomed here than at Black Mountain. If I've squandered the opportunity with Adam, I can still make a good life here. I'll be running into him every now and then, I hope we can remain friends. Tonight, I'm going to make it a good night.

* * * *

After two weeks of living with vampires, Willow found the vampire mystique to be quite different from their true lives. Who could live with cinematic drama? For the undead at Erne Castle, their evenings tended to be domestic. Willow knocked on Rick's suite door. Anna opened it, holding a giant coffee table book under one arm.

"Hey! Good evening! You've brought siestas to Ireland. We thought you'd wake up, eventually. We were waiting for the continued stories of Pegasus shifters." She hugged Willow. "Your scent is different. Do you feel okay?"

Willow smiled. "I'd say I'm wrung out. I feel like I could hibernate. You know, it's the gray sky."

Anna trailed a look back at her while she led them into the living room. "Okay." Her smile froze.

Cat's head rose from over the onyx and marble chess set. "I'm beating Rick. Come on over and watch me bring him to his knees."

"Dear, dear, fledgling." He sighed wearily. "The things I put up with for you! You will never, *ever*, beat me at chess. I have checkmate in two moves."

"What?" Cat squeaked. "Then, I guess I'll have time for all the good gossip."

There was a knock on the door, and the dinner cart was rolled in. Rick nosed over the offerings. "Willow, this smells divine!"

Willow dutifully sniffed what should have been a delicious dinner and felt queasy instead.

They sat around the dining table, and there was much to catch up on.

After dinner, Rick excused himself. "Our Dungeon Master called out, and I'm back in the saddle…" he winked at Willow, "…so to speak, for tonight. You ladies, behave." He pointed to Cat and Anna. "I expect Willow to have a calming influence on you two."

Anna lifted a brow. "Maybe, Fitz, we'll lead her astray!"

He paused at the door and Anna raised her index finger, then four fingers, then three fingers. His grin was positively smitten, and he closed the door behind him.

Cat and Willow shared a curious look. Cat couldn't let it go. "What is that? You two do it all the time."

Anna slid back into the soft chair. "The first time Rick did that, it was on video, and he didn't tell me what it meant. I held him down and threatened to tickle him if he didn't tell me. He's very ticklish. It's his sign language for 'I love you'. One finger, four fingers, three fingers. Now you know all my secrets." She blushed like a teenager, hard for a vampire.

Cat and Willow gushed at the "cute" of it all. "Rick is full of surprises!"

Anna handed Willow the phone. "Speaking of romance, when are you going to call Adam?"

The phone sat in Willow's lap as if it were a snake. "We miscommunicate enough face to face. How am I gonna talk to him over the phone?"

"You start with hello. I miss you. How are you doing?" Cat reasoned.

Willow stared at the phone. "I just can't."

* * * *

"I got some disappointing news from the weather center in Scotland. A big snowstorm is headed in with high winds. They expect a delay in air travel of three to five days."

Adam groaned. "Well, that's gonna set us back some. I was hoping to get out of here next week."

Matt and Adam stretched out on their bunks. Matt watched him with a scrutinizing eye. "Why do I get the feeling this mood isn't just about the weather? What's going on?"

He raised a jaundiced eye to Matt. "Women are high maintenance."

Matt broke out a bottle of single malt and passed it to Adam. "You're just figuring that out? No shot glasses. That bottle is all yours."

Adam's lips turned up as he received the bottle and down when he spoke. "Some more than others."

"And the some we'd be discussing is…" Matt egged him on.

"Willow," he admitted at last. "She's back in Ireland, but I haven't heard from her." Adam took a big swig.

Matt opened his bottle, dropped some A Positive into the neck and rolled it, then tapped it to Adam's bottle. "Maybe she's waiting for you to call *her*. Is she who you want?"

Adam's gaze riveted to Matt's. "Yes. And, no."

"Aren't you decisive?" They both swallowed a swig.

Adam frowned. "Okay, pros and cons."

"She's beautiful, but she's insecure."

Adam nodded thoughtfully. "She's smart and funny but also distant and moody."

"True. She's sexy, isn't she? But, I'll bet she's a brat."

"She's a brat all right, but that's fun." They drank again. "What isn't fun is her tendency to run when she doesn't get her way." Adam brooded.

"Emm. She's a shifter, and unlikely to die on you." Matt pointed with the bottle.

Adam swallowed his shot. "Is that a pro or a con? Till death can be a long, long, time."

Matt gave him a challenging look. "Hey, you're not perfect either. Does your kink match?"

Adam shrugged and swallowed. "Mostly." He looked around the tent. "Are you writing this down?"

"I'm a vampire, not a stenographer." He turned the bottle up and guzzled the last of it. "But, let me summarize. She's beautiful, smart, funny, sexy and a shifter. But she's high maintenance, insecure, moody and bratty." He stared at Adam sharply. "Have you considered all the negatives are because she's been hurt?"

"Who hasn't been hurt in relationships?" Adam's eyes were heavy-lidded.

"You've been hurt when your women die. From what Cat told me, Willow's never found a fraction of the love you were given."

Adam was chagrined by Matt's words. He looked up. "Have I been high maintenance, too?"

Matt's stare was direct. "Little bit."

Adam lowered his chin and scratched his stubble. "What a jerk!"

"Little bit."

* * * *

Over dinner, Cat and Anna continued to press Willow about calling Adam. They exchanged troubled glances. Anna's eyes lit up. "How about this? You text him. Just a friendly text."

"I could do that!" Willow's expression held hope. "Will you help me?"

Both women's brows furrowed, but in the end, their combined wisdom produced a text Willow felt comfortable in sending.

"Hi, Adam, this is Willow. I'm back in Ireland. I can't wait to talk with you face to face. I hope this message finds you well."

* * * *

Adam's aching head burrowed into his insufficient pillow. The next pain was a ruthless vibration.

Make it stop, God, please! Make it stop!

He reached for the vibrating phone under his pillow. In an unapologetic formality, his phone said, "One new text message." He squinted at the damning light.

Is this how vampires feel in the sun? Balls! What's next, a plague of dysentery?

Matt threw back the tent flap. "Hey! You're up!"

Why is Matt always so damn happy? Because he's never hung over.

Adam fought to sit up and read his message.

"You were really wasted last night. I was going to let you sleep." Matt stuffed dirty clothes into a laundry bag and sat on his cot.

"Someone just had to text me, and that woke me up." He forced his bleary eyes to focus.

"You look patriotic today!" Adam squinted back. "Your eyes! They're red, white and blue."

"I'd say you are the cutest right before you die, but I'm too miserable to stake you and cut off your head."

Matt pulled on clean socks and nodded. "Good to know. Today's project is the septic system. We'll be drilling. It's going to be noisy.

Adam's large hands clutched his aching head. Then he rose abruptly and covered his mouth. He was barely out of the tent when Matt heard retching. "Can you make the next drop further from the tent?"

"I hate you. You did this to me."

"Did I hold the bottle to your lips?"

"Shut up. Shut up." Adam staggered back into the tent, shielding his eyes from what felt like incinerating sunshine. "How do you vampires put up with the light?"

"With age comes power. Before that, powerfully dark sunglasses." He inclined his head toward Adam's phone. "What's in the message? If we have to spend another month out here, I quit."

Adam palmed the phone and slumped onto his cot. He read and re-read the message. "It's from Willow." He said soberly. "She says she wants to talk face to face."

Matt's sober tone matched his. "Do you remember what we talked about last night?"

Adam raised a wry brow. "The part where I'm a jerk? Yeah, I remember." There was a long pause.

"Are you going to text her back?" Matt prodded.

Adam rolled the crappy pillow into a ball and laid back with the phone over his heart. "I'm thinking about what to say." He began to type.

"I am well. Glad you're back in Ireland. I should be home in another seven to ten days. I look forward to talking with you, then. Text me any time."

* * * *

The air was crisp, but the sun was bright, and the day was cloudless. Still, Willow couldn't shake the fatigue dogging her since she got home. The sunshine suited her mood perfectly, she felt sensitive. In fact, she held back tears of joy, which was entirely out of character for her. Adam responded! He invited her to text again! He wanted to talk to her! Things were looking up!

Nothing smelled as good as horses. Their barn was heated to a pleasant fifty-five degrees, and the warmth of the horses themselves made up the rest. She'd venture to say the horse's accommodations were better than many children's summer camps. That morning, she slipped into the side entry. Cassius, the stallion, whinnied for her to join him in his stall. He sent her happy pictures of trail-hunting adventures with Rick. He butted her middle gently and sent picture after picture of foals running in the fields.

"Do you want us to find you a girlfriend?" He butted her again, and there were more images of foals frolicking. "Spring's coming, are you feeling the fever?" Willow smiled at the great horse's mood. "I'm looking forward to spring too."

The horses munched the horse chow in their stalls, and she greeted each horse fondly and was delighted they'd found special happiness at Erne stables.

An insistent scratching sounded from door to door. Finally, General, the Dandy Dinmont terrier, barked to be recognized and let in. Mephisto did the horsey equivalent of rolling his eyes. "That dog has a Napoleon complex."

Willow admitted the yappy terrier but explained it was meal time, and a time everyone needed to use their indoor voices. Mephisto actually stopped chewing and turned around to look at Willow, equal parts amused and astonished when the little dog did her bidding.

Daisy stuck her nose out, no longer hiding in the corner. "You don't see that every day!"

Playboy nickered softly. "Who knew Daisy had such a great sense of humor?"

Willow walked to the mare's stall. "Are you happy here, Daisy? Are you teaching Cat to ride?" Willow received a groundswell of love from the formerly abused white horse.

She turned to the herd in general and asked, "Are all of you enjoying your work?" Everyone responded with individual gratitude. Everyone, except Mephisto. She turned in concern and drew close to the massive Clydesdale. "Mephisto? Baby, what's wrong? What don't you like?"

Mephisto hung his head. "They think because I'm big, I'm slow and stupid."

Willow stroked his face. "Well, sweetie, is there something you want to do, that you can't do? Do you want to run in the field? Or pull the wagon?"

"No, I don't want to pull a wagon! Just because I'm big…"

"Okay, okay, you don't have to pull it if you don't want to. What do you want to do?"

Mephisto threw his head up, arched his neck and wore a defiant look. "I wanna dance!"

Willow recognized he was being pigeon-holed in the same way she was on returning to her herd. "Poor Mephisto!" She laid her face against his. "You can dance if you want. You want me to teach you to dance?"

Mephisto stomped a feathered hoof. His mental tone was incredulous. "Do you know how?"

"Well yes, I do. At least enough to get us started."

His tone became wistful. "I want to do Aires above the Ground."

Willow's brows drew together with concern. She remembered seeing a demonstration of the Lipizzaner's from the Spanish Riding Academy. They guided their graceful horses through the incredible feats and jumps called the Aires above the Ground. The moves took many years of training and conditioning to execute without injuring the horse. She patted Mephisto's neck. "I'm willing to start conditioning you if you're willing to go through the training. You have to realize; those moves were created for a different body type. I don't want you to hurt yourself, so we'll start with dressage, and we're going to need a saddle to fit you and a better bridle."

The mammoth horse buried his muzzle in Willow's neck and gently snorted. "I can't wait to start. Can we start today?"

"Well, I'll tell you what, we need to order the equipment, and that's not easy to come by. It could take a few days. Will you be patient?"

The great Clydesdale nodded.

"Until then, let's start by having you run laps in the pasture."

By sunset, Willow was satisfied with her day's work. She'd lost count of the laps Mephisto, walked, trotted, cantered, and galloped in the small square pasture behind the barn. Once she bathed and dressed for dinner, she stopped when she saw Rick's open door.

With a gentle knock, she heard his wry comment. "You could bathe in Chanel No. 5, and I'd still smell horse. Come on in, Willow." Willow sniffed at herself. Rick tapped his nose. "Hope you're not offended, it's the old vamp nose. On the other hand, I can't fly. But, that would be cool, wouldn't it?"

Willow folded her arms over her chest and giggled at his sense of humor. "I need to ask a favor."

Rick capped his fountain pen and sat back in his chair. "And that is?"

"I need a large dressage saddle and bridle."

"Dressage, huh? Okay, how large?"

"Ah…Mephisto wants to dance."

Rick stared at her a long moment, trying to process the request. "But he's a Clydesdale."

"He's a Clydesdale who wants to dance. Think how unique he'll be in horsey circles. Can't you just see him in competition? Won't it be fun?"

"Do I get to ride him?" Rick stared in the general direction of the stables.

"If you buy the equipment, you can." She winked at him. "Right now, we're just working on conditioning. I'm sure the poor dear is exhausted in his stall tonight."

"Absolutely, I'll make the call myself. Did you measure him?" Rick stretched out a hand to receive the list. "Of course you did!"

* * * *

Willow's days were full between managing the stables, interviewing the therapist for the equestrian program, riding herd over the cottage remodel and, of course, teaching Mephisto to dance. As she settled in, she looked forward to Adam's return with great anticipation.

Dinner with Rick, Anna and Cat became a nightly ritual. Rick raised a goblet. "Three more nights until Matt and Adam return."

Cat raised her glass. "It can't be soon enough! I'm thrilled! Matt says they're coming home ahead of schedule. We've never been apart this long, and I never want it to happen again."

"Spoken like a newly-wed," Rick observed, and Anna kicked him under the table.

"I got a text from Adam today saying he wished I was there to see how beautiful it is. He thanked me for alerting him about the threat, and he thinks the community will flourish." Willow put down her fork and sipped water. "Izzie is sending me a thank-you gift. Something marvelous she made. I hope it fits!"

Anna's gaze sharpened. "Are you having problems with your clothes?"

Cat, ever the co-ed, popped in. "Don't you hate that time of the month when everything feels like a sausage casing, and not in that sexy way?"

Anna laughed. "I don't miss that a bit! The best gift of vampirism—no more periods."

"I thought I was the best gift!" Rick objected.

"You know what I hate?" Willow agreed. "All these clothing manufacturers are getting stingy. I know they're cutting their sizes. I've been ordering from this one company for years; I went online to replace some riding wear. I paid for overnight shipping because I need them. And damn it! They are all too tight!"

Cat nodded enthusiastically. "I hate that! I swear they want to fat shame—like that could even be possible with you!"

Willow's dinner sat heavily. It was up to the chef's usual excellent quality, but Willow felt queasy. Maybe she'd picked up some kind of Pegasus virus at Black Mountain? They had a doctor there, after all, maybe they had viruses? *Yeah, it would probably explain not feeling up to par.*

The four of them retreated to the comfortable living room after dinner, and the conversation focused on the remodel of the Manor House. Rick and Matt decided since it was not a permanent home, one spacious building could house two mirrored master suites, meeting in the middle with a communal great room and kitchen.

Cat held a sample in her hands. "This granite is phenomenal. It's like diving underwater!"

"I can't wait to see it on the counters!" Anna accepted the sample and turned it, watching the light bring out different hues. "These counters will positively glow! What do you think, Willow, there will be enough to use on your cottage too, if you like it…"

They turned to Willow for a response and heard gentle snoring. Anna shrugged. "So much for our lightening-sharp observation skills. How long has she been sawing logs?"

Rick lounged in the wingback recliner. "I was waiting to see how long you'd chat before you noticed she was asleep."

"Fitz, we've never seen her like this. Am I the only one who scents something different about her?" Anna's voice carried enough concern Rick rose and circled their sleeping friend.

He knelt over Willow. Without disturbing her, he scented inside her elbow and behind her ear. He bit his lip, and the two women hovered. In subtones, he explained. "Cat, I spent time as a physician directly after being turned. My mate and I used our vampire skills as healers. Tsura was a midwife with many miraculous deliveries. I diagnosed the diseases that could be confirmed by my vampire senses, and I haven't scented this in three hundred years."

"What is it?" Cat asked nervously.

Rick stared at Willow's abdomen. "She's pregnant, and it's not going well."

Anna clapped her hand over her mouth. "Do you think this is why she left Adam? That she thought he wouldn't want a child?"

Rick stepped back from Willow and scrutinized her appearance. "Her face and hands are a bit fuller. She mentioned her clothes were tight. Did we have her do a pre-employment physical?"

Cat and Anna shook their heads. "We don't have a Helen here to handle those things. And shifters don't get sick, so…"

"Anna, don't we have a house physician for our guests?"

Anna scrolled through her phone. "We have a couple, if she's feeling poorly, we can refer her."

Rick paced around Willow's sleeping form, and then he gently took her pulse and felt the bounding rate. Once again, he knelt in front of her, gently touching her shoulder. "Willow, dear, how do you feel?"

Willow startled when she saw him in her personal space. "I'm tired." Her voice was cranky.

"Have you been having headaches?"

Willow rolled her eyes at him. "I thought you were my boss, not my doctor. I'm fine, I probably just picked up a little virus."

"Humor me." Rick sat back on his heels. "Have your blood pressure checked. We have house doctors; they'll see you anytime. I'd like to call one."

Willow tilted a look at him. "What's going on?"

Rick stood, and in his Dom voice, he said, "Let's see what the blood pressure tells us. Anna, call right now."

Two hours later, Willow sat with a blood pressure pill in her hand, with Rick and the doctor standing over her to be sure she took it. The doctor looked appropriately concerned. "With blood pressure this high, I'd like to admit you to hospital, but since you've refused," he cast Rick a disgruntled look. "I'll agree to monitor you at home, as long as you agree to take this medication without fail."

Willow frowned and nodded, but Rick sensed the mutiny under her accepting demeanor.

After the physician left, Rick turned to her, serious and commanding. "I don't care what this doctor says, I want you to have some blood work done. Something's gone awry, I scent it on you, and I believe the high blood pressure is just a symptom. The blood work will tell us the cause."

"You're scaring me. I've never been sick a day in my life. I got perfect attendance in school—for twelve years." Willow flinched. "What do you expect the blood work to show?"

"Could be a lot of things. Have them check everything they'd run on a woman your age."

How can I tell you about a pregnancy you probably don't even know about? Whose child is it? Damned if I do, damned if I don't.

"Okay, doctor nebulous! Humor me. I'll get the blood work if you tell me why you're so damned curious." Willow insisted.

"If anything happened to you while Adam was away, he'd never forgive me. I'm simply protecting his interests." He clapped his hands together. "Now, time for bed. Why don't you stay down here tonight?"

Willow's lips curled downward. The bratty sub emerged. "I really don't want to." His gaze sharpened. "But, I'm tired, and I'm already in yoga pants and a tee shirt, I guess I'll stay."

"Good choice. My ears will stand watch. Cupcake, why don't you show Willow the guest room?"

* * * *

Willow approached Mephisto. "Today is your seventh day of conditioning. And I think you've come so far that today we'll begin to dance." The massive animal projected sweet images of their prancing in the pasture. "I'm grateful to see someone who doesn't bug me about my blood pressure. Are you ready?" He nickered. She felt like she was heaving hay bales when she hoisted into his saddle. "Today, we're expecting the guys back. Won't you be happy to see Adam?" If a horse could laugh, it would be the image he projected.

The day was bright, and an azure sky stretched to the horizon. *What a good day to be alive!* Willow started him off with a warm-up, walk, trot, and canter. From there they worked on the half pass. Mephisto moved diagonally across the ring, not an easy move for a Clydesdale.

* * * *

Adam stopped at the front desk, and his first inquiry was about Willow. Told she was at the stable, he headed there directly. He could see her on the mammoth horse from yards away, and he was approaching the paddock fence when he saw her go limp and fall from much too great a height. Mephisto stopped on the double, his muzzle gently snuffling over her as Adam leaped the fence and ran to them.

Afraid to lift her, Adam dialed emergency and called for an ambulance. He watched for a few anxious moments until her eyes fluttered open and she blinked up at him. "Adam?"

She blinked again and made to sit up, but he pressed a gentle hand on her shoulder. "Don't move. Are you hurt?"

"I don't know. What happened?" She stroked the anxious horse's muzzle now nosing her neck. "I'm okay, sweetie." Again she glanced at Adam. "What the hell happened?"

"I don't know. One minute you were in control, the next you were on the ground. I think you passed out."

Rick bounded across the field at vamp speed and slid to a stop beside them. "Ambulance is pulling in, now." He looked at Willow. "Did you get those test?"

"No. And I don't need an ambulance! Let me up!"

"No, Lolo. You're getting checked out first." It was unmistakably Adam's Dom voice.

* * * *

The doctors sedated Willow immediately after her designation of Adam and Rick to make medical decisions if she was unable. Adam paced outside the emergency department gulping in air and talking with Anna and Cat while Rick conferred with the obstetrical staff.

"I guess Rick suspected it since she came home, but they just confirmed it. She's pregnant with a condition called eclampsia, it sends her blood pressure sky-high. She had a convulsion on the way to the hospital, and they have her heavily sedated to prevent another one."

"Oh, Adam, is it yours?"

"No. Impossible given the gestational time. It happened at Black Mountain."

"But, she didn't have sex with anyone there. I know she didn't."

"Yeah, well, there's no such thing as shifter immaculate conception."

Cat was adamant. "I can't explain this, I don't know how it's possible, but I guarantee you, she didn't know she was pregnant, and she didn't knowingly have sex with anyone but you."

Adam was too tired to argue. "It doesn't matter now. They're prepping her for emergency surgery, she's hemorrhaging. Rick's talking with them right now."

"Oh, my God, we'll keep vigil here. Will you call us when she wakes up?"

"Of course, I'm sure Rick will be in touch before then."

* * * *

What should have been an hour's surgery at most, was heading into an hour and a half, and Adam paced, half out of his mind with worry.

Rick handed him a large cup of chamomile tea, infamous for having a tranquilizing effect on dragons. "Drink up, dear boy, before you wear out the floor tiles."

Adam shook his head. "I need to stay sharp."

"Oh, believe me, you're sharp enough. This will take the edge off. Drink it." It was a command, not a request, and after some hesitation, Adam ceded and drank.

After a time, he let Rick lead him back to a plastic chair, dwarfed by his stature. He gave Rick a helpless look. "How did the wheels fall off this bus? How can she be pregnant?"

Rick raised a brow. "I know you're not asking about biology, so, I'm going to agree with the girls. She didn't know she was pregnant, which leads to the conclusion that she didn't willingly have sex…"

Adam stood, his agitation over-riding the chamomile. "You think she was raped and didn't tell us?"

"That's possible, but, you'd think that kind of trauma would spill out as soon as she was in a safe place." He thought deeply for a moment. "Once you eliminate the impossible, whatever remains, no matter how improbable, must be the truth. Or so says Sherlock Holmes. I believe that's true, and I would guess she was drugged in some fashion and impregnated. They wanted to produce an heir."

Adam was bleak. "No wonder she made a run for it." He turned to Rick in agitation. "Did I drive her to that? And what the devil is taking so long?"

The words were no sooner out of his mouth than a nurse dressed in surgical scrubs sought them in the waiting room. "Dr. Lachlan?"

Adam's hand flew up. "Here."

She looked at Rick, but seeing no objection from Adam, gave her message. "The surgical team asked me to convey their progress. The majority of the surgery is complete. There is a complication."

"That is?" Rick pressed impatiently.

"They're having trouble controlling bleeding. We're giving her clotting factors and platelets and whole blood. We're hoping to have her re-stabilized and in intensive care within the next hour. If there is any other family, you may wish to call them in now."

"Good God!" Adam sank back into the chair. "Alright. Thank you."

Rick joined him in the uncomfortable chairs. "She's a shifter, that means she's strong. She's young, and she has her love for you to fight for. Don't give up."

* * * *

Willow was aware she was in between realities. The tunnel, built with bricks of light, changed colors as she was propelled along by some unseen mode of smooth transportation. At the end of the tunnel was light so brilliant she thought it would hurt her eyes, but in fact, it was warm and welcoming. She was in a meadow, the most idyllic pasture she'd ever seen, and from a distance, she saw two Pegasi flying toward her. She hadn't seen them in thirty-one years, yet she knew them in a flash. They were her parents.

She recognized her mother's soft telepathic voice and realized she'd heard that voice in her mind many times. "As much as your father and I want you here, you have far too much to do to join us."

"Why am I here? What happened?"

"We never wanted that life for you." Her mother's voice was sorrowful.

"What kind of life?"

Her father stepped forward. "A life without real love, a life with only duty. That's why we fled."

"After all we went through to get you out of there, I can't believe you were drawn back in."

Willow was still confused. "But, I got out. Why am I here with you, now?"

Her mother gestured with her wing and a window, into another world, opened. Willow saw herself in her Black Mountain bedroom, but her bed was reconfigured like the beds in labor and delivery rooms. Her feet were in stirrups, and the 'kindly' Dr. Frasier was inserting something between her legs. Willow didn't know how she knew, but she understood this was artificial insemination, and the Willow in the bed was unconscious.

"They did that to me?" Willow demanded.

"Yes." Her mother waited a long beat. "They are afraid their species is dying."

"For good reason!"

Her father nodded sadly. "Yes. But, they are not your concern. Your concern is that young man, who is your destiny." She saw Adam, distraught, hands clenched between his knees, head down, waiting anxiously in another room. "We can never know why things happen as they do. Perhaps seeing us will remind you that you are worthy of love."

Her mother brushed her face with a feathery wing. "Go back and accept love and freely give it."

The vivid world around her began to fade into nothing, and darkness encroached from the edges until Willow's awareness was gone.

* * * *

There was comfort flowing, it was suspended in the air around her bed. Her free hand was gently held within two strong hands. "I know you can feel what I'm going to say, you have to know this. There was never any doubt in my heart that our love began before either of us could express it." Willow felt his hands tremble as his words caught. "What's mine is yours to make your very own."

A woman was calling Adam's name. She heard it repeatedly, and slowly it dawned on her, it was her voice.

"I'm here, Lolo." It was Adam's deep voice again, and she felt the pressure of his hand. Why couldn't she see?

The nurse at her bedside removed a cool cloth covering her eyes.

Oh, thank goodness.

She smiled weakly up at her golden dragon. "I thought I heard your voice." She struggled to sit up.

Rick's hand on her shoulder gentled her without hesitation. "Take it easy. You've just come out of some serious surgery. Let's not disturb the healing process. Okay?"

"Okay. My mouth is cotton. Can I have some water?"

"How about some ice? Let's start with that. It'll make you feel better."

Willow was desperate. "I *have* to tell you."

"What is it, Lolo?" Adam's gorgeous aqua eyes were compassionate.

"I know what happened. I saw it. My mother showed me." She saw Adam and the nurse exchange a look that clearly said she'd been hallucinating. However, Rick's eyes were focused and empathic.

"What did you see, Willow?"

"At Black Mountain. They inseminated me. They drugged me, and while I was out, they used Iago's sperm." Big, hot, tears gathered in her eyes and spilled down her cheeks.

The nurse gasped. "That's rape!"

Willow turned her face toward the sympathetic woman. "It is, isn't it?" She said slowly. "…I've been in surgery…what happened?"

Adam took a chair next to her bed and looked up at Rick and the nurse. "Will you give us a few moments, please? I've got this." He turned back to Willow. "Lolo, there's a drug called Scopolamine, that will not only knock you out, but it'll also make you forget anything ever happened. I'm guessing that's what they used on you. Today, there was a crisis with your blood pressure. They found you were pregnant, and the pregnancy was ectopic— outside your womb. That caused hemorrhaging, and they…" He swallowed hard. "I'm sorry, there was a lot of damage, and they had to remove your uterus, they had to take everything. The baby was never going to survive, and I'm afraid you'll never have another child."

Willow stared at him but said nothing.

"Do you understand what I've told you?"

"I can't have children. And I had surgery because the child was in the wrong place."

"That's right. It could never have been born."

"Okay," she murmured dully.

He stroked her head lovingly. "You're in emotional shock, it's perfectly natural. It protects us from more than we can handle at one time. I love you. I'm right here with you. I won't ever let you be hurt again."

"I'm really, really tired."

He smiled. "I'll bet. Me too. And Mephisto, I'm sure, is out of his mind with worry."

She smiled wanly as she drifted off. "You should tell him I'm okay."

"You'll have to do that yourself."

* * * *

Less than a week later, Adam opened the car door to help her out. Willow was still sore from her incision, but she was out of danger, eating and drinking, and starting to get her strength back. She heard Mephisto's whinny all the way across the field. She projected mentally, as loudly as she could, she was doing fine, but dancing lessons would wait a few weeks.

Cat and Anna fussed like old aunties as they got her settled in a comfortable chair. Adam gave firm instructions for Player to stay on the floor by her feet. Cat was excited. "This letter came registered mail for you, from Kentucky."

Willow tore into the envelope. "It's from Brad. All it says is, please call me at once." Adam frowned but produced his cell phone. He hit the speaker button. "One wrong word and you hang up."

The call connected. "Brad?"

His voice was urgent. "Willow. Are you well?"

"As a matter of fact, I'm not. I just got out of the hospital." There was a long pause. "Are you there?"

"I came across alarming news. I don't know any other way to tell you, except to say it." Another long pause. "Dr. Frasier, Olympia, and Iago artificially inseminated you. God, Willow, I'm so sorry."

"How did you find out?"

"When I was crowned King, Lily came to me. I want you to know, I exiled them, but I think you should seek medical attention."

"It's been taken care of."

"Are you alright? I hope this didn't come between you and Adam; I'll offer proof if needed. You're actually registered in the pedigree database."

Adam's deep voice assured everyone. "I don't require proof, Brad, but thank you for letting us know."

Brad sighed audibly. "Some bad things were going on, Willow, this was only one of them. I'm grateful, and your herd is grateful, that you made me your successor. We won't let you down, if you visit, you'll find it's a different place."

* * * *

In another hour, Adam was able to shoo their friends out. It felt like years since he and Willow were alone together.

Willow grinned at him, relaxed and confident. "So, is this the end of turmoil, and the time we'll take to get to know each other?"

Adam slanted a wry glance her way. "It can be whatever you want."

Willow huffed. "Well, do you want the politically correct answer, or what I really want?"

"I don't understand. What's the politically correct answer?"

"That answer is, of course, we should take this time—amount unknown—to get to know each other."

"Unh huh…and what do *you* really want?" He prodded.

"What I really want, is for us to be together, forever."

Adam grinned and picked her up from the chair to deposit her gently on the bed, against the wall of fluffy pillows. "You know, that's what I want, too. We'll have all the time in the world." Adam stepped to the other side of the bed and arranged his pillows. He slid off his loafers and slid into bed and with great care settled her in his arms.

Willow plucked at the bed linen. "I won't be able to give you little dragons with Pegasus wings…"

Adam's voice was serious. "I never thought that would be possible, anyway." He smiled down at her. "I've been pitching woo for nine hundred and ninety-five years with enumerable fertile mortal women and never fathered children. I thought it was me. I never counted on a fire breathing Pegasi. All I ever wanted was you." He watched her closely. "How do you feel about it?"

"I never saw children in my future. It wasn't my fantasy to have the home and the picket fence."

"We could adopt if you really want to. Or, you could channel maternal feelings in another way, say, with students."

"Having students would imaginably be best. They'd be like grandchildren, at the end of class I can hand them back to their parents."

"I love you, Willow Greer." He nuzzled her neck. "You'll be the best teacher in the world."

Epilogue

Five Years Later — The Beach House

The Malibu sunset was exactly what Matt sought to capture his emotion. High above the beach in his third-floor studio, he painstakingly placed the whipping post where Cat, dressed in a diaphanous ice-blue gown leaned alluringly. Her heart-shaped face peeked at him over her left shoulder. Ah, the memories of their meeting in art class stirred his undead heart. "Sorry to keep you tied up this long, baby, but I'm waiting for that particular ray that flatters you at this time of day." Cat wiggled a bit, and the chain at her wrists made a delicate jingling noise.

"Hold it there." Matt worked in a flurry of vamp speed. When he caught this one last aspect of the total image, he knew this was his masterpiece.

"Are you done yet, babe?" Cat's china-blue eyes twinkled at his enthusiasm.

"Two minutes…"

When indeed, two hours and twenty minutes passed, Cat descended from the model's platform and swept behind her mate.

Her light hands hugged him fiercely after he put down the paintbrush. "Oh, I can't fathom how you see me this way, but it's heavenly." Matt swept her into his lap, and they gazed at the huge portrait together.

Once their lives settled down, they moved into the beach house and added the top floor art studio. Matt produced life-sized works of art, posing Cat, Anna, or Willow in an evocative pose, using subtly hidden references to aspects of BDSM. Art lovers flocked to his shows, with the majority of them missing the flogger, or as in tonight's painting, the golden chain handcuffs. The linchpin of the coming show was Cat, painted in sinuous lines. She was the center of the evolving, elegant designs. Matt's emphasis on linear contours took precedence over color.

"The New York show will be this painting's debut. We'll see if the rest of the art world is ready for BDSM in Art Nouveau."

Cat's gaze followed the flowing line of her arms, held together with dainty chains. She giggled, "If you didn't mention it, the average art enthusiast wouldn't even know that I was wrapped around a whipping post."

Just then, Matt broke the fourth wall and spied you, the Reader. He winked. "Don't you have other vampires to spy on? We're about to get busy here, I'm an artist. Oh, I guess you've seen my 'work' before. G'night."

****

The Los Angeles Penthouse

Sometimes, for no reason, other than to peel the intoxicating layers of evening wear off Anna, Rick proposed a formal night in. The music was eclectic. Most nights they'd cha-cha, or almost break a sweat with a Lindy Hop. Tonight, they dialed history back a notch, and wearing his best Fred Astaire cutaway, Fitz knocked on Cupcake's dressing room door.

"Cupcake? Ready to cut a rug?"

"In a minute. There's a reason Fred didn't like Ginger in feathers."

Rick waited outside patiently, practicing a couple of dance moves in place. "But, I adore you out of them, after we dance." When the door opened, she was a vision from the 1930s. All that beautiful hair of hers was twisted and marcelled in place. Diamond earrings the size of grapes danced on her earlobes. She held out a satin-gloved hand, and Rick swept them toward the living room.

Nights like these, the furniture was pushed back against the walls, and the lighting was iridescent and low. Rick nuzzled his mate and whispered as they waited for the cue. "There's music and moonlight, and love and romance, let's face the music and dance…"

From months of wearing out movie DVD's, Fitz and Cupcake polished several of Fred and Ginger's dance routines. Tonight, their elegance celebrated the night she originally told him, "I don't like you." It was a memory they both laughed at, these days.

As they danced the quickstep, their nimble feet bounced them along in each other's arms. Their passions flared back and forth, as the bliss of being in their partner's embrace accelerated. After almost six years of being with a Master Dominant, Cupcake finally learned to let Fitz lead. As the music drove them to pirouettes, side by side, they recognized the song was drawing to a close. With a masterful lift, Fitz drew his Cupcake into a spin, and they caught their Peeping Tom.

Rick gave a leering grin. "After all these years, she's finally let me lead. I'm glad I've got you, to witness this. Now, go away, we're about to get to the naughty parts…"

* * * *

Erne Castle

A group of totally entranced seven-to-ten-year-old girls watched Willow indicate different anatomy points on Mephisto, who patiently allowed her to use him as a teaching tool. "Ears, forelock, forehead, muzzle…" They intoned as one. Adam caught her eye as he ambled up to the fence. He spent his days as the General Manager of Erne Castle. He spent his nights as one half of Dr. and Dr. Adam C. Lachlan.

It was a gorgeous spring day, and he was not ready to abandon his wife to her adoring charges. Not today, someone else could teach horsey anatomy. He rested his muscled arms on the top split rail and one large booted foot perched on the bottom. He caught her eye and Willow wrapped up the class. "Alright, girls. Thank Mephisto for teaching us the parts of the horse. Liam is teaching your class today; I want everyone to work on trotting and posting."

"Yes, Dr. Lachlan," they chorused, and each offered Mephisto a portion of carrot he took with good humor. Adam almost laughed out loud when he remembered the first time he'd ridden the huge horse, and the stable hand referred to him as a 'killer'.

Willow dropped Mephisto' s lead line, and the great horse ambled back to the barn. Sly grin in place, she met her mate's sensuous stare and swayed over to him at the rail. With casual grace, she pulled herself up to the top rail and watched the class disperse. His hands on either side of her luscious hips, Adam buried his nose in the thickness of her long, wavy, dark chocolate hair. Just the scent of her cachet beckoned him to grab a lustrous hank and twist it. "You smell deliciously alluring." He whispered into her ear.

None of the preteens could resist a chance to beg Adam's attention. The ringleader, Fiona, gazed up at him with adoring cornflower blue eyes. "Where are you taking Dr. Lachlan, Sir?"

"We're going to Williamsburg, Virginia, in America, to unveil an art exhibit." He looked down at the girls, charming as ever, and his voice was deep and sweet.

There was a chorus of "Oooh" from the students.

The tiniest rider frowned. "What's an art exhibit?"

"Well, in this case, it's a series of paintings from Dr. Lachlan's family. Do you know what a family tree is?"

Fiona piped up. "It's pictures of all the family before we got here."

"Very good, Fiona." The little girl beamed. "There will also be magnificent horse sculptures, created by a friend of ours."

Willow put on her mock stern look and admonished, "Your mounts are waiting."

"Yes, Dr. Lachlan." They parroted and scattered with longing looks back to Adam. Willow cupped his face and gave him a sound kiss. "Am I going to have competition in about twelve years?"

He pulled her over the fence and scooped her into his arms like a bride. He sing-songed like the girls. "No one compares with you, Dr. Lachlan."

They walked toward their cottage. "Brad's sculpture of the Pegasus pair was pure artistic genius." Willow sighed.

Adam gazed over the land and the bounty of the animals enjoying the harmony of Erne Castle. "That old romantic! I saw the photos of the finished sculpture. It's him and Diana, isn't it?"

He swung her hand in his. Willow giggled. "Don't you think it's sweet how he has his wing over her, protecting her as she grazes?"

Adam made an incredulous face. "Sweet? Yeah, sure."

"It's hilarious we've convinced the gallery these are racehorse bloodlines from colonial America."

"It must have been your Ph.D. It gave that whopper credence."

* * * *

Each time is better than the last.

Adam began a kiss he hoped would signal the shedding of their everyday lives and start them on their romantic yearly "honeymoon." Their expansive abode was quiet this late afternoon. He pulled Willow into his arms. Home, the estate's residence, was where they built their lives together, surrounded by the fields and stone outbuildings of Erne Castle.

Flirting, Willow took a few steps from him with a come-hither look over her shoulder. His long legs stalked her until he stood before her. His hands encircled her waist, and he pulled her close. Her eyes were half-lidded, and with a finger under her chin, he tilted her head back. She gazed at him through long, dark lashes. He lowered his head, lips centimeters from hers, and ran his determined tongue over her bottom lip, and then bit that full lip. Grinning, he thought of all the times she'd bitten him in a sensual frenzy.

* * * *

Through her lashes, Willow adored his aqua eyes, and through those hypnotic eyes, felt she could see into his mind. Willow lifted her face, closing the distance between their lips unhurriedly. The instant his lips touched hers, she raised her hand to his face, running the backs of her fingers over the stubble of deep blonde beard growth. Her hand traveled down his neck to rest at his heart, as his hands caressed her upper arms. His grip tightened, pulling her closer. They shared the same breath as he inhaled her sensual sighs. She tilted her head to the left, his tongue tracing her bottom lip. She opened her mouth for a breath, and he took advantage of her hesitation, exploring further with his tongue. He slid his hand down and around her. The world was banished, and all she heard was their pounding hearts.

They were in the moment and in the kiss. It didn't need to be more than a kiss. The kiss was sublime and lasted a long time. A 'first taste' amount of time. Their marriage was an amazing flower, layers of petals sometimes opening, sometimes closed tight like a fresh new bud. Each morning they awoke, willing to pull back the layers to smell the new, rich, buried fragrances hidden at its core.

It was just that kind of kiss.

All the while, Adam unbuttoned her barn coat and slipped it off her shoulders onto the mahogany floor. Issuing an invitation as he began to ease his kiss, she bit his lower lip, and then gently sucked it. After she released his lip, he raised his head. She opened her eyes fully and viewed his handsome face, framed by his windblown golden blonde hair.

* * * *

They left a trail of discarded clothing, and he continued to worship Willow's body. It was his personal philosophy, when it came to making love, Willow's pleasure was his pleasure. He caught the scent of leather and freshly strewn hay.

"Shower?" He pulled the sumptuous bath sheets from the shelf. She stepped out of the last piece of clothing, her sheer peach thong, and he drew it into his hand and held it against his nose and mouth. "Your scent makes me forget about anything but plundering your sweet flesh."

He pushed his hands up her outer thighs and with a wicked grin, sensually drew his palms down her inner thighs. He knelt, and his lips crept up the inside of her legs. Deft fingers dallied at the delta of her body, feeling her creamy warmth in the moist folds of her pussy. His kisses traveled, planting soft caresses, leaving a moist trail. He teased Willow at first with determined fingers, running them back and forth over her wet flesh, his thumb searched avidly for her clit, all the while he nibbled toward his reward.

Willow shuddered, drew in a shaky breath, and leaned back against the wall. She threw her leg over his shoulder, quivering from Adam's touch. She pulled his face toward her, so his mouth covered her pussy, urging him to devour her. *What else can I do, but her naughty bidding?* His tongue dawdled over her most sensitive flesh. He teased, losing track of time until she begged him to 'take her' in the shower. He didn't fully give in to her demands. First, his tongue laved back and forth between her lips. Her breath hitched when he took her clit with his flattened tongue, swirling it around the source of her need. The questing index finger of his left hand slid inside her, and with a few teasing strokes, she sang his name, as completion overcame her.

I love the sight of her long, chocolate hair wet and caping her shoulders while I make her come. I know how wet and wanting her pussy is, how tight and silken it will feel when I push her against the wall and wrap her legs around my hips.

"Let me…love you, Adam." Her heavy-lidded eyes begged and how could he deny her that pleasure?

Willow knelt on the floor and positioned herself between his strong thighs. Her teasing began by kissing the insides of his muscular legs. She took his hard cock at its base and stroked softly and playfully before she engulfed it in her mouth. Willow's tongue toyed with the head of his cock. His shudders began before she swallowed him in his entirety. Adam gazed adoringly at her lips around his thick shaft, always impressed by her oral skills. Even better, it was obvious to him, she enjoyed using her lips and tongue to make his toes curl.

"Oh, Lolo, I'm going to lose it right here." Her playful response was to form a smile around him and maintain her onslaught. Her hunger made him shiver and planting his hands against the shower walls, he came hard. "It takes every bit of my strength to stand here, right now. I've been hungry for you all day."

"I wanted to take my time, how about we tear up the sheets?" She rose and embraced his still trembling body. They eventually made their way to the bed after stops to exchange plundering kisses. His lips silently conveyed the message, *there's no place else I'd rather be.* They kissed, their hands caressing each other's faces as if to say. "Never leave my grasp."

He lay down beside Willow and cuddled with her in his arms, their bodies seeking every inch of naked flesh. Empathically, they measured each other's energy and began a slow and comfortable screw. Their lips moved together leisurely at first, but that didn't last long. They were soon locked together in feverish passion. He felt her tongue playfully meet the tip of his. She was tasty, like the first piece of chocolate after a fast. With a lazy roll, Willow straddled him and played with the swirls of blonde hair on his pecs.

"You know, I can be ticklish, Lolo." He momentarily caught her wrists and kissed the palms of her hands. She accepted his invitation and ran her fingers over his well-kissed lips, then pressed her index finger between them. He caught her hand in both of his and gently suckled it.

"I see your interest…growing…" Willow slid back to watch his cock harden again. They shared a smirk, and she enticed him further by sliding back and forth on him, her slick flesh inviting his turgid, velvet cock into her. She ran her other hand down his broad chest, combing her fingers through his golden hair. His fingers found her nipples, and not-so-gently squeezed them, fondling them in his palms. She moaned as his thumbs passed over them.

* * * *

Impatient, her hand slid down his hips and around to grasp his cock, her smile innocent, and curious. He caressed her hard nipples, and then encircled each one with his lips and tongue. "My body and soul are alive with what you do to me, Sparky."

"That nickname makes me grin like a teenager as if I'm necking in the woods."

Willow was eager to harness all that aching tension building inside. She slipped his hard length into her hungry pussy. Balancing on her knees, she deliberately rose and fell on his pillar of flesh, eliciting fevered sighs.

He held her waist and thrust up meeting her strokes. "Lolo, the sight of my flesh splitting yours is pure heaven." Hungry arms reached for the blessed weight of her breasts and body on his. Her weight shifted forward, and her lips left a trail of kisses from his earlobe to his jaw. Every fiber of her body yearned for their next move, while in the back of her mind, a voice screamed, *stay right here, ride him until his moans fill this room.* The warmth within them grew with momentum.

* * * *

Adam's hands gripped her ass.

Who'd have thought all the time in the leather saddle made her such a great rider in our bed?

His masterful fingers stroked and caressed her thighs as he slid one hand between them to play with her clit.

I want you crazy with the pleasure only we can give each other.

Long sighs and moans were their soundtrack as they moved through their favorite postures.

I could do this all day and stay hungry for her caresses all night.

"There now, steady love." He arched, seeking every centimeter inside her. Willow's body radiated heat. Her cachet flared his nostrils, it was fuel for his body and soul. Their joy multiplied in consuming each other.

He spied their onlookers, the Reader. "You don't suppose you get to come, too? The book is over. Go to sleep, now."

The End

Other Paperbacks and eBooks by Amber Anthony
Appetite for Blood, The Prequel to The Blood Trilogy
Blood Rising, The Blood Trilogy Book One
Blood Emerald, The Blood Trilogy Book Two
Blood Dragon, The Blood Trilogy Book Three
Blood Fugue, Tales from the Gaoler Book One

Arise, My Darling
Becoming Gabriel

Roman's Revenge, Roman's Adventures Book 1
Roman's Rules, Roman's Adventures Book
Roman's Return, Roman's Adventures Book

Do you enjoy tea with your reading?
We have blended teas for each book and a few of our characters.
They are grouped by Key Word: Amber Anthony
Amber Anthony, Romance Writer By Patrice Bader
Although we do not profit from these teas, 5% go to charity.
https://www.adagio.com/signature_blend/group.html?group=16228

Blood Dragon is a tea is as smoky and complex as our Dragon Shifter, with Lapsang Souchong, Assam Melody, Oriental Spice. Blended With Lapsang Souchong, Assam Melody, Black Tea, Natural Spice Flavor, Orange, Cinnamon, Ginger, Cloves & Cardamom

Pegasus Paradise, Willow Greer is the apple of Adams eye. Apples and cinnamon will please you, too. Blended With Black Tea, Rooibos Tea, Apple Pieces, Cinnamon, Natural Caramel Apple Flavor, Natural Creme Flavor, Natural Cinnamon Flavor & Natural Apple Flavor

Appetite for Blood, Prequel to The Blood Trilogy

A revolution is roaring into the 1920s! Vampires, who previously killed to feed, now *thrill* to feed.

The revolution is led by a four-hundred-year-old vampire, Rick Hiatt, and his newly turned ward, Matt Brenner. This is not the first time Rick has encountered the brutal treachery of the Moreau family of vampires, but he and Matt seek to make it the last.

Los Angelinos mortal and immortal are under attack by the entitled, remorseless Moreaus. Dragon-shifter Adam Lachlan and seductresses Venus and Luna, team up with Rick and Matt to put an end to the siege. Brute strength won't take these hellions down, but they might be hoodwinked into exposing themselves.

Read about the origins of the fast friendship between Matt, Rick, and Adam, and see how their BDSM empire grew from humble beginnings to an international conglomerate.

Blood Rising, The Blood Trilogy Book One

Drop dead gorgeous alive, Matt Brenner has never lacked for feminine attention. Undead, he's even more potent. Immortality would be stellar if only he accepted his life as a vampire. Matt and fellow vamp Richard Hiatt created a BDSM empire catering to Vampire/Doms and willing donor/subs who trade sexual ecstasy for blood. The clubs have made Matt's existence manageable, if uninspired.

Inspiration comes in the form of Catherine Temple.

Matt's made it a rule not to get emotionally involved with human women, and he sticks to it. Cat is the woman who can entice him to break all the rules. When Matt is introduced to a controversial drug that allows him a human lifetime with Cat, it's too exquisite to resist.

Powerful elements of the vampire nation are against it, and though Matt tries to protect Cat, love must be stronger than death.

Blood Emerald, The Blood Trilogy Book Two

SDV (Single Dom Vampire) unknowingly ISO compassionate, sincere, spontaneous SMW (Single Mortal Woman). Extra points for patience, brains and beauty. Handsome, powerful, Rick Hiatt has managed romance and sex within the roles of Dom/sub relationships for five hundred years. What if there is something more? What if the delicious Anna Curley, shielded from the world of dark sex games, can show him?

Rick returns to the helm of his international BDSM Empire after confronting a disaster within his vampire Family. His nemesis, Veronique Moreau, could destroy the fragile veil between the Vamp/Mortal worlds, leaving vampires exposed. He meets Anna, a guileless young woman with enough savvy to see trouble coming in the form of a vampire hunter.

Their worlds collide. Swept into the dangers of preternatural conflict, Rick and Anna experience exquisite passion and heart-stopping peril. Is love enough? They could lose their lives as well as their hearts.

Blood Fugue, Tales from the Gaoler Book One

Fugue: [fyoog] *noun*

Psychiatry. A period during which a person suffers from loss of memory and often begins a new life.

You think your memory stinks?

Meet **Harry VanAlt**. An apex predator with fading memories of mortal life. Along with his memories, his exalted vampiric powers have faded to vampire-lite. *Great taste, less exciting.*

Along comes **Dr. Lizbet Mitchell**, a police profiler who has not yet opened the right door on her future. Thirty-four and questioning, when Harry rescues her from a rogue vampire, she invites him into her button downed life.

Her fascination meets his reticence as flashes and images from some other life intrude on his own. A 16th-century ceremony reveals Harry's memories and unlocks his powers.

When Lizbet challenges Harry and they take steps toward a new and powerful immortality, there are two flesh and blood details to reconcile. *Harry closes the door on 1951 and settles a score.*

Becoming Gabriel

Meet Gabriel Lee, if he were a young billionaire, his last few years would have earned him celebrity status. But, he's a mechanic in Baltimore's inner city. Past regrets haunt him. Can he ever win in a rigged system?

Opposites attract when Grace Lerner trades abusive privilege for freedom. Suddenly homeless, she meets Gabriel and in their unlikely bond, they find soulmates come from the darndest places.

When Gabriel's ghosts endanger their joy, criminals cause a painful separation. Will their devotion deliver their happily ever after?

#Romantic Literary Fiction, Urban Life

Roman's Revenge, Roman's Adventures, Book One

Jax Roman is the image of courage, nobility, and strength. A clever mind and agile body propelled Roman to the head of his SEAL class. Handsome and disarming, Jax is in charge of his world, vertical and horizontal. Now, at the pinnacle of his game, he leads his own team until…the Lobos Cartel, the worst Jax has ever fought, sets out to eliminate him.

Lovely and compassionate, Dr. Kameo Alana meets Jax in his most desperate hour. Her family has borne the cartel's punishment. Without Kameo, Jax would not be free to topple the depraved cartel.

Kameo is more than a balm for his pain. Together they sizzle white hot. Jax's mission for a 'happily ever after' with Kameo is an exercise in 'taking no prisoners', SEAL style.

Roman's Rules, Roman's Adventures, Book Two

A complicated situation...

Kirk Roman knows he is the reason his relationship with Jordan Perry has never gotten to first base. His insecurity has been an ongoing barrier between them — until the day a sultry woman with her eye on him makes him re-evaluate his feelings for Jordan.

Jordan Perry is a fighter — and she is a survivor. She thought being widowed at thirty-seven was the worst that could happen until her diagnosis seven years ago. Clean, cleared, but scarred from her battle with breast cancer, Jordan silently dreams of the one man who has kept her going — Kirk Roman.

Kirk's inner battle with his desire to date Jordan isn't only about his insecurities. Jordan is a friend and an employee — two things he doesn't want to jeopardize. What he doesn't expect is the arrival of his estranged adult son and his wife.

The complications escalate when the sultry woman after him has a murderous past. Will all this kill his chance of finally telling Jordan how he really feels about her?

Will Roman's old rules work in this new situation?

Roman's Return, Roman's Adventures Book Three

Conner

A young cowboy with his boots in the Texas dirt and his heart set on flying fighter jets, until love makes a course correction on a flight to meet his unknown father.

Skyler

An artist gifted beyond her years stands up for herself and wins a place at a prestigious art institute. A stalker shadows her path and drives her back to the last place she was happy.

Their Fate

Each had dreams tailoring their perfect futures. Will their long-held dreams nurture their love? Or, will the tolls of achieving their ambitions drive them apart?

Arise, My Darling

Strangely gifted Jacob King finds Cricket Nielson in his meditations between worlds.

Delightful Cricket is a woman trapped first by injury and then her husband's villainy.

Captivated by her buoyant spirit, intrigued by their elusive meetings, Jake uses his psychic talents to locate this imprisoned beauty.

Their meetings on the astral plane reveal they have loved each other for eons. This newly reignited love calls Jake to draw on every spiritual resource at his disposal. He convinces sympathetic law enforcement professionals to hear him out as he discovers a series of murders and knows Cricket is next.

Will the forces of the universe unite Jake and Cricket before the insidious serial killer strikes again?

#MetaphysicalRomance

www.ingramcontent.com/pod-product-compliance
Lightning Source LLC
Chambersburg PA
CBHW021111110726
47900CB00007B/2130